BLOOD RENEGADE

Book Two of the Blood Herring Trilogy

To Mom & Papa Bear. We should all be so lucky to have our parents as our biggest fans. I love you.

CHAPTER 1

LILY

When that book came out with the sparkly vampires, a lot of my kind were pissed. I didn't get it.

Inaccuracies just like it had saved my ass more than once. Some hack vampire hunter would stake me, then I'd have to provide a soap-opera worthy death scene while they sauntered off like a big shot. Imagine my relief when teenagers the world over started thinking I would sparkle like a disco-ball. Much less painful.

And yeah, there was the silly insta-romance. It was wish fulfillment for a bunch of lonely girls. What did people expect? The stalky bits were creepy, but that kind of played to another vampire stereotype. Easy enough to dismiss.

But I did wonder, why Washington? Why not Oregon?

Oregon was just as overcast and our landscapes were just as beautiful. Maybe better. The November rain was chilly, but the clouds weren't yet thick enough to properly block the sun. I might need to reapply my sunscreen.

Most of the leaves were green and lush, excess moisture making their fallen brethren stick to the bottom of my boots everywhere I went. While the rest of the country had changed colors or forfeit their foliage, Oregon took on a healthy sheen as the heavy rains nurtured them, giving the hills a wild look.

The few trees that did submit to Autumn broke the vast expanse of green with deep bursts of scarlet and honey.

Even sitting on a motorcycle in a mall parking lot, it was breathtaking.

I inched the sunglasses down my nose to better see the big building ahead, snapping photos from my phone repeatedly while sitting astride my Harley. I usually brought the car to stakeouts, but Maria had needed to do some shopping. She couldn't exactly balance the grocery bags on my handlebars. Not that I would have trusted her to take my bike. Ever.

So I took pictures with my cell phone, trying to look like I was fiddling with my GPS. How exactly does one look when they're lost?

My phone chimed and a text appeared on the screen. Alex.

He's out of the basement.

Another chirp, Maria this time.

He's still asking for you.

I swallowed and flicked both texts off my screen, silencing the phone to focus on the mall entrance. It was probably another dead end, but it gave me an excuse to stay out of the house.

The heavy double-glass doors slid away from each other with a big swoosh. A short woman with a large handbag walked out. A fuchsia scarf peeked out through the thick mass of dark hair shrouding her face. I sat up straighter, trying to see her features. That damn hair blocked my line of sight.

The woman had the stance of the insecure, trying to turn herself into a tiny ball while still walking. She hunched her shoulders, staring at the ground and shoving her hands deep into her pockets. She could be hiding her face out of habit, but that scarf... It was a bit irregular for someone with low self-esteem to wear something so bright.

I hardly wanted to go after a woman with self-confidence issues. Then again, the whole Court wanted my target's ass on a silver pike. Would a vampire on the lam wear something so flagrant?

A light wind rustled the woman's hair and she lifted a hand to smooth those dark strands. Her skin was the right shade of olive. She started to push the loose hair behind an ear before quickly finger combing it back over her face.

Too late.

I snapped three photos in quick succession.

Click. Click. Click.

Pinching my fingers, I zoomed in on the image, just to be certain it was my target.

"Gotcha." I grinned and dismounted my bike. I could chase her on it, but she might run somewhere the bike would become a handicap. Better to leave my baby here. I checked my saddlebags one last time and pulled on the hood of my sweatshirt, making certain my hair was hidden. Finally, I shoved the oversized sunglasses back up my nose, obscuring my features as much as possible.

I kept my distance, waiting to see where she was going. Every background check told me the twit had stayed in Portland, but I had no clue why. Credit checks showed she hadn't used any of her credit cards to rent a room; she'd just used them to purchase cosmetics and clothes, of all things.

So where had she been hiding out? Had Elias been stashing her somewhere?

The large shopping bag thumped my target's waist with every hasty step. She turned a corner, exiting the large parking lot. Down a crack riddled sidewalk, then through a half-dead park with poorly designed paths, and finally into a residential area with the same cookie cutter houses repeating every third property.

I reminded myself to give her plenty of space, even more than I would if I was following a human. I didn't skulk or crouch behind cars. This wasn't some bullshit detective movie.

Instead, I walked casually, looking at the overcast sky like I was considering the various hues of gray instead of the woman ahead of me.

A quick glance under the rim of my sunglasses kept her in view without staring. I nodded politely to the people who greeted me, not wanting to actually speak but also not wanting to be rude. Either one might draw attention.

I could hide my wild blonde hair but not my accent and my quarry knew me pretty well. I really should have gotten with the program and taken steps to eliminate the lilt like everyone else living outside Court. Everytime the Court had to redo my papers for a new identity, it only caused extra work explaining when I'd immigrated. But... I just could never seem to get around to it.

A group of children ran past me, maybe playing tag, and waved as they passed. I gave a small waggle of my fingers in reply. They stuck their tongues out at Anna and a small boy with a mohawk called her some silly playground name that made me smirk. Hey, not my fault the kid had good instincts.

She looked down at them for a moment before looking away. Suddenly, she turned a corner sharper than I'd been expecting. I sped up, just a little. I turned the corner and scanned the few people walking on the sidewalk. No fuchsia scarf. No short Latina woman.

Shit.

I ran, throwing caution to the wind. Maybe if she'd just turned another corner but I had to assume she realized she was being followed. Aside from her, all I had on this case was a bunch of mismatched computer files compiled by a psycho little twit.

If I lost her, Ivan would have my ass.

I bumped into a burly man on the sidewalk.

"Watch it, lady!"

"Sorry." I stumbled past him. My gaze darted down each alley and street corner I passed.

Nothing. Nothing. Nothing.

Dammit. Dammit. Dammit.

A flash of black hair caught my eye and I turned a corner, then another.

Smack!

Her fist shot into my face, shattering my sunglasses, crunching my nose. Several tiny shards scored my skin, narrowly missing my eyes.

"Heya Lils." Her greeting was chilly as she punched again.

My cheek-bone cracked and I staggered backward. Anna sprang forward, trying to land another blow. I shot my foot out. It landed square in her gut and she flew backward into a fancy brick fence, her body cracking and the impact forcing all the air from her lungs in a heavy gasp.

"Heya, Anna." I grinned wickedly. "How's tricks?"

I ran forward, trying to smash her against the wall again. She raked her nails across my face, catching me off guard and embedding some of the shattered glass in my eye.

I don't care who you are, glass in your eye fucking hurts.

I reeled backward and shook my face wildly to lose the busted shades, blinking rapidly. My cheek and nose snapped back in place, audible little clicks as the bone mended itself. My eyes welled with tears as the slivers popped out one at a time and I hissed in pain.

"I'm not going back!" Anna stormed forward, just a blurry shadow in my good eye right before her knee slammed into me, shooting my stomach into my spine. I coughed blood, scrounging to grab her leg before she could go again.

"Yes, ya bloody are!" I barely grabbed her ankle in my half-blind attempt.

She must not have been ready for that, because she fell to the ground, her body slamming into the walkway.

I snatched her throat and pushed all my weight into her windpipe before she could scream. She flailed and kicked against the ground. I looked both ways down the walkway, my eye finally shoving the last bits of glass out.

No audience. Not yet.

She continued to kick wildly, gasping out little words without any air to carry them. I kept my grip firm. We were about the same in strength, but only one of us had bothered learning how to use it. She clawed at my hands, tiny trails of my flesh ripping under her well-manicured nails.

When that didn't work, she pounded her fist on my arm, like a feverish toddler in the midst of a tantrum. She kept mouthing something with every blow, but I didn't let up to find out what.

How had I ever called this woman a friend?

I leaned down, just enough to whisper. "We need to talk."

I shook her, snapping her head into the asphalt. Blood showed on the ground in a shiny dark splatter. Pure hate-filled those copper eyes as her head lolled and her body went limp as a wet towel.

I took a second to wipe sweat off my brow and looked her over; her right hand looked like she'd broken her thumb, the bones slowly coming back in place with tiny snaps. A dark chuckle escaped me. Bitch didn't know how to throw a proper punch.

Her clothes were washed and her skin was clean. Even her make-up was perfect.

"Well, ya haven't been living on the streets." I continued my examination, trying to ignore the itch of healing claw marks on my hands. They'd be gone soon enough. "So where the hell have ya been all this time?"

I looked up and down the alley again, deciding it would be best to continue this later. I patted her down, not finding anything but the credit card Darren had already traced for me. Seriously, what fugitive doesn't carry a weapon or even a burner phone? And where was that giant bag she'd been carrying earlier? I didn't see it laying around and there weren't a lot of solid hiding places for it.

Finally, I stood and lifted her, one arm supporting her knees and the other under her shoulders. Her head remained as loose as a newborn's. She could be faking it, but I wasn't too fussed about that. I could always drop her on the asphalt and go for round two.

Just as long as she didn't turn to a pile of ash. I had some questions first. Or at least, the Court did. The back of her head would heal, but if I was lucky, she wouldn't wake right away. I cursed my lack of a car. Next time, Maria could take the damn bus.

I looked around trying to find a place to hide my old friend, my eyes landing on a set of rubbish bins. They were tall with big company logos on the side. There was enough space between them to shove Anna's limp body out of immediate sight. I looked around again.

The neighborhood was clean and well kept. If someone saw me sitting here with an unconscious woman between the bins, they wouldn't just ignore us and keep walking. They'd stop, probably call 9-1-1.

"Shit."

It was kind of annoying that I had to worry about people being decent to each other. I gave the rubbish bins another look. But if Anna was inside the bin...

I kicked a few before the sound echoed back to me. I plopped her on the ground and kept a wary eye for any movement, lifting the lid. Empty or not, the receptacle stank.

Good. It was no less than she deserved. I checked my surroundings again and hauled Anna up, letting her fall none-too-softly on her head. She slid in with a heavy thump, her body contorting into an unnatural shape to fit the container.

I closed the lid and hoisted myself on top of the bin, seating myself over my captive. She would move the bin if she woke, giving me time to react while I waited.

I pulled out my phone, hunting through my contacts and stopping at the Cs before hitting the little green phone icon and pressing the phone to my ear.

"Hello." The male voice was like melted butter, the echo bouncing off whatever surrounding he was standing in.

"Cy! How's it goin'?"

"Lily." The smooth tone dropped and Cyrus' natural speech took over, rough with what remained of his Norse accent. "That is not the way to greet someone you're about to ask for a favor."

"Who says I'm askin' for a favor?"

"Drop the act. We both know you need something."

"Yeah but it's not a favor. I need a pickup." I used my phone's GPS to relay my location to him. "I found her."

"That only took you two weeks," Cyrus grunted and I heard someone howl in pain in the background.

"I've had a lot of balls to juggle, asshole." I winced at another howl. "Are ya seriously torturin' someone while we're talkin'?"

"It's called multitasking," he grunted and another wail issued from his captive. I held the phone away from my ear as someone pleaded for mercy. The cry finally stopped and I tentatively brought the phone back to my face.

"Knock that shit off. I don't want to hear it. And send someone for Anna." I barely heard him say it would be twenty minutes as I hung up. The screen filled with my normal background and I saw the time.

"Fuck." Now, on top of everything else, I was going to be late for my meeting with the new Captain of the VPB. I gave the overcast sky an annoyed look. "Okay, I get it. Thanks."

I hunted through my contacts again, stopping at the Hs this time.

CHAPTER 2

GABE

How could the simple rhythm of a heartbeat be so intoxicating? The two pulses were out of sync, monotonous drums that filled the air. Still, my whole body quaked as I fought for control.

Darren and Maria wore twin expressions of practiced calm and moved slowly. They looked like field mice, ready to retreat from a predator.

"You can do this." Maria moved to place her dark hand over mine.

I flinched, as though she were the monster. "Don't."

God, this was a bad idea. Should I still be in the basement, caged like the animal I'd become?

The only reason I wasn't running for the concealed entrance of the basement was the second vampire sitting next to me. Alex's posture was rigid, like a steel trap ready to snap the instant I lost control. I stared intently into the red liquid of the coffee mug before me. I didn't dare grasp it. I was sure I'd shatter it, breaking my twenty-four-hour streak.

"Is it always this hard?"

"Our blood has life in its cells. Yours doesn't." Maria gave me a small smile as she continued to speak, her tone gentle and encouraging. "When we give you blood, your body stores the life and uses the energy until your next feeding."

"Same way our bodies use calories." Darren this time, his tone shy and his posture hunched over a magazine. The cover page article title was labeled '*Bigfoot at 50; Evaluating a Half-Century of Evidence*'. His eyes continued to skim through the pages while he spoke. "For a newb, it's like they wake up starving after being in a fast during boot camp. It can be a lot to handle."

Understatement.

"Take your time." Maria drank from her glass. The red wine was a few shades deeper than the blood infront of me. The multi-colored beads in her long hair clicked together as she tilted her chin. A large lump appeared in her throat, drawing my gaze in as she moved the liquid down in several delicious swallows.

I knew I should stop looking but the simple motion hypnotized me. The slow sound of each gulp was a torturous siren, beckoning my ship towards the rocks. The thought of her blood slicking my throat made me want to vomit and feast all at the same time. The more I tried to resist the images, the smells, and the ideas, the harder they fought to resurface. Echoing with each swallow.

"Gabe." Alex's raspy tone said he'd been trying to get my attention for a while. His dark eyes were cold and stern. "Keep it together."

"I'm trying," I gagged, coughed, and finally swallowed, forcing the feeling of starvation down. I just needed to sit here and not think of murdering someone. Why was that so hard?

"Don't try, just do it."

"Yeah, okay, Yoda." Though he didn't have the ears for it. The only feature on Alex that wasn't sharp or scrawny was the circular ears that protruded from his skull.

His scowl turned to a slight frown. "I thought we agreed I was Obi-Wan."

"With that line, you're either Yoda or Nike. Take your pick." I gulped and looked back at Maria. "Sorry."

She shrugged. "I'm kind of used to being viewed as a juice box."

The image made me grimace as I reached out to the mug, slowly gripping the curved handle and lifting it off the smooth surface of the kitchen island. My hand shook and the thick contents wavered in the cup before I put it back down. It shattered on the counter.

"Dammit." I ran my hands through my hair, registering the slick oils of my own scalp with disgust. I already knew I stank; the smell wafting off me had made it a lot easier to learn I didn't need to breathe. But the feeling of my hair actually holding a shape beneath my hands reminded me it was time for a shower.

"I got it." Maria sprung up and had the paper towels out before I could react. Alex picked out the bits of glass and tossed them into the bottom of the ruined mug.

"Lils will be pissed, she liked that one."

Good. But I still felt awful for the mistake.

"I could really use a beer."

"Sure." Maria turned, the front half of her body disappearing while she rummaged through the fridge, glass and plastic-ware making small chinking noises. She emerged with a bottle before quickly combing through a drawer for a bottle opener. It snapped then popped as she removed the cap and placed the open beer before me on a coaster in the middle of the kitchen island.

I gave Maria a dubious look, then transferred it to the bottle before me. Could I really drink that? I hadn't thought about it.

Why not? I'd seen the group play a drinking game once, their only remark being that vampires couldn't get drunk. And I'd seen Lily drinking a martini before I'd realized what she was.

Lily. The memory of her irritated me. Ever since she'd changed me, she couldn't even be bothered to stop and talk. Even Alex was running out of excuses for her.

"What, not your brand?" Maria looked worried, like she might have offended me. The idea was just plain laughable. Maria wasn't capable of offending anyone. She was so considerate it made me feel like a grade A asshole, even when I wasn't debating tearing her throat out.

"It's not tha–" Intense pain cut my sentence off. I clutched my chest and hunched, unsuccessfully willing it away.

At least this time, I didn't mistake it for a heart attack. It was as though someone had tied a noose around my heart and kept pulling, yanking me to God-knows-where. Beseeching me to help a woman who hadn't even bothered to come down a set of stairs.

"Son of a bitch." Alex sat next to me, scrunching his hawk-sharp nose and gritting his teeth, like he was waiting for a dentist to stop drilling. Then again, he'd had around a hundred years of practice.

The sharp pull finally shrank and I panted like I was regaining air after drowning.

"How can you be so relaxed?" I clenched my teeth. "She doesn't show up for days and then subjects you to *this*."

Maria tensed across the table, watching Alex like he was a bomb ready to explode. I glanced over, only to find Alex gritting his teeth and staring at the island. Darren gave me a look that said he was debating seven different ways to kill me.

"Sorry." I waved the question away.

"No." Alex shook his head and gave his partner a sad smile. "Just so you know, it's normally bad manners to ask someone how they were turned."

"I didn't ask." My tone was more defensive than I meant.

"No, but I'm not sure how else to explain this to you." He sat back in his chair. "You remember when I told you that Lily gave me the best part of my childhood?"

Hard not to remember that day. The image of Lily scream-ing on a hospital bed while the doctor pulled silver out of her heart almost tempered my anger. Almost.

I nodded and he continued, "I was in New York while the gangs were still fighting for the Five Points. I was just trying to survive and stay away from the Bowery Boys or the Dead Rabbits. But they wanted every man they could get... And the Bowery Boys offered something I didn't have."

I swallowed. "What was that?"

"Food." Alex chuckled but it held no humor. "My parents had died two years prior. I was a dirty street urchin living through pick-pocketing but I knew it couldn't last. Someone would catch me and with my luck, it'd be the kind of someone who'd kill me."

Darren put his magazine down and reached across the table, laying his hand over his partner's. Alex squeezed it but kept his eyes on me.

"So I joined. I was young and skinny, so they mostly used me to run errands; fetch their food and pass messages, that sort of thing. But I got older and started to realize how I felt about my best friend. I tried to hide it, but I guess I didn't do a very good job."

Alex paused and I waited. Something in his tone made me know this was no time to interject. Not like I had any idea what to say.

"He and a bunch of our friends jumped me. They beat me until I blacked out and I wouldn't be surprised if they'd kept going after that." Alex let out a chuckle that made my spine shiver. "I'm not sure if they thought I was dead but they left me there, bleeding in a back alley next to a pile of rotting trash.

"That's where she found me." He finally smiled and it seemed genuine. "I woke up in a run-down apartment with this weird Irish chick hovering over me. Weirder yet, I couldn't find so much as a scratch on me, no idea how I'd healed. Just assumed I'd been out longer than I realized. It made sense, since I also felt pretty drunk at the time.

"She didn't prod about what happened. Just asked if I needed a place to stay. I ran out." Alex's smile grew and he sat back, shaking his head. "With her accent, I figured I'd just escaped the Dead Rabbits. Even if that wasn't the case, no way I wanted to be seen with one of the *Irish.* I was relieved she didn't chase me.

"After that, I went back to pick-pocketing. I had to dodge my old friends and our gang, but I kept seeing her on the streets. Never saw anyone with her and I didn't ever see her stealing. She just kept checking on me, asking if I was doing alright. Come Christmas, I couldn't resist a warm place to stay any longer.

"We lived together for a few years, working odd jobs to pay rent. She never questioned me about my family or where I'd come from. It was like I'd gained this weird older sister." The smile dropped with his tone. "It broke me when I came home to find her packing her bags."

He swallowed and just stared off for a second. Maria and Darren shared a quick glance but no one said anything.

"I don't know why she didn't just black-eye me and leave. Not sure she knows either, but I understood why she'd never pressed about my past. She laid it all out, even showed me her fangs when I thought she was crazy. I knew I'd never find a better friend, so I asked her if I could come along."

"Wow." Talk about inadequate word choice. I tilted my beer back and took a swallow, remembering there wasn't much consolation in the bottle anymore. I didn't even really taste it, but it gave me something to do with my hands.

There we were, Lily's little rescues.

Maybe Alex meant we owed her some kind of patience for this, but he didn't strike me as someone who'd just blindly follow their sire.

The woman who saved my life, twice, and took in home-less-Alex, how could she also be the woman who avoided me for two weeks straight? I drew in a deep breath trying to clear my thoughts. The intake of oxygen comforted me until I got a whiff of the noxious odor crawling off my own body. God, I needed to clean up.

"Stop your huffing."

"Breathing helps me feel alive."

"Lily makes that same excuse." Alex shook his head, his round ears wobbling as he did. "You both need to drop the illusion."

"At least we know she's really working." I blew out a final breath, ready to change the conversation. "That or she's a masochist."

"That was probably just a couple bitch slaps. Just wait 'til she's in a real fight."

I glowered. "I really hope I can just take your word for it."

"Yeah, good luck with that." Darren shrugged and straight-ened his ragged beanie before picking up the magazine again. Alex glowered but nobody added anything.

Guess the conversation ended there. I returned my atten-tion to the beer before me. The bottle was still cold and little drops of perspiration beaded down the brown glass, making it appear bejeweled in a way I'd never noticed before.

"Yes?" Alex let the single word draw me out.

I realized I was gawking at the beer and shook my head, opting not to tell them how poetic it looked. I already felt crazy, no reason to sound it.

"I wasn't sure if beer would be any good." I picked up the open bottle and sniffed. It still smelled the same, though there were some undertones I'd never caught. Hoppy, yet sweet.

"In some ways, it's better." Alex grinned. "I mean you can't get drunk on a bad day, but you also don't have to worry about developing a beer belly."

He drummed his flat stomach for emphasis.

"Cheater." Maria playfully glared at Alex and drank from her stemmed glass again.

I looked away before I could see that enticing lump rise in her throat. "So I could down this whole bottle on an empty stomach and I wouldn't even feel it?"

"One reason I don't switch teams," Maria teased with a wink.

"No doubt." I would have killed for a little intoxication right about now. Then again, I needed all the self control I could muster. I took a tentative sip, the glass cool against my lips as the chilly brew slid over my tongue. Yup, tasted the same. Decent, but not as good as blood. "So really, nothing will change?"

That part was still too surreal. Not only would I never develop wrinkles or a bad back. My green eyes would never need glasses and my hair would always stay the same near-black color, the curls lingering around my ears. I'd always have the scruff I'd been too busy to shave that week.

"Nope. Our bodies enter an odd kind of stasis when we turn. Every strand of hair, every limb, even scars. They all grow back exactly as they are if you lose them. Except the head–"

Pain sliced into both of us again. I almost dropped my beer, slamming it down on the island with a heavy thump that caused half the liquid to erupt like a volcano.

CHAPTER 3

LILY

Only one couple had walked by, giving me rather curious looks. I waved and smiled, trying to act like sitting atop a rubbish bin was a perfectly normal activity. Being a PI had given me a lot of acting practice but there really was only so much one could do. They started walking faster and I went back to kicking the air, mentally turning every minute into five.

Finally, a delivery van turned down the alley. A set of silver and red flowers decorated each side, dark silver letters advertising *Byblis Flower Delivery* in barely legible cursive. No phone number. We needed the van to look legit instead of creepy, but we didn't want anyone checking the yellow pages for us. I looked up and down the alley, confirming we were alone before starting in on the driver.

"You're late."

"Yeah, well, I had an extra stop." The warden stepped out of the driver's side and strode towards me, several tribal necklaces clinking together as she walked. Her dreadlocks were thick and decorated in an array of colored strings and ribbons, the original ebony peeking through individual pieces to contrast with her tawny skin.

"Cyrus said twenty minutes."

"It's going to be even longer if you keep complaining." She surveyed the ground before realizing where I was seated. "She's not..."

I shrugged. "I needed her out of sight while I waited."

"Disgusting." Melody scowled and motioned for me to hop off the bin.

"Which one of us hangs out in dungeons all day?" I obliged and we tipped it sideways, pulling Anna's unconscious form out by the ankles.

"Even I wouldn't stuff someone in a trash can." Melody tossed Anna over one of her petite shoulders and grimaced. "And if I did–"

Anna chose that moment to wake up, suddenly kicking and beating Melody with the energy of an animal about to be caged. Her windpipe had healed and her screams were as wordless as they were loud.

"A little help here?" Melody gave me an irritated look as she hugged the prisoner's legs to her chest. A mean little part of me really wanted to let Anna go on kicking. Then again, her screaming would attract attention.

There was no time to retrieve a blade from my boots, not with her making such a racket. I sucker-punched her skull. It took three times before a satisfying crunch filled the air and Anna finally slumped.

Followed by a gasp so tiny I almost missed it.

I looked up and down the alley, checking the source of the softer noise. "Shit."

A little girl in pink overalls stood at the end of the alley. Her eyes were cartoonish in their size. A small ball rolled away from her feet towards the street as she stared at us, her mouth open and her knees shaking.

"You got her?" Melody nodded at the little girl as she headed towards the back of the van.

"Yeah." At least this didn't require me to be particularly *good* with kids. I walked towards the child, my hands up like I was being arrested. "Hi sweetie."

The girl shook so hard the lopsided pigtails on each side of her head trembled. Poor kid couldn't be older than five. She probably had no context for the violence she'd just witnessed. At least she wouldn't remember it long.

"It's okay." I kept my tone soothing, halting at least five feet from her to kneel. "Ya don't need to be afraid."

The girl's face relaxed, her jaw going slack and her eyes returning to a normal size. Good, I had her. Without my sunglasses, I knew my eyes had pulsed from their typical light blue into a solid black.

"Ya never saw the woman gettin' hurt or the van, okay?"

"Okay." The confirmation sounded like it came from a mouse.

"Where's your mum?"

The girl raised an arm and pointed down the sidewalk. I walked closer and looked around the corner. No one was outside. Probably pointing to her house. I looked down the other way, confirming it was empty. Nothing. She'd probably been playing in her front lawn when she'd heard the noise.

I knelt in front of her again, making sure to leave more than an arm's length between us. No reason to scare the rug-rat's neighbors; they could be looking out any window.

"Okay, I want ya to go home."

The girl tilted her head, still speaking in her relaxed tone. "What about my ball?"

I almost laughed. I hadn't phrased the last part as a command, so her little brain hadn't considered it one. Kids were good at re-interpretations when something was too inconvenient. I looked around the girl. The pink rubber ball was still rolling in the street.

"Wait here, I'll go get it for ya." I held up a palm, even though the gesture was useless. I looked both ways before walking into the residential road and picking up the pink ball with one hand, returning to the street corner. "Here, now go home."

"Okay." The girl took the ball, turned, and slowly walked down the sidewalk. I watched her go until she turned into a picket fence and walked up the stoop to her home. I watched another moment, just to be certain, before turning back to the task at hand.

The double doors at the back of the van were secured shut. I pulled on the latch and stopped, staring in near-blind fury at the inside of the delivery van.

"Who the hell said ya could touch my bike?" That wasn't the worst, but it was the only thing I could actually say something about.

"You're welcome." Melody was hard at work securing Anna. She'd jammed a knife through Anna's spinal cord, temporarily severing the brain's signals to move if she woke up again. After that, she'd secured Anna to an overhead bar, using a heavy-duty set of cuffs with silver barbs that would drain the blood slowly and keep our prisoner weak. This last part was obvious overkill. Just like Cyrus had taught us.

"Ya better not have scratched it." I climbed in and started to check my Sportster with the precision of a parent investigating their child for boo-boos.

It was a useless check, Melody had propped my bike with heavy-duty motorcycle stands and secured it upright with rope ties to the side of the van's interior. Still, I'd rather double-check than look at what Melody was currently working on.

"Edwards..." Melody reached past me, closing the door with a heavy slam.

"I mean it." I glared at her before returning to my check. "How'd ya even know where I parked?"

"Last Thursday, you said the moron kept using her card at that mall. I knew you had to park close to watch the entrance, took about five minutes to find it."

"Yeah, but how'd ya even know to look for her?"

"You called the Court for a pickup." She shrugged. "No way you had a car."

"Well, thanks." I stood, having to hunch in the back of the van. "Saves me a walk back to the mall."

"Especially since you'd be walking from Court." She walked to the front of the delivery van like what she'd just said wasn't ridiculous.

"Excuse you?" I crossed my arms and continued to hunch in the back of the van. It probably wasn't as imposing as I'd have liked.

Melody produced a folded slip from her pocket, forcing me to come to the driver section to get it. I stalked forward to snatch the little paper. My boss's uneven scrawl was unmistakable, as were his words.

Kid, stop being dramatic.

At least now I understood Melody's gesture of picking up my Harley. She was a hostage. I crumpled the paper in one hand and shoved it in my coat pocket. "I'm already late for somethin'."

"Captain Harper has already been informed you will miss your meeting." Melody grinned. "Ivan called him before I left. He said he'll meet at the same time tomorrow. He apparently has some stuff he wants to put together and a phone call to Detective Collins he wants to make."

"He's not a detective anymore," I grumbled, flopping myself into the passenger seat and buckling myself in. "Let's just get this over with."

"I'm sorry." I stuck a finger in my ear, acting like it must have too much wax. "Let's try that again."

"Kid, stop being dramatic." Ivan kept his voice annoyingly level.

"Come up with a new line first." I leaned back in his plush office chair. "I do have a business I'd like to reopen."

"We're paying you." He laced his big hands together and gave me a level look. His face, full of disproportionate features, held no hints of amusement or irritation. "And we're already behind schedule."

"Hey, I worked as fast as I could." I crossed my arms, not caring that I sounded like a child.

"I understand that but we're still three steps behind. We need answers and I don't have anyone to assign to this. Unless you'd rather team up with Cyrus–"

"No!" It flew out before I could stop it.

"I thought as much." Ivan tapped the large desk with his heavy hands a few times. "Kid, we need to understand what Elias was doing with the Cheri Coke scheme and we need to figure out his next move."

"So I'm supposed to have an epiphany looking at a bunch of random missin' person fliers and some maps with doodles?"

He sighed and dragged a hand down his face. "You're the professional PI. You tell me."

"No deal. I brought you Anna, end of case."

"Not according to Ritti."

"Meanwhile, the 'Out of Office' sign stays hanging." I slumped into the thick seat. "Do I have any say in this?"

"After the stunt you pulled with Detective Collins..." Ivan shook his head once.

Melody was occupied, so Cyrus gave me a ride back to the house and helped me unload my bike. I'd offered to drive but

Ivan insisted. Probably thought I'd crash just to get out of this assignment. It was worth consideration.

The van still stank of Anna's blood. I muttered a thanks and started to close the back door of the van.

He placed a calloused hand on my shoulder. "Are you alright?"

"Let's see, I'm supposed to find the answer to some mastermind scheme in a bunch of files that are little more than loony ravings and you're about to torture someone I used to call a friend." I let out a dark chuckle. "'Alright' doesn't even know my zip code right now."

"We'll sever her first."

"Yeah, that helps." I grimaced. Severing was a give-in in this situation. Unless Cyrus nearly killed Anna, letting her body start the automatic cremation process just before feeding her a massive amount of blood, her tether would pull and tug on anyone she sired. While this might be hurting other traitors, it wasn't a risk worth taking.

Though I was rather surprised Cyrus didn't leave the tether intact just to rule out any more rats on our sinking ship.

"You do know there are other forms of communication besides sarcasm, right?" Cyrus tilted his head, his long mohawk falling over the Celtic tattoo on that side of his skull. The rest of the dragon still curled over his scalp.

"Go flash some of that Viking charm at Court." I pulled away from him and started to walk my bike towards the garage.

It was harsh and unwarranted, but I didn't much care. I'd had a bad day and I didn't want to sit around chatting. I barely caught him muttering under his breath, "Knows full well Viking is a verb."

I didn't look back to see if he was still there. Seconds later, I heard the heavy slam of him getting back into the van right before the engine roared to life. I found my garage door opener and waited for the door to lift completely before parking the bike next to our car and heading in.

"Maria, tell me ya picked up some whiskey," I called out, starting to unzip my jacket. After the day I've had–"

My sentence stuck in my throat, pushed back by a nervous lump. None of my usual roommates sat on the large sectional. But there was Gabe, his dark hair dripping onto the shoulders of a button down shirt while he sat still in the middle of flipping a page.

His green eyes took me in with a cocktail of fascination then anger, his mouth pursing into a thin line as he snapped the book shut.

CHAPTER 4

GABE

It was like seeing her for the very first time. It was still Lily, her wild blonde hair barely contained in a ponytail. Her motorcycle jacket was the best cared-for apparel on her, while her jeans were shredded and the hem of her tank top stretched from constant tugging. Her eyes were still the color of sky, her face was still thin with that elf-like nose.

But her hair wasn't just one shade of gold as I remembered. More like a field of sun-drenched wheat as it moved in the wind, various hues of yellow and pale orange dancing under the light. Her eyes ranged in shade from the lightest blue to deepest gray, like clouds just before a storm. Her porcelain skin wasn't as smooth as I remembered, but a little gaunt. Especially in her cheeks and neck. I didn't know if finally seeing her was more shocking because of the changes in her appearance or because she was actually here.

"After the day I've had–" She stopped in the entrance, the zipper half drawn down on her jacket. "Um... hi..."

That pulled me out of the trance and I realized I'd been staring. It also reminded me that I was irritated. I snapped *Odd Thomas* shut, belatedly realizing I'd forgotten to mark my page. "Two. Weeks."

All the question left her eyes and she stood straighter. "Yeah, I know how to read a calendar."

"Great. Do you also know how to read a text? I'm pretty sure you understand English, so surely you know I've been asking for you since day one."

"Look, we can do this later." She headed towards the stairs, her coat still partially unzipped. "Now's not a good time."

"I took a bullet for you." I stood and walked in front of her. Lily was almost a foot shorter than me, so I had to literally look down my nose at her. "I betrayed a man I've known for years."

Seriously, how did she not get this? I'd had a life before, a job and home. Not much, but everything I had I'd worked for. And with one bite, she'd taken that away. I didn't know what I could return to and I also had no clue why she'd done it.

"And? It's not like he was a fuckin' preacher!"

True, Captain Murphy's betrayal still stung. I'd trusted him, only to find him selling out humanity. Still, that didn't change the facts.

"I told you never to feed me that shit and you *changed* me!"

"Would ya rather be dead!?" Her bottom lip trembled and her hands shook.

Oh, you got to be shitting me.

"*That's* why you've been avoiding me?" I lowered my voice to a growl. "You were worried I would ask you to put me down?"

"Hmmmm, ya weren't super fond of vampires and now I turned ya into one." She tapped her chin with one finger in mock thought. "Yeah, the thought crossed my mind, among other things."

"Such as?"

"Does it matter?" She looked up at me and deflated, all the rage leaving her expression as she rubbed her eyes. "Look, just yell at me and get it over with."

"No." I crossed my arms.

"Then let me by." She stepped to the side and I moved in her path again.

"No."

She leaned back on her heels and spread her arms in a helpless gesture. "So what do ya *want*?"

There was the million dollar question. What the hell did I want? What could she possibly do? Could she say anything to alleviate my confusion? I'd been so certain that having her in front of me would make everything make sense. But now she was here, worried I might want to commit suicide, and I was even more lost.

I pushed a hand through my hair, glad it was free of the earlier grease. "Sit."

"Huh?" She looked perplexed.

"We're having this out." I motioned to the large sectional. "So, sit."

It wasn't an interrogation room, but it would have to do. I was getting some answers if I had to ring them out of her.

"I know I can be a real bitch, but I'm not a pup." She made her way to the large sectional, unzipping her jacket and the heavy boots as she sat. "Let's have it."

"Oh no." I sat kitty-corner to her. "This is all you."

"What do ya want me to say?" She set her boots aside and leaned into the couch, crossing her legs under herself. "I'm sorry? It was the only way to save your life? I didn't know what else to do?"

"Yeah, let's start with that. I woke up a vampire with a huge hole in my shirt. What the hell happened?"

"Murphy shot you." Her look of disbelief was almost comical. "Didn't Alex tell you?"

"Yeah, he didn't have a whole lot of detail, seeing as he wasn't there." That sounded snide even to me, but I wanted answers. "And I told you never to even feed me blood again, but you did *this*?"

I held up my hand, not even sure what I was showing her. Maybe my complete lack of melatonin.

"We didn't know what else to do!" She twirled her hand in exasperation. "Your heart stopped with the damn bullet in it. I couldn't heal ya with your heart shut down, and if Harper had done CPR, your heart might have shredded."

"So *this–*" I pointed at my chest, "was your solution?"

"It was *our* solution! Are ya also mad at Harper?"

I opened my mouth with a retort but the name of my partner slapped it down. Was I?

He'd been there that night, but I didn't know his part in the whole situation. Lily could easily overpower him, and I'd never thought to ask about it. Anytime I spoke to the big guy, he didn't really want to talk about it. I'd assumed it was either trauma or vampire compulsion.

"We did the best we fuckin' could. Harper said if ya didn't like it, we could stake ya in the morning, but at least you'd have a choice."

That snapped me out of the fog. "*Harper*, chose?"

"Like ya said, you didn't even want me feeding you blood again." She gave a helpless shrug. "So I left it up to him."

The knowledge that Harper had made the final choice, leaving me to war with a new monster inside my stomach, did that change it at all? I was still the same kind of creature that had killed my father, and though I'd recently realized that was a very limited view I still wasn't sure how to feel about it all.

"Look, if you want out, I can do that. Kind of part of the deal." She sagged, melting into the couch. "But is this really that bad?"

That snapped my attention back to the moment. "I can't."

"You can't what?"

"I can't... check out." I didn't know what I was going to do with this life but I still had it. It was all I had now.

"Okay..." She didn't sound convinced. "So what do you want to talk about then?"

"Why else were you avoiding me?" I clasped my hands together and leaned forward. "I haven't known you long, but these two weeks seemed uncharacteristically chicken-shit of you."

She gulped and looked around, like the living room contained a magic escape hatch. Hell, considering the vampire holding cells hidden behind a secret door in the pantry, maybe it did. When she finally spoke, it was like a verbal white flag.

"Ya remember the night we met?"

"Yeah, you were dressed up like a goth chick. You gave Harper and me a lousy excuse about being late on your rent."

"At the party, before you guys busted it up, I was dancin' with this kid. I was using him to get to Joey, the dealer."

"Okay..." Where in the hell was this going?

"I implanted a suggestion, just like I did with Harper. But I forgot to set a limit on it."

"Limit?"

"Alex hasn't explained that yet?" She tilted her head in interest. I shook my head and she shot the open upper level a nasty glare before turning back to me. "Vampire glamor is everlasting. That's why I could tell Harper never to reveal what I was to anyone and leave it at that. It only comes undone if a vampire removes it or the subject dies."

"Okay, so you implanted a suggestion on some kid at the party and forgot to put a timer on it?"

She nodded. "I needed to question Joey, but he would have recognized me as another vampire. So, I gave directions to this kid, Dean. But then you guys broke into the party and I ran for it. I forgot about Dean. He kept pesterin' Joey at other parties and it gave them a captive."

"The body." Memories swirled with the image of a corpse lying next to a blood-splattered Lily. "When I came to get you, there was a body next to you."

"That was him." She nodded again. "Mrs. Stafford shot him in front of me. Punishment for killin' Joey."

"That's why you went without telling me." I hadn't had much time to ponder what she was doing rushing into danger. Like she said, we didn't know each other well. And even if we did, I'd been a bit busy trying to find her and get her out alive.

"Yeah." She scanned my face as she spoke. "And now, looking at ya, I just see that poor kid I got killed."

"Huh?" I looked down at my hands like there were mystic runes written on my skin. While I wasn't nearly as pale as her, my skin had lost most of its natural tone after the change. I looked like I hadn't seen sunshine for years.

"He's dead and you're only a vampire because I dragged you both into this mess."

"Ah."

"Yeah." She gulped. "Go ahead and try to tell me it's not my fault if ya like. The others have tried."

"But I can't."

She looked like I'd slapped her and I realized I should clarify.

"I got someone killed too." I swallowed. I'd only met the young man for a short moment, but I could still feel his hand wrapped around mine in a sturdy shake. Just before I'd left him. "Campus security offered to guard Kimberly when I went back for you."

"Shit."

"Yeah." I shook my head, trying to clear my mind. "I'm not saying everything is your fault, but actions have consequences."

And who knew how any small change would have shifted everything. For better or worse.

"At least that makes some sense." She gave me a small smile. "I'm sorry, I should have been here sooner."

"Yeah, you should've." I looked away from my hands and into her eyes. "What about the silver? Alex said there's possibly some long-term damage due to silver poisoning."

"The cuffs and the bullet." She encircled one of her frail wrists and rubbed it. "They'd already started to pollute my blood. By changin' ya when I did, I transferred some of that over. Between that and the few minutes ya went without oxygen, we had concerns about how well you'd come out."

"What do you mean? Alex wasn't specific."

"Alex doesn't seem to have told ya much." She emphasized the last three words, aiming them towards the second level before returning her attention to me. "The fact that ya woke up able to talk and have all your memories is a great start. Truth is, we won't know if there is damage until it shows. You're probably fine though."

"Probably?"

"Life doesn't have certainties." She shrugged. "Even for the undead."

Fantastic. "Anything else I should know?"

She snorted. "There's always somethin' to learn, right?"

"What about my eyes?"

"Your eyes?" She scrunched her own to examine mine. "They look fine to me."

"No, I mean–" I gestured at all of her with the wave of a hand, "I recognize you, but it's like watching stained-glass move."

"Oh, that." This time, her snort sounded amused. The sound seemed to release some of the tension in her body. "Don't ya remember what I told ya about vampire vision?"

"Being undead has its perks, yadda yadda." I nodded. "And I remember seeing more clearly with the vampire blood you gave me; I could see in the dark. It still wasn't like this. I didn't really notice the difference until you came in."

"I'm going to flog Alex senseless." She stood, grabbing her boots from the side of the couch. "Do ya like motorcycles?"

"Huh?" I got up and followed her, more for answers than anything else. "God, do you even know what a segue is?"

"Yeah, a useless piece of conversation meant for those who can't keep up." She walked and yanked on the boots in a clumsy hobble. "I know you don't own a bike, but you've been locked up for two weeks. I assumed Alex was tellin' you what you had to look forward to. Apparently–"

"What the hell are you thinking?!"

We both snapped our heads up at Alex's raspy voice. He was clutching the banister from the upper level, the wood groaning beneath his grip.

"I think we have a new vampire with a serious need to see the world!" She shot back, jabbing her finger in his direction. "We're having a chat when I get back!"

"Oh, you're one to talk." Alex started toward the stairs, taking three at a time before he stood before her. "He's not even off the blood bags!"

She didn't look intimidated. "Ya felt he was in a good enough place to handle being left alone. I think he can handle a ride on the bike."

"Lils–"

"Alex, I'm not arguin' with ya." She turned her attention to me. "Ready to go?"

"Huh?" I shook my head at the sudden twist in conversation. This was the most bizarre verbal tennis match.

"His face is *all* over the news!" Alex indicated me with an arm.

"Do I get a say in this?" I was getting tired of being talked about in the third person.

"Alex, the helmet will shield his face from the public. Gabe, ya want to go or not?" She shoved her way past Alex and jerked the door to the garage open. I followed her. My stomach churning between excitement and trepidation.

"You're serious?" I stepped into the cool space of the garage, looking over her blue Harley.

"Do you want to get out of here or not?" She grabbed a second jacket from a hook on the wall and shoved it into my chest.

"Hell yeah!" The jacket was tight, maybe two sizes too small, but I didn't see another one around. I left the zipper down and reminded myself that breathing was indeed optional.

"The helmets have Bluetooth, so don't yell." She handed me one without kitty ears before grabbing her own and smacking a large button to open the overhead door. It hummed and groaned as it rose, and I fought the urge to cover my ears.

I didn't know how everyone was so calm around all this racket.

"No problem." The helmet was snug, but not as tight as the jacket.

She hopped on the bike and the engine roared to life. Again, I pondered ways to drown out the ever increasing thrum of the engine.

"Well?" Her voice came through like she was speaking directly in my ear. "Get over here."

I climbed onto the back, gently placing my hands on the motorcycle to steady myself into an awkward position. We sat still and I started to wonder what we were waiting for.

"Hopeless cabbage." She reached back, grabbing my arms and drawing them around her waist. "Do ya want to fall off?"

The muscles of my stomach clenched at the sudden change in proximity. Her thin body curled against me, fitting snug with her back against my chest. Even through the helmet, I could smell something sweet and citrusy on her. Before I could protest, she backed out.

A long country road rose and fell several times before I lost sight of the two long lanes of blacktop. Despite the tinted visor of my helmet, it was like watching God paint. I could see the individual grays and whites of light snow, both fresh and old. The speckles of asphalt and road salt sparkling in the setting sun. The whole scene was teeming with life, yet completely still.

She turned the bike onto the first hill and we descended. I watched the colors of the world flash by, blue shifting to deep purple and gray as the sky transitioned to night. Individual leaves flew across various fields, shimmering with moisture. The grass was a thick green, but richer and more lively than I knew was possible. Hills and mountains were strewn throughout the moving countryside, and I picked out tiny little spikes that had to be the few barren trees littering their sides.

"Was it always this vibrant?" I tightened my grasp around her, trying not to fall off. But I thought I felt her ribs, and loosened my grip, worried I might be crushing her.

"Perks." I could hear her smile. I looked up right as stars blinked into existence, outlines of blue, violet, and red circling the tiny diamonds in their cobalt backdrop.

Maybe there were. I guess I'd find out.

CHAPTER 5

LILY

The next day's drive wasn't as much fun. Maybe that was in part because it was for business. But at least my contact was good company. Plus, he always chose interesting places to meet.

Tasty 'n' Sons was one of those hole-in-the-wall types. The exterior of the building was nothing special; just painted concrete sporting a black metal sign with cream-colored cursive for the name of the establishment. It was the end cap of a strip mall, set next to a salon and neighboring a house that the owner had turned into some sort of herbal shop.

I parked the Harley in front of a yoga studio two doors down and walked in, carrying my helmet with me. Restaurant chatter and kitchen clatter enveloped me while the scents of eggs, bacon, pork, and steak all flooded my nose at once. Though the smell didn't make my mouth water, it was still pleasant, especially when compared with the cooking smells typical in my own home.

Where the outside didn't stand out in any way, the inside was unique on a plate. One wall was the standard drywall and plaster, painted the color of faded parchment while the other was bricks painted in a roasted red. The parchment wall sported a decal of an old-fashioned bicycle, the kind with a large front wheel and an itty bitty back one. The red wall sported a few abstract paintings of what I assumed were flowers, lined with a large colorful bar with several bottles shining in the overhead lighting. The parchment wall was set up with several tables and chairs pushed against a long booth bench that covered the wall all the way back to the kitchen and bathrooms.

The Captain of the VPB sat in the booth directly in the middle, furthest from both the kitchen and front door. He had a large shopping bag next to him and wore a suit that just didn't look right on his big frame. A manila file sat next to his glass on the table.

He sipped at his soda and droplets clung to a huge dark beard. He didn't seem to notice as he intently studied the menu. I chuckled and strode forward, picking up the napkin from my side of the table and offering it.

"Ya got a little somethin'."

James Harper looked up, his umber face covered in a well-used set of laugh lines and his beard breaking to show me a large smile. He ignored the napkin and stood to hug me. Vampire or not, I could still feel like someone's trying to compress me in a vice.

"How's it going?"

"Ya know, same shit different day." I shrugged and we sat. "Sorry about yesterday, had a rough start."

"Oh?" Harper's beady little eyes stopped twinkling and he frowned. Before he could speak, a waitress arrived pulling a notepad from her apron. She seemed surprised when we already knew what we wanted.

Harper ordered something called the Shakshuka. I requested a cup of coffee and nothing else. The waitress returned with the coffee soon after and left to put the order in. I returned my attention back to our conversation.

"Nothin' to do with him." I waved a hand at the notion. "Well, a little to do with him but nothing ya have to worry about. He's still in rehab."

"Yeah, he called the other day." Harper shuffled the salt shaker between his hands. "He sounded... rough."

"We have rebuilt him. We've made him stronger. Faster," I mocked an old TV show, not sure if he would get the reference. "It's a lot to deal with. Kind of like your promotion, I imagine."

"Don't even go there." Harper let out a single laugh. It sounded like a jolly bark and a few heads turned at the sudden noise.

"I kind of have to, remember?" I waggled my brows at him. "I'm your *liaison*."

"Yeah, speaking of which—" he slid the folder my way "see what you think?"

I flipped open the cover, grimacing immediately. "What the fuck am I lookin' at?"

Someone at the next table glared at my curse. I sneered at them and turned my attention back to Harper. It wasn't very ladylike of me, but the image was gruesome. A family sitting like they were watching TV, except they sat on a concrete floor and their posture was limp, like a discarded stuffed toy. Their level of decomposition was similar but seemed to progress more and more from left to right. Blood had pooled on the floor, soaking their clothes from the bottom and sides.

"Meet the Cassidys." Harper's voice was low, keeping anyone from overhearing our conversation. It was also filled with a sorrowful kind of humor. "Second scene like this. Whole family, taken to the basement and... well, you can see for yourself."

I flipped the page and couldn't help flinching. The second angle emphasized the fact that I was looking at *things* that had once been people. Each family member was sitting next to the other like rag dolls on a shelf, their eyes open and lifeless. It was all the more unsettling for the peaceful expressions on their faces.

Several puncture wounds littered their arms and necks.

Even the children.

I closed my eyes and willed myself to flip through the rest of the crime scene photos. It was a good thing I didn't have food on the way.

"How long?"

"They'd been missing for a week. Another family was found about three days before that."

"Take it the other family shared this... pattern." I squinted at the bite marks on one of the children. There was something off about it. Or was that just my disgust?

"Yep." He let the 'P' pop for emphasis.

"What did your medical examiner think?"

"He said the punctures were too perfect to be fakes. Most people try to use a fork or something; it misses the dental impression the teeth would leave behind and doesn't have the same shape."

"Makes sense." I handed the folder back. "Anythin' odd in the family's histories leadin' up to their deaths?"

"Yeah, each called out sick from school or work, one by one. From what the ME tells me, it was the same order they died in."

I pondered that. "Probably multiple vampires livin' in the home."

"But how'd they control the other..." He let the words hang then shook his head. "They mesmerized them into acting normal."

"That'd be my guess, but that's not the odd part."

"What?"

"How clean the victims are." I sipped my coffee. Harper crunched his face and I clarified, "If you were about to die a gruesome death what would your reaction be?"

"I'd scream, probably piss my..." Harper's eyes lit in under-standing. "Oh."

"Yeah." I swallowed my coffee but still had a lump in my throat. "Whoever was in that house, they cared enough to tell the family not to be scared in those final moments, even enough to let them go about their days without anyone notic-ing anythin' until they called out sick. You've got a group of monsters with a hint of a conscience; they wanted to make it easier."

"So why not just take the little they need and head out?" Harper looked at the closed folder, his dark eyes losing all their natural twinkle. "Why kill them?"

"Could be a number of reasons. They could be mental. Could be some of Elias' goons hidin' out after the fallout, avoidin' exposure. From that last one we helped ya bag, he's not thrilled with his Portland team. Probably pissed they got caught and lost him a valuable pawn."

He let out a sigh and started playing with the salt shaker. "Remind me why I took this job."

"Because ya didn't want another crackpot in the position and didn't feel like dealing with a new partner. And because we offered to ease the way." I tried to give him a reassuring smile. "The suit looks nice."

"Liar. I'm just a big gorilla stuffed into a tux."

I chuckled softly. The description was pretty accurate. "So how's the new job treatin' ya?"

"Awful. There's about ten times more paperwork than my old job and I don't have a partner to pawn it off on. Then there's the media having a circus over how the Cheri Coke sales seemed to almost stop after Captain Murphy died and Collins went missing."

"It's been two weeks. They're still on ya?"

"They're vultures, circling over dead meat. That's one thing the old Captain used to say that I still agree with. If not for the cases you helped me solve, they'd be ten times worse."

"Well, at least they didn't make ya shave the facial hair." Granted it added to the gorilla bit.

"Yeah." He scratched his chin under the large Santa-style beard. "I think your little friends at Court had something to do with that."

"They can certainly be persuasive." I nodded. "So, any other business?"

"Sure." Harper bobbed his bald head once. "Adrian St. Claire's case has been officially closed. My testimony of the events of that evening has been put on the record. They also found a burner phone in the Captain's possession, same as Kimberly Ashland's."

"And Gabe?"

"Collins remains a missing person, but the department is operating under the assumption that he's dead. Your turn."

"I finally found Anna. That's why I was late yesterday."

"That's the traitor nurse, right?"

I nodded.

"How'd you even find her?"

The waitress interrupted to place a bowl before Harper. It looked like tomato soup with a giant fried egg on top and I could smell sausage somewhere in the mix. The waitress warned Harper the bowl was hot and turned back to me.

"You sure there's nothing I can get you?"

"Actually yeah." I pointed at the bowl. "The recipe for that."

"Um, we actually have a cookbook." She offered me a tentative smile. "Do you want a bowl to test first?"

"Nah, just the book will be fine."

She nodded and walked away.

"Why the book?" Harper slurped some of his stew and looked like he was in Heaven.

"One of my roommates loves to cook and one loves to butcher it." I shrugged. "Someone will get use out of it."

"Ah. Anyway–" he dabbed his chin with a cloth napkin, completely missing the bits of soda from earlier, "what were we talking about?"

"How I found Anna," I reminded him. "The little cabbage was still usin' her credit cards. Mostly on clothes, but either way, she was in Portland. I figured she might be stayin' with humans and takin' advantage of them, but that doesn't fit with where I found her."

"So where do you think she's been hiding?"

"No clue. I was tryin' to tail her but she must have noticed."

"Anything else?"

"Yeah." I swallowed a sip of my coffee, giving myself a moment to think. "Ya remember those files you found in Kimberly's dorm room?"

"The missing persons files and maps of the US. Yeah, why?"

"Well, we can't exactly figure out what they mean." I let out a weary sigh. "My boss is houndin' me to find some kind of meaning. Or else."

"How long?" Harper slurped his soup again.

"Not long, his superiors aren't exactly thrilled with me." Not to mention Ritti and I had a history. "Also, Gabe's out of solitary."

Harper's face lit up like it was Christmas morning. "When can I see him?"

"I don't know." Harper's face fell and I hated myself a little. "I guess he handled his first session with Maria and Darren very well, but they're trained on how to react."

"Trained?"

"You're given a lot of training on how to approach a suspect or someone armed, right?"

He nodded.

"Kind of the same thing. Coming out of solitary is really hard. One of Alex's clients used to be an alcoholic. He said it was like withdrawal combined with the most violent urges he'd ever known."

"Ah." Harper looked like he was starting to get the picture.

"Maria and Darren are trained on how to move and act around a new..." I looked around, reminding myself not to use the V word in public. "Well, someone new, and even then Alex is always present to prevent any..." I fought for the right word. "Slip-ups."

"Okay." He still looked sullen. Between that suit and his expression, it felt like a completely different person sitting in front of me. I tried to smile.

"I don't think he's gonna check out."

"Yeah?" A little of his usual cheer lifted back into his eyes.

I nodded, electing to leave out the part when Gabe had looked like he was seriously considering my offer. "Said so last night. He's still getting used to everythin', but I think he's startin' to see the bright side."

"Like what?"

"Enhanced vision for one thing. Ya should have seen his face after I took him out on the Harley–"

"Wait, wait, wait." He held up a large hand to silence me. "You got him to get on a motorcycle?"

"Yeah, it was the only safe way I could take him out of the house. Why?"

The waitress chose that moment to drop off our checks with my new book. We thanked her and handed over our payment. I gave her a fifteen dollar tip for the five dollar coffee. She'd been polite about me taking up space and ordering so little.

All the while, Harper looked like he was scanning me for some great mystery or hidden code.

"What?" I almost laughed.

"I've been trying to get him to even learn about bikes for years; he just pretends to listen. But you've known him less than a month and got him to *ride* on one."

"He was just feelin' cooped up."

"Uh huh." Harper was back to batting at the salt shaker.

"What?"

"Nothing."

"Uh huh." And I was about to start sleeping in a coffin.

CHAPTER 6

GABE

It didn't matter how I slept. Rough concrete always greeted me first thing every morning. It was familiar, even oddly comforting while infuriating at the same time.

So it was strange, even unnerving, when I opened my eyes to a textured white ceiling. I turned over and found painted walls and simple furniture. The air didn't carry that vague dank smell, like a man made cave. It was absent of any odor, clean and fresh.

Guess I'm dreaming.

It wasn't the first time, though usually I dreamed of the station's continuous chaos or my quiet studio apartment, everything I needed packed into one little room.

Then I remembered; no more concrete cells. I sat up in bed and checked the alarm clock. Seven AM. Our next session with Maria and Darren wasn't until ten.

Could I go downstairs before then?

Alex hadn't said otherwise. He'd let me wander after yesterday's session, just warned against being alone with the human roommates.

This must be what inmates feel like. Everything planned and scheduled, day in and day out. No free will in the matter.

I decided a cup of coffee would do me good, even if it wasn't technically nourishment. Then again, was coffee ever nourishment?

I pulled on a t-shirt to leave the room, stopping in the hallway to look around. Only one other door was open. Was that Lily's? I vaguely remembered stumbling out of that door when we first met, but I could be wrong. I had been drunk on vampire blood at the time.

I scanned the main level through the open rails. Sure enough, she was seated on the sectional. Her hair was in a sloppy bun at the nape of her neck, several strands escaping over her shoulders. She was hunched over a laptop without typing.

On one hand it comforted me, knowing that someone without a pulse was downstairs. On the other hand, maybe I should stay upstairs. Sure we'd ended our last conversation cordially enough but there was still tension hanging between us once we'd removed the helmets.

It had only gotten worse after she and Alex had *talked*. I hadn't heard the majority of it; they'd started upstairs and moved to the basement when it was clear they weren't going to agree any time soon. I had gathered that Alex didn't appreciate his work being upended for Lily's rash decision, or that she was interfering with his methods. Lily, for her part, just kept getting in his face about helping me learn about everything I could appreciate in this new world. Going back to bed would be easier but I couldn't avoid her forever, and *forever* was actually a factor to consider now. I didn't have a job or an apartment anymore. My parents' family home was probably going to go under foreclosure soon enough, since I couldn't make the payments.

Officially, I was still a missing person, but unless someone magically found a way to get my heart thumping again, I had to stay that way until the world forgot about me. All I had now was a very long, very uncertain existence ahead of me. And I didn't know how long I would need Lily or Alex to navigate it.

I took a deep breath in and made my way down the stairs, each step groaning and creaking in a way that seemed far too loud. Like I was about to shoot my whole foot straight through the step. Despite my elephant-grace on the stairs, she didn't look up from her task as she greeted me, "Mornin'."

"Hey."

"Shite!" She snapped her head around at my voice, nearly knocking her laptop to the floor. "Um... wasn't expectin' ya."

"Sorry." Though I wasn't sure what I'd done. Things may be awkward but that seemed like an over reaction.

"No, my fault." She shook her head, trying to smile. "I just assumed it was Darren or Maria. They walk heavy."

"Gee, thanks." I made my way across the living room, trying to take softer steps and failing.

"It's nothin' to be upset about." She snorted and turned her attention back to the screen, one of her long fingers scrolling on the mouse pad. "It's just muscle memory. Takes a while to rewrite."

"What do you mean?" I threw the question over my shoulder as I dug through cabinets, wishing I'd paid more attention to Maria's movements the day before.

"Did Alex at least have ya try push-ups?" There was a hint of warning in the question, like maybe Alex's life depended on my response.

"Yeah. I pushed myself into the air and broke my nose when I fell back down." I opened another cabinet. "Why?"

"I'm guessin' your second push up didn't require your bones to stitch back in place?" Her laptop snapped shut and suddenly she was next to me, digging into a cupboard three doors away before holding out my prize. I took the coffee filters in one hand and a can of grounds in the other.

"How'd you know?"

"About the push-ups or the coffee?"

I debated that before answering, "Both."

I made my way over to the shiny coffee maker and started to prep the machine.

"Same answer I guess." She shrugged. "Been there, done that. It takes a while for most vampires to lose a taste for their human favorites. Ya chugged coffee like it's from the fountain of youth."

I bit back a sarcastic remark about the tumbler glasses I always saw in the sink. "And the push-ups?"

"Who do ya think taught Alex all his rehab tricks?" Her grin was wicked but playful.

I'd actually forgotten about her smile. Not the sarcastic one or her smirk, but the genuine one that released that individual dimple from its hiding place.

"Great..." I hit the start button on the machine. "You're Qui-Gon Jinn."

And just like that, the smile fell into an ugly sneer. "Those prequels were bloody awful. At least give me Yoda."

"Yoda didn't train Obi-Wan." The coffee pot began to groan and the kitchen filled with the smell of hazelnut roast. It was pleasant until the drips started to hit the bottom of the pot.

They were monotonous and deafening. One big drop pounding against the metal, then another, and another.

I gripped the counter and groaned. "So how long does the hearing take?"

"You're still strugglin' with that?"

"Yeah." I gulped and tried to ignore the drips. It was like trying to ignore a battering ram at my front door. "The eyesight is great, but this..."

The smallest sounds are visceral.

"Is it like this with all noises or just some?"

"Your voice is normal but those damn drips are killing me."

"So you're hyper-aware of the small stuff?" Her probing tone was just as grating as the stupid drips.

"Yeah! What's it matter? Just tell me how long it's going to last!"

"I've got work to do if you're goin' to be an ass." Her tone lost the concerned quality, becoming pointed with irritation.

She spun to walk away and I reached out, gripping her elbow. "Okay. Okay. I'm sorry, what were you getting at?"

Silence filled the kitchen for a moment, those drips breaking it with punctuating agony. She turned and wrenched her arm from my grasp, scrutinizing me with her lips pinched and her body held tight. It felt like hours before she gave me a single sharp nod.

"Stand up straight and face me."

She still looked pissed, so I kept my mouth shut and just did it.

"Hold still." She pressed her forefingers to my temples and massaged in deliberate, small circles.

The building headache started to ebb, a little more under each soft circle of her fingers. I breathed in, the scent of coffee and her orange soap mixing in the air, light and clean. I closed my eyes, my pounding head relaxing.

"Better?" She was still rubbing my temples.

"Yes," I let the word out like a prayer.

"Coffee maker back to normal volume?"

I popped my eyes open and stared at her in disbelief. She was right. I could still hear the drips. But the sound was more standard, easily ignored. Then it started to grow. Quickly and just as bad.

"It was," I groaned.

"Now it's turnin' back up?" She dropped her hands.

"Yeah." I winced. "Why?"

"Because you're lettin' it." She reached up and started to rub in those delicious circles again. "Vampire hearin' is odd. It's like different layers in a song, and ya can control which layer ya turn up. If ya focus on somethin', your hearin' will increase it automatically."

"But your voice is normal. I was focused on you." At least I was pretty sure I'd been.

"Ya were focused on the content of what I was sayin', not the actual sound of my voice. Don't think about particular sounds and they won't crank up." She started to pull her hands away, the motion drawing my attention to something I'd never noticed before.

"Your pinkie." I stared at the marred finger.

"Huh?" She looked at me confused.

"Your pinkie." I nodded to indicate her hand. "It's crooked."

"Oh, that." She let out an amused snort and looked at the digit like it was sporting a shiny ring. The top third was bent at an angle away from the rest of her hand, not a lot. Just enough that you could tell if you happened to look.

"What happened?" I resisted the urge to reach up and touch the odd little bend. Vampire healing was remarkable; I had seen whole limbs grow back. What could have happened to leave this evidence?

"Not much. My brother and I were playing with the yard tools instead of usin' them." Lily grinned. "Cillian and I decided to have a sword fight. He won."

"No splints?" I scrutinized the crooked finger again. A childhood break seemed so... ordinary and out of place.

"Did ya forget my upbringin'?" She arched a pale brow at me. "I'm lucky they didn't have to cut the damn thing off."

"Yikes." I hadn't forgotten about her history but her answer still surprised me.

I'd been expecting a battle story of some sort. Of course it was simpler than that. As a human, she'd been the wife of an Earl. Before that, she'd been one of many siblings in a poor family. Silence passed between us and I tried to picture her, little and playing with her brother. I couldn't.

"What?" She looked a little self-conscious, hiding the finger with her right hand. "It's not that bad."

I shook my head, giving her a rueful grin. "My dad would have given both his kidneys just to talk to you."

She let out a half laugh, half snort, some of the tension leaving her body. "Who sucks at segues now?"

"I'm learning to keep up," I shot back. "Seriously, you saw the man's book collection. He loved history. Found it fascinating. He used to say we were better off without all modern conveniences."

"I don't know about that. I'm rather fond of the internet." She gave her laptop a weary look. "It certainly made sortin' through this mess simpler."

"Cheating spouse or what?" I rubbed one of my temples; the spot now felt cold.

"Huh?"

"Your work." I filled a mug three-quarters before searching the fridge for creamer. "Since the Cheri Coke case is closed, I assume it's from your PI business."

"I wish." She grimaced. "The Cheri Coke case is only closed for your old team, the sales are down to a trickle in the area. How'd ya even know that?"

"Harper told me." I took a sip of my coffee and almost sighed with disappointment. Nowhere near as good as blood. God, that sucked. "So what are you looking into?"

"I'm tryin' to figure out how all this ties into Elias." She headed back to the couch. "Startin' with Kimberly's files."

"Wait, what?" I followed and sat next to her. What could that lunatic have to offer?

"Yeah, we haven't had any luck sortin' out the meanin' of these fuckin' things." She pulled the laptop into her legs and started scrolling. A long list of file names I faintly remembered from before. "I was lookin' through the Portland files."

"Where'd you even get those?"

"Harper made me a copy." She leaned back into the sofa. "He figures the information should go both ways."

I smirked.

"Yeah he mentioned that, but I didn't realize you were still working on *this*." I looked at her, finally realizing we were both sitting here talking in our pajamas, like this was the most normal conversation to have first thing in the morning. I coughed and made sure to look straight at her face instead of the ratty tank top or sweatpants. "Why sort them?"

"A hunch." She minimized the open image, a missing person flier featuring a little girl, opening a new file with color-coded circles and lines spreading across the United States in a seemingly random array. "Ya see all the circled cities?"

"Yeah." I leaned in, seeing Portland circled in deep purple among many other locations around the country.

"I think that's Kimberly's doin'. The colors are all bright and gaudy, like her dorm room." She scrolled around on the map pointing out at least seven other cities with the same marks. "At first I thought it might be a lead for the Cheri Coke traffickin'."

"Not anymore?"

"I had Darren look into it. Before we took out Miss Stafford, we found at least seventy cases in Portland hospitals that could have been people sufferin' from Cheri Coke use."

"Jesus." That was news. "When were you going to tell me?"

"I found out right before..." She let the words trail off.

Before everything had changed.

I shook my head trying not to be annoyed. If she had just called me and asked for help, things might be wholly different. But then again, I wasn't so sure I'd have made a different choice. And we'd never know, either way. "Okay, so what's that have to do with the map?"

"Darren looked into every other city on this map for me. *None* of them show the same pattern. High drug use was only here."

Thus, eliminating the drug angle. "So what do you think they are?"

"Ya see the pink lines?" She indicated one on the map. I started to follow the neon lines spiking out from each circled city. They were short and didn't lead anywhere noticeable, or resemble each other in any other way.

"Yeah."

"It took a little diggin', but I *think* they are marks for the missin' people."

"What?" I looked at the pink marks in a sort of horror.

"Yeah, I noticed it right before ya came down." She pulled up the picture of the little girl again. The background told me it was probably a school photo. The effect was lost with her plain hair and the missing front tooth in her smile.

A smile that looked more like a grimace.

"Olive Taylor, reported missing three years ago." My gut rolled in a sick little circle as I read the poster. "Eight years old at the time, reportedly taken on her way home from school."

"Yeah, her caseworker didn't realize she was gone until the next mornin'."

"Caseworker?"

"Yeah." Lily frowned at me. "She was an orphan. A whole lot of them were."

That made my stomach churn. Kids in the system already had it hard. That only made it easier to target them for a lot of awful things.

Lily brought the map up side by side with the little girl. "She was the last to go missin', came from 'round here."

She pointed at a pink line in Oregon leading back to the Portland circle. "I found three others with this same pattern. I think those pink lines sync up with the missin'. Some of them at least."

"What do you think it means?"

"Not a fuckin' clue." She rubbed her forehead. "I wish I did, then I could get back to work."

"Huh?" I sat up and looked at her. "What do you mean?"

"Ritti's insisting I figure this puzzle out before I reopen my business." She wrinkled her nose.

"She can do that?"

"She's the one that controls how and when they renew my credentials." She blew out a breath and gave the ceiling an offended glance. "And she's pretty pissed at how things turned out."

"What about the vampire case you're helping Harper with?"

"I get paid for the liaison shit, but it's apparently not enough."

"No, I don't mean that." I waved the idea away. "The killer started right after we took out Miss Stafford, so probably a minion for Elias, right?"

"Yeah..." The implied *duh* in her tone made me want to roll my eyes. She'd looked right past the connection.

"Well, if you catch them, maybe you'll get something that opens for more research here."

"Shite." Her eyes bugged in an odd mixture of delight and frustration. "Why didn't that occur to me?"

"Too close to trees to see the forest." I shrugged. "So when do we head out?"

"Huh?" She looked taken aback and I couldn't help a smile.

"When do we check out the crime scene?"

"Um..." Lily worried her bottom lip with the flat of her teeth. "I'm not so sure–"

"You're taking me."

"Gabe..."

"No." I sat up straighter so I'd have my extra few inches. "Look, you yourself said you owe me for ditching me these last two weeks."

"Yes, but–"

"*And*, you want to see results." I gave her a level look. "You need a fresh perspective."

And I needed something worthwhile to do.

Lily continued to bite her bottom lip, scanning my face before shouting, "Hey, Alex, wakey wakey!"

A door squeaked open and the sandy-haired man shuffled towards the banister of the second level, rubbing the sleep from his eyes. "What?"

She still held my gaze when she said, "We need to argue about me takin' Gabe for another field trip."

CHAPTER 7

LILY

G abe flung himself out of the car like he might kiss the asphalt. "You are the worst driver!"

"Oh, I'm not that bad!" I got out and stretched, using the action to look around.

"You're right, that's insulting to actual drivers." He slammed the door, wincing at the hollow thud that echoed into the empty street.

"Now you're just being dramatic." I walked towards the sidewalk, stopping to stand behind him. "Ya better not have done any damage."

We'd already had to argue with Alex for over an hour. Last thing I needed was to come home with a dent in the door.

Gabe was bent low, running his hands over the metal as he checked. "I don't see any."

He really needed to learn to watch it. What if this had been a glass door? My stomach twisted. I really didn't like this idea. Not at all. But Gabe was right, I was hitting a wall and I did owe him one. I just hoped I wouldn't live to regret this.

He stood, glowering at me. "How can someone who's so good at driving a motorcycle be so bad at driving a car?"

"Drama queen." I rolled my eyes before stuffing my hands in the pockets of my jacket and started walking. He took two long strides to catch up before falling in pace next to me.

"I'm driving back."

"Have it your way." I shrugged.

No use fighting over it. Yes, there had been a few disgruntled people on the road, but they'd misunderstood the proper use for a gas pedal. Instead of arguing, I used the short walk to take in our surroundings.

"Middle class?"

"I'd say so," Gabe replied.

The Cassidy's had lived in a pretty standard neighborhood. It was well-kept and clean. A few unkempt houses and a few nice ones, but most of them were just okay. Almost all of them were littered with little lawn decorations or shriveled flowers going dormant for winter. A dog barked somewhere in the distance. Other than that, the street was nearly barren of anything but parked cars. Not surprising since we'd come here in the wee hours of a Saturday morning.

Harper's bike sat ahead, a large silhouette on the side of the road in the purple sunrise. His Ninja didn't have the old school look of my Harley. My bike was all curves and classic angles, Harper's was sharp, like a hunched wildcat ready to pounce. It looked kind of funny under the large man who sat atop it. Especially with him playing on his phone.

"Not Candy Crush again," Gabe teased.

"Nope, just. Amber Wright is still looking for an interview." Harper looked up from the small screen, his bandanna at odds with the wrinkled button-down shirt and gray slacks. His jaw dropped in mild surprise before he let out his signature laugh. "That you, buddy?"

I eyed my work with mild pride. Maria and I had spent a half hour applying make-up, creating shadows and wrinkles where they didn't normally exist on Gabe's strong face. The effect was a nose that looked more narrow than it really was and cheekbones that appeared much lower than they really were. Add this to an over-sized beanie, threadbare jeans, and a flannel shirt, he looked nothing like the man in khakis who'd tried to arrest me only three weeks ago.

"Don't try to change the subject." Gabe looked like he was having a heart attack. "You were doing business on your phone?"

I snorted and Harper glared at me.

"It's not like it never happens."

"No, but it's bloody rare." I grinned. "Shall we?"

"First things first." Harper climbed off the motorcycle and wrapped his old partner in a giant bear hug, thumping Gabe on the back several times. I immediately felt embarrassed, like I was intruding, and tried to stare at my shoes, pretending to give them privacy.

Gabe coughed and hugged back. "Not ashamed to be seen with me like this?"

Did he mean the cosmetics or his undead status? I fought the urge to blurt the question out; it could wait until later. Harper apparently assumed it was the former.

"Buddy, you could wear drag for all I care." Harper held Gabe out at arm's length, taking him in fully. "Just... don't die again, okay? That really sucked."

"Yeah, I'll try." Gabe coughed again, giving me a quick glance before eyeing the houses. "Can we work, please?"

Harper snorted but thumped Gabe on the back once more and led the way. "Only one uniform on duty, just guarding the place. With the media all over this, we didn't want to risk leaving the house unsupervised."

"Media?" Gabe raised both his brows in interest.

"You haven't seen?" Harper grimaced. "Two days ago, some local news made the connection. They're calling him 'The Doll Maker.'"

"What is it with humans and serial killers?" I sneered. "Why not just come right out and say 'We're going to make this guy sound like a low-grade superhero and downplay how awful he is with a silly name?'"

"What? Vampires don't have a serial-killer-fandom?" Harper looked entertained by the mini-rant. Gabe failed to suppress a chuckle and I shot him a dirty look.

"We consider them more of a–" I struggled to find the right words, "learning experience."

At this Gabe stopped, turning on his heel to face me, his eyebrows furrowed. "Learning experience?"

The anger in his voice surprised me until I understood he hadn't taken that the right way at all. I thought he was passed these prejudices but I guess I was wrong. A knot twisted in my guts at how he was processing the change but I shoved it down. Now wasn't the time.

"Considerin' the first known serial killer was sort of our fault..." I let the sentence hang, hoping this wouldn't make matters worse.

His eyebrows tried to meld together before they disappeared into the giant beanie and understanding dawned. "You're kidding."

"What?" Harper looked like he was still playing catch up.

I kicked a small stone away and pursed my lips. "'The Ripper was ours."

"The ripper?" Harper took another second, then barked out a surprised laugh. "*Jack* the Ripper?"

"Keep your voice down," I snapped. "We're not exactly proud of it."

"I would hope not. The guy ripped how many women to shreds?" Gabe stared in disbelief. I wondered if he still thought his dad would have invited me over for a chat.

"It was five, okay?" I hissed. "And it wasn't exactly sanctioned by the Courts. Some dumb cabbage turned a nutter. The eejit thought a crazy vampire would be a bunch of laughs."

"Five that you know of." Gabe still looked stunned. "They never caught the guy."

"No, the *humans* never caught him." My look was more than a little pointed this time and I let the meaning sink in.

"Wait, were you *there*?" Harper looked at me in wonder. That's right, I hadn't told him how old I was. His human brain still probably guessed my age from appearance.

"No. I'd already immigrated when Jack started up. That was all the European Court." I snorted, a little amusement shining through. "Do ya two even remember why we're here?"

I walked past Harper and Gabe, strolling towards a two-story house with a police cruiser sitting across the street. Harper opened his mouth, probably to stop me, but Gabe placed a hand on his big shoulder.

"Let her."

I stopped and turned, a single brow raised in challenge. "Are ya waitin' for a written invitation? Get your ass over here."

Harper laughed again and Gabe shot him a look before walking the extra length between us.

"What?"

"Who do ya think is going to mesmerize the cop?" I smiled and continued to walk forward.

"Wait, what?" He followed after me, stumbling once in surprise.

I didn't answer, just approached the cruiser and rapped a knuckle against the cool surface of the window. The door mechanism hummed and half of the glass disappeared into the frame as the officer inside turned down a decidedly political bit of radio.

"Can I help you, ma'am?" The officer's voice was thick with a southern accent. He sounded less than concerned at our sudden appearance. More like he was annoyed at being interrupted. The half-finished breakfast sandwich in his lap made that easy enough to understand.

"Why, yes." I lifted the large sunglasses off my face, resting the lenses on the crown of my head. "Ya can sit still and listen."

"Yes, ma'am." The cop's voice became automatic. Gabe approached the open window, finding him slack-jawed and staring at me.

I grinned. "Your turn."

"And I'm supposed to do this, how?" He let a fair amount of sarcasm shine through his words.

I knew he wouldn't like this, but it was part of my deal with Alex. Gabe couldn't mesmerize Maria or Darren and he needed practice for when he got back into the real world. If that would be possible...

"There's not a manual." I lifted a shoulder. "Ya just do it."

"Why? You're more than capable."

He said capable, but something in his tone made me think he meant comfortable. Too bad. He'd insisted on this little outing and I had a promise to keep.

"You're not gonna live with us forever, right?"

He looked stunned by the question.

"What if someone sees your face? What if ya need to feed and you've run out of blood bags?" I arched a brow at him.

He scanned the air like he was reading, probably trying to find a reason not to do this.

"Come on, we don't actually have forever." I grabbed his elbow and pulled him closer.

Gabe swallowed as he looked into the slack face of the cop. He opened his mouth a couple times but stopped himself before anything came out. After a mental eternity passed, he simply shook his head.

"No." He spun away and strode towards the house at a clipped pace.

"Eejit," I grumbled. Part of me wanted to chase after him, but making a scene wasn't on my agenda. Instead, I bent low before whispering orders to the cop, "Ya never saw us or James Harper here this morning. Nobody has entered the residence and no one will be leavin' it. Do ya understand?"

"Yes, ma'am." The cop intoned. Imagine that, even under mind control he had manners.

I stood there another moment, mentally double checking for loop holes or open timers. Satisfied, I joined Gabe on the stoop.

"This isn't over." I put some gravel in my tone.

Gabe didn't respond, just watched as Harper snapped a set of latex gloves on and fished in his pockets before producing an evidence bag containing a key ring. It jingled as he sifted through each key before unlocking the door. A heavy creak echoed beyond the doorway and Harper snapped the yellow tape blocking our path down. "I've got more on my bike."

I moved to enter the residence, mentally drawing my emotions back. If the photos I'd seen were any indicator, I was in for a rough time. Even if the bodies had been removed. Plus, the smell of rotting blood was liable to mess with Gabe on every level. I'd have to shove my heart in a box.

Gabe gripped my elbow. "Wait."

"Why?" Harper looked as confused as I felt. Surely Gabe didn't intend to have it out right here?

"Gabe, if you're about to give me grief–"

"Shut up." Something about the low intensity of his tone made the hair on my neck stand. His eyes were fixed on the second floor of the home.

I glanced up to where he was staring & rocks fell in my gut. "Harper, did your team leave any windows open?"

"Of course not!" Harper sounded offended by the idea, as well he should be. Leaving a closed crime scene open to the elements would be a grave offense.

Still, a pale curtain fluttered against the glass of a closed window. No wind could have rustled it and the fabric on the opposite side stood still as a sentinel. Someone had pulled it aside or flipped it in some fashion.

Gabe was still staring at the mysterious curtain as the motion ceased. "Is anyone supposed to be here today?"

"No, why?" Harper stood, still holding the ripped crime scene tape.

Gabe finally averted his gaze. "Second floor, someone's watching us."

Harper looked like something had stung him, backing away from the door and looking up. "Did you see them?"

Gabe shook his head. "Just the curtain moving."

This wasn't right. I took in a deep breath, expecting the smell of decay and rotted blood to overwhelm me. It didn't. I spat out a curse. Gabe looked down at me, concern in his gaze.

"What?"

Fuck this was bad.

"Lily?"

Dammit, I shouldn't have brought him. Any insight he might offer wasn't worth the risk. He might hurt Harper. Neither of us would ever forgive ourselves if that happened.

"Lily, what is it?"

I swallowed the lump in my throat and finally looked at him. "Smell."

Gabe looked confused but stood straight, closing his eyes like he was getting ready to meditate. He drew in a long breath before gasping. He instantly hunched, breathing heavily. I grabbed his shoulders, steadying him and making sure he couldn't lunge away.

Gabe was already drooling, the thick streams all over the sleeves of my jacket. I forced myself to hold his gaze; it was like staring into the eyes of a hungry bear.

CHAPTER 8

GABE

The air was delicious, like walking into a bakery first thing in the morning after starving for a month. It was thick and warm and every nerve in my body quivered with need and expectation.

"Collins?" Harper moved like he would come to comfort me, his big frame edging closer in my peripheral.

Dear God, no. Don't let him get close. Not when I'm like this.

I wouldn't be able to control myself if Harper came any closer. He took another step, the single thud accompanied by the steady thrum of his pulse, the volume slowly rising into an intoxicating rhythm.

Bum bum. Bum bum. Bum bum.

It was taunting me.

No! No! No!

"No!" Lily snapped the single word as my mind continued to rail. Her gaze stayed locked intently with mine. "Stay where ya are!"

"What's wrong with him?"

"Stay there!" I couldn't tell which of us said it.

Harper flinched but stayed quiet while Lily continued to grip my shoulders. Would she be enough to hold me back? Some vampire legends stated vampires grew stronger with time. But Lily was still incredibly skinny compared with me. I had more muscle on my skeleton; did that transfer over in this life? I didn't know and I was terrified to find out.

I closed my eyes, trying to focus on any other noise. Anything beside the delectable beat of my friend's heart. The steady thrum of blood in his veins pulling me in. I was shaking, my fingers digging so deep into her jacket I might tear the leather.

"I don't get it," I gasped out. I'd been in front of blood before. Hell, I'd been in front of a whole person thinking about their blood in my mouth, and it still hadn't been this agonizing.

"The blood we're smellin' is fresh." She breathed in heavily. "Not even an hour old."

This crime scene was days old; how was there fresh blood? It must have something to do with the intruder but my mind was too rattled to piece things together.

She looked around quickly. "Ya gotta pull it together, fast."

How could she ask that of me? Just standing here was a challenge, even while I was being held like a baby learning to walk. And she wanted me to sally forth and possibly eat Harper.

"Gabe, we don't know who's inside." Lily's voice turned cold. "I can't watch out for Harper from two fronts."

Shit.

I closed my eyes, taking one long breath and forcing myself to steady under the aroma. It didn't work. The air begged me to find the nearest source of blood and devour it. To feast until I could slip in the warmth of a gory food coma.

That brought my mind to a real massacre, children screaming in the background. Some for their parents, others in agony. But instead of the face I knew from that day, I saw myself, gorging on innocent people foolish enough to leave their house when the world didn't even know vampires were real.

Dammit, no! I have to be a vampire but I will not be a monster.

I forced myself to sit with this image. To live with the very idea of inflicting that kind of pain on someone. I put Harper in place of the victim in my head. I inserted my father.

My body turned from feverish to freezing.

I blinked several times and finally looked at Lily. "I think I'm okay."

"Ya sure?" She didn't sound certain. I barely managed a nod and she let go.

The loss of support felt odd and I had to suppress an urge to reach out for her again. I *would* do this. Streams of saliva made the sleeves of her jacket shine and an obscene part of me was embarrassed. We had a fresh crime scene in the house and I was worried about spit.

She ran her hands down each elbow, smoothing the slick trails away and shaking her hands dry before walking forward. I wiped my chin with a sleeve and squared my shoulders, facing towards the open door. To an outsider, I must have looked ridiculous. Treating the entrance of this suburban home like the entrance to a dragon's cave.

"Let's get this over with." I gulped and entered the beast's lair before either could respond, forcing them to scramble after me.

"Do we have time for these?" Harper scooted in, taking time to cover his shoes with blue booties. He held back, probably waiting to make sure it was safe to approach me.

"Yeah, toss us some gear." My voice shook and I closed my eyes for a minute. I started to breathe but stopped short, remembering that might start me up again. So I tried, instead, to focus on facts.

The techs had already been here but there was apparently a new crime scene in the mix. Either we were about to be attacked or find new evidence. Unless our enemies came barreling down on us, Lily and I would have to be very careful not to contaminate the scene. Harper's presence could be excused, but either of ours would only make the investigation more challenging going forward. Since they hadn't assaulted us, chances were whoever was watching us had already high-tailed it.

Lily shut the door and stood next to me, watching me like a lion loose in the zoo. Her vigilance gave me little comfort. If I got overwhelmed again, I wasn't sure God himself could stop me.

Harper gave Lily a questioning look and she nodded, giving him permission to approach. He handed us each a set of boot covers and gloves. My hands shook as I pulled on the booties. Lily pulled the gloves on quickly enough but seemed to have trouble balancing as she covered each boot.

"Here." I offered an elbow for balance.

"Thanks." She placed a hand on my arm, putting her weight on the limb as she pulled on one cover then the next. I took the opportunity to catalog our surroundings.

The entrance was lined with tile-print linoleum. Not a single crack or stain marred the surface, so it was either new or very well cared for. The entrance banked off a living area with carpet that showed several signs of use, grooves from someone wearing trails as they paced or maybe got up to retrieve something from the kitchen. The furniture was all old but clean and well kept. The room was spotless and even showed trails in the carpet from being recently vacuumed.

These people didn't have anything extravagant but they had cared about their home.

I swallowed once. "Crime scene?"

"Basement." Harper and Lily said together, their tones equally glum.

"Should we call for vampire back-up?" I gave the stairs to the second level an evaluating glance.

"No point." Lily shook her head. "By the time they get here this will be taken care of."

"Fine, let's get going." I looked at my old partner. "Harper, stay at the end of the hall, just in case."

Hopefully, no one with fangs would get past Lily or me. If they did, Harper stood very little chance.

"No need to tell me twice."

There wasn't anything more to be said. We needed to clear the rooms one at a time.

I walked towards the stairs and ascended into a short hallway, several closed doors before me. I stopped at the first door to my right, listening. No noise from inside the room.

I looked down, unsurprised to find Lily right next to me. She scanned the rest of the hallway before turning her gaze to mine. I reached out, placing a hand on the knob and raising my brows in question. She gave the door a wary look but nodded.

Harper appeared at the top of the stairs, his service pistol drawn and ready. I turned the handle, checking to the side and behind the door before entering any further. A bathroom, barely big enough for two people to stand in. No window inside, so the curtain hadn't been here. But the tub was wet, the shower head dripping slowly. No steam had shrouded the mirror.

Someone had been here, but it had been a while.

Lily and I nodded and moved onto the next door, unsurprised to find a linen closet. No boogie man or gremlins jumped at me. I moved across the hall to the next door, even if the window had been at the front of the house, it was a bad idea to leave the room unchecked with Harper here.

It turned out to be the master bedroom, a queen-sized bed on a simple metal frame. The dresser looked like something you probably had to assemble yourself, with a lot of visible allen-wrench settings and peeling faux wood and a small TV on top. The master bathroom had a stand up shower with an eighties-style glass door and yellow shell-shape vanity. A quick look in the closet, under the bed and into the master bath revealed no ghosts or goblins.

The next room down the hall turned out to be another bedroom, and I checked it as I had the last few, Lily standing guard at the door. The offending curtain turned out to be in this room, but no one lurked behind the door or amidst the cheap furniture.

The room was painted dark and lined with movie and music posters. A dark arrangement of clothes were hung messily in the closet, while counterparts were sprawled all over the floor. A rebelling teenager maybe?

My mind flashed back to the details Lily had given me. She'd kept them vague, only telling me the basics so I wouldn't be shocked at the grizzly scene. Still, one thing stood out in her recollections of this place.

This had been a family of five.

My heart sank to my shoes as I went back into the hall, my eyes landing on the final door. There were only three bedrooms up here. Sure the parents would share one, but there had been five bodies, not four. It was bad enough imagining a whole family slaughtered, but this. From the punk-rock room, I already knew one life had been snuffed out before it had really begun. My gut writhed at the thought of what lay beyond the last door.

I walked down the hall, the smell of fresh blood becoming stronger with each step. My hands trembled and I felt the sharp twist of fangs tearing my lower lip, but the churning sickness in my stomach overwhelmed the aching hunger. This door was cracked open, but not enough to see inside. I pushed on the hollow oak with two fingers and my chest clenched.

A child's room with two single beds. An open window between the beds let in cool air that slowly curled the curtains and stirred the scent of fresh blood right to me.

One half of the room was organized; filled with books, movies, animals, and other various toys to separate them like bookends. I didn't look but I was willing to bet they were shelved alphabetically. Where the neat side was bright and cheerful, the scattered side was oddly muted but for the comic books and clothes that were piled on every surface.

The blood was directly in the center.

Crimson footprints moved from the window, around the beds and back again. Several tracks, the hues ranging from rotted brown to a bright scarlet. Most of them stemmed from a single spot in the floor, where several deep layers of red pooled in various shades on top of one another, blending into the macabre collage, topped with a corpse.

His skin sagged and his bowels had emptied, staining his pants. No bloating yet, nothing indicating he'd been out long. There wasn't a smell of decay, just blood.

I swallowed the saliva flooding my mouth. I was staring at a crime scene, something I'd done hundreds of times. I was meant to be queasy and outraged at this sight of him. Instead I was salivating.

"Gabe?"

"Give me a second." My voice was harsh, shaking. As were my hands.

I closed my eyes and thought back to my training. Look at the facts. Start with the basics and move your way up.

Okay, let's look at the person.

The man was ordinary in every way possible. Middle aged, white, and a little pudgy around the middle. A worn button up and abused pair of slacks were his only clothes. His brown hair was simply styled in something that could pass any work environment. His eyes were wide open and rolled back, making the color hard to determine.

Even his features were bland. Something about him made me think of an extra in some B-rate movie.

"He hasn't been-" I coughed and swallowed my drool. "He hasn't been here very long."

She walked up and knelt by the body. "Agreed."

The footprints continued from the body, going in and out of the closets, diminishing in size as the blood had dried on the bottom of the intruder's shoes. They either didn't care about leaving a mess or didn't have the skill to clean up after themselves. But that wasn't what bothered me most.

Those are some very small shoes.

I tapped Lily's shoulder, motioning to look at the trail around the room before pointing towards the left closet then to the right. Lily nodded, heading to the left. I checked the crevice behind the door before proceeding toward the right. We both placed a hand on each of the bi-fold doors and I nodded at Lily to go first.

Hers was already cracked open, a hoodie wedged between the open doors, so she didn't have to move it much to look inside. She stuck her head into the open closet, looking back and forth before turning back and shaking her head. I turned back to my set.

It was a silent action, aside from a low swish of the door wheels winding in their tracks. No demon waited in the dark. Just clothes, organized as methodically as the books and movies. I poked my head in, checking the corners and shelves. Nothing. I turned and shook my head.

Lily eyed the open window and fluttering curtain, annoyance twisting her lips. She sniffed the air and grimaced. "Shit."

"What?"

She inhaled again. "I think we know where Anna's been–"

The monster jumped out from under one of the beds, a cyclone of brown and purple streaking towards the window. She was halfway out when I jumped across the bed, grabbing for one tiny ankle and drawing her back in. She howled, kicking her other foot into my face as she hit the ground.

I cursed and let go as she landed a direct hit in my eye. Lily jumped over the bed, reaching to grab the girl. The little monster bit her hand, sinking her teeth deep into the flesh and pulling away like an angry shark.

"Fuck!"

In the mayhem, the girl clawed to get out from between us. Both of us made a grab for her again, only to smack our skulls into each other and the little brat elbowed me in the groin. Her little bones made the blow sharp and it took everything I had to avoid doubling over.

"Guys?" Harper's voice was quickly followed by his heavy steps running down the hall.

Lily fought to grab the small waist, but the brat squirmed free, kneeing Lily in the chest and running for it. We scrambled after her, but not before she'd made it out of the room and into the hall. I flew after her, Lily right on my heels.

"What the–" Harper gasped as the girl jumped up, grabbing his face and looking directly into his eyes.

"Put a bullet in your head." The command was stern but small-voiced, like it came from a demonic pixie.

My soul lodged in my throat as Harper raised his gun. "No!"

I urged my feet to go faster right as the scene unfolded before me. Harper brought his gun up, but instead of pointing it at himself, he slammed the butt of his service pistol down on the girl's skull and she sagged onto his shoulder.

I stopped in my tracks, staring, confused. Lily came forward and took the child in her arms.

She shook her hand like she'd only gotten a nasty papercut. "Little gobshite took a chunk."

"Want my bandanna to wrap it?" Harper went to remove the cloth from his head, looking a little green at the missing piece of flesh.

"It'll close in a minute. Thanks." She looked at the offer briskly and turned her attention back to the girl. "Dammit, this is bad..."

"Excuse me!" My mind caught up and released its iron grip on my mouth. "How are you still standing?"

"Huh?" Harper looked bewildered. Lily blinked a few times before looking back to him.

"Ya didn't tell him about the blood, did ya?"

"Oh, shit." Harper put his pistol away and smacked his forehead with the heel of his hand. "I forgot. Sorry, buddy."

"Blood?" Like I didn't already know.

"Yep." He let the 'p' pop as he pointed at his skull. "Regular transfusions to keep them out of my noggin.'"

I thought about it and wanted to slap myself. Of course, what better way to protect an ally?

"So—" I nodded to indicate the little girl, "should we check for others?"

"Turn up your ears." Lily was already on the stairs. Her tone was solid rock. "If someone else is here, they aren't movin' a muscle. When they do, a floorboard will creak or somethin.'"

Harper looked between us in confusion before turning back to me. "Turn up your *ears?*"

"Fancy vampire hearing." I walked past him and gave the bandanna another look before snatching it off his head. "Thanks."

"Hey!" His big palm slapped against his barren scalp in protest.

I followed Lily into the kitchen, watching as she gently seated the girl in a dining room chair. The sweaty bandanna made a pathetic offering when I held it out.

"Really, you too?" She rolled her eyes. "You've seen me heal from far worse."

I grimaced at what I was about to say. "It's for her mouth."

"Oh, yeah. I guess." Lily took the cloth from my hand, kneeling to push the girl's wild hair from her face. The kid was a crazy mix between Cousin It and a yeti. "It won't last long, but if we can get her to hold still, we might have a chance to talk to her."

"Can we not gag her?" Harper stood behind me, shifting back and forth on his feet, the gesture awkward on his big frame.

"Sure." Lily held up her hand, the missing flesh slowly materializing. "Ya wanna hold her mouth shut?"

True, the sight of her gnawing at the cloth would be disturbing, but we couldn't have her screaming and getting the neighbors' attention.

Harper looked like he was going to vomit but kept his opinion to himself.

I knelt next to Lily. "Are children common?"

It hadn't ever occurred to me before. The very idea was foul but I was new to this world.

"No." Lily was still combing the tangles away from the unconscious face, her tone was clipped. She'd just finished her task and readied the bandanna, rolling it before getting ready to tie it over our captive's mouth. She froze, the gag inches from the girl's face.

"Fuck." Lily's eyes bulged to cartoonish levels and she slapped a hand over her mouth in disbelief.

"What?" I looked at the girl, expecting to find some type of injury. Ridiculous, considering the circumstances, but it was my gut reaction.

Nothing stood out. The girl was filthy, her lax face covered in various smudges and hues, red all over her mouth from her recent meal.

My insides coiled around themselves as I imagined this *child* attacking the man we found upstairs. Pondering how she'd lured him here and avoided detection. I decided I didn't want to know. Not yet.

Was the gruesome visual too much for Lily?

Lily still wasn't responding, falling slowly back to her knees examining the unconscious child.

"What?" I repeated, turning my attention to Harper. He looked about as enlightened as I felt.

"Olive." Lily's voice was so soft I'd almost missed it.

She swallowed and looked at me, her eyes probing. The name was familiar but my brain struggled to find the source. Olive. Olive.

Then it clicked.

The small girl posing in her school photo with a lost front tooth, missing for over three years. Olive Taylor. I looked down, past the dirt and the wild mass of hair. Her brown locks were far longer than the photo, hanging well past her shoulders despite the current chaotic state. She was older than her photo, maybe ten. Her face was also leaner, sharper. But there, in her pointed chin and her slightly widened nose, I could still see traces of the girl smiling awkwardly for the camera.

"Shit." True, she was no different than any other little girl to me. I'd only seen her picture for a moment. But this added a layer to the crime, an aspect I didn't understand, not with so little to go off. "What do we do?"

Lily worried her bottom lip, staring at the little girl, not even seeming to have heard my question.

I placed a hand on her shoulder. "Lily?"

She looked up slowly, her eyes swimming with uncertainty. "I've got to go."

CHAPTER 9

LILY

Whatever Gabe had expected me to say, that wasn't it. "What?"

I didn't have time to address it. "Harper, can you take Gabe home?"

"What?" They both looked like I was speaking an alien language. But I didn't have time. I'd known what I'd have to do the minute she crawled from under that bed. There wasn't any other choice.

Now those fang marks in the photos made sense; they were too small. I should have known, I'd seen it all before.

"You'll have to call Court later." I pulled out my phone, snapping it over my knee and breaking off Gabe's next question in a shower of glass and metal before tossing the two halves to the side. "They'll need to know what's happening to the youngsters."

Harper stuttered. Gabe wasn't much better but he got the question out first. "What's going on? Why can't *you* call them?"

"Please, Gabe, you've got to trust me." I started pulling open drawers in the kitchen, slamming each shut when it clearly didn't have what I needed. Finally I stumbled upon an overstuffed, miscellaneous drawer with phone chargers and batteries on the top of many layers. Duct tape... I hated the idea but she'd probably wake up fighting. "They'll kill her."

"What?!" Gabe stepped back into my path, his face stretched in shock and apparent horror.

"Why?" Harper sounded worried, looking between the two of us like it was a tennis match waiting to start. "I mean who's to say she's our killer?"

Normally, Harper's optimistic nature was endearing. Right now it just made him seem naive in the face of... well, the girl's face. She was covered in fresh blood. Even if she hadn't been the original murderer, and that would be one hell of a coincidence, she was definitely the killer for the guy upstairs.

Still, no child just woke up a vampire and anyone who'd be brash enough to turn a youngster probably hadn't helped her figure out alternative ways to feed after transition.

"Yeah." Gabe ground out the words, cold fury hardening his eyes. "Doesn't she even get a trial? Or do vampires not have that?"

"It's not about that." I *so* didn't have time for this shit. "It's illegal to turn children."

"So what?" Gabe's volume started to raise and he squared his shoulders. "Surely the Court can understand she couldn't have consented to this? She's just a kid!"

"It doesn't matter." I needed him to get this and get it fast. I didn't want to fight him or Harper but I needed to get out of here. "It draws attention when someone so young *never* changes"

"What does that matter?" Gabe looked like he'd swallowed raw sewage. "They don't want to babysit a bunch of vamp kids through the craze? Your race kind of sucks."

"It's *your* race too," I hissed back. "Sorry, it's just as imperfect as the last one."

"So you just kill them all, don't even give them the chance to try?"

"I don't do a damn thing!" I shouted despite myself. "You are the worst kind of eejit if ya think I'd ever bash a baby's brains in!"

Some tension in my stomach relaxed when Gabe's shoulder sagged a little.

I didn't have time to explain this now; I just knew I had to get going. Give us some distance. I wasn't sure what the hell I would tell Ivan this time but it didn't matter.

Olive was still dangerous, but there was another solution to the Court's.

Harper stared at us, stunned into immobility.

"I'll take her out of town. Once I get her far enough away, you two tell the Court. They still need to know what Elias is doing." I stepped forward, my hand outstretched and my eyes pleading. "Please, I know someone who can help."

"No."

"Please Gabe, just tell him I overpowered ya or threatened Harper. Ivan will give ya the benefit of the doubt."

"No," Gabe repeated. "You're not going alone."

Oh, hell no.

"You almost *ate* Harper–" I pointed at the captain, and he jerked back like I was threatening him, "but ya wanna go on a bloody road trip?"

"Can you watch her every second of every day?" He gave me a pointed look.

"Ya were just complainin' about *coffee drips* in my kitchen." I flapped my arms in the general direction of my house, like it was available as evidence. "How are ya goin' to handle the noise of a traffic jam?"

Dammit, I didn't have time for this. Ivan was expecting me to check in any minute. He knew I'd brought Gabe here, we'd had a rather heated conversation about it. When he called my phone and it went to voicemail...

"I need the practice." Gabe shrugged but it didn't look convincing.

"Your face is all over the news!" I fought to find anything that might knock some sense into him."Ya can't wear a motorcycle helmet everywhere!"

"Lily, you can either keep arguing with me until the Court gets here–" he let that thought hang for a moment before continuing, "or we can leave now."

I stared at him, trying to think of anything I could say that might sway him. I already had a violently turned child, I really didn't need a newb to train at the same time.

"If ya come with me, you're givin' up Court protection." It was my last card to play.

"What's that mean?" Harper, finally able to speak again.

"It's a lot like being an illegal alien," I tried to explain quickly. "You're technically protected by law but–"

"Those same laws condemn you, making you an easy target." Gabe hunched like someone had loaded the weight of the world on him. "So we'll be fugitives from the Court right after we exposed Elias' drug operation in the city?"

I nodded. "Precisely."

Gabe's eyes started to dart back and forth before he nodded once. "Okay, let's get going."

My jaw fell but words wouldn't form. He was a bloody moron. He had to understand what that meant. Coming with me made us both fair game for Elias and his merry men. But he still wanted to come and I couldn't stop him...

Shit.

"Give me the girl."

"I'm comi–"

"Give me the girl," I repeated more harshly. "And help me restrain her."

Understanding dawned and he complied, taking the roll of tape and letting me walk past him.

I picked Harper's bandanna off the ground and gagged Olive before swooping her into my arms. A sharp *zip* ripped the air as Gabe pulled a long, shiny piece free.

"You sure about this, buddy?" Harper's voice was an octave higher than normal and shaking. At least I wasn't the only one panicking.

"I don't see another option." Gabe's voice shook as he stuck the end of one long strip to the counter and began to tear another.

"But..." Harper's face drooped.

"I know." Gabe paused to pat his friend's shoulder. "But we don't have time."

⋇

It was an hour before Gabe spoke. "Are you sure they can't track us from the scene?"

His voice made me jump; I'd been so focused on the road. As though staring would make us go any faster.

"Our scents will be too subtle after we got in the car. Even if it wasn't, they can't exactly put their nose to the ground in that neighborhood. It would draw too much attention."

"We managed to get a bound child into the car." His tone was pointed.

"Yeah, and that was a fuckin' cake walk."

He considered this. "Fair enough. So what's the plan?"

"Right now." I blew out a breath and glared at the ceiling of the car. "Ditch the car somewhere Ivan can find it; he'll make sure Alex gets it back. We need somethin' he can't trace anyway."

"Makes sense, Court might ask Harper to put an APB on the plates." Gabe flicked his eyes to the rearview mirror. "After that?"

"I'm kind of wingin' it." I looked into the back seat. "Any ideas?"

I didn't get a response; Olive was still out, her limp form draped over the backseat, the seatbelts wrapped gently around her and breaking up the shine of tape on her ankles and wrists.

Gabe tapped the steering wheel and turned like he was checking his blind spot. He eyed me a few times before asking, "Why'd you ask Harper to tell Ivan?"

"Huh?"

"You knew Ivan would..." He let the words trail and glanced in the rearview mirror again. "You knew, why tell him?"

I thought about it; I hadn't really debated it at the moment, but I knew the answer even before the words formed in my mind. I couldn't let it happen again, but...

"It's a clue, even if I don't have any fuckin' idea what it means." I swallowed, trying to find the right words. "I owed Ivan that much."

"And you said you know someone that can help?"

I nodded. "I have a place that will take her in."

"So who are these people?" Gabe flicked his eyes away from the road to the mirror again. "How do you know them?"

I stared at my feet, shame washing over me. "Long story short, they ran a ring of child protection the Court took down in the fifties."

"Huh." Gabe chewed on that for a second. I let the silence fill the cabin, hoping that would be enough.

"If the Court took them out, how do you know about them?"

I sighed. Of course that simple answer wouldn't be enough. This man was freaking curiosity on a stick.

"I helped."

"What?" The single word was crisp through tight lips.

"I..." I struggle to come up with anything. "I didn't have a choice."

He gave me another sideways glance before turning his attention back to the asphalt ahead. "Explain."

Great, another fucking Q&A.

I rubbed my forehead with the palm of my hand. "Look, can we do this later? I'm tryin' to think."

He turned to face me, just long enough to say, "And I'm deciding whether or not I keep going with you."

"You're insane!" I squawked. "First ya badger me to take you now you wanna pull a U-turn? Make up your mind!"

"If you can't tell me what you did and why, then how are we going to work together?"

I opened my mouth but only a squeak came out.

"We've been through a lot—" he continued, "but I still hardly know you. Give me a reason to trust you."

Shit.

Could I get Olive away on my own? Gabe didn't know where Melissa hid or how to get in contact with her. He also could still go back and claim I'd forced him or something.

But hadn't I burned enough bridges today? Even if I did get away with Olive, doing this by myself was still more than a little impractical. He'd been right about that.

But would he really trust me if I told him?

He sighed. "Fine, I'll drop—"

"It was a woman hoarding child vampires!" I blurted it out, trying to end his thought before it began.

He blinked several times. "Excuse me?"

"Sometimes vampires, mostly women—" I struggled to force the words out, "can't handle the idea that they'll never be a parent. Usually one's enough, but this one went way off the deep end."

"Oh, cause turning a kid, that's sane."

"Of course not!" I snapped then looked into the back seat before lowering my voice again. "Obviously, those women are sick pups. This woman was just... worse."

Mental images of corpses and feral vampires resurfaced, the memories struggling for air after I'd tried to drown them for so long.

"She had several children in her home. She wasn't teachin' them through the hunger, just turnin' them and then lettin' them loose. That's how we found her, the bodies kept turnin' up."

I paused, not sure how to continue. If he hadn't already thought low of me before, this would sink me to the deepest depth of hell in his mind.

"Keep. Going." He was clutching the wheel so tight I could hear plastic cracking.

Dammit. He really wasn't going to like this. I didn't.

"When we realized it was youngsters, we had one lead us back to the nest. During the interview, we realized some were missin' and had been for weeks. We put the first batch down and looked for the stragglers."

He inhaled sharply, and exhaled slowly "When you say put them down..."

"They killed them," I croaked, needing this over with already. "*We* killed every last one."

Gabe pulled over and turned off the engine. "How many?"

This man had once called me a 'fucking fang head.' He'd refused to use my name in the beginning, referring to me as 'vampire.' Still, those two words were the coldest thing I'd ever heard him speak.

"Twe.." I choked on the number, forcing it out like slow vomit. "Twent... Twenty-eight."

When he got out of the car this time, he did leave a dent in the door. I let out a breath and debated if I should follow him. Did he need answers or space?

A furious grunt from the back seat startled me. Someone definitely wanted a little room. I glanced in the rearview, only to see Olive wrenching her arms apart, slowly tearing the tape. I sighed and tapped my head against the headrest. It didn't have the effect I was looking for.

There was no point in leaving the restraints. She'd just rip out of them. I might as well earn some goodwill. I dug in my boots for a knife.

"Here." I reached into the backseat and Olive's eyes grew to the size of fish bowls. She scooted away and thrashed as I grabbed her wrists. I made the business quick, cutting the remaining tape on her wrists. She stilled as the silver strip snapped, her fingers stiff as she stared.

"We'll be back in a minute." I tucked the blade back in its slot. I had the distinct feeling she'd rather get the rest of her bonds on her own. "I'm kind of havin' a shit day, so please don't make me chase ya."

I let the sentence hang and watched her eyes. They were wary and I couldn't exactly blame her. Either she'd run or she wouldn't. Either way, I knew I could catch her.

I followed Gabe, stopping to engage the child locks. Olive could get through them if she really wanted, but at least she'd make a lot of racket before she got out. The air was cool as I looked up and down the barren two-lane highway.

We were near a larger city, so even if someone did happen by, a good samaritan was unlikely to stop and offer help. It was as good a place as any to get this over with. I closed my door and walked to the front of the car, sitting cross-legged on the hood while he paced.

He finally turned back to me, his eyes twin slits. "You killed twenty-eight kids?"

I stared at my lap trying to find a way to explain it. "Ivan said that the loss of these children would save hundreds of children from being turned."

"And you just accepted that?"

"I begged them not to!" I didn't mean the shout, but now I couldn't stop. "Why do ya think everyone at Court hates me?!"

The final word seemed to hang over us, echoing through the highway.

"*That's* the favor you cashed in for Anna?" He breathed in deep, the idea settling. "That's why Ritti punishes you."

I let out a dark chuckle. "They forced me to be quiet. Said we needed to band together as a team for the sake of the court."

What a load of shit.

"So, if you took them out, how are these people still out and about?"

"We captured the kids but I let the operation escape."

"How?" He looked confused.

"They made a break for it after we found them." Memories threatened to surface and I pushed them back, trying to focus on facts so I could get this out. "I found 'em a couple years later and gave them a few tips to fly under Court radar."

"And they trusted you, after everything?" He sounded impressed and disbelieving at the same time. "How'd they know it wasn't a trick?"

"They didn't. It took a lot of time and only mutually assured destruction helped us get along."

"And how do you know they're still in business?"

"We have a friend in common."

He didn't have time to question that as glass shattered and metal crunched in the car behind me.

CHAPTER 10

GABE

G lass poured over the ground like jagged drops of rain, sparkling on the blacktop. Each kick produced a small thunder to accompany the storm. I would have to deal with everything I'd just learned later.

As I rushed past Lily and down the passenger side of the car, Olive was frantically kicking the door with both legs, like she was trying to propel herself through the other side. From the basketball sized dents, she'd gotten in at least seven good kicks. Not all the glass had broken on to the road, some of it glittered on Olive's clothes as she continued to kick and scream.

"Olive, stop!" I yanked the door open. She paused at the sound of her name, then tried to kick my face. I dodged one foot, then the other, as the opposite door opened.

Olive's shrieks grew even louder, her thrashing even more panicked as Lily reached in, pinning her to the seat. "Knock it off!"

Olive spat and snapped her teeth, but Lily kept her arms just out of range.

"If ya don't stop, I'll punch your lights out!"

"Lily!"

"Ya got a better idea?"

The girl stilled, her face pinched in a gremlin state, staring at Lily.

Uncomfortable silence hung between us all and I shivered, not just from the cold afternoon. A car passed and reminded me that we had to move, and soon. God knew what this looked like to anyone passing by.

"We need to get goin'." Lily glared a warning down at the girl. "I get that ya hate me but–"

"This isn't about you!"

She flinched and Olive looked baffled by my tone. I pushed a hand through my hair and sighed, keeping an eye on our tiny captive and trying to calm down. Now was not the time. It wasn't the place.

The silence stretched between us, a thick substance that swallowed every precious second. We needed to move. As per usual, we'd have to talk later.

"So how will we proceed?" Olive intoned. Her voice came out less demon pixie, more precise and clipped than seemed suited to a child, breaking me from my thoughts.

"Right now–" I looked between them, "we need to keep moving away from the Court. And you–" I pointed at Lily, "are going to tell me everything."

I needed to know who the real Lily was. Once and for all.

"Fine." Lily nodded. "Since you're already pissed, we need to talk about somethin' else."

Her words came out so tense, my own body went rigid. I tried to steady myself. "What?"

"Ya need to feed from a human. Tonight."

"Are you kidding?" My tone turned chilly. Really, she wanted to push this agenda *now*? "After what just happened, you want to introduce that complication?"

"We're at least a few days away from where Melissa holds up. We'll all need to feed between now and then. Do ya have another solution?"

"We'll steal from a blood bank or something." It sounded pathetic even as I said it. "After what we just saw, you want to expose a human to her?"

"I am right here." The little urchin wiggled her foot to emphasize the point.

"Yeah and you just tried to escape." I gave the battered door a meaningful look.

"And who's fault is that?" She glanced between us both.

Lily seemed to ignore this entire transaction "So, you'd rather take donated blood and add more exposure to this trip than learn somethin' ya need to know anyway?" She arched an eyebrow in her typical routine, but it annoyed me more than usual.

"And Olive?"

"We can obviously overpower her." Lily glanced down. "You'll behave, right?"

Olive glared back, blinked a few times before nodding once, sharply.

"Good girl." Lily let off her and slammed her side of the car closed.

Olive gave me another glance and I watched Lily get back in the car before kneeling to her height.

I let out a breath. "You going to try that again?"

She looked hard between the two of us and shook her head. "You've proven your point and I clearly lost my advantage when your human failed to shoot himself."

Her disappointed tone made blood boil in my veins. The mere mention of what she'd tried with Harper made me reconsider the restraints, but I held my tongue.

"Don't think that I won't be watching you."

"Don't imply that I'm foolish." The girl sat up and buckled herself back in.

"Ya are foolish." Lily rubbed her temples. "If I wanted ya harmed, handin' ya over to the Court would have been much quicker, ya eejit."

Olive looked taken aback, looked down and pinched her chin between two fingers before finally nodding. "You have a valid point."

Lily turned to look at the girl, staring at her like she was trying to put a square peg in a circular hole.

"Have ya always been so–" Lily twirled her hand as she hunted for the word, "formal?"

I was wondering that myself. I'd had to interview children for the VPB more than once. Rarely were they so straightforward about life or death scenarios, and they weren't known for sitting to evaluate them. Olive had done so and explained her situation like a soldier. It was... unsettling.

Olive blinked several times. "What do you mean?"

Lily eyed the girl for another moment, then shook her head. "Never mind. We'll talk more when we get to a motel or something."

Shutting the door, I snorted at the bumpy surface between Olive's door and mine. Anyone passing would most likely give us a lot of space, assuming we'd had one hell of a wreck.

I got in, turned the engine over and pulled back onto the two-lane highway. I didn't think I could engage Olive in standard road trip games, the Alphabet or I Spy. Nothing would make this less awkward. Might as well continue the conversation.

"What was the favor?"

"Huh?"

"You used a favor to save Anna. It obviously wasn't how you handled the kids. So what was it?"

"What's that matter?" She looked at her boots again.

"You did something for the Court. Something that saved that worthless woman." I pretended to pay careful attention to the road, not wanting to see her face. "And I doubt the united front was that high in price for Ritti."

Just yesterday, she'd massaged my headache away. Before that, she'd shown me the *perks* in this existence. Now, she was a child murdering accomplice, trying to save one kid. Just when I thought I understood Lily, new information would change everything, like the now falling snow obscuring the image through our windshield.

Each word fell from her lips like a cold stone. "I assisted in the executions."

I closed my eyes, just for a second, then turned them back to the road. It took everything in me to stay calm, but the next question was frosty on my tongue. "Why?"

"At first, I was hopin' I could get close enough to sneak one out, but Ivan caught me." She made a choking sound that made me certain she was crying, but I couldn't bear to look at her. "If I didn't go through with it, I would have died with them."

I wasn't sure what to make of this. Would I have done any better? I wanted to say that I would have, but I didn't know. From the sound of it, either way, the kids would be gone. What lengths would I go through to save them, and could Lily have been any use to them if Ivan had reported her? What would the repercussions have been? Did I even want to know?

"Stop there." Lily pointed at an exit for a truck stop, pulling me out of my inner monologue. Right, the car. My stomach churned in on itself, thinking about what else this stop would mean.

"I think we should wait until we get to the city." I pulled onto the exit. "I hate to steal a car from someone in the middle of nowhere."

Sure, they might be able to get a taxi, but that wouldn't be cheap. The nearest city was at least a half hour back. Or they might end up driving with a stranger, and God only knew how that would end.

"We're not stealin' anything." Lily looked offended at the notion. "Whatever gave ya that idea?"

I clamped my mouth from saying the other things I never thought she would do.

"It would be efficient but it would also draw police attention," Olive noted in a monotone, her eyes still examining our surroundings out the window.

"There's that," I acknowledged. "*And* the fact that we'd be hurting someone who did nothing to earn it."

"You're running from two vampire Courts." Olive turned her attention to us but her expression was bored at best. "Collateral damage is to be expected."

Lily and I shared an uneasy look. Jesus, what was with this kid?

I didn't see the point of arguing ethics with her, not yet anyway. But her words still left a question. "Two Courts?"

"The Americans and Elias."

I didn't have long to ponder the implications of what she was saying, as Lily indicated a parking space in the huge truck stop. Eighteen-wheelers and various cars were split into two groups. A worn down but clean gas station sat just beyond two giant pump stations with several bright advertisements for food, showers, and other utilities painted in big bubble letters.

Lily pointed to a faded parking spot further away from the building, maybe for people to rest their eyes on long trips. Hopefully far enough away to avoid the establishment's cameras. I pulled into the space backwards just to keep the mangled door on the driver's side from view.

"So, if we're not stealing a car, how are we getting out of here?" Olive's precision-tone was back in place.

"Hitch-hikin'." Lily gave me a rueful smile that didn't quite meet her eyes. "After we grab a quick bite."

I sighed and turned off the ignition. *No time like the present.* "Fine, how do we do this?"

"Watch and learn." Lily propped her feet on the dash and leaned back. "Bit like a stakeout."

The simple analogy gave me some relief. A stakeout I could handle. I wondered if she chose that particular comparison for my sake or because of her PI experience.

"I'm glad you didn't agree to the blood bank." Olive leaned forward with intent in her hazel gaze. She looked like she was on a secret mission, her statuesque posture a little disturbing. "This lasts longer."

Her casual comment made my stomach curl and I clenched my fists to keep them off the keys. Flashes of the dead man in the child's bedroom circled in my mind. We'd have to address that, figure out what the hell had happened. Obviously, Olive was dangerous and very capable. But I refused to believe she couldn't be rehabilitated.

A few minutes later Lily sat up and bobbed her head. "Him."

She used her chin to indicate a large man waddling towards a big rig and snacking on a Slim-Jim. He didn't look particularly remarkable to me.

"Why that one?"

Lily looked at both of us as she explained, "First of all, he's got snacks but no liquids. Second, his truck's not at the pump."

"So?" I wondered.

"Usually a sign they're about to crash in their truck. Most of them have beds in the back. If they only get a small snack but no drinks, they don't want the drink to get warm or the ice in the cooler to melt. They wait until they have finished nappin' to buy the rest of their supplies." Lily tugged at the edge of her tank top and checked that her hoodie was zipped up. "Give me a minute, then meet me on the passenger side of his truck and don't let anyone see ya. Truckers are a close bunch."

"What's your plan?"

Lily smiled, a mischievous little grin. "Just gonna show him these boots are made for walkin'!"

Olive looked as confused as I felt. Lily cut off any reply when she got out of the car and swayed her hips toward the stranger, waving him down. He stopped, almost letting the jerky slip from his mouth. Lily stepped right up and started talking. After a moment she started twirling her hair and visibly giggling while she squeezed the large man's biceps playfully. He said something and she bounced up, holding her hands up as she squealed before hugging the big man around the shoulders.

"Doesn't that hurt?" Olive's voice was curious.

"What do you mean?" I gritted out.

"Your hands are starting to turn white." She leaned between the two front seats and gave my hands a meaningful look.

Sure enough, my knuckles were pressing against the skin, turning deadly white. I relaxed my grip and my knuckles started to regain their normal color.

Unresolved issues with Lily aside, she was right about one thing. I'd chosen to come along. There was no way to keep delaying this.

I gulped, closing my eyes to calm my thoughts. Instead I was met with the mental reel of my father's funeral. The look on the coroner's face when he told me identifying him wasn't only not needed; it wasn't possible.

Could I really feed on someone, the same way they had done to him. The same way Olive had taken that man back at the house. Something about the scene nagged at my mind. Something other than the carnage.

"They're moving." Olive was back to her mission tone.

Sure enough, Lily and the large man were walking over to the nearest truck. Lily still swayed her hips, the motion grabbing every male set of eyes around her. She'd pulled a similar trick when I met her, wearing boots with a short skirt that made her legs more memorable than her face. The trucker opened the door for Lily before she bowed her head and smiled bashfully.

I placed a hand on Olive's shoulder, forcing her to look at me. "Do not try anything."

"Didn't we discuss this already?" Olive looked at the door and waited for me to disengage the child locks.

I got out, pausing to open the door for Olive. We began walking slowly toward the truck until we saw Lily sitting like a statue in the passenger seat. The trucker nodded at whatever she said and went to the back. Lily moved over to the driver's seat before opening the passenger door for us and we approached more quickly. I hoisted Olive up before entering the truck myself.

The little girl clamored between the two front seats and looked into the back. The large trucker sat on a makeshift mattress with a sedate grin that made my stomach roll into knots.

Was his head bobbing? I opened my mouth to ask about that, but Lily spoke first.

"I'll have to give him a good memory-overwrite when we leave."

"Huh?" I looked back to her, forgetting my previous question.

"Oh, he'll think..." Lily paused and gave Olive a meaningful look before continuing. "Somethin' more *fun* happened back there than what we're really doing."

Realization hit and I felt my jaw clench. Lily must have seen something in my expression because she cocked her head to the side.

"Nervous?"

"Let's just get this over with." Even I heard the hard edge to my tone.

Her expression was wounded but she nodded and got up.

"Okay, if you're new to direct feeding, the palm is the best place to start."

"Why not the neck?" Olive chimed, though I was wondering that myself.

"You watch too many movies. The neck has some very important veins that you can nick." Lily went back and lifted the guy's hand. "Blood flow to the palm is very limited. Harder to overdo it when you're just getting started."

She looked into the large man's gaze and smiled. "Jason, ya don't feel anything in your hands. You're happy just relaxin' here, singing your favorite song."

"Wait, that's what you've got him doing?" I all but laughed. He was bobbing to the beat.

"It's easier for them to ignore what's happenin' if ya give them somethin' pleasant to focus on. Easiest option these days is visualizing a TV show or listenin' to music." Lily gestured to me. "You first."

I looked out the truck window to see if anyone was watching. No one was and the trucker's bed was hidden from any exterior view. I slid into the back and sat opposite the large man, next to Lily. She lifted the man's hand, palm up.

"See that real fleshy bit 'round the thumb?" I nodded and she continued, "That's the best spot to go for. Now give him a directive, something ya think would feel relaxin'."

"Um." I coughed, unease filling me all over again. "How?"

"Same way ya learned to crawl." Lily lifted a shoulder. "Don't think, just do it."

I looked into Jason's face and cleared my throat. "So, you just keep listening to that song and stay real calm. This doesn't hurt."

Jason made no motion of understanding, just kept slowly rocking out.

"Try again." Lily's tone was one of mild reproach. "And this time, mean it."

"Mean it?"

"Yeah, it doesn't work if ya don't want it to. Bit like changing ya over. I could have fed ya every drop of my blood and ya wouldn't have risen unless I really wanted it."

Something in her tone made me hold back the reply I'd had in mind. Unless she really *wanted* it. So she didn't just change me out of duty or desperation. With everything else I had learned, the thought was comforting somehow, but it didn't resolve the current dilemma.

"Then it's never going to work." I pushed my hand through my hair and looked into our donor's complacent face. "How could you be comfortable taking away someone's free will?"

"I'm not." She worried her bottom lip before going on. "But my other options are starvin' or terrifyin' the man. To me, that's not much of a choice."

Starve? What would a starving vampire even look like? I blinked, taking a single second to take in her already frail figure. Given the vampire stasis I'd seen, I doubted they withered away in the traditional sense. Would vampire starvation even resemble the human counterpart, or would it look more like a mindless corpse, hungry and everlasting? I shook the thought away, filing it away for later. I already had a problem to solve right now, no need to make up a puzzle.

"You don't realize you're being fed from and this doesn't hurt."

Still no reaction. Lily sighed. "Don't worry, happens to almost everyone their first go. That's why I put him under first."

Olive giggled. The carefree note made me turn in surprise. It took everything in me to keep my jaw from hanging slack. I regretted it instantly, as the little lights in her eyes died and her face lost all expression.

"Sorry." Though I wasn't sure what I was apologizing for.

She gave me a weary look and I turned back to the literal task at hand. I gulped instinctively and looked down at the palm held up to me.

At least it looks clean.

I brought the beefy hand up to my face. My canines poked my lower lip, my teeth adjusting with a small nudge through the gums, extending automatically with the growing certainty of nourishment.

I went to bite, backed up, and repeated this ritual about three more times before sinking my teeth in. There was a strange sensation, like sinking my teeth into gelatin and leaving them there. Then, the warm blood filled my mouth and I gasped, drawing in even more of the ambrosia.

CHAPTER II

LILY

G abe growled low in his throat with every swallow. The sound grew, urgent and fierce. I counted each swallow before tapping the top of his head.

"Alright, that's enough."

I can't explain the change. His eyes were still closed. But something in me knew, like a rat too close to a snake, that the next growl was now aimed at me.

"Come on." I nudged, cautious not to jostle him too much; his fangs were still buried in Jason's flesh. The next growl shook his whole body, reverberating through him and vibrating in his throat.

My jaw fell open, but words wouldn't come out.

Fuck, had we done this too early? He'd been so hesitant. But I'd pushed it, been a fucking know-it-all. If I had to wrestle him off Jason, could I?

Before, when he was human, I could have lifted Gabe off the ground. But now he had the same preternatural power boost as me.

I was so stupid.

Hell, one of Alex's clients had once tried to chomp his hand as he'd tried to take a blood bag away. And that guy had *asked* to be changed.

Just as I was about to push Gabe off the trucker, the look in his eyes halted me.

He'd finally opened them, but they weren't on me, the one who might take his meal. Gabe stared at his own hands, quivering as he slowly pulled them away from the trucker's forearm. I reached for his shoulders again, but another low growl warned me off. He lifted his gaze to mine. It was only a moment but it spoke to my soul.

Those deep green eyes were angry, territorial, yet he was slowly pulling his hands off Jason.

"Gabe, ya need to decide what kind of vampire ya want to be." I put as much ice as I could manage into each syllable, but the words were brittle, cracking under my uncertainty.

What if I had to fight him off? I eyed Olive, making sure she was still seated. She was but she looked like a coil ready to be released. If I had to control Gabe we would lose her, simple as that. We could chase her at the house because it was enclosed. Here was too open. There were too many witnesses.

"Pick," I repeated. "Can ya control yourself or not?"

His eyes pleaded with me.

"Pick." I got more stern, pulling my hands away from him and showing him my palms. I'd been too cocky, thinking I knew everything. Our only chance was for Gabe to get control on his own.

He quivered and took one more swallow, closing his eyes like he was in utter agony. Finally, he pulled away, saliva dripping from his mouth onto Jason's hand.

After a few deep breaths, he wiped his mouth with the back of his wrist, scarlet smearing from his arm in thin streaks. He didn't say anything, just let out a long breath and shoved his hands through his hair.

A small bubble of pride welled inside me before I could pop it. Gabe's self-control was his own, nothing for me to be proud of. He climbed into the front seat, his eyes cast to the floor. I debated trying to comfort him, but given all the shit he'd just learned about me, I doubted he would take much solace in what I had to say.

I coughed to knock the thought loose and turned to our charge. "Your turn."

Olive took Gabe's previous place and sat with her hands in her lap, turning her gaze to Jason's large face. While Gabe had struggled to mesmerize the man and failed, Olive's eyes filled with black instantly, like someone flipped a switch in the back of her tiny head.

"Sit still and don't scream." She leaned in immediately.

"Whoa, whoa! Olive!" I stopped her as she leaned over his palm.

"What?" The little girl looked genuinely confused.

"He's still goin' to feel the pain if ya leave it like that."

"Oh." She looked taken aback by this notion, but she turned back to the teddy bear of a man. "Sit still, stay quiet, and... this doesn't hurt."

With that she sank her fangs into the same mound Gabe had drunk from. No hesitation. Her swallows were slower as well, controlled and methodical. My insides turned to solid ice.

There was something I'd seen in her eyes right before her second set of instructions. I looked over to Gabe and his brows were furrowed like he was sorting through a puzzle. We exchanged looks of confusion.

We'd rushed into this so fast, and it was steadily becoming more apparent we had no idea what we'd signed on for. I shook the idea away, turning back to monitor her progress.

"Alright, that's enough."

She pulled away from Jason, licking her lips discreetly and marching to the front seat as though it was a thousand miles off instead of a few short steps.

I took my own meal, estimating that we'd all taken about a pint from Jason combined. When I pulled away, Gabe piped in, "What about the holes?"

"You ever remember seeing any marks on Maria or Darren?" I wiped my mouth with the back of my sleeve. Gabe shook his head and I continued, "There's something in our saliva, has a lot of the same healin' properties of vampire blood."

I held up the trucker's hand to show the six tiny holes closing. I spat on the end of my sleeve, using it to clear off some of the excess blood. Kind of gross, but better than him waking up to find that mess all over his palm.

"Ya found this money on the way back to your truck earlier." I pulled twenty from my pocket and pressed it into Jason's hand. "We seem like nice folks and ya offered to give us a lift. You're not gonna be startled by anythin' we say and you'll drive your planned route as normal. Got it?"

"Yes." Jason nodded mechanically.

"Great." I climbed into the back, flopping onto the mattress. "Go get yourself a couple gallons of orange juice."

The trucker nodded and climbed out clumsily.

"So..." Gabe still sat in the front seat. "Where's he headed?"

"East."

"We're in Oregon." Gabe's tone was dry. "East is all there is."

I flicked my eyes to Olive, whose glower deepened. Gabe's brows knit together. Any chance of conversation died as Jason returned with two large jugs of juice, holding one up to Gabe as he hoisted himself back into the truck. "You mind popping this in the cooler?"

"Sure thing." Gabe took the jugs and dug at his feet for a large cooler before climbing back to sit next to me and Olive. The girl crawled into the corner, as far away from any of us as she could get. She sat there, glaring for about an hour as the vehicle rocked and we made polite small talk with Jason. Finally, she seemed to nod off and Jason ignored us as the road began to fill with heavy layers of snow and ice, hail pattering against the exterior of the truck.

"So…" Gabe broke the silence first. "How often do ya give guys hugs for food?"

The question caught me off guard and I laughed. Jason seemed to chuckle up front but kept his eyes fixed on the slick road.

"Jason here seemed shocked that I was talkin' to him. He thought I was a hooker at first and was politely trying to turn me down."

"It's not every day a woman like you approaches a guy like me." Jason sounded a little embarrassed and I could see a blush overtaking his ears.

"Well, they don't know what they're missin'." I winked towards the mirror and had the pleasure of seeing his blush deepen. True, Jason was not my type. Still, he seemed awfully sweet.

"I don't think you realize the effect you have on people." Gabe gave me a sideways glance.

"Oh really." I crossed my arms. "Got an opinion?"

"No." Gabe smiled. "Just observations."

"And they are?" I snarked back.

He chewed on his cheek a couple times before speaking.

"You're gorgeous and any sane man would consider attention from someone like you a miracle." He didn't say it like it was meant as a compliment. More like he was stating a fact. Jason started to whistle something that seemed off-tune, loudly.

I blinked stupidly, unsure what to say. I shifted in my seat for a moment before clearing my throat. "Um, thanks I think."

"Nothing to thank me for, I didn't build you." Gabe pointed a finger skyward.

"So, you're a believer?" I don't know why, but the idea surprised me.

"Yeah." He glared again. "Got a problem with that?"

"Not at all." I held out my hands, hoping I hadn't shattered the moment of peace. Any more arguments would kill me. I was too fucking tired. "No judgments. I just didn't think it was your shtick."

"Learning all sorts of things about each other today." Gabe's face relaxed and he tried to smile, but it didn't reach his eyes.

"How about you?" His soft question threw me off guard and I didn't get his meaning at first.

"Huh?"

"So what's your *shtick?*"

"I don't really have one." He looked disappointed and I quickly added, "But vampires do."

"Really?" Jason stopped whistling, a little surprise entering his cheerful tone. "I didn't know that."

"Yeah." I chewed on the thought, deciding how to explain this. "Ya remember the Garden of Eden?"

"Yeah, yeah. Adam and Eve. Hard to forget the story of the apple." Jason leaned forward, watching the road more intently. "What about it?"

"Do ya know about Lilith?"

"Who?" Both men sounded like I'd said a foreign word.

"Adam's first wife?" I asked, trying to sound conversational.

"Adam only had one wife," Gabe said quickly.

"According to vampire lore, and some others by the way, Eve was his second. He was made from the ground. Lilith from ashes, so they were equals. Still, Adam wanted Lilith to be—" I glanced at Olive's slumbering form. Extraordinary child or not, I wasn't ready for *the talk*. I finally found the word, "subservient. Lilith didn't care for that idea, so she left the Garden and she became neither dead nor alive."

"Wait a second." Gabe's voice was filled with humor. "You're telling me that the Garden of Eden is in Vampire Sunday school."

I scowled. "Humans don't have a monopoly on religion any more than they do politics."

"No, I get it." He laughed, and this time a little of the smile reached his eyes. "It's just a surprise."

Was he trying to get past the tension? Maybe offering an olive branch?

"So what happened to this Lilith?" Jason sounded truly interested.

"Some stories talk about her sleepin' with demons and procreatin' a new race." I shrugged.

"Doesn't sound like you buy that party line." Gabe leaned towards me.

"Not sure I buy any of it, seein' especially as I've never met a demon before. I guess castin' her out of the Garden *could* have changed her and she simply spread the change the same way we do today."

"So why is one species from the Garden immortal and the other not?" Jason again.

"Ya already said it." At his look of confusion, I added, "The apple."

"Huh?" Jason spared the mirror a befuddled glance.

Gabe looked like he was about to shout aha! "Lilith was cast out without a bite, so she kept her immortality."

"Exactly." I smiled, comforted that he didn't look disgusted by this development. "So, what do ya think about *Bloodsucker Bible School?*"

Gabe tilted his head a bit before nodding. "I kind of like it."

"Me too," Jason said a little too enthusiastically. I smiled at him again before turning back to Gabe.

"Really?" I arched a brow. "I'd have thought our faith touchin' yours would be an issue."

"Nah." Gabe shook his head once, his eyes still locked on mine. "Makes me think that maybe the two worlds aren't so far apart."

I smiled but didn't say anything, not wanting to push my luck. That's exactly what I'd told Ivan when he'd given me the history of Lilith. The rig rocked, the heavy motion breaking my musings, and I looked out the windshield.

"Shit."

The storm had grown heavier, a full blizzard that made the road hard to see, even for me. Jason had to be having a bitch of a time.

"What?" Gabe leaned to look over my shoulder.

"This storm's gonna make the drive slow."

"Meaning we can't put as much distance between us and the car," Gabe filled in.

"Yeah, nothin' to be done about it now though," I grumbled and rubbed my eyes, the exhaustion of the day finally catching up with me. "Jason, ya mind if we crash on your bed?"

"I'd say it's a little late to ask." The big man nodded to indicate Olive, her soft snores barely audible in the cabin.

I giggled and looked back to Gabe. "Ya want first shift or second?"

"You're already settled." He nodded at the mass of pillows behind us. "I'll keep a lookout."

"Thanks." I crawled back, fluffed one of the pillows, and curled up, trying to leave Olive enough space on the other end of the mattress. It wasn't until that moment, when the loud hum of the big engine and gentle swaying of the cabin lulled me, that I realized how glad I was that Gabe was with me. Without him here, I'd have to stay awake the entire trip to keep the trucker safe.

CHAPTER 12

GABE

If Olive wasn't sleeping, she was an excellent actress. She even included drool. After watching her sleep for a while and making idle chatter with our chauffeur, I finally grew bored. My other *Sleeping Beauty* candidate proved mildly more interesting.

Lily was always moving. When she talked, it was with large gestures of her hands and extra inflection in each word. Even when she sat, she fidgeted. I'd seen her unconscious once; even then she'd mumbled to herself and writhed.

Sitting on the edge of the trucker's bed, leaning against the vibrating cabin wall, I finally saw her still. Her face was snuggled into the pillow, mouth hanging open with that pointed nose buried out of sight. It was the most relaxed state I'd ever seen her in, even if it was clumsy and ineloquent.

A stray hair fell over her mouth, fluttering with her occasional murmur. I reached out, gently moving it away from her face. She stirred and I froze, worried I'd woken her, but she just reached up and limply swatted at the air before passing out again. I took in a breath and found a pleasant mix of soap and oranges in the air around me.

"How long have you two been together?" The trucker's words snapped my attention back in place and I shook my head.

"We're not a couple." I turned away from her and faced forward.

"No." Jason eyed me in the mirror and smiled knowingly. "I asked how long you've been *traveling* together."

"Oh. Just..." I'd almost said a few days, but that didn't seem right. In such a short time, how had we been through this much? Whole weeks felt insignificant for everything that had transpired.

"Well, maybe you can answer this." Jason chortled a funny little laugh, his eyes crinkling in the rearview mirror. "Since you're not a couple, what are you?"

Again, the words that came to my mind weren't right. *Coworker* was the first thought I immediately dismissed. Coworkers don't pull each other out of fires or risk their lives as instinctually as Lily and I did. And *friend* was too flippant; it didn't allow for the complexity.

I'd only had a relationship like this with one other person.

"She's my partner," I decided.

"Not sure I understand the difference." He shrugged noncommittally. It took a minute for me to understand his response but it didn't seem worth correcting.

"We've been through a lot together," I admitted, suddenly realizing it was creepy to sit around watching her sleep. "Mind if I come up front?"

"Go for it." His grin was immediate. "Hand me my drink? I have this crazy craving for OJ."

"Really?" I couldn't help the scoff that escaped me as I climbed into the passenger seat. I reached into the cooler, the half-melted ice chilling my skin as I pulled out the large jug. "You got a travel mug or something?"

"In the bag to your right."

I searched the foot area again before finding a small backpack. It took me a few minutes of fishing through hats, gloves, and spare shirts before I found a water bottle for which to pour the neon excuse for juice. "Here you go."

"Thanks." He took several grateful gulps. "Forgot how thirsty I was, listening to her. Interesting stuff."

The beverage moved down his throat and I forced myself to look away. My hands started to tremble and I shoved them together to keep them still. I closed my eyes, trying so hard not to focus on the sound of his pulse. Even the heavy engine couldn't drown the steady beat, calling me like a siren.

Thump, thump. Thump, thump.

"Something wrong?" Jason wiped his mouth with one sleeve before plopping the bottle into a cup holder.

"Nothing, just a little car sick," I lied and looked out the window. "I'll be fine in a minute."

I focused harder on the sound of the truck rushing down the road, willing the noise to drown out Jason's pulse. The trees and foliage of the roadside were being buried and dusted under the heavy snow. A large green sign shined in the truck's headlights, drawing my attention like a beacon. It announced several upcoming exits and cities, but the bottom one made me jump. Boise, 50 miles. Idaho? When had we crossed the state line?

"Okay then." The trucker drank again and we fell into silence.

Lily might have told him not to be shocked by anything we said, but I didn't think it was fair to tell the guy I wanted to shotgun all his blood and then lick it off my fingers.

Somehow these thoughts rambled over to a ridiculous Dracula impression Harper had tried once. *"I want to suck yo' blood."*

I'd been swept up in everything taken from me. Only now was the weight of what I had given up settling in my mind.

True most of it was gone thanks to my undead status. My job, my home, my parents' old house, even Hammy's Pizza.

Even then, I'd still had Harper. Would I ever see him again? What about Lily's roommates? I barely knew them, but I'd started to consider them friends, and I didn't make those very often.

I looked into the back at the two snoozing forms. Lily with a pool of drool beneath her pillow. Olive was kicking in her sleep, like a dog chasing an imaginary rabbit. Would these be my only companions?

"Can I ask what's the deal with the girl?" Jason seemed to notice my moment of illness had passed. "Kid looks like she tried to wrestle a hurricane."

It was an apt description. We'd have to find somewhere to let Olive clean up and fix her hair. Then something hit me.

"Shit." I sat forward and stared out the window.

"What? What!?" Jason looked around wildly and I realized I must have startled the big man.

"Sorry, nothing on the road." I rubbed my chin. "Just thinking."

"Don't do that! These roads are slick as it is!" He glared. "And this would be a bad load to crash."

"Wouldn't any?" I responded automatically, my mind back at the crime scene. The bathtub had been wet with the shower faucet still dripping. It had been the second indication of someone being in the house after the CSI team had finished. I'd automatically assumed it was Olive, but she was filthy and her hair looked like it hadn't seen a brush in over a month.

"Yeah, but this one's for a hardware company. I have over two tons of spray cans and other flammables in the back." He lifted one hand off the wheel and mimed an explosion. "Boom."

"Good to know." I was barely keeping up with the conversation, my mind bending around that damn faucet over and over. Who else had been in the house? Had they been there when we'd caught Olive or were they already gone? And if they were using the shower, why hadn't Olive? Why did she look like a street urchin when soap and water had been readily available?

"Can I ask something else?" The trucker tried to make the question conversational but his tone betrayed an urgency that drew me back to the present.

"Shoot." I shook my head to clear my thoughts. Lily and I could talk about it later, but even if we figured out the meaning, there wasn't much we could do about it from here.

"What's with the make-up?"

"Huh?" Then his question sank in. The make-up Lily had applied to distort my features. I didn't know if I was embarrassed or surprised he'd noticed, given that he'd been watching the road so carefully.

"Hey, it's not like I care, to each their own, but you should know it's all messed up." He reached over and deftly flipped the passenger-side visor down. Sure enough, the mirror showed half of my face covered in Lily's perfect handy-work, while the other looked like I'd let a farm animal apply it, blush and eyeshadow smudged in random streaks.

"Great..." I started to rub the products off with the cuff of my shirt. I hadn't enjoyed having that trash on my face anyway, but it had been pretty convincing. I guess we could get more at a convenience store or something. Did they have makeup in gas stations?

"Here." Jason produced a small packet from his pocket and offered it. Turned out to be a moist towelette with the KFC logo on it.

"Thanks." I ripped the packet open eagerly. The alcohol stung and the sickly sweet smell of disinfectant flooded my nostrils as I scrubbed my skin with the cheap tissue. I looked like I'd baked in the desert sun for a week by the time I was done but at least I didn't pass for a cheap *Phantom of the Opera* imitation anymore.

I turned to ask Jason where to toss the trash, but his expression stopped me.

"You!" He was swiveling his head back and forth between the road and me, like a deranged bobblehead. "You're that cop on the news!"

Guess the makeup was even more effective than I'd realized. I tried to come up with something but he whipped his head back to the road and swore loudly. Before I could react, he was turning the wheel of the truck and standing on the brakes. I slung forward, only to be yanked back by my seatbelt. Something flew past me and smacked the windshield with a sickening crunch.

The loud squeal of the big rig stopping was deafening and my hearing automatically honed in on it. My head felt like it would burst open to the deafening crescendo and I clutched my skull like I might be able to hold the pain at bay. Suddenly, all noise was replaced by a single deafening whistle.

I looked up, finding Lily in front of me. She had several lacerations on her face and her nose was wiggling from an unusual angle. She was speaking, her expression urgent, but I couldn't make it out over that damn whistle. I shook my head and yelled, "Speak up!"

At least, I thought I yelled. I couldn't even hear myself.

She looked stunned and grabbed my face, turning my head to one side. The quick motion made me dizzy and I dry-heaved. I struggled until the view through the windshield stopped me.

I'd assumed the shock of recognizing me had caused Jason to stop the truck suddenly. I was wrong. Through the spider-web pattern of broken glass, Cyrus stood in the middle of the road, his arms crossed and his lips in a tight grimace.

CHAPTER 13

LILY

The cabin rocked hard, reminding me of my original passage to America. Just like before, the motion roused me. I rolled over, punching the pillow to get comfortable again.

"You're that cop on the news!"

My eyes popped open as the word *cop* sank in. Shit. I'd told Jason that nothing we *said* would shock him; I hadn't thought about concealing the identity of my travel companions.

Rookie move. Again.

Sitting up, I found Olive staring at the pair, breaking her concentration long enough to catalog me in a glance. She looked like a cat ready to pounce, her feet on the edge of the bed and her hands clutched to the side of the vehicle.

As I opened my mouth to warn her against running, the brakes of the truck squealed and Jason shouted. I flew forward, landing with a heavy slam against the windshield and shattering it along with several of my bones before falling to the floor. I groaned as I rose, my bones cracking back into place. I was unsteady and not just because the huge truck was still swinging wildly. Jason looked stunned, his lip quivering like he was trying to form words but nothing was substantial. He was alive, a good start. Gabe was clutching his head, red trails running down each side of his neck.

"Gabe?" I stood before him. He looked up, his face growing concerned as he scanned my face.

"You okay?" I started to check him over. Nothing I could see but the blood and a nasty bruise where his seat belt had done too good a job.

"Speak up!" His shout echoed in the truck's cabin.

I grabbed his head, twisting it to see the side. The blood coming from his ear. He gagged, drool coming up as his body tried to push something out when it couldn't.

Shit.

His eardrum must have ruptured. Still, minor injury, it would only be inconvenient for a minute.

"How'd he find us?" He was still yelling, completely unaware of his temporary state.

I snapped my attention to the windshield. Cyrus stood, fractured in the broken glass and falling snow, like a spider sitting comfortably in his web.

"Dammit." I grabbed Gabe's face, bringing his attention to me and pointing at the ground. "Stay here with Olive."

The little imp was still crouched behind his seat, ready to bolt.

"Shouldn't we run?" Her voice didn't shake, her eyes looking around like she was solving a complex equation.

"I know this asshole." I climbed over Gabe and popped the passenger door open, he was still shouting protests and reaching for his seat belt. I shoved him back and leveled him with a look. "Let me talk to him."

Snow sprinkled my skin, tiny ice needles as I exited the truck. The smell of burnt rubber singed the tiny hairs in my nostrils. The large engine of the semi was still running, the heavy thrum churning in the night air like the vehicle might surge forward at any moment. The cabin of the truck must have insulated us from the noise because I hardly heard my boots against the asphalt as I walked forward. The vehicle growled, low like some mythical beast, its headlights glowing twin eyes staring into the night.

The main cabin was blocking both lanes of the highway, bent at a near right angle from the load. No other cars were visible and I didn't hear any commotion from oncoming traffic.

Cyrus had staged his grand entrance well.

I joined the Viking in the headlights, casting half his body in blue-gray shadow as I crossed my arms. "Did ya have to scare the trucker?"

"It's not like I could call you." His tone was gravel.

"Who all's here?"

"Small team, finishing a road block before they join us."

Ah, so the lack of cars wasn't just a happy coincidence. I should have guessed. Cyrus had far more practice than me finding vampires on the run. And he'd had to work throughout centuries when our kind was still considered to be akin to the Boogeyman and Santa Claus.

"You shouldn't have run."

"I didn't have a choice." I shoved my hands in my pockets, more to hide my fidgeting fingers than keep them warm.

"Lily–" The confidence left his tone, his gray eyes pleading with me, "come back."

I snorted. "Ya tried that line before, remember?"

"If you come quietly, you'll both still be part of the Court. But if you fight me..." He let the sentence hang in the brittle air.

One of the truck doors slammed heavily behind me.

"You heard the lady." Gabe stood next to me. He wasn't shouting anymore.

"Please..." Cyrus rolled his eyes.

Gabe ignored him and mimicked my stance. "There's more on the way."

"How many?" I murmured, more out of habit than anything.

"Not sure, we just saw the headlights in Jason's mirror."

"A team of three." Cyrus' grin was more frigid than the snow.

Fuck. Gabe had police training and Cyrus had taught me most of his moves, but that wasn't near enough in four-against-two odds. To top that, Gabe still had no handle on his vampire strength, he might punch with all his force or he might punch like a human. We might as well have brought a knife to a nuclear fight.

"We'll make do." Gabe grimaced, his fangs extending into the expression.

Something further behind me snapped, the sound so quick I almost thought I'd imagined it. I kept my eyes fixed ahead but Cyrus peaked towards the back of the truck in interest.

"Got something up your sleeve?"

Something metallic scattered across the asphalt far behind us, like tiny bells receding into the night, barely audible under the engine.

"You weren't the only one who left the truck just now."

Gabe shrugged.

The back doors of the rig slammed open with a heavy bang in the night, like someone kicking a huge metal drum.

"You let the brat out," Cyrus growled.

Before I could let the idea sink in, Olive's little voice came from the opposite side of the van. "Hey, assmunch."

Cyrus turned, but he didn't have a chance. Olive smashed the buttons on two twin aerosol cans, releasing two streaks of gold, glittering in the truck's beams and coating his face. Cyrus couldn't dodge fast enough, the spray paint blinded him and covered two-thirds of his face and mouth.

"You little shit!" He swung with wild purpose but Olive ducked and came out on the other side.

"Missed me!" She ducked again as Cyrus reached for her and ran towards us, pointing urgently to the woods behind us. Cyrus swung again, his fist connecting with the side of her skull and sending her down. She landed hard against the road.

Headlights crept around her body, turning Olive into a deep silhouette as her head smacked hard against the blacktop, bounced up, and came back down again. The long trails of blood arched up just long enough for me to see their red gleam. The roar of the engine swallowed my scream.

All this couldn't have been for nothing.

Relief filled me as she stayed solid, though unmoving, on the road. Knocked out, not dead. Gabe rushed forward, narrowly missing a still blindly flailing Cyrus as he scooped Olive into one arm and tossed her over his shoulder. The shine of the headlights grew, the street becoming more yellow than gray as the cars drew closer.

"Let's go!" Gabe grabbed my hand, running into the frozen forest.

Car doors slammed behind us, footsteps crunched in the thick frost, all followed by a symphony of men and women asking, "Sir, what happened?"

"Leave me!" Cyrus shouted. "Get them!"

Snow crunched under our shoes, branches beat my face and hands. Heavy shoes thudded behind us, shouts for the group to spread out rising over the cold air. A web masked my face, it's gossamer strands clinging to my eyelashes and lips.

I spat and blinked, trying to rid myself of the sticky construction as I forced myself to keep running away from the thunder of boots behind me.

"Over there!"

The loud blast of gunfire was my only warning before the bark of the tree nearest me exploded, showering me in dust and wood that coated my webbed face and lips with its raw film. The next round dug into my shoulder, fire tearing a shriek from me. Then another, flashing through my innards and ripping my side apart. Another in my leg brought me down, making me stumble.

Gabe howled. Olive landed hard; Gabe fell over the girl as a shield as he dug his palms into the frozen soil. Cold air left his mouth in large plumes. He shuddered, clutching his chest.

Fuck, the tether. He was feeling his own pain plus my own.

I reached for him, reminding myself to keep moving. The wounds would heal but we had to go. "Gabe, we–"

Another bullet cracked the air, then another. Something sharp pierced my ear and sliced my cheek. Red peppered the snow like cherry paint on a fresh canvas. Gabe gagged and croaked, trying to speak as he pressed one hand to the side of his throat. Blood oozed through his fingers.

Another bullet whizzed overhead, the loud crack of the shot followed by a sharp buzzing.

I searched the surrounding woods, trying to find options. Footsteps grew closer and the men chasing us started to shout a chorus of, "Over here!"

"Olive." I shook the girl, trying to rouse her. We might be downed, but I didn't think they'd hit her. She might be able to get out while we put up a solid fight. We'd lose but at least she'd have a snowball's chance.

"I'm awake." Her voice had that precision tone again. Sure enough, she looked alert when her eyes came up, scanning the clearing. "Let me go."

"You'll need to... run fast." Gabe's words were wet and bubbly, gurgling past the hole in his throat.

"No need." Olive squirmed away from Gabe. "I'll take care of this."

Before I could question how she would take care of anything, something snapped next to me. A twig under someone's shoe. It didn't surprise me to look up into the barrel of a gun.

CHAPTER 14

GABE

Maybe it was her expression. Maybe it was that damned tether. Or maybe it was just years of protecting my partner out of habit. Whatever the case, the gun in Lily's face re-focused my attention, the throbbing aches of my throat and leg forgotten.

These monsters were pinning her under their gunfire when all she wanted to do was save a kid. I searched for a solution. Anything. But my racing mind found nothing but problems.

Three soldiers flanked us, every one of their guns trained on our skulls. The closest soldier, a man with a ridiculous cowboy hat and sharp chin, reached out.

"Don't even think about it." Lily angled herself between Olive and the man. Olive crouched next to her legs, her eyes still scanning the clearing and evaluating the situation.

"Like you get to boss us around anymore." A second soldier pointed her gun squarely into Lily's eye.

Lily hissed, a cornered animal delivering a warning. The sound was low and the message was clear.

We have nothing to lose. Try it.

I gulped and tried to think, which was getting harder to do every second. We had no weapons and no hope. Praying had quickly become our best option.

"I got her." The first soldier, with the hat, stepped forward, pushing past Lily. She hissed again, burying her fangs deep into his outstretched arm. The man howled and yanked his arm back right as the woman pulled the trigger. The shot tore through Lily's side and her sharp shriek echoed in the woods, like thousands of women crying out from a single gunshot. I swore and ground my hand into the dirt as my heart wrenched inside my chest, as if someone was wringing it for every drop.

"Huh." The woman seemed amused. "I didn't realize you'd broken your hiatus, Edwards."

"Fuck off, Melody." Lily glared.

The woman just chuckled. "Randy, aim for Edwards. She and the newb are tethered."

"No shit!" The man in the hat responded with a long whistle. "Never thought I'd see the day."

"Move again and I'll plug a bullet in your head." Melody's tone left no doubt. "We all know how much you'd regret putting anyone through that."

Lily just continued to glare but her body shook, going from an impenetrable dam to a flimsy wall in a hurricane. She growled low. I panted in agony. We'd put ourselves through all this for nothing.

Cyrus appeared up higher on the slope. He was still covered in paint, the gold streaks glittering in the faint glow of moonlight. It would have looked ridiculous any other time. Right then, those sparkles were war paint on an ancient combatant. His silver eyes lit brighter than his face, anger glowing behind them.

"You never choose the easy way." He walked briskly down the hill and glared at Olive. "That spray paint was a nasty trick. Good try, though."

Randy reached down and jerked Olive up by her shoulders, the girl thrashing and screaming like a heathen.

When he finally had her standing and at the ready, Olive exploded into motion, tackling him without a sound. She reached into her jeans and something gleamed in the moon-light. She plunged it down, sheathing it deep in the man's eye socket. Randy had no time to cry out. A small gasp escaped his lips as his skin darkened and the body crumbled. Lily moved to stop her and fell immediately under another gunshot. The noose around my heart tightened again but I couldn't take my eyes off the little girl wreaking such carnage.

What the fuck?!

Cyrus ran for Olive in the chaos. She grabbed his arm and used it like playground equipment, swinging from one victim to the next.

"Tag." Olive twirled around his gun arm with the ease of a monkey before coming up under his chin. Cyrus stilled like he'd been flash-frozen. "You're it."

While her words were playful, Olive's tone was anything but. The earlier gleam solidified into one of Lily's knives, the tip buried into the soft underside of Cyrus' chin. His skin sizzled against the silver. His eyes were locked on his attacker, orbs stretching past their capacity.

"Olive!" Lily clawed at the snow, trying to get up. Blood still gushed from her side. "What have ya done?!"

"Let him go!" Melody bellowed authoritatively.

"Stop!" I jolted to my feet, pain slicing into my still-healing leg and bringing me back to my knees.

"Everyone stay still!" There was no negotiation in the girl's tone. She twisted the knife like the handle of a faucet, letting a gush of red flow over her without even flinching. Cyrus shook, garbling incoherently.

"We're leaving." Olive looked down at me and Lily, like the clarification of *we* was required. "Any of you follow us, he dies."

"Little bitch." Melody held up her hands in a tense surren-der.

"Gabe, pat him down for weapons." Olive barked the order and her tone turned my bones into brittle ice. I'd seen more sympathy in serial killers.

"No." I wouldn't participate in this ugly hostage situation.

"Do it." Olive glared down at me. "The longer you hold off, the more pain he'll be in."

Cyrus had punched my lights out the first time we'd met, then proceeded to call me a whelp. I had no fondness for him. Still...

"Fine." I hobbled forward, my leg finishing its gruesome repairs far too slowly for my liking. The sooner we got out of here, the sooner we could reevaluate what we'd learned about Olive.

I knelt next to her captive and patted his pocket and sides, seizing a gun and several clips. I loaded them into my own pockets before finally nodding. "Clear."

"Okay, let's go." Olive re-positioned herself, still keeping the knife deep as she re-angled herself like a backpack on the man.

"No!" Melody stepped forward, her body rigid and her gun aimed at the pair. "You're not taking the commander."

"Melody." Cyrus gave the barest nod.

"Ya need to report to the Court anyway," Lily grunted as she rose, her eyes wavering like twin pools.

The two women stared at each other for a long moment, the tension palpable. Finally, Melody dropped her gun and growled, "This is all your fault."

"Yeah." Lily was holding her side to stem the bleeding. "I'm aware, thanks."

"We can't let you leave!" another soldier barked, his gun low but ready, prepared to re-engage in an instant.

"I don't think any of us have a choice." I gave Olive and Cyrus a pointed look before glancing at the fresh ashes on the ground.

"Let us go." Cyrus garbled around the blade.

"Don't move." I crouched and dipped my hand into the pile of ashes. They were moist from the fallen snow; gray flakes stuck to my hands.

"Leave him be!" The soldier lifted his gun, lowering it immediately after Olive growled.

I ignored him. My stomach churned as I sifted through the remains. A few bones were still working on their fiery decomposition, melting under my fingers. Finally, I found a partially charred wallet. I flipped the warm billfold open.

"Good, we need money." Olive kept an eye on the two remaining soldiers, gathering my movements with quick glimpses.

I didn't respond, just read the ID quickly. Randy Jones. He had deep dimples. The hair under that giant hat had been brown. I removed the license and tossed the rest back in the pile.

"Sorry," I muttered the apology over my shoulder without turning to our adversaries.

Lily's side was still bleeding, something I could tell from the persistent pulls on my heart more than from sight. I offered an arm for support. She fell on it and hobbled up the hill with me. Cyrus carried his deadly passenger close behind us.

He walked backward until the last minute, letting Olive see that the others weren't following us and giving his team a look I couldn't interpret. It took less than ten minutes to get back to the main road. We'd come out a little ahead of the semi, still parked in the middle of the road.

Another vehicle was parked further down with doors open and the engine running, the headlights mingling with those of the semi and highlighting the stalky form of the trucker. Jason walked around his beloved beast, probably looking for damage.

He spotted us and held up his hands in defense.

"Please, please." A large bruise showed on one shoulder, probably extending diagonally on his abdomen under his shirt. "No more. Just let me go."

He didn't ask if we were okay and I didn't blame him.

"Don't worry, we don't need your help again." Lily patted my hand to let her go and limped forward. "I just need to clean up my mess. Ya never heard gunfire in the woods, ya never gave any vampires a ride. Ya lost control when a deer ran into the road but nobody's hurt and everythin' is okay now."

Jason nodded mechanically and sagged in relief. "It's all okay."

"It really was good to meet ya." She turned away and we all started walking up the road. Our travel was silent, only partly because we were all watching the barren forest for movement.

I thought about the meager change in my pocket and debated if I could maybe get a six-pack later. Hamm's was pretty cheap. Then I remembered the alcohol wouldn't have any of the desired effects and my mood grew even darker.

"Whose idea was the paint?" Lily's breath rose in gray plumes against the dark night.

"Hers." My tone was just as numb as my nose and ears.

"And you let her?" Lily's face was incredulous and she stopped next to a road sign sporting three different upcoming cities and towns.

"I figured it was better than leaving her with Jason." I gave a pointed look at the hostage situation.

She held my gaze a moment longer then nodded. "We'll let him go here."

"Gee, thanks." Cyrus looked annoyed but one of his shoulders sagged.

"No." Olive grasped her captive tighter. "I need to make sure you two don't try anything."

Oh, fuck this.

"Then you might as well just kill him now."

CHAPTER 15

LILY

Gabe's shoulders were back, his chin set in a solid line, and his eyes drilled Olive with none of the uncertainty swarming in me. It took several minutes and I kept worrying a car might drive past and notice our little drama. Battered, bloodied, with clothes torn, and a knife stuck into Cyrus' throat, we were not winning any awards for being inconspicuous.

Finally, Olive just nodded. "Point the gun at his head so I can climb down."

Gabe nodded and pulled out the gun he'd retrieved from Cyrus earlier, pointing it directly at his head. The little girl, though it was getting harder to think of her like that, disentangled herself from Cyrus and fell to the asphalt with an audible plop as her sneakers hit the road. The knife gleamed black with blood as she walked back to us and I blew out a weary breath.

"You're still protecting her?" Cyrus ground out.

"Our little monster acted in self-defense, we'll deal with it." I held out my hand. "Hand it over."

I sounded more like a schoolmistress than someone demanding a weapon.

Olive looked at her weapon and back to me a few times before shrugging and giving me the knife, hilt first. I wiped the blade on my shirt before returning it to my boot and counting. The rest were there.

Olive had initially said she was staying with us because she couldn't outrun us and that might still be true. But clearly, it wasn't everything. She'd just murdered a man more than twice her size and taken a centuries-old Viking hostage, all in under sixty seconds. There was more to this than we knew and that wouldn't do.

As I stood, I grabbed Olive's little hand. She tensed like she might pull away but something in my face must've made her decide against it. She relaxed a little, drumming the pads of her fingers against the outside of my hand.

I had to hold myself back from clenching Olive's hand tighter as the rat wheels of my mind twirled. What the fuck had we gotten into?

"Will ya take Gabe back?" I blurted the question before I even realized I was going to ask it.

"What?" Both men's faces looked precisely how I felt, shocked and confused.

"Gabe came with me without any warnin' as to the consequences. He isn't responsible for his actions, he's new to our world and ignorant of the laws." I gave Gabe a warning look before turning my attention to Cyrus. "Will ya take him back to Court?"

It was a long shot, but Cyrus had no proof either way. He didn't know what I had or hadn't told Gabe. Not only that but Gabe had been turned without giving consent. That would go a long way in setting the belief that he'd gone into this blind. He still had the chance.

Cyrus squared his shoulder, eyeing the man who still aimed a gun between his eyes. "Detective Collins, did you go into this situation without a full understanding of the consequences?"

Gabe gave me a cursory glance before his eyes started to do that air-reading thing. He looked at me again and nodded slowly.

I closed my eyes, willing myself not to cry. This was my burden, I should be happy he wasn't going to be taking it on anymore. Happy he could get back to assembling his shambled life. And yet...

"No." Gabe's response was soft. "Lily warned me that this action was a large offense. She didn't tell me the exact consequences, but I didn't ask. Any ignorance is my fault, not hers."

"Gabe!" I snapped my eyes open, ready to smack him.

"Very well." Cyrus nodded and I swore I saw a hint of respect cross his features. "Lily, your request is refused. Anything else?"

"What are ya thinkin'?" I ignored Cyrus, punching Gabe in the shoulder with my free hand. Unsurprisingly, it didn't fix a damn thing. I went to do it again, hoping I could beat a little sense into him.

He caught my wrist and held my gaze, his dominant hand still pointing the gun at our hostage. "If you're going down, I'm going with you."

We held that stare for a mental eternity, only the occasional snowflake broke our eye contact. His eyes weren't reading the air anymore, they were steady and unwavering. Unmovable.

"Stubborn eejit." All my prior melancholy was swallowed in irritation. "Fine, let's go."

"We can't just leave him here." Gabe bobbed the gun to indicate Cyrus.

No we couldn't, but I had a solution to that.

"If I recall—" I tried to smile but I was too damned tired, "he gave you a pretty nasty goose egg the day ya met."

"Why yes." Gabe turned his attention fully to the Viking. "Yes, he did."

This day just kept getting better and better. I glared at the sky in an angry plea. I needed a shot of whiskey and a long bath. And to call Alex.

Olive's face matched my mood, her eyes steady on the road ahead and her fingers flexing against my hand, probably itching for freedom.

In the middle of my musings over bars and child warriors, I realized we were passing yet another exit sign. It's a truly screwed-up world when a small child with two adults walking on the side of the highway can't draw enough pity to stop in a snowstorm. Luckily, that drop in human decency was to our advantage. We'd only been honked at so far.

Cyrus and his team weren't going to try again so soon after. Besides, they had a huge mess with the trucker to clear up. Olive might have damaged the truck when she pulled the spray cans out, it was the Court's responsibility to account for that and make sure Jason didn't face any consequences for the vampire influence on his evening. Then there was reporting Olive's battle skills to Ivan.

Yeah, the Viking had his hands full and needed to regroup.

We still needed to get as much distance between us and him as possible and the biggest threat to us was currently clutching my hand.

I walked up the exit ramp, Gabe turning at the exact same time.

We stopped in a gas station bathroom to clean up. It smelled foul but at least it was warm and private. Spikes of pain shot through my fingertips as the skin changed from ghastly blue to palest peach. It took several paper towels to dry my hair. The tangled mass was still moist when I was done but at least the icicles wouldn't pull at my scalp.

Olive followed the similar procedure with far less care for her brown snarls. We cleaned our faces and hands, finally coming out looking like a homeless family instead of apocalypse survivors.

Small victories.

Another walk down the main road found us a no-name motel, cheap enough to host hourly rates. A perfect place to avoid security cameras. Gabe and I pulled just enough cash from our pockets to get a room. We were running out of money fast and needed new supplies; our bedraggled clothes kind of made that a requirement. Not to mention the rest of our trip.

We'd deal with all that later, we needed shelter now.

We could have black-eyed our way into the room for free but I already felt like a shit person for what we'd done to Jason. I couldn't take much more. The idea either didn't cross Gabe's mind or he had similar hang-ups.

The people in the room next door made me question my conviction. A couple entered, the woman looking at least twenty years his junior in a belt she'd forgotten to attach her skirt to and a tube top that was being stretched by her robust figure.

The skimpy outfit was accessorized with several bruises in various stages of healing and a busted lip.

"Move!" The man slapped her ass and it wasn't playful. The woman shuddered as she forced her key into the lock and ran as fast as her three-inch-glitter heels would carry her. Their grunts and moans started as soon as the door clicked shut.

Only his groans were of ecstasy.

I considered snapping his neck, but we had our own troubles. Gabe glowered as he opened our door.

The carpet patterns were seizure inducing so you didn't notice all the stains buried in the overlapping diamond shapes and worn-out colors. The walls were partially covered in a solid sepia wallpaper that peeled at the corners. The beds were stiff and Olive almost bounced into the ceiling as she sat on her mattress. She still hadn't said a word since letting go of Cyrus, just nodding and shaking her head when applicable.

"Talk." Gabe closed the door with his foot and turned on the low-watt lamps. They hummed with the pulse of electricity before flickering to dim life.

"About?" Olive crossed her legs and sat ramrod straight.

"Dealer's choice." I drew the curtains across the only window before crossing my arms and leaning against the wall.

Apparently, these walls weren't originally sepia. They'd been colored by years of various smoke and chemicals; my jacket was sticking to the residue.

Fuck it.

The feeling only added to the natural disgust in my tone. "But ya may as well start somewhere, because Lucy, ya got some 'splainin to do."

"Huh?" Olive cocked her head like she was trying to sort out the meaning of an ugly piece of modern art.

"Does anyone get your jokes?" Gabe gave a deflated chuckle "Ever?"

I glared at him and pointed at the wild child before us. "Stay on topic."

"You first." He turned back to Olive and sat on the second bed. "Why don't we start with who else was staying in that house?"

I tried to keep my face neutral but I wasn't sure how well I succeeded. Still, I managed to keep my questions to myself.

She had to see us as a team in every sense of the word and my earlier offer to let Gabe run for it might not help the situation.

"I thought you already knew." Olive's head cocked to the other side and her hazel gaze turned to gold in the cheap lighting. "You said her name."

"Huh?" I racked my brain. What name had I said in front of her today? There couldn't be that many.

"Anna." Gabe almost spat the two syllables. "She was the one using the shower. That's why she was so clean when you found her."

CHAPTER 16

GABE

The news that our least favorite nurse was the one primping in that house was less than surprising. In fact, the answer seemed too easy.

"Who else?" I prodded.

Olive gave Lily another look. "Didn't you recognize their scents?"

"A bloodhound couldn't sort through all the smells in that house." Lily looked like a spring ready to burst, the tension winding tighter and tighter. "Why would I know 'em?"

The woman next door let out a sharp cry of pain. Lily shot our adjoining wall a glare that I understood all too well. I would have appreciated a punching bag right that moment and the pimp seemed like a great option.

"Your..." Olive stuttered, blinking several times. "Your accent. You must know him."

"Know. Who?" Lily ground the question out.

"Our captain." Olive turned her head to look between us. "He sounds just like you."

"You mean Irish?" I clarified.

Olive nodded once and we all paused, letting it sink in.

"Fan-fuckin'-tastic." Lily threw her hands in the air. "Great way to represent the home country."

"You said he was your captain?" I tried to keep Olive's attention before Lily could derail this train.

She nodded, watching Lily out of the corner of her eye. "We were trained how to hunt and kill in teams of five. He trained the team leaders, like Anna, and they kept an eye on us."

Something curdled in my stomach, rotten with premonition. "How many teams were there?"

"They changed a lot as we graduated from boot camp." Olive looked thoughtful and began to tick off the numbers on her fingers. "Last I counted, six troops had been sent out with their leader and seven remained in boot camp."

"Thirteen?" Lily stopped her pacing to gape. "You're tellin' me there are thirteen groups of vampire children ready to create those nasty little family massacres?"

I did the math in my head. Sixty-five brainwashed child soldiers.

Olive shook her head. "That wasn't our core purpose."

I knew I'd regret asking, "Then what was it?"

Olive gulped, inching back on the bed. "Graduation."

I closed my eyes and braced. "What were you graduating to?"

"Infiltration."

"How?" My stomach rolled like the back of a cement truck.

"That's easy," Lily spat before looking at the girl. "Security wouldn't question a lost child?"

Olive nodded and looked at the window like she could see through the curtains. She flinched when the woman next door cried out after a sharp slap.

"And why are ya stayin' with us?"

Olive blinked in confusion. "I told you–"

"Ya fed us a line of horse shit," Lily interrupted, coming to sit next to me on the bed.

Olive blinked at her. Then turned to me, maybe hoping I was still falling for her act. I shook my head.

"You can't expect us to buy that line anymore. Not after what you just did." I blew out a sigh and dug in my pockets, finding Randy's ID and holding it out for the girl to see. "So, why are you complying?"

Olive looked away from the photo, finding something very interesting in the bedspread. "He would have killed me."

"Yes, it was self-defense." I placed the ID on her lap and the girl flinched as if the plastic card burned. "But you were also willing to keep Cyrus on a leash to control us. That was a calculated decision. So what's the plan?"

Olive's eyes flicked between the floor to the driver's license several times before she sighed.

"You said you knew someone who could help me." Olive set her shoulders and picked up the ID, analyzing it as she spoke. "I'm already tired of running."

A home. Our murderous Orphan Annie just wanted a home. I couldn't decide if that made me feel better or worse. Lily leaned forward, so close to Olive that the girl backed up to give herself just an inch of space. They sat there, an odd staring contest, neither blinking.

"Fine." Lily sat back. "We'll take you to Melissa, but no more lies."

Olive looked disconcerted at the proposition. "How do I know I can trust you?"

"You don't." I shrugged. "But you don't have a whole lot of options."

Olive eyed us both in turn before giving a single nod. The solemnity of the moment was broken by a guttural groan from next door.

"Enough." Lily shot to her feet, slamming the flimsy door before I'd fully registered her opening it. Several loud thumps sounded next door and the pimp told Lily to go fuck herself.

"Stay there." I pointed at the bed and followed Lily.

She was still at the door, her eyes large discs of pure black as she continued to slam her fist on the door, shaking it with each blow. The man shouted something about teaching her a lesson; his footfalls sounded from inside the room. The woman mumbled something, her voice preceded by another loud slap.

"Shut up, bitch!"

"Oh, fuck this!" Lily drew her hand back like she might punch the door.

"Wait!" I grabbed her arm at the elbow. "He's coming, just wait."

Unlikely the motel would call the police for a broken door, given the level of hygiene and security, but it wasn't worth the risk.

The door cracked open, a security chain snapping between us and the pimp. "What?!"

"Move please." Lily shot her foot out, slamming the door open and snapping the chain. So much for not breaking things.

"What the fuck!?" The man flew backward, sprawling on the floor in all his glory. "You're one of them monsters!"

He scrambled for a bag on the ground, pulling a pistol out. I stepped forward, jerking the gun from his hands. It let a single shot loose, the rapport filling the room with the quick muzzle flash. The barrel seared my hand and I gritted my teeth as I yanked it free.

"Would you like to take old mythology for five hundred, Alex?" Lily looked around the room until she found the woman. I followed her gaze, gritting my teeth so hard my jaw ached.

The woman was naked below a see-through sheet. She shivered bland rubbed a huge red spot that took up a third of her face, licking a fresh laceration on her lip to prevent the blood from dripping. She didn't even take an interest in us, just stared at the bed and waited.

I snorted in disgust. "And you call her a monster."

"Bitches get out of line, man." The guy put his hands up and tried to sit up straight. "You know how it is, right?"

His eyes flicked to Lily and she flew forward like she might claw his eyes out with her bare hands. I turned, grabbing her under the waist with my free arm.

"Let me go!" She pulled and stretched, wild animal cries falling from her throat.

I wanted to let her loose. At heart, I agreed with her.

How many times had this wretch degraded, beaten, or raped this woman, only to send her back to the streets to make him money? How many more were under his thumb?

No, not a thumb. Claw. The claw of a wicked and vile thing and my most primitive instincts snarled for action. Smite this evil, have done with it. But my police instincts and years of training kept my arms firmly latched around her.

I pulled her to me, cradling her head against my chest. She continued to struggle and I had to aim the gun away from anyone just in case she jarred my hand. Suddenly, those animal cries died in her throat. She whimpered once and then fell into heavy sobs, clutching my shirt to hide her face. I froze, my arms still clenched around her.

All the strain from our long day was ripping from her in raw emotion.

Unsure what else to do, I forced myself to relax, draping my arms gently over her shoulders. The floor shifted in a soft creak and I looked up, finding the pimp in mid-step a few inches away from the door. The energy of all my pent-up emotions pulsed in my eyes, like a new heartbeat, completely out of place. "Don't even think of moving."

The man lost his rigid tension and his face fell slack as he nodded. I would have mentally whooped for joy as I realized I'd finally managed to get past the vampire milestone but for everything else.

I pulled Lily closer, stroking the top of her head. It was all I could do for now.

The woman on the bed finally took an interest in us. Her eyes were filled with envy, pain, and longing as she watched us.

Movement caught my eye and I glanced back at the open door. Olive stood in the doorway, her eyes were calculating as she took in the room. Yet, behind that cold appraisal, I saw a glimpse of what I'd seen in the prostitute's face.

"Olive." My tone was clipped and harsh, bringing the girl to attention. I inwardly berated myself for the slip-up. Maybe this girl had a chance to find a life and become something other than a tool. If so, we needed to start now. I swallowed, forcing myself to be more gentle despite my surroundings. "Please take this young lady over to our room."

The woman and Olive exchanged confused glances before they turned back to me. I swallowed and tried to use the same practiced tone for interviewing. "It's okay, miss. We'll be right there."

Given everything we'd learned, I didn't think Olive would make a snack out of the poor woman. The prostitute looked at the broken door and her frozen pimp, clearly going through a mental tug-of-war. Either she realized we didn't mean any harm or saw her options just as limited as Olive did. She stood, wrapping the sheet around her again to cover herself a little better before leaving with Olive for the room next door.

I turned my attention back to the pimp. He still stood where I'd left him, shivering with fear. He hadn't bothered to grab his boxers from the ground, something I hadn't noticed in the initial calamity. Between the shivers and the slow trickle of urine on the carpet, it was becoming harder to ignore.

"Get dressed and gather all your other belongings."

The pimp nodded and began to mechanically gather his clothes, dressing robotically and stuffing various belongings into his pockets.

Lily stopped shuddering, backing up and wiping her eyes. "Shit. I ruined your shirt."

I looked down. Yep, her bloody tears had stained the flannel and even the t-shirt below. Probably into disuse. "We'll pick up another one."

She nodded but she wouldn't stop looking at the mess she'd made. "What's the plan?"

I blinked several times, the cogs in my mind coming to a short halt. *Did she just defer to me?*

"Simple." I lifted her chin, forcing her eyes off my chest. "We're going to get everything of use off him and send him to the nearest police station to confess."

She scowled. "I'd rather rip his spine out."

"Me too, but we're going to be better than that."

She nodded glumly. Her expression made my heart wrench from its silent place in my chest. I leaned down and kissed the top of her forehead.

CHAPTER 17

LILY

He wasn't human anymore; his skin was the same temperature as mine. So why were his lips impossibly warm on my skin?

I was still fighting to control my mind, steadying it. I couldn't go reading more into his kindness than there really was. Gabe had just been comforting me when I'd been about to murder this piece of shit. I still wanted to, butI suddenly too tired. It was like all the anger had sucked out my energy.

"We better see if he's got any cash or cards." I pulled my head back, avoiding his gaze and trying to figure out what the stain at my feet was. Coffee, maybe? Or old blood. "We're going to need a lot to get off the grid and still make it to South Dakota."

Gabe coughed once like he was trying to clear more than his throat. "South Dakota?"

He still didn't release me; his broad arms felt safer than any stronghold. I gathered my courage and looked up.

His green eyes were fixed on me, not even scrolling through the air in his current thoughts. A scared little rabbit jumped around my insides, spurring me to look back down. For fuck's sake, I'd just dealt with a child soldier, a murderer, and an abusive pimp. Why was looking into Gabe's eyes suddenly so hard?

Was it because he knew the worst of me and had still stuck around? Must be.

"That's where Melissa was holed up, last I checked." I swallowed and checked in on the progress of the pimp. He was fully dressed, his dangly bits covered in a set of baggy jeans and red boxers he'd pulled higher than Urkel's belt.

I swallowed and tapped Gabe's arm meaningfully. "Ya can let go now."

"Oh, right." He coughed again and released me, the sudden loss of his support almost making me drop to the ground. He gave me a quizzical look, a check for my condition.

"Just tired." I shook my head once before turning back to our prey. "Ya got any cash?"

"Just the bitch's pull for the night." He started to dig in his pocket. And just like that, all my exhaustion was lost in annoyance.

"You'll never insult any of your employees again." My tone could have seared a hole through the floor. "You hear me?"

"Yes." Despite my command over his mind, the pimp's voice shook like a brittle branch in a strong breeze. The acrid smell of urine strengthened the air and I relished the stench. About time someone made the little prick fear for his life.

"Lily." Gabe placed a hand on my shoulder, his breath low in my ear. "You're making a mess for housekeeping."

"Look at the carpet." I waved a hand to indicate the room. "Ya really think they care?"

A whole day of unearthly stress circled in the dark carousel of my mind. The least I could do was torture this asshole. It wouldn't make the world right but it was a start.

"The longer you're terrifying him, the longer Olive is alone with a scared and abused woman." Gabe's voice was a soft reproach.

Fuck. He had a point.

I sighed. "Give me your wallet and all your other valuables. And stop pissin', ya can hold it."

I didn't bother telling him to not be scared, he hadn't earned it and I wasn't feeling charitable. Gabe looked around the room once more, stepping away to check outside the door for any bystanders.

The pimp handed me his wallet with several prepaid Visas inside and a small wad of cash. I stuffed both in my jacket pocket and zipped them up before accepting a fancy watch.

Definitely not a *Rolex*, it didn't have the right feel in the band's metal. I found the brand name on the face. *Ball*. I searched my memory, not sure I'd ever come across it before. Still, the watch was nice. One Isaac would have liked for sure. We might be able to pawn it if we found a seedy enough joint and agreed to skip the paperwork.

I looked up to give the pimp a sarcastic thanks and immediately shielded my eyes again. "What the fuck are ya doin'?"

"These are *Dolce & Gabbana*." His tone was a muddled mixture of confusion with compliance. The man had his trousers around his knees, bent down halfway through the gesture of pulling one leg over his foot.

"Keep your pants on!" I kept my hands up, warding the image of his naked body about as effectively as a finger-cross.

"But we'll take the shirt." Gabe snickered and I glowered his way. He didn't wash away the look of amusement quivering at his bottom lip.

"What for?" I arched a brow at my partner. "You'll swim in it."

"The woman." Gabe hooked his thumb towards our room. "Her clothes didn't cover much, and that shirt is pretty baggy."

"Fair point."

"You've had how long to practice this whole vampire gig?" He was leaning against the door frame, shifting his gaze between us and the outside.

"Pardon me if I'm not practiced in unarmed robbery." Even I heard how childish the defense sounded. "Whatever, let's just get out of here."

"Sure." As we left, he told the pimp to stay put and be quiet. He also neglected to tell the bastard not to be scared.

Back in our identical room, Olive and the woman sat next to each other, flipping through local channels on an old tube TV. They looked awkward next to each other but not terrified. At least that was something. I took the opposite bed and Gabe closed the door before sitting next to me.

The woman hit a button on the remote and the TV shut off.

"Now what?" She turned to us, still holding the wet paper of a sheet to conceal her body. Her voice had a southern quality to it, but not a full drawl, nothing like the faux-erotic moans from earlier.

"Here." I held out the shirt that was at least six times too big for her. "That sheet can't be too warm."

The woman gave Olive a wary look. Despite the child's crazy hair and filthy appearance, our new guest probably didn't want to strip down in front of her.

"You can use the bathroom." Gabe pointed at the tiny cupboard this motel touted as a washroom. "Take your time."

"Thanks." The woman took the shirt from me and gave us a grateful but weary smile. Her arm was all bone and skin, the knob of her wrist sticking out sharply. I resisted the urge to order a pizza there and then. We didn't need any more witnesses.

The cheap sheet dragged behind her as she shuffled to the bathroom, like the train to a worn gown. She took ten minutes, coming out in the large shirt and her long hair wrapped in a flimsy excuse for a towel.

The bruise was growing bulbous and purple on her right cheek. She looked to be of Asian descent, with almond-shaped eyes and skin the color of baked honey. The shirt hung off one shoulder, exposing a bright tan line from wearing too many spaghetti straps on blistering days. Her bare feet showed similar tan lines and blisters, probably from wearing strappy high-heels that were too small for her feet. Despite the heavy tan, her legs and arms were littered with hues of purple, blue, and yellow. She looked like a macabre watercolor.

My jaw started to ache and I realized I was clenching it. That pimp's spine was starting to sound like a pretty nice trophy.

"So, what's your name?" Gabe backed away as the woman sat on the other bed, giving her extra room from his presence. Good idea, she might not be a big fan of men. She didn't look freaked out, but her occupation required a certain ability to swallow emotion.

"M— Mink." She said the name like it was forced and practiced at the same time.

She sat back down and the towel fell off her head, showing long black roots that edged into a shade of platinum that stood stark contrast against her eastern skin. Olive scooted away from her, looking a little disturbed by their proximity.

I leaned in conspiratorially like we were talking about boys next to our lockers. "Is that your name or is that what the human pile of shit next door calls ya?"

'Mink' looked stunned then bubbled into a slow laughter, confusion and humor exchanging places on her face faster than I could keep pace.

"Tara." She put a hand in front of her mouth, looking embarrassed by her moment of enjoyment and trying to stifle a laugh. "Sorry."

"No need to apologize." Gabe gave her a sympathetic smile.

He was doing really well with her. Of course, he'd been a cop for years before we met and probably had been working with victims all the time.

"So, Tara—" I forced a calmness to my tone I didn't feel, "do ya have any family ya need to get back to?"

Tara shook her head, the wet locks of her hair nearly swatting Olive's face. "Life with them isn't any better than it is with Calvin."

The little girl looked annoyed as she dodged the incidental whip but otherwise watched the exchange without comment.

"Fair enough." I fished in my pocket for the folded batch of bills and offered them to her. "From what I understand, this is yours."

Tara wrinkled her nose at the cash in my hand. "Consider it payment for getting Calvin off me."

"You sure?" Gabe prodded.

"I wouldn't be able to spend it anyway." She grimaced. "Though I guess I just have to make more when I leave, at least it won't be for him."

An idea hit me. "What if ya didn't have to?"

The girl looked intrigued and I pressed on, "What if ya could go somewhere else, all expenses paid."

"I'm not interested in going..." Tara seemed to struggle for the right words, eyeing Olive for a long moment. "Full-time."

"Full-time?" I tilted my head in confusion. What the hell did she think I was offering? Gabe nudged me with an elbow and leaned in.

"She thinks you're offering to make her part of a brothel or something."

"Oh no!" I backed away, looking embarrassed and aghast at the idea. "I'm offerin' a place at Court!"

I didn't have anything against people who chose sex work but I'd also never met someone who wasn't doing it out of desperation or manipulation. Hell, a couple of my childhood friends had gotten stuck in the trade when the famine started.

"Court?" Tara's eyes became twin slits of dubious interest. Olive sat up straighter, her eyes faceted on the door to our room. I shot her a warning look and pointed the conversation back to our guest.

"Look, ya know what we are, right?"

She nodded. "Not exactly worth a Double Jeopardy question."

I snorted despite myself.

"And you're not scared?" Gabe sounded like he was still trying to catch up to everything. Hard to blame him. He was taking the crash course on vampires, with a heavy emphasis on the crash.

Tara averted her gaze. "What you just saw wasn't new for me."

"Well, I've got somethin' different in mind."

"Hold up!" Gabe held his hand up to me like a traffic cop trying to stop a stampede. "How the hell are we going to get *her* to Court?"

"And what would I do there? I mean, if I'm not–" Tara teetered her head this way and that, "entertaining, what would my job be?"

"Feeding hungry vampires and takin' iron supplements," I said bluntly, turning to Gabe when he gasped. "It's not like we could advertise on Craigslist."

He looked stunned. Olive looked freaked and ready to bolt. I didn't have time to coddle either of them. I'd had a hell of a day, but dammit I was going to help this one person.

"That's it?" Tara looked the calmest. "I just give you guys blood?"

"About a pint a week. And you obviously can't tell folks what ya do for a living."

"I'm kind of used to keeping secrets." She gave the room next door a pointed look. "What about him?"

"We'll take care of him." Gabe finally recovered his countenance.

"Do I want to know?"

"Best to worry about yourself." I shook my head. "Especially considerin' my terms."

CHAPTER 18

GABE

Tara waggled her fingers slowly from her seat, high in the Greyhound as the long bus lurched forward. A quick spurt of exhaust rose from the back before the engine roared and the gray cloud lifted. I flinched at the loud wheeze of some mechanism in the breaks, chiding myself for instinctively focusing on the high pitch.

"Clever conditions," Olive remarked from her lower position on the sidewalk, a neon hood covering the majority of her head and neck. Her hair was still growing back, barely down to her chin now.

Tara and Lily had spent hours brushing the tangles out. Finally, both women conceded it was a lost cause and cut the nest from her head. The little girl hadn't even protested when Lily had used a knife to saw through the ratty mess. Just turned around and sat still through the motions, impervious to the awkward, girlish chatter Tara tried to engage her in.

"Thanks." Lily waved, a Walmart shopping bag fluttering from her elbow. She looked proud under her *Cubs* baseball cap. "It keeps her from telling the Court where we are."

"And that cocktail we gave her will keep anyone else from removing it." I pushed a huge set of aviator sunglasses up my nose. We'd decided to keep our disguises simpler going forward, the old sunglasses and hat trick.

"Exactly." Lily sighed. "Shame she wouldn't let me erase some of the memories before last night."

"Nah." I watched the back of Tara's head as she turned in her seat. "She didn't want to risk becoming someone different."

Olive eyed me in interest, her arms stiff at her side under the sparkly pink hoodie. "What do you mean?"

The coat looked wrong on her, her soldier posture rigid under the sequins and shimmer, but it was all they'd had.

I debated my words for a second. "Our experiences shape us, right?"

"Right." She nodded sharply, causing her short hair to bob inside the hood.

"Take those memories away, you give up a piece of yourself."

Olive tilted her head down and eyed the concrete. "So she chose to preserve who she is and suffer?"

"Yup." Lily didn't look up, fanning our tickets away from her face and examining the overhead signs to figure out where our bus would be in this concrete maze. "This way."

She extended her hand and Olive took it without a second's hesitation.

The small girl still curled and uncurled her fingers automatically, her arm tense at the contact. "She was foolish."

"Why do ya say that?" Lily looked a little worried by the comment, despite being the one to offer the memory swap in the first place.

"She wasn't in control of what that bastard did to her," Olive said succinctly. "Why should she carry those consequences?"

A little old lady gasped at Olive's use of profanity and looked at us like a flaming bag of crap left on her doorstep. I suppressed a chuckle as I leaned down.

"Olive, you can't use words like that." I elbowed her and nodded at the offended crone. "You might upset someone."

"People shouldn't eavesdrop." Olive walked on without a second glance backward.

The old lady turned several shades of scarlet before running off and shouting, "Harold!"

"Ya do remember we're tryin' to keep a low profile?" Lily snorted and walked a little faster, but the corner of her lips twitched like they were being pulled by an insistent marionettist.

We rushed to our bus despite final boarding being twenty minutes away. Lily handed our tickets over, smiling and making pleasant conversation with the conductor while Olive and I found our seats. I moved to take the window when I caught my young companion's furtive glance at the glass pane. She was bouncing on her toes, those hazel eyes locked on the sheen of glass behind me.

"You want the window?" I worked my way over the three seats and back into the aisle, gesturing for her to go ahead.

"It..." She hesitated, then blurted out, "It provides the best location for vigilance."

She ducked her head in embarrassment before climbing into the seat and I suppressed a smile. Olive looked so much like.... a child. Even as she sat, she drummed her knees with little fingers as she watched the people on the pavement below.

I was having a hard time merging this fidgeting little girl with the brutality in the woods last night.

"Here." Lily plunked into the aisle seat next to me, shoving a book in my face and obliterating my thoughts entirely. The title was illegible until I plucked it from her hand and held it away from my face.

"Odd Thomas," I read aloud and looked back at her. "You used our meager savings to get me a book?"

The paperback couldn't cost much, but still. We'd spent half the night making Calvin the Pimp tear through various cushions and loose ceiling tiles of his home to give us a decent stash. Even then, between the bus tickets, new clothing, a decent meal for Tara, and a couple burner phones, we weren't rolling in the Benjamins.

"You weren't done readin' it." She shrugged and fished in the shopping bag before producing a magnetic bookmark clip. When had she managed all this? "I think ya were on page one hundred and twenty-somethin'."

"What, you counted the pages with your fancy vampire vision?" I teased, ignoring the garish cartoon kitten on the bookmark. Ugly or not, it was less destructive than dog-earing the corner of each page.

"Ya left it out on the coffee table a few days ago." She averted her gaze. "I was curious what made ol' Tommy odd."

I let out a loud laugh, drawing the attention of a few passengers. She clearly hadn't read the beginning of the book. Her embarrassment was quickly replaced with her normal spit-fire energy, and she opened her mouth, no doubt to say something snarky.

Luckily, the bus driver garbled something about the various stops and safety procedures, the crackled intercom interrupting her comeback as I continued to laugh. Olive eyed us in apparent interest before turning back to her coveted window.

At least the long ride gave me a minute to catch up with *ol' Oddy*. When I finally decided to give my eyes a rest, my ears honed in on several fast clicks in the seat next to me.

It was a basic flip phone with no internet access and only the core features, perfect for keeping the Court out of our business for as long as possible. Granted they shouldn't even know about the phones since the whole point was to use them to contact each other and Lily's friend. Yet, there was Lily, pushing the plastic buttons of her new phone with the enthusiasm of a teenager on her first cell.

"Melissa?" I guessed, marking my book and putting it aside. She shook her head. "Alex."

"What?" I barely restrained myself from raising my voice. We were in public so I settled on hissing, "Are you crazy?"

My tone was still harsh enough to catch Olive's attention, bringing her wandering eyes away from the window.

"Calm down." Lily just continued her fast typing.

"Calm down?" I reached for the phone, but she leaned away. Reaching for it again would only make a scene. "You're in the middle of giving the Court our exact location and I need to calm down?"

This was unbelievable. Lily had been a PI for God's sake, she knew the risks. That was why she'd insisted on the cheapest, oldest phones money could buy. Hell, they didn't even require IDs on the prepaid service; we'd just told them we were Mr. and Mrs. Smith.

All that work was being obliterated with every click and tap.

"I'm gettin' Melissa's number." She hit the final button and pocketed her phone.

I made a mental note to confiscate it later and lose it in a large body of water.

She sighed and glared at me. "We kept a phone just like this in the house in case somethin' like this happened. It's registered under a similar ID and Ivan has no clue about it."

"Oh." Mental note erased. I sagged back into my chair. Olive did a great imitation next to me. "Sorry."

"Ya should be." Lily's eyes were set like storm clouds. "Besides, after all that shit in the forest, Alex has to be freakin' out."

God, that hadn't even occurred to me. I'd at least known why it felt like someone stuck my heart in a vice but Alex had been clueless for almost half a day. Wondering must have been excruciating.

"Sorry." And I was. I rested my head against the cushioned headrest and ran a hand through my hair. "What'd he say?"

"That he's gonna have a word with ya about keepin' me out of trouble." She snorted and looked past me to Olive. "Hey kid, do ya like fairy tales?"

CHAPTER 19

LILY

I t had taken eighteen hours, a flat tire, three bus changes, and a taxi ride. We were exhausted when Storybook Island finally stretched before us, Christmas lights flickering weekly in the afternoon sun. Children ran in every direction, screaming with joy and climbing on everything. Parents chased them about with warnings on their lips or cameras in their hands.

"Why don't they turn the lights off durin' the day?"

Gabe's eyes followed the direction of my gaze. "They probably just forgot while they were pulling some kid out of Yogi's basket."

Sure enough, a youngster was climbing the colorful sculpture of Yogi Bear, trying to stick his leg in the cartoon characters' mouth. His buddy was on the ground directing and recording with his cell. A park employee stormed towards them with an exasperated expression.

Gabe looked at our departing cab like he was losing a friend. "Why'd you choose such a public place?"

"People will be so focused on the scenery, unlikely anyone will recognize you."

"Also, the Court can't make a scene here," Olive analyzed. Her hair had finally grown back and was cascading out of her hood.

"That too." I smiled with approval even though my guts twisted. This child understood my tactics.

"I guess that makes sense, God knows it's colorful enough here." Gabe shoved his hat further down his face. He had a point about the color but I kind of liked it.

From Snow White's cottage to Humpty Dumpty hanging mid-way through his infamous fall, there seemed to be hundreds of statues representing childhood favorites. We walked down a clean path, Olive holding one of our hands in each of hers.

"It's a shame we can't stay longer." Olive's gaze fell on a gorgeous carriage bejeweled in the strands. "I bet the lights are pretty."

Gabe smiled and gently elbowed her. "You just want to ride in Cinderella's carriage while it's lit up."

"And?" I gave him a warning look.

"That girl waited for a man to rescue her." Gabe eyed the life-size prop that held three giggling teenagers. "Another Disney damsel."

"Cinderella did *not* wait for a man!" Olive guffawed, wrenching her hands free and placing each tiny fist on her hips. Gabe looked to me for support but I raised my hands, washing myself of the business.

"Think about it," Olive pressed on, her tone emphatic."Her first song is about making your dreams come true and never quitting no matter what people tell you. There is no mention of a man, it's about hopeful defiance."

I gawked. "When the hell did ya see *Cinderella?*"

"It was my sister's favorite movie." Olive shuffled in her shoes. "Rose and I used to stay up late just to watch it."

Gabe looked worried, trying to perk up in his tone. "So, really? We're defending the girl who let her stepmother walk all over her."

"Since when do ya blame the victim?" I arched a brow in challenge.

"Besides–" Olive started slowly, "she gets her ass to that ball just so she can have a night off."

"Okay, okay." Gabe held both palms up. "First of all, you've made your point. Secondly, stop swearing."

"Lily swears!" Olive's voice was downright petulant. It was kind of cute.

"Hey!" I stiffened in mock disgrace. "I was on your side!"

"But you do!" Olive glared up at me.

"Ya better change your tone." I tried to keep a straight face but it was damn hard. "Especially if ya want a photo in that carriage, missy."

Olive gasped, her hands over her mouth and her eyes fixed on the now empty setting. "Really?"

"Go for it." I pulled out the crappy flip phone. The picture wouldn't be great, but it's what I had to offer.

Olive squealed, actually squealed, before bounding off.

Gabe stepped next to me as I followed Olive and hunted through my phone for the camera function. "Nice of you."

"She needs it." And I kind of needed it too. We stopped walking, waiting for Olive to figure out what pose she wanted.

Gabe tilted his head in interest, his eyes starting to shift from side to side. "Seems there's more to her than we realized."

"Yeah, she was actin' very different on the bus ride." I waited, giving him a minute to bring up whatever he was thinking about. After a mental eternity, I gave an exaggerated sigh. "Out with it."

"What?" His eyes stopped shifting, landing squarely on my face.

"Your eyes are doing that air-readin' thing." I gestured vaguely at his face before snapping a photo of Olive and telling her to pose again.

"Air-reading?" His brows knit together.

"Yeah, your eyes shift back and forth like your readin' words in the air whenever you're thinkin'." I snapped another before shouting to Olive, "Wait, let's do that again. It was blurry."

"It's not my business." Something in his tone seized my throat, choking any response for just a moment.

I tried to speak twice before swallowing a lump and coughing out the word. "What?"

Gabe kicked a rock a few inches from him. "Did you ever want kids?"

"Oh." I turned back to Olive, directing her move so the glare of the sun wouldn't catch her face. It gave me a second to think. "I thought I was barren. I mean after so long with Isaac..."

A hand strayed over the flat of my stomach before I could catch myself.

"That's not what I asked." He sounded like he was reading a map to find some lost treasure.

Dammit. He wasn't going to let this go. It wasn't even that big of a deal, just... not something most vampires asked each other. Not exactly a fun topic. But his question wasn't unreasonable. And he had come all this way with me.

"I grew up the oldest of five." I swallowed again, flipping through the photos on my screen as I spoke. "Having a quiet house always felt wrong."

"Five?" Gabe blinked at me in shock.

"Yeah." I looked at the crooked pinkie on my left hand. "Before I knew that Isaac couldn't give me children, his news that he didn't want any broke me."

"I'm sorry." His voice was filled with a pity that stung more than any scorn.

"Where there are perks, there are costs." I snapped my hand into a fist, shielding the broken finger from view. "What about you?"

"Me?" He looked confused by the switch.

"Yeah." I smiled wryly. "Don't think you get to ask somethin' so personal not get some of it dished back to ya."

He considered that a moment before nodding.

"Living through my folks' deaths tore out a chunk of me and I wasn't leading the life of a stockbroker or librarian. Putting someone else through that never felt right to me." He chuckled darkly, looking over at Olive as she approached. "Of course, now, that's not really a problem."

Guilt seized me, making me shiver even more than the frozen air around us. He looked back at me, his face not even an inch from mine. If I leaned in, just a little, our noses would touch.

When had we gotten so close?

"Gabe..." I licked my lips and forced myself to focus.

"Yeah?" He had to lift his eyes from my bottom lip.

I swallowed before speaking. I wished things were different for him. Better. He deserved so much more. "I–"

"Let me see!" Olive barreled into me, crushing all the air from my lungs.

"All right, all right." I wriggled free and handed her the phone, offering a small chuckle. I looked back at Gabe, expecting amusement. Instead, he looked annoyed. At least, I thought he did, but Olive shoved the tiny screen in his face and the expression melted into a grin.

"Yeah, I see." He used the arrow buttons to scroll through images as they walked back to the path. "These are great. We should get them printed."

"Not off that crummy phone, you're not."

Gabe and Olive stopped, the authority in the woman's voice freezing them in place. Butterflies tickled my insides and I smiled wide, looking for her in the bustling crowd.

It didn't take long.

She wasn't a traditionally beautiful woman, looking to be in her mid-forties with soft wrinkles and a broad nose. Her skin was the color of creamed coffee and her hair was a cascade of long dreadlocks. But her smile was dazzling. All the world's compassion and tenderness came to light with the smallest curl in those chocolate lips.

I smiled wider and yelped in glee, "Melissa!"

My feet were light on the ground and I had to remind myself to stay at reasonable speeds. My little stunt gathered a few onlookers but I didn't care. I needed one of Melissa's hugs.

Melissa opened her heavy arms wide, letting me fly into them with the practice of a grandmother being tackled by several children a day, keeping herself upright despite the immense force from my run. She squeezed me tight, crushing my sides before putting me down.

"Oh good Lord, chil'! There is no putting weight on you!"

"Nope." I laughed heartily. "Been that way for a while."

Melissa stretched her stubby neck to look around me. "That her?"

Gabe and Olive were shuffling their feet towards us.

"Yup." I nodded, still smiling. "Thanks for meetin' us. Especially given the... complications on this one."

"Maria said something about her being a chil' soldier." Melissa's voice was a worried whisper, far too low for anyone to catch her words with all the happy shouts and running feet around us.

"Yeah." I let the smile fall. "Elias did a number on her. We're still not sure of the damage."

Melissa pursed her lips and let out a sad sigh. "Another one."

CHAPTER 20

GABE

Even after clearing the frost from the concrete picnic table, melting snow soaked my pants. Still, it was better than talking inside. While there were plenty of people crawling over the scenery, none had stopped to sit in the brittle winter air.

"Okay, girly." Melissa reached across the table, leaving her palms exposed.

Olive wrenched her hands away as though the old lady were a serpent ready to strike.

"Now, now. That won't do." The broad woman wiggled her fingers insistently.

"She's particular about being touched, ma'am." Not adding the term of respect just felt like addressing my grandmother by her first name.

"Hush." Melissa's tone was sweet, like a southern belle. There was something strangely familiar in her accent.

I opened my mouth but Lily gently elbowed my ribs, shaking her head softly. I shut my mouth with an audible click.

"Now." Melissa leaned forwards, her hands still up. "These nice folks tell me you're looking for shelter. A place to call yo' own. Is that right?"

Olive didn't speak, just gave us a wary look. I gave her a thumbs-up and immediately felt like a simpleton. Seriously, the only encouragement I could offer her was about as effective as an emoji.

Olive rolled her eyes and looked back to her possible foster.

Melissa just left her hands on the table. Her face was patient like she was waiting for an apology for some silly misdeed. Olive wiggled in her chair, looking frail and uncertain.

"Oh for God's sake girl!" Melissa's reprimand had humor behind it and she shook her large hands. "You act like I'm going to rip your arms off! I understand not wanting to reach out, but how hard is it to answer a question?"

"I don't want your shelter," Olive mumbled.

"Oh?" Melissa cocked her head, her eyes turning into beady little slits. "The way I understand it, you murdered one man, threatened another, and helped to kill a whole family."

"Now, wait a minute!" I shot to my feet, knocking my knees against the heavy table.

How dare this old bat. True, the girl had to deal with all that someday, but that wasn't her job. Not right now.

"Gabe." Lily's soft voice drew my attention. She was still seated, her hands folded in her lap as she twiddled her thumbs below the tabletop. "Sit."

Her eyes were fixed on the pair but none of my anger lurked in those turbulent blue depths. She watched like it was some sort of ritual. A rite of passage from some ancient society, ready to inaugurate Olive into their ranks.

I didn't want to sit. I wanted to tear the old crone a new one. But Lily knew her. She insisted on letting this scene play out.

"Woof, woof." I sat, crossing my arms and leaning on the icy table top. Lily snorted while Olive eyed me, confusion lurking in her open scrutiny. I waved a hand absently. "Answer her."

Olive's eyes grew wide and her lip shook, despite the brick wall of her posture. Her voice didn't even tremble. "Yes, I did those things."

"And you're on the run from Elias and the American Court?"

"Yes." Olive looked into her lap, still refusing to hunch her shoulders. "But I don't want to go with you anymore."

"And why is that?" The extended hands of the elder woman became more urgent, without so much as twitching.

Olive shuffled on her butt, finally giving up her steady posture. "The hooker."

"Huh?" Melissa blinked as she turned her attention to us. "Am I missing something here?"

"They rescued a hooker." Olive nodded to indicate us. "And the first time I fed from a human with them... they made sure I told the man not to be in pain. None of it was necessary."

"Sounds like good people." Melissa nodded approvingly. "But how's that change your situation?"

"They're going to have to fight... " Olive swallowed and tapped her knees. "Forever... because they... risked everything for me and I..."

Her voice trembled more as the sentence progressed, slow gasps escaping between words. Finally, she reached into her pocket and slapped something on the table, hard enough to garner some attention from passersby.

Randy's driver's license. Tiny black X's were inked over each eye, the pen marks so deep that the plastic was peeling and cracked. "Monsters don't get homes."

Before I could respond, Melissa flew around the table and pulled the girl against her in a thick embrace.

"Shh, chil'." She smoothed one of her large palms over Olive's head. The girl pulled away once before bouncing back against the plump woman's bosom and breaking into loud sobs that reverberated in the open air.

A few people slowed down to gawk but Melissa paid them no mind. She just rocked the girl from side to side in their standing pose. "You think you can turn that clock back and make it all better?"

"No!" Olive's loud wail was muffled by the big woman's frame, barely understandable. "But, I can fight!"

Her last word rang out into the still air, repeating itself amongst Snow White and her dwarfs before whispering back to us.

Lily walked over, kneeling next to the pair. "What do ya think we've been fightin' for?"

Olive kept her face buried in Melissa.

Lily reached out, hesitating once before smoothing a hand over the girl's quivering back. "We did this to give ya a chance."

Olive finally pulled her face free of Melissa. "It's my fault."

"No, it's not." I grabbed the ID still laying on the table and stood next to Lily. I took one of Olive's tiny hands and laid the small plastic card in her palm. She winced and I squatted to put my face right in front of hers. "Your job is to lead the best life you can. You owe that to him, don't you?"

Olive looked down at the little card, her eyes owlish and terrified as the tears ran down her cheeks. Finally, she looked at me and nodded slowly.

Someone nearby screamed, breaking the moment. "Oh my god, look at her eyes!"

We looked up to find a small crowd, maybe ten people. Some just standing in slack-jawed bewilderment. One had her phone out, clearly recording.

I looked down, taking in the red stains of Olive's tears against Melissa's clothes.

Lily hissed. "Shite."

"We got to go." I grabbed Lily's hand. Melissa grabbed Olive and we bolted for the entrance.

The Court hadn't needed to make a scene. We'd done it for ourselves.

CHAPTER 21

LILY

"*And here–*" The video jostled like the camera had been in shaky hands as the reporter continued, "*you can clearly see Gabriel Collins, the missing VPB detective from Portland, Oregon.*"

Well, at least we got our fifteen minutes of fame. Check that off the bucket list.

A kid on the floor in front of us popped his head up, blocking the view.

"Adam, get outta the way." Melissa shooed the boy with a wave of her hand.

Adam jumped and hopped to rejoin his fellow orphans on the rug. Seven children, a collage of backgrounds and ages, their eyes reflecting pale reproductions of the TV more effectively than any shop window. Half of them watched with the glazed vision of a true child, others sat to the side with their noses buried in books or other distractions. All except two.

Olive sat between myself and Melissa on the cramped couch while a gangly boy sat doing a puzzle at the coffee table, only looking up occasionally, as if checking his surroundings.

"*Is there any good reason that Detective Collins would be in South Dakota?*" Another reporter appeared on screen, tapping a stack of papers on her desk. The screen shifted, showing a woman in front of the Oregon Police Department, her wild hair whipping in the wind.

"*Captain Harper, the newest VPB captain and Detective Collins' most recent partner, was unavailable for comment. However, Collins has not checked in with his office since his disappearance in October.*"

"Dammit." Gabe pushed a hand through his thick hair. "Now they're pestering Harper."

"Language." Melissa's reproof was soft but firm. She didn't shift her eyes from the screen. "And your friend's a police captain. I'm sure he can handle the heat."

Gabe scoffed, covering his mouth with one hand and tapping the other on his knee.

"Harper's new to the job." I twirled the remote in my hands, trying my best not to break it. Melissa didn't have a lot and we couldn't afford to replace anything.

Gabe shot me a grateful look that I didn't understand before turning his eyes back to the TV. The reporters were going over basics about Gabe's history in the VPB and the Cheri Coke case we'd been working on when I'd turned him. As well as his father's death in the original vampire massacre. They hadn't given any attention to Olive yet, which just seemed strange.

Gabe started to tap his hand more anxiously at the mention of his father, the rapid pace vibrating the couch cushions.

At the second drop of Jack Collins' name, I muted the television. "Didn't even take them two hours to identify us."

"They identified *me*." Gabe continued to watch the silent TV, his eyes scanning the scroll bars of text for additional information. His knuckles were turning a ghastly gray as he clenched his fists. I dropped the remote and grasped his hand in both of mine, forcing my fingers into his palm.

He stilled instantly, lifting his hand a little higher to take in the visual before turning his attention to me.

"Flogging yourself for this shit won't help." I made sure not to blink, squeezing his hand in my best attempt to reassure him.

"Language."

"Oh shut it, Melissa." I glared at her but I couldn't hold it long. "I love ya, but we both know all these kids only look like children."

Melissa looked like she was sucking on a ripe lemon.

"And you." I turned back to Gabe. "If you weren't here, there is no way I would have made it this far."

He searched my face, his eyes darting back and forth over every crevice before nodding. "How do you want to deal with this?"

"Maybe you two should pop up on YouTube," Melissa offered. "Tell yo' side of the story, give the humans someone to root for."

"We need more than just a good public face for Gabe turnin' vampire. Besides, they didn't seem to notice his change in the video." I shook my head. "Yet."

"The Court let Elias have control of the narrative when the vampires came out and failed to respond." Gabe poked his thumb out, running the appendage over my skin. It tickled but I kept my hands still. "Maybe if they had reacted publicly, instead of trying to keep to the shadows, we would have more faith in your kind. We might not have reacted so harshly."

He was drawing soft circles over the long healed break in my pinkie.

"Fine." I swallowed, trying to keep my mind on topic. "How do you want to take over your narrative?"

"Me?" Gabe looked up, his thumbpad still on my knuckle. "We're both on candid camera."

"I'm on the news sitting right next to Melissa, no way I'm getting my life back." I shook my head. "Besides, I was due for an alias change anyway."

"Alias?" Gabe tilted his head, his brows meeting in the middle. "I thought your married name was Edwards."

"It was." I smiled though I didn't feel it. "We update our names and lives every decade or so, and move to a new location. Only way to keep people from noticing their neighbors never age. Last time I was forced to update, it was close to our anniversary."

"Huh." Gabe looked back to my hand, his brows were still scrunched together. "How we tackle this affects both of us."

"And, you know, everyone else." Melissa's tone had a lot of *ah-hem* implied.

We disentangled our hands and I turned back to her, coughing a couple times. "How so?"

"You'll be the first vampires to speak to the public." Melisa expanded her broad arms, showcasing the outdated living room as though it was the whole world. "How you present yo'selves could make or break our whole case."

"Shit."

She was right, the weight of the world was riding on how we did this.

"And that doesn't even cover what yo' going to do when the Court comes gunnin' for you." Melissa slapped her knees as she stood, her body creaking. "Oh, Lord. I wish I'd been turned like you two. Young and sturdy."

"You never know how that might have impacted ya," I reminded her. "You might not have Maria."

"True that." Melissa nodded and began to make her way towards the galley-style kitchen. "Soup?"

"Wait." Gabe looked between us. "What's this got to do with Maria?"

"The mutual friend." I smiled sheepishly. "And Melissa's daughter."

"But, vampires can't reproduce." Gabe looked at Melissa again, giving her features more scrutiny than he'd shown previously.

"Nope." Melissa turned her attention back to the group of kids. "Y'all better wash up for supper. Hop to it."

The kids created a miniature stampede and the old staircase groaned as they rushed upstairs. All but two.

"Come now. The both of you." Melissa waved her hands towards the second floor.

Olive looked at us uncertainly before we both nodded. She sighed in resignation and followed the other kids. The gangly boy popped another puzzle piece in place before trudging up the stairs behind everyone.

Gabe waited for the last sneaker to disappear before starting again. "Okay, I'm guessing Maria is adopted."

"Quick on the draw, isn't he?" Melissa gave a mischievous and familiar grin before waddling over to the kitchen.

"Play nice," I followed her to see if I could make myself useful.

"That was nice and you know it." Melissa pointed at the fridge. "Twelve ought to do it."

I crossed the cracked linoleum and opened the fridge, pulling out the requested blood bags and laying them gently on the counter.

"To answer yo' question, I found Maria when a woman was about to change her back in the 1800's." Melissa pulled a huge metal pot from the bottom drawer. I thought I saw Gabe respond but couldn't hear him over the metal clang as she fished out a lid. "What?"

"But–" Gabe cleared his throat and his eyes started to shift in thought, "the Maria I know is in her early twenties."

"Oh good lord, child!" Melissa gave me a dark look. "Please tell me you didn't turn him without giving him the basics."

"It was a rush job," I stammered. "However, I did tell you that the blood I gave you would add twenty years to your natural life, remember?"

He stared at the hideous couch for a moment before nodding. "Yeah, I just didn't think that effect could be... cumulative."

"Regular transfusions basically halt aging." Melissa sifted through various jars and bottles laying salt and oregano out on the counter next to the large pot and blood bags.

"But why not just change then?"

Melissa slowed in her meal prep, the blood dripping from a bag for several seconds before she finally put it down.

Gabe looked at me expectantly. Shame made it impossible to meet his eyes. "She doesn't want to have to make the choice."

"Choice?"

"How she'll die." Melissa emptied the last bag and threw them in the trash.

Gabe went rigid. "Excuse me?"

"Have you ever noticed how most vampires aren't that old?" I laughed at myself. "Duh. Of course, ya haven't."

It wasn't like every vampire walked up and gave their backstory and date of their change.

"But Ritti's from Egypt. Ancient times."

"Yeah, that's why she's queen." I snorted. "I may not like her, but livin' as long as she has is pretty remarkable. She and Cyrus are the exceptions and *he's* busy workin' in the dungeons."

"What are you saying?"

I sighed. If he was struggling to come to terms with vampirism before this wasn't going to help.

Melissa gave us a side glance before waving Gabe away from the fridge. "Out with it, girly."

Gabe stepped out of her way, letting her fish some ingredients out, still eyeing me. I swallowed.

"Most of our kind checks out after five hundred years. Some a lot sooner."

Gabe went still but he didn't look surprised. "All the moving. No aging. Not interacting with anyone."

I nodded. "Watching everyone around you die. Maria would rather just wean off the blood when she's ready to go."

Gabe's eyes held mine more and more intently. "What about you?"

I shook my head. "I'm not thinking about punchin' my ticket just yet."

Gabe's eyes started to scroll back and forth over the floor. He took in a deep breath before letting it out. "What about Harper? He's getting blood."

I smiled. "Harper's transfusions are too shallow. Any more than a pint a year, people might start noticin'. But he could increase the dose if he wanted, he'd get the extra years. Be clear of almost any disease."

"And you guys kept that healing property to yourselves?" Gabe looked in interest at the growing pile on the counter. "I mean, we've been trying to find the cure for cancer for how long?"

I snorted rudely.

He turned his gaze back on me. "What?"

"We're not a pharmaceutical company." I decided to address his use of *you guys* for his own species in private. If he was alright with being turned, then I was about to sprout bat wings. "Can you imagine the military and medical uses that would be abused if you started applying vampire blood to the human population?"

He opened his mouth to argue then thought about it. "Every government would start dosing their soldiers the minute they saw the patient results."

"Exactly." I propped myself on the counter. "One of the few vampire laws even Elias agrees with. Never give the humans outside Court a drop."

Gabe winced. "So when you fed me–"

"Ivan was willin' to overlook it." I shrugged, a little pang filling me at the thought of Ivan. I decided to derail that thought train, segue or no. "So what do you want to do about the exposure?"

He rolled his eyes but kept his opinions to himself. "I have an idea but I don't think your roommates are going to like it."

"Oh?" I perked up.

Gabe explained the plan and I grimaced. Sadly, I didn't see any other options, so I just groaned and pulled out the burner phone. "Ya got Harper's number?"

"Not memorized."

"I'll contact Alex, see if he can help. Anythin' else?"

"Yeah, we should probably start taking shifts." Gabe leaned against the wall, bobbing his head to talk around Melissa as she emptied the remaining blood bags into the large pot. "We only have one gun but we can trade off."

"Keep it." I hit the send button on my rather long text and waved the idea away. "I'm not great with 'em anyway."

He blinked. Melissa hummed, loudly.

"What?" I shifted uneasily. His gaze was growing heavy on me.

Gabe's jaw tensed. "I assumed you knew how to work one."

"I know the mechanics, kind of needed in my line of work." I looked at the floor, staring at a spot where an oil burn had browned the fake tile to the color of aged parchment. "But I don't like them."

It always felt weird killing someone from afar. The act of taking someone's life should never be impersonal.

He stared another moment before strolling across the kitchen and grasping my hand in his. "Come on."

"Heh?" I barely got the response out as he pulled me off the counter.

Gabe looked over my head, not even deeming to respond to me. "Melissa, may we use the back acre?"

"Go for it. There's an ugly fence about a mile out if you need something she can aim at." She turned her head, her eyes gleaming with mischief. "'Fraid I don't have any barn sides for target practice."

"Come on." He pulled my wrist, yanking me through an old sliding glass door before I could come up with a kid-friendly retort.

"Gabe, knock it off." I pulled, wiggling free of his grasp and stopping a few feet from the door. "It's not a big deal. I have my knives."

"No big deal. Right." Gabe glared at me. "We're on the run from two vampire Courts and all over the news. But it's all good. You'll just fight the armies off with the knives buried in your boots and a wicked come-back."

"Fuck off." How was that for a wicked comeback? I turned to go back inside but he looped his arm around my waist and pulled me back.

"Get back here." He turned, lifting my body off the ground and carrying me further out onto the frozen acre like a gym bag. The frozen dirt crunched under his shoes.

"Let me down!" I had to hold my tank top down to ensure I wasn't showing any plumber's crack.

"You're my partner." He kept walking, looking around as he talked. "I count on you to keep me alive."

"Your point?" I made sure my tone was irritated but the word partner made me smile despite the awkward position.

"You know what I'm getting at." He plopped me next to him in the snow, keeping his hands out to make sure I stayed upright. "Don't be belligerent."

"That's rich!" I crossed my arms and stood like I had a rail for my spine. He was still taller than me but damned if I'd be cowed. "Especially coming' from you."

"What's that supposed to mean?" His breath came out of his nose in a huge plume.

"They. You guys. Why don't vampires?" I inched my face closer and closer with each statement. "You think I haven't noticed how ya refuse to call yourself a vampire out loud? You still won't own up to what you are! Bet you felt all freaked out by how much you enjoyed ol' Jason's blood, huh?"

Yeah, it was harsh, but it felt pretty good having somewhere to aim some of the pent up rage.

"This coming from the girl who wants to take the blame for everything including global warming?" He set his jaw in a tight line. "And *avoided* me for two weeks."

My jaw dropped before I remembered to fill my mouth with words. "We settled that!"

"Yeah, yet you're still trying to ditch me like bad luggage." He inched closer to me. "Trying to tell Cyrus I didn't know what I was doing coming along?"

"I offered ya a way out!" I gestured with my hands towards the house as if it held some secret passage back to his old life. "I dragged you into this—"

"Would you knock that off?" He glared. At my look of surprise, he continued, "You tell me how I should feel. You tell me what I should do. You tell me what I am going to do. They're all your choices and I'm just along for the ride, right?"

I opened my mouth to respond but he kept on, "Wrong! I'm a grown man. Younger than you, sure but so is most of the population. That doesn't make me a child. Stop making everything about you, for once!"

"Oh really?!" I didn't care that I was yelling. Didn't care that every word was echoing back to a house full of vampire ears. I stood on my toes, placing my face only inches from his. "If I'm so damned annoyin', then why do ya insist on stickin' around?"

"Because I think I love you, you Irish idiot!" He looked as shocked as I felt.

I let out a single laugh and fell back on my heels. "Points for originality."

Silence filled the field before he raked his hair and grumbled, "Dammit, that was not how I meant to say that."

"I wouldn't worry about it." My chest contracted, like my heart was trying to beat, and I struggled for composure. "It's not like ya meant it."

"There you go again." He blew out an irritated breath, the mist filling the air between us. "Telling me what to think."

I didn't have time to respond. He pulled me to him, covering my mouth in a hard kiss.

CHAPTER 22

GABE

I'd only just figured it out. I hadn't realized how much I wanted to touch her until she grabbed my hand. Even more so when she'd pulled away. I'd already resolved we'd have to discuss this, but I hadn't meant to blurt it out in the middle of a field. Still, I couldn't say I was sorry for the Freudian slip.

She gasped in surprise, then moaned softly as I ran my tongue over each half of her lip. They were chilly from the night air. My body heated at her nearness and I used the small of her back to press her even closer. She responded slowly, first stiffening then relaxing and sliding her hands over my shoulders.

When I began to explore her mouth more fully, I felt the soft push at my chest and pulled away. Her eyes were hooded and her expression was embarrassed as she stared at the spot just below my chin. "Gabe..."

I knew that tone.

"If you even try an 'it's-not-you' excuse, I'm going to pick you up and hold you here until we settle this."

She glared up at me. "I really miss the days I could lift ya off the ground one-handed."

"Your own fault." I released her, smoothing a stray hair from her face. "Look, I don't expect you to say it but it's not like I can take it back. We may as well get this elephant out of the room."

"What's there to talk about?" She arched her blonde eyebrow. "Ya kissed me in the middle of what was supposed to be a shooting lesson."

"You kissed back." I smiled at her look of indignation. "It doesn't take a detective to tell when someone's tongue is in my mouth."

"Ya surprised me!" She defended and I laughed.

"You could have pulled away. I wasn't exactly holding you down." I crossed my arms and gave her a level look.

"You're hot!" She snapped and then looked a little annoyed. "I might not buy every piece of art I see but I can still appreciate them."

"Cyrus isn't exactly a mutant, yet I didn't see you throwing yourself all over him." I flashed her a satisfied grin. "And thanks for the compliment."

She blanched. "How'd you know about *that?*"

"He's not subtle." I shrugged.

She started to say something else and I held up a hand.

"Look, I already said I'm not looking for any declarations here. I'm just asking you to admit that maybe you feel something too. Maybe–" I laced my fingers through hers, holding our joined hands up as an exhibit, "there's something worth considering."

Sure, we had a lot to sort out. Her past, my hang-ups. But that didn't mean it wasn't worth trying.

She looked at our combined hands but made no move to pull away. "We're kind of in the middle of somethin'."

I scoffed. "Like that's unusual."

"You've known me for less than a month."

"Time has nothing to do with this." I leaned my forehead against hers.

"So what, ya like everythin' about me?" She shot back.

"Nope." At her new look of shock, I chuckled. "Your habit of taking the blame for everything annoys me to no end, your driving scares the hell out of me, I've never understood your humor, and you have got to be the most vulgar woman I've ever met."

She looked like the words stung but I didn't want her thinking I was viewing her through rose-colored glasses. I didn't love her *despite* her flaws.

"You know why I didn't take that deal the Captain offered?" I kept my eyes locked with those sky blue depths. "Because when I thought about sacrificing you to save my ass, I'd rather be dead."

She worried her lip but she didn't look away. She hardly even blinked. "You still haven't accepted what ya are."

Okay, she had me there. "Hey, a month ago, I thought all vampires were scum. Give me–"

"And ya seriously need to catch up on TV," she interrupted, her tone playful. "Everyone has seen *I Love Lucy* for fuck's sake."

"Huh?" I drew my eyebrows together.

"What, you're the only one who gets to start this with a laundry list of faults?" She arched a brow. "Oh, and–"

I cut her off with another kiss. Our teeth clashed but I didn't care. I relished the feeling of her lips smiling against mine and her chuckle escaping into my mouth. I pulled my hand free, running my palms over her sleeves before cradling her head. I wanted to run my fingers through her hair but that damn ponytail was in the way. She nipped my bottom lip, her fangs grazing the soft skin without puncturing it. A low growl rumbled in my throat.

"Ahem." A deep male voice grunted.

We both stilled, her teeth on the edge of my lip and my hand on the back of her head.

"You're giving the kids a show." A dark man the size of a locomotive stood, his arms crossed over his chest and his big lips pursed in a grin. "Care to introduce me to your new beau, Lils?"

"Um..." Lily scrunched up as much as our tangled posture would let her, her arms still draped over my shoulders. "Gabe, this is Thomas, Melissa's husband. Thomas, this is Gabe, my..."

"Boyfriend." The large man snorted and extended an arm bigger than most tree trunks. "Nice to meet you."

"Thanks." I took my hand off Lily's waist and let it disappear in the man's large grip, taking the moment to take in his features and suppress my surprise.

I'd assumed Thomas was a son or friend until Lily said something. Melissa looked about mid-life with gray hair and a plump figure. Thomas looked young, maybe early thirties, with a muscle form Atlas couldn't gain, no matter how many planets he held.

"Dinner is ready." He released my hand and whistled a merry tune as he walked back to the house. Sure enough, the children were stationed at the back door, pointing and laughing. I looked down to Lily, then to the fence we'd been intending to shoot. Guess target practice would have to wait.

We followed Thomas back to the house, pushing through the mini mob and jeers. The smell of blood and salt made my mouth water. My fangs threatened the still tender skin of my bottom lip.

The children continued teasing us until Melissa glared from her position at the stove.

"Do y'all really have nothing better to do?"

The children silenced one at a time, a few mumbling apologies while others shifted on their feet. Thomas headed to the kitchen, sticking one beefy hand into the pot before licking his finger.

"Needs more pepper." He stuck his hand in again to confirm the thesis.

"Get yo' hand out of there." Melissa swatted his wrist and he chuckled before placing a kiss on her cheek.

Despite their physical differences, nothing in the moment seemed artificial or forced. It looked odd, a young man being so tender with someone almost twenty years his senior. Not like it didn't happen in the human world but still. Somewhere in the kitchen a phone started to ring, saving me from further gawking.

Lily pulled the phone from her pocket. She hadn't even finished her whole greeting when she yanked the phone about a foot from her face, scowling at the flip screen. She waited for the squawks on the other end to die before gingerly returning it to her ear.

"Yes Alex, I'm still here." She waited, making the talking-too-much gesture with her free hand. "Yes, yes, I know we're on the news. Did ya ring Harper for us?"

Another pause.

"Yeah, it was, but it's not like–" Another loud squawk and she shoved the phone into my hand. "Here!"

She tossed her hands in the air and leaned against the counter. I sighed, hesitantly putting the receiver to my ear. "Hey, Obi-Wan."

"Don't you start," Alex growled. "You seriously want to go on the news *again*?"

"Fight fire with fire." I plunked into a seat at the table, feeling several sets of eyes burning the back of my head. "Did Harper have the info I wanted?"

"Yeah, he does." Alex sighed heavily. "Here."

Before I could respond, a far more jovial voice bellowed into the receiver, "That you, buddy?"

"Harper?" I couldn't keep the grin off my face. It was like coming home from an awful vacation.

"You bet!" He barked a surprised laugh. "You two okay? That video looked pretty rough."

"We're alright," I confirmed. "Hey, is Amber Wright still looking for that interview?"

CHAPTER 23

LILY

"It was sitting straight the last five times." Gabe smirked as he watched my handy work.

"Shut up. I need something to do with my hands." I smoothed his collar again, concentrating on this one stubborn wrinkle.

I'd already helped Melissa clear the entire background behind us. Top that, Darren had walked me through some procedures, making sure the laptop couldn't be traced for the video. I'd had no idea what I was clicking and he'd growled every time he described a 'big blue button' and 'black windows with the white text', but I trusted the result.

Gabe tweaked his brows at me with a sly grin. "I can think of something."

I glared but I could feel my mouth twitching at the corners. "Cool it, tiger."

"Yeah, *tiger*." Melissa's tone was dry as she stood sentinel at the bottom of the stairs.

We sat on the lumpy sofa, the laptop before us on the coffee table. Amber's backdrop was a modern office, all sharp silver angles and abstract art.

Meanwhile, we looked like we were in a well-maintained farmhouse. Granted, that's exactly where we were staying but that didn't make me feel any better.

Melissa's glare silenced the children as they sat, captivated, on the stairs. They were allowed to watch so long as they didn't come on camera. Or make a peep.

We faced the built-in camera of the little laptop and took the call off mute just as Amber finished introducing us, "And now we're joined by Detective Gabriel Collins and Lillian Edwards."

Olive stiffened at the intro, becoming a rod on the bottom step.

Gabe swallowed and smiled nervously. "Hi, Amber. Thanks for having us."

"Oh, I knew I'd get you on camera someday, Detective." Amber Wright gave a small wink. "But having you here is a lovely addition, Miss Edwards."

Her brown hair was pulled back in a huge bun that made her square jaw more pronounced. She wasn't traditionally pretty but there was still something pleasant in her features. I'd been picturing a woman wearing a pro-vampire t-shirt. Instead, the leader of V.A.P.E. was poised like a journalist, her navy suit setting the perfect tone. Meanwhile, I was in Walley World rags that had barely made it out of the dryer on time.

"Yeah, sure." Wow, what an entrance. I swallowed, forcing myself to look at the camera instead of our image on the screen.

Man, after that bit on the news Ivan had to be having kittens. Just wait until he saw this...

"So, Gabe, let's get right to it." Amber looked down, presumably checking her notes, clicking her pen a couple of times before she looked up. "You disappeared at the end of a vampire-crime case, no word and no trace. What happened?"

"Well, I was hunting vampires." Gabe shrugged, trying to make it seem like no big deal. "I found one and I ended up working with her."

"Wasn't that against protocol?"

"It was, but this vampire put me in a tight spot." Gabe gave me an indulgent grin.

"Ms. Edwards, am I to understand you were that vampire?"

I nodded, coughing once before I managed to speak. "Afraid so."

How the fuck was Gabe so confident right now?

"Why did you agree to work with Detective Collins?" Amber's tone was neutral. "Did you think he had leads you needed? Were you using him for your own benefit?"

Luckily, a huge lump acted as a cork against the words I came up with. It must have shown on my face, because Gabe took my hand below the table, squeezing it once for reassurance.

Amber wasn't attacking me or anything. She'd warned us that she'd have to ask some pointed questions the public would want to know. Or they wouldn't take us seriously. She waited for me, not even looking phased by my slow reply.

God, why did we do this live? I could see the counter ticking up with every new viewer and my tongue weighed a thousand pounds.

I closed my eyes, breathed deep, and tried again. "Honestly, at first I was worried we would get in each other's way." I gave Gabe a sideways glance. "But he wouldn't back off."

"Oh really?" Amber's voice was a little less neutral as she clarified.

"Don't get me wrong, this man can be a real pain in the ass." I slapped a hand over my mouth. "I'm sorry! Should I not say ass?"

Gabe chuckled next to me and I glared. Amber let out a single laugh and waved away the question. "I think we can deal with it, Ms. Edwards."

"Okay." I considered my words for a second. "I mean, I can't exactly pretend I didn't benefit."

Gabe's chuckles abruptly stopped but not like he was gaining control. Or maybe I'd surprised him. Now wasn't the time to ask, so I just smiled and turned back to the camera. "Gabe's a great investigator. I'm lucky to have him by my side."

Something in Gabe's posture deflated but I didn't have time to consider it.

"So Gabe, why are you still hiding?" Amber leaned forward, her look growing intense. "Why haven't you come back to work?"

"At the end of my last case–" Gabe swallowed and looked down, "I found out Captain Sean Murphy had been helping to undermine the already tenuous vampire-human relationship in Portland. I wouldn't play along and he shot me."

"But Captain Murphy is gone." Amber tilted her head in interest. "Surely you're not hiding from him."

We'd already told her this part as a fair warning. It had been the winning argument for an interview.

Still, Gabe didn't look thrilled at having to say it. I squeezed his hand, trying to comfort him through the sweaty palm clasped over mine.

He swallowed. "Captain Murphy shot me in the heart. I died and Lily brought me back."

"So, you're not coming forward because..."

"Because I would be put to death for simply existing." He looked away from the monitor.

"And what of Captain Harper's recollection of the events?" She looked down to review her notes again. "He says that he didn't see you there the night Captain Murphy died. And it was his gun that killed Captain Murphy."

"Murphy's vampire associate had been beating Lily when I found them. Harper came in after the fact."

Not technically a lie. We'd agreed to word it as best we could to keep Harper out of trouble. He'd probably still get some pushback but the Court would help with that. Harper was a court investment now.

"And your sudden appearance in South Dakota?" Amber's eyes glittered like the edge of a knife. Damn, the woman was a keen actress. "Was it harder to hide out in your hometown?"

"No." Gabe shook his head, readying himself for the next question. "But we had an emergency."

"Does this have anything to do with the little girl in the video? Or the woman we saw you with?"

"The girl you saw is named Olive." I smiled, trying to look non-threatening, but it was stiff. "She went missing several years ago. We found her a few days ago."

"And why didn't you bring her back to her family? They must be worried."

"I wish we could..." I paused. Wording was key. "Olive is alone in the world. And I don't think a lot of places would take a child with her unique needs."

Not to mention keeping her out of the Court's hands. If the humans found out how we handled youngsters, it would not help us with the whole monster image.

"Are you confirming the theory that Olive is a vampire?"

Not much of a *theory* after that shot of her crying blood. But I kept the opinion to myself. Amber was just trying to be polite.

Gabe nodded as he said, "She was turned against her will."

As if any child could ever consent to something so permanent. But we had to say it.

"Is turning a child *common* in vampire society?"

"Absolutely not!" I caught myself shouting and settled down. "The turnin' of a child carries the death penalty. To take the experience of growin' up out of someone's hands is considered one of the most vile things ya can do."

"And has Olive's sire been punished accordingly?"

Gabe set his jaw. "We're working on it."

"So you know who turned her?"

"The same group that attacked humanity in the original massacre."

We took turns, laying out all the pertinent details. Ritti had once said that continuing to hide had given Elias control over the narrative. Well, she'd made the same mistake with Gabe and me. Now it was our turn, and if we did it right, we might just be able to force their hand. Served her right.

"Well thank you both so much for your time, but before we go, I have one more question." Amber flipped a page in her notes before looking back up. "What will you do to save me?"

I reeled back. Gabe recovered more quickly. "Excuse me, Amber, I'm not sure I get your meaning."

"What would you do to save me?" Something was wrong. Her tone, her demeanor, everything was off. "It's a simple question, no?"

Out of the corner of my eye, Olive stepped closer. I kept my hand low, out of the camera view, gesturing for her to halt. She stopped but she was still leaning in.

Something was very off with Amber. Even her posture was different...

Fuck.

"What would the two of ya do to save this woman?"

I stiffened.

It wasn't Amber's voice. In fact, she was drooling, staring blankly through the monitor. The new voice coming from the computer speakers was male. And Irish. And too fucking familiar.

CHAPTER 24

GABE

O live collapsed to her knees with a heavy thunk and let out a strangled noise, like someone was choking her. Her whole body quivered. Melissa rushed to her side but Olive didn't pay her any mind. She just kept shivering, shaking her head slowly. "No. No. NO!"

She was screaming it. There was no way of blocking the sound. Everyone watching the live stream would hear her.

It took a minute for me to realize Lily was speaking too. Lower, not even a whisper. "It's not possible."

I didn't have a chance to ask. That second voice spoke again. "Ah... so the little maggot is there."

Olive started to rock and scream continuously. Lily shoved her whole fist in her mouth, only small squeaks escaping past the impromptu bite guard.

"Líle..." A slender hand wrapped around Ms. Wright's neck. It didn't squeeze, just pulled the reporter to the side. Lily gasped as he spoke again. "Come out to play..."

He'd pronounced it Lee-leh. Just like the Queen. I'd never asked Lily about the name, figuring it could have just been an old pronunciation from her Egyptian ruler. Yet here it was again, encased in a voice Lily and Olive both recognized instantly.

The stranger's face had three jagged marks that tore from above his hairline and down to his cheek. His left eye was clouded and grayed over. But his right eye was the blue of a stormy sky. And his nose, while kind of cute on Lily, looked anything but charming on this stranger.

Lily reached out to the screen, flinching twice before tracing the scars on his face in horrified fascination. "Ci...Ci...Ci llian?"

"Lily." I placed my hands on each of her shoulders, trying to still her. Olive continued to sob openly. I had to ask; I had to be certain. "Who is this guy?"

"He's..." Lily's tears gleamed with the contents of the computer screen. She shook her head slowly, not daring to take her eyes off the patchwork face before her. "He's..."

"Her brother," Cillian finished with far too much menace. "And if I'm still knockin' about, dear sister, are you so certain we don't have little Rose too?"

If I'd ever imagined a malicious Cheshire Cat, he would have smiled like Cillian. As his lips twisted, the scars curled like they were in on the joke. "Of course, I could be lyin', but do you really want to risk it?"

Cillian leaned over and licked Amber Wright's neck and face in a long motion, keeping his eyes on the camera.

"Stop!" Lily looked away, a single dark tear streaming down her cheek. "Why the fuck are ya doin' this?"

"We all have our marching orders." Cillian gently bent the reporter's neck. Amber stared ahead, limp to any adjustment he made.

"What do you want?" I growled.

"I'd like to talk to my big sister." He smiled again, those scars stretching into even more unnatural lengths and twists. "In person."

CHAPTER 25

LILY

The whiskey burned my cheeks and throat but it did little else as I chugged straight from the bottle, a little grateful I didn't need to stop for breath. As I licked the big bottle free of its final drop I couldn't help but suck in a bit of liquor-flavored vapors.

Sometimes, it really sucked being a vampire. Ha, ha. Funny, right?

It was freezing outside, the snow drifts slowly building in the field, but at least I was alone. Even Melissa had let me be this time.

Giving up, I let the bottle fall from my hands. The glass plunked into the snow with a hollow thud. The night air sang on the bottle's edge, an empty whistle.

I'd often wondered if I could remember what my family looked like. If I closed my eyes I could pull small details out, my father's eyes or the shape of my sister's chin. I wasn't sure how accurate these were; I figured I'd never find out. Downfall of being turned at a time when food was scarce and photographs were a new fangled thing.

How I wished for that obscurity now.

Cillian was alive. Okay, not *alive* alive, but he was walking and talking. Who else was out there? What about Neasa? My mum or dad?

And why was Cillian working with Elias? And why did his boss want me so bad? Was it just because of the role I played in that whole Cheri Coke shenanigan?

Surely Elias couldn't be that petty. But I didn't know. Cillian hadn't said. He'd only said that I had three days to decide.

As though there was a decision to make. I'd be there with bells on and a shit-eating grin. Even if Olive's sister wasn't alive, Amber Wright was only in this mess because she was trying to help us. And I doubted very much it was just her. Most podcasts had crews, producers, or editors. Who knew how many hostages Cillian had?

I couldn't let someone else die for my sake. Not again.

Soft crunches interrupted my dark musings, the footsteps breaking the thin sheets of ice and snow as Gabe rounded the corner of the house, a fresh bottle of Powers Whiskey in one hand and his burner cell in the other. I held up a hand, curving it to receive the bottle.

The glass was warm against my hand and my fingers were stiff as I worked the lid off. Jeez, how long had I been out here?

"Alex said the Court's already working on moving him and the rest of the gang. Apparently, Miss Wright had posted the impending interview on her site, so Ivan had a little warning."

"Must be how Elias found out." I upended the bottle. Rinse and repeat. My gulps were thick, echoing over the empty field.

"He also said he's sorry he can't be here for you." Gabe sat in the snow.

I snorted, some of the whiskey burning a new path up my nostrils and I coughed. Gabe thumped my back until the fit was done. "Drinking won't solve anything."

"Yeah. But I'm not in a tea and crumpet kind of mood, so..."

I began to lift the liquor again, but Gabe slipped his hand over the mouth of the bottle, his eyes locked on my face. "I'll let you drink out here alone all night if that's what you really want—"

"It is." I worked to gently push his hand away. I wasn't ready for this conversation yet. How could he understand? And dammit, we'd just decided to give this whole thing a go. Now... well now.

I'd been wrong, the universe didn't just have a sick sense of humor. She was an evil masochistic bitch and, right now, she was the only drinking company I wanted.

"But I meant what I said last night." His tone was forceful and he didn't remove his hand. "I've let you wallow in it for over an hour and all you've got to show for it is the malodor of whiskey and blue lips."

"Fuck." I lifted my free hand and touched my lips self-consciously. I couldn't see the color but they were numb. And my speech couldn't be slurred by booze.

"Yeah." He slid his hand from the bottle and smoothed a stray strand of hair from my face. "So, how about we try talking?"

"Nothin' to talk about." I put the bottle down, wrapping my arms over my knees and clutching myself.

"I disagree."

"Of course you do." I snorted. "But we can't leave them to die."

"Oh, no, that part I'm a hundred percent on board." He began to shrug off his coat.

"Don't." I placed a hand on his elbow. "It's freezing out here."

"That's the point." He continued to work out of the jacket.

"Gabe, come on."

"What kind of boyfriend do you think I am?" He looked mildly affronted.

A little lump rose in my throat. This really sucked.

"My mother would roll in her grave if she saw you like this and I *didn't* offer my coat," he said it so simply.

"Gabe, do ya hear yourself?" I grabbed his coat collar, forcing him to stop and look at me. "We just found out I'm a key pawn in a hostage exchange and my *brother* is apparently trainin' child soldiers for Elias."

Why did the words sound so cold on my lips? Were they just that numb? Or were my ears frozen too?

"Yeah, and we started this relationship while we were on the lam." Gabe smiled and pulled me close, folding his open coat over me and wrapping me in his arms. "Before that, we became friends while taking down a drug ring and dethroning a bad police captain."

"Your point?" My teeth started to chatter. It was getting harder to ignore the cold now that he'd pointed it out.

He rubbed his big hands up and down my arms, "Our relationship has always been complicated. I didn't think things were going to get easier just because our status changed on Facebook–"

"You don't even have one."

"Heh?" He looked surprised by the interruption.

"Facebook. You don't have one." I finally looked up at him. Sure enough, his brows were trying to form a big caterpillar over his eyes. "I looked into you and Harper at the beginning of the case. He had a profile, you didn't."

"Why were you looking?" He seemed amused.

I punched his chest. "So I could avoid you, jackass."

"Sure," he drew the word out playfully and leaned his forehead against mine. "You mind grabbing the booze?"

"Why?" I fumbled behind me in the snow and gripped the neck of the bottle.

"Because it'd be rude to leave it out here and my hands are full." He stood, slipping his arms under me and chuckling as I shrieked in surprise. I flapped, spilling some of the whiskey in the process and he scowled. "Great. Now we both smell like a bar."

"It's your own fault." I glowered up at him, locking my arms around his neck as he started to walk back toward the house. "And you're leavin' a bottle behind."

"That one's empty, I'll get it in the morning." He stopped at the back door. "Want to open that?"

"My legs work ya damn cabbage." I squirmed. "Just put me down."

"Stop being a pain and open the door for me." He nuzzled my neck, sending the little hairs into a dancing gesture.

Deciding he'd put me down faster if I just played along, I reached down and wiggled the glass door open. It took a bit of effort with my fingertips still numb.

He had to push it the rest of the way with his foot, but it wasn't long before the heated house shocked my nerves, stinging them into a weary ache.

"Ow, ow, ow." I blew on the knuckles of my free hand, trying to warm them faster, but my breath was just as cold as the rest of me. And why couldn't I see my hands as well? Usually, their pale color stood out like a light in the dark.

"What is it with you and cabbages?" Gabe used his back to slide the door shut again before crossing the kitchen, still refusing to let me down.

"What?" I shook my free hand, trying to will the sting out of it. I was starting to be grateful he wouldn't let me walk. If this is how my fingers were reacting, my toes might not do much better. Right now they just felt numb, but that probably wouldn't last long.

"Cabbage." He started to ascend the stairs, lowering his volume as we got closer to the second-floor bedrooms. "You use the insult a lot. I don't get it."

"I don't know." I was still shivering and only the threat of breaking glass everywhere kept me from dropping the whiskey bottle. "Just thought it was a more interestin' way of insultin' someone than just directly calling them an eejit."

No one had ever questioned it before. Even my roommates just assumed it was an Irish thing. It was, but I'll admit I over-indulged.

"Huh." Gabe gently nudged the last door on the right open, revealing the tiny bathroom shared by the whole house. A wide arrangement of books were stacked on a shelf in one corner, while several types of shampoo and soaps lined the floor at the edge of an old claw-foot tub. The ceramic tiles were cracked in several places. New grout contrasted with the original application. The mirror and vanity were the only updates this bathroom had seen in ages, both less than ten years old and providing extra storage.

Gabe placed me on the vanity. After he felt confident my balance was intact, he closed the bathroom door and walked over to the large tub, turning one faucet up high. "You like it really hot or just kind of warm?"

I was stunned into silence. What the hell was he up to? When I didn't respond, he looked up from the slowly filling tub. "What, more of a shower girl?"

"What the fuck are ya talkin' about?"

From across the hall, I heard a motherly cough, reminding me that we were in a house full of vampire ears and no sound-proofing. Bad combo for a talk.

"Here." He flicked the lights on, scorching my eyes for a moment. "See?"

And I did. My fingers weren't just numb. They were gray and black at the tips. They probably would have fallen off if my body hadn't been working to fix the frostbite. I shuddered, wondering what my face looked like. I probably looked like Death's icy sister.

He walked over, taking my face in his two hands and keeping me from turning my head.

"Trust me when I say not to look in the mirror." He kissed the top of my head. "We'll sort the rest out after we warm you back up."

"You just want to see me naked." I teased, though rocks sank in my gut. Another *ahem* informed me our audience was still active.

"Maybe when you don't resemble freezer-burned meat." He smirked and took the bottle from my hands, taking a quick swig before coughing and sputtering. "Damn! Do you actually enjoy this?"

"It tastes like home."

He eyed the label quizzically. "Here I thought Jameson was the name brand for the Irish."

"This is a lot smoother." I reached to retrieve it. "Don't waste it."

He pulled back, placing it just out of reach on the shelf.

"Drunk or not, you've had enough." He looked over the steaming tub, like he was mentally measuring something. "You going to need help?"

I shook my head. "I can take care of it myself."

I propped my still-sore hands on the counter and hopped off. My legs were just as fucked up as my hands. I slipped and Gabe caught me, pulling me back upright just before my head would have cracked against the counter.

"Why do you think I carried you in here?" He placed me back on the counter and started to undo my hoodie. "The tether started ringing a low-level alarm about a half hour ago."

"Please." I caught his wrists, holding his hands in place at the bottom of my tank top. "I'll warm up without the water."

He looked down at our hands then back up to me. "Is this about your body?"

I flinched again. I'd really hoped he wouldn't guess but it wasn't exactly a far leap.

"This is about whatever makes you pull on your top, isn't it?"

I didn't have words, just looked at him in stunned silence. When had he noticed that?

He smiled, cupping my cheek in his palm. "Whatever it is, I don't care."

I snorted again. "We just started seeing each other."

"Yeah, and I think we just discussed the rate of courtship here." He tugged at the bottom of my top again, not pulling it up, just making his point. "We might as well get everything on the table."

No one had seen it since Cyrus. There was nothing I could do about it. Not like it was uncommon for vampires but that didn't make me feel any better.

He kept looking at me and I fell into his gaze. Those green eyes always reminded me of the rolling hills of home. I swallowed and held my arms up. He took it slow and I wanted to yell, just tell him to get it over with. But no, he inched the tank top, slowly revealing my stomach.

CHAPTER 26

GABE

Her belly was concave, not grotesque but just a little too thin. Her creamy skin stretched tight, making the puckered pink crescent of the scar stand out even more. It curved around her abdomen, stopping just under her breasts while a thin line disappeared into the hem of her jeans.

I reached out to run a finger over the scar and she sucked her stomach away from my hand.

"How?"

She snorted and shoved the dirty blouse back over her skin. "How do ya think?"

"But I thought Isaac was your first." He'd paid a good bridal price, securing both her and her family's survival. And he couldn't have impregnated her.

"I told ya some men in the town had taken notice." She leaned against the mirror. "Isaac was my parents' pick, not mine. I liked a boy, someone I'd grown up with. We'd managed to get our hands on some church wine and I thought I could take destiny into my hands."

"But you didn't marry him?" My knowledge of history wasn't as extensive as my dad's but I was pretty confident that was the standard solution.

"Couldn't." She shook her head. "He died about a week later."

I looked again at the scar. I already knew she hadn't had any kids... But I didn't think I had the right to ask.

"It came early." She averted her gaze, her face smothered in shame. "I was too unhealthy to bring it to term."

She placed a hand on her stomach and let the next sentence out in a sad sigh. "I'm told it would have been a boy. I think I would have named him John."

"Did Isaac know?" He'd offered a high bride price for Lily. He couldn't have. But the scar was impossible to miss.

"Yeah." She snorted and a dark tear welled in the corner of her eye. "The whole town did. But he still said he would have me. My parents were almost as shocked as me."

So he'd saved her family, knowing everyone would judge him for taking a promiscuous wife. He'd chosen to love her in spite of the indiscretion. Meanwhile, she sat here waiting for me to ridicule her.

"You're such a cabbage." The insult felt unnatural but it got her attention.

She snapped her head up, blue eyes darkening with her tone. "Excuse you?"

She was right. Watching her expression change was fun. I fought a smile.

"That's why you avoid relationships. It's not just because you're picky or you're hung up on Isaac."

"Ya didn't exactly look like you were concealin' a hard-on just now!"

Someone coughed a correction out in the hall.

"If you don't like it, then mind your own business." Sure, it wasn't nice to insult our hosts, but they could pop in some headphones or something. "And, yeah. I wasn't turned on; I was thinking."

Her irritation relaxed into a confused look, but she didn't say anything.

"I watched my mother disintegrate, lose everything she was, all because of a sick pull in the medical lottery. Then I watched my father get ripped apart in a nasty tug-a-war before I even realized it was vampires I was watching. All while I lay there, presumed dead under another victim." I closed my eyes and breathed, letting the memory of those dull eyes wash through my mind. "She had lavender perfume. I can't stand that smell."

"Gabe..." My name was a cough on her lips. What could she say? We'd both heard every condolence. Even when the words were heartfelt, they were useless.

"I can't imagine carrying a constant reminder on my skin." I smiled up at her and reached for the hem of her shirt. "Now stop trying to break up with me. If you don't want me, that's one thing, but stop trying to spare me your baggage."

This time, she didn't stop me, just sat there for a stunned second before nodding her head once. The shirt slid up her slender frame and I tossed it aside. I reached around, finding the clasp to her bra.

"Count of three?"

Those sky eyes searched my face and she shook her head. "Just get it over with."

I nodded and released the hooks deftly. She undid her pants and pushed them down as much as she could, guiding my hands down to pull them off where she couldn't. Her gaze filled with uncertainty. I didn't look down.

This wasn't how I'd pictured seeing her naked the first time, but that didn't matter. I lifted her in my arms and set her down in the tub, the water splashing over the curved edge and sloshing under my shoes.

She hissed between her teeth as her frozen flesh touched the steaming water, pulling her legs to her chest and leaning her chin on her knees. The water started to gray as her hair swirled behind her.

"You want shampoo?" I knelt on the ground and looked for the fruitiest-smelling one available. Nothing citrus but there was a strawberry one.

"Yeah but..." she paused, then blew out a breath and looked between her knees. "I may need help with that too.

"I think I can accomplish that." I sorted through the bottles a second time before holding a matching bottle to the shampoo. "Body wash too?"

She looked over her shoulder, read the bottle, and shook her head. "I can go without if that's the best they've got."

Really, she smelled like freezerburn and whiskey, but strawberries were out? I rolled my eyes and put the bottles back.

"Anything specific you want?" I looked again, landing on a brown sugar and vanilla one.

She examined my choice over her shoulder. "That'll do."

It took a long soak and another wash under the shower spray before her skin was finally back to normal. She was still exhausted, probably using a lot of energy healing when she was outside. We'd have to get a meal in her.

She didn't argue when I pulled her out and patted her dry. She just sat on the edge of the tub, wrapped in an extra towel, watching me work up her feet and legs. "Who was your last girlfriend?"

The question surprised me and I stopped to look up at her. "Why?"

"Just curious." She shrugged. "It's not like I thought either of us was coming into this as a newb."

I looked back down and kept pat-drying her legs. "Captain Murphy's sister-in-law."

"Seriously?" Her question was part laughter and part surprise.

"Yeah, not my finest moment." I sat next to her, patting her hair and squeezing the moisture out. "Michelle's clever and a fantastic lawyer. We hit it off, initially."

"So why didn't it work?" She leaned into my touch.

"Her reasons." At her confused look, I added, "For the work. You know why I joined the VPB."

"Ya thought you'd be rightin' a wrong."

I nodded.

"And her reason?"

"She likes the attention." I patted Lily's neck and shoulders dry. "And the success. She sees the vampire outing as her chance to rise in the ranks. Even without that, we wouldn't have worked; we didn't understand each other."

"And we do?" Lily's laugh was self-deprecating.

"Odd Thomas." The book title stopped her. "You knew I needed a mental escape before I realized it."

She looked down. "It was just a guess."

"Yeah sure." I lifted her chin and filled the gap before she could respond. This kiss was darker, deeper, and more intense than before. I slowly molded the flesh of her sides beneath the towel.

"Before you start thinking I don't mean it." I pushed the towel aside, running my fingers over her scar. She gasped in instant ecstasy and I took the chance to taste her mouth, sweet under the bitter bite of whiskey. The scar fit perfectly along the curve between my thumb and forefinger, like they were designed for each other.

She reached over, tentative at first until her hands curved over my abdomen. She ran her fingers slowly down until she found the scars. Three jagged little puckers I'd earned in an off-duty shooting. Her touch electrified every nerve. I never wanted it to end.

Bang! Bang! Bang!

"Hey, get a room!" Thomas' deep voice cut through the electric currents. The door shuddered again beneath his thundering fist. "Hard to mind our business when yours is echoing!"

His heavy footfalls were accompanied by the sound of girlish giggles and wicked snickers in the hall.

CHAPTER 27

LILY

One moment, we were lightly dozing, his legs still curled around mine, little hairs tickling the back of my calves. The next, those same legs were tangled and tripping us as we both tried to lunge out of bed, alert in a way no alarm could ever manage.

"Pants?" Gabe looked about wildly before I tossed his trousers over the bed, hobbling along with my own, one leg at a time.

"Did she scream in the truck?"

"No. Not even a whimper."

"Shit." We were out the door and down the hall.

We should have expected this. Hell, I'd lost my husband over two-hundred years ago and I still had nightmares. Olive had only recently escaped and god knew how she'd managed that.

And then, just when she was starting to feel safe...

I'd been so caught up in the shock of seeing my brother on that screen I'd completely forgotten her, selfish little shit that I was.

"Did she say anythin' to ya last night?"

Gabe shook his head. "She just sat in the corner cradling herself. That boy sat with her but it seemed companionable."

"Companionable?" I squashed the thought as we reached the edge of the hall and rounded into the room.

Some girls stood at the edge, their arms crossed and their bodies tense. Others sat on the ground and covered their ears to block out the sound as they cried. One sat in her bed, her hair sticking up at all angles, making her wide eyes appear small as she stared.

But none of them tried to help. None of them knew what to do as Olive thrashed and cried. They hadn't dealt with their own nightmares enough to help someone else.

I lunged forward, lifting Olive from her bed and wrapping her in my arms in one swift motion. She still screamed, kicking wildly, her feet pounding on my flesh and the cheap metal bed frame with sharp rings. I hugged her tighter, waiting. I hated when people shook me awake or screamed, but now I understood the urge.

Finally, she slowed, the screams suddenly dying as she went limp and her kicks turned sluggish. At last she stilled, looking up at me. "I'm done now."

I nodded and lowered her to the ground. "How long have ya had 'em?"

She blinked at me, solemn and calculating. "You first."

I snorted. "Before ya were born doesn't begin to cover it."

"Are yours because of something that happened–" she looked away, her small fists tightening, "or because of something you did?"

"Bit of both." I knelt down to her level. "That's two questions for me."

Olive looked over her shoulder. The other girls were still staring.

True, Mellisa found kids in bad situations. They had their own trauma in all kinds of ugly, unique little snowflakes. But that didn't mean they wouldn't judge Olive for this. I caught Gabe's eye and indicated the peanut gallery.

He nodded. "Alright, everyone out. Pretty sure Mellisa taught you better manners than this."

The girls stood ramrod straight at the name and marched out, quickly and quietly. Gabe grabbed the door knob after the last one and closed it behind everyone.

I listened intently for the final footsteps at the bottom of the stairs. "Alright, out with it."

Olive eyed me warily.

I sighed and stood straight. "Do ya want a new life or not?"

She continued to stare, only her eyes wavering.

I sighed, counted to three in my head, and tried to keep my tone level. "Look, ya didn't ask us to stick our necks out but we did. Didn't even back off when ya killed a man–"

"You took me just after I killed someone."

Now it was my turn to stare.

She looked up at me but it only lasted a second. "The man on the floor when you found me. That was what I was dreaming about."

I gulped back my first thought. And my second. True, we'd suspected that but I hadn't known the details. I'd been holding out hope that he'd attacked her and she'd made the best of a bad situation. Either way, was I ready to hear about this? Did I really have a choice?

"Alright." I swallowed again, but even then the words were a croak. "What happened?"

Olive sat on the bed, her eyes locked on the clasped hands in her lap. "I got hungry. It had been days since I left the group. I found him passed out in an alley."

I covered my mouth but the small whimper still escaped me.

Olive finally looked up. Red rimmed her giant hazel eyes, the drops barely clinging to her lashes. "It was easy; he was drunk and no one was around. I figured the police had finished over at the Cassidy's. It would give me some privacy."

And then we'd shown up and spoiled that.

"What'd ya dream?"

A tear finally fell and she looked away before visibly forcing herself to face me. "He was hurting me. Getting me back for everything I did. I didn't mean to break his arm, he'd struggled. But he didn't care about that. He wanted to make sure I could feel everything he did."

I had to learn to think again. My brain broke trying to incorporate this new knowledge. I knew she'd been raised to be a monster, to treat humanity as livestock. But I had hoped that her escape, however she'd accomplished it, meant she hadn't gone this far.

How naive.

Olive hadn't been innocent for a long time. She never would be again. But that wasn't the point of all this.

Olive stared at me, another tear streaking down her other cheek. "Are you going to turn me in?"

I shook my head. I didn't trust myself to speak.

And with that the waterworks opened, tears pouring freely. "Why not?"

"Because it wouldn't bring him back." I kneeled in front of her. "I can tell you from experience, no matter what ya do goin' forward, he will remain dead. So will Randy."

Her face turned sour but she couldn't stop crying. "I know that."

"So your best bet is what Gabe said." I took Olive's hand in mine. "You have to live and grow."

"What if I can't." She sniffed. "What if I'm too far gone?"

How many times had I asked myself that same question? After Isaac. After putting those kids down. And then getting Dean killed a couple weeks back. But Gabe had been right about this too. "You owe it to them."

I left Olive after she'd cried herself back to sleep. Good thing Mellisa always bought black sheets and pillowcases; guess she'd learned that lesson fast hosting a bunch of traumatized kids who cried blood.

Gabe was waiting in the hall. "How is she?"

I shook my head.

Gabe took one step forward and folded me in his arms. "Pretty sure the other kids listened through the walls."

"Shit."

"They were going to find out eventually."

"Yeah, but I was hopin'..."

"For something."

"Yeah." I leaned my forehead against his shoulder.

"Something else we need to discuss."

I let out an exhausted sigh. "Amber Wright?"

"And you wanting to charge off and sacrifice yourself for her."

That made me stand up straight. Those green eyes pierced my gaze. I couldn't lie to him.

"We can't leave her."

"No, we can't."

"There's no other way."

He cupped my face with his hands. "There has to be."

"They wanted me from the beginnin'." I gulped. "Who the hell knows why."

"Maybe this was Cillian's doing. Murphy said it was some kind of surprise." He leaned against the wall. "But you're right, they have some kind of purpose for you."

"Yeah, I've gathered." I squirmed. "So?"

"So, handing yourself over might give them more assistance than you realize."

"How?" I wasn't exactly tied high with the court, even before this stunt.

"Your guess is as good as mine." Gabe reached out, taking my hand in his. "My personal feelings aside, I doubt you're just a pawn to them."

This was getting nowhere and I was already exhausted. Had I really only woken up an hour ago?

"I have to go. Ya know that."

"You're just looking for reasons to get back to your brother." His tone was cold. "Not that you need much of one to go marching into a lion's den."

"What if it was your father?" I hated myself the instant I said it. That was further reinforced by the look of despair on his face. Still, I had a point. I pressed on, "If ya found out your father had survived the attack but been turned, could ya leave it be?"

He shook his head, his jaw clenched. "Don't use him like this."

"I'm not. I'm trying to explain."

"It's a lousy explanation." But he wouldn't meet my gaze.

"Only 'cause ya know I'm right."

"You don't even know how Cillian was turned." Gabe's eyes were still averted. "Or where he's been all this time."

"That's part of the problem."

"Lily, even if you find him, figure out how he became a vampire, hell, even if you two talk it out on some psychologist's couch–"

"I know!" I raised my voice. "He's tortured and turned children! He's helped Elias! He's always going to be number two on vampires-most wanted!"

My head was starting to ache and my eyes were threatening to burst.

I leaned against the opposite wall and crossed my arms. "Even if I magically convinced him to stop everythin' right now, it wouldn't absolve him of his crimes. I know all that."

After all, it wasn't like raising Alex or helping Maria find a home had absolved my relatively smaller sins.

Gabe's eyes danced over my face for several seconds and he let out a long breath. "But he's still your brother."

I nodded. "Even if Amber Wright wasn't at risk, I'd need to know."

Neither of us did much but blink at the other for a while. Finally, he nodded. "What if we could bring him in?"

"Heh?"

"What if we could bring him in, alive?" Gabe's eyes started to shift back and forth through the air. "We could get more than just answers for you. We might even be able to get some good intel on Elias."

"And how would we accomplish this miracle?" I arched a brow, mostly because I lacked the energy for anything more. "We're two vampires against a damned army!"

"Maybe we bring our own damned army."

"You want to *what?*" Thomas put down the bowl of blood he'd been slurping and gaped.

"Please tell me you're not on board with this." Melissa glared holes into my skull.

"Unless you're willin' to let me take their offer—"

Various forms of 'no' rose from every side of the table. Everyone but Olive and the gangly boy, who both stirred the blood in their bowls without comment.

I raised my hands in mock surrender. "If anyone has another plan, I'm all ears."

The other children had finished their breakfast and pretended not to listen from the living room. I didn't really see the point of excluding them. Especially with the puzzle-boy sitting right here. I wasn't sure why Olive had wanted him here, but he hadn't spoken against it.

He hadn't said anything, matter of fact.

When no one offered anything new, Gabe leaned his elbows on the table. "So it's settled."

"Dagnabbit." Melissa stood, gathering the dishes and storming to the sink.

"They have a point, dear." Thomas looked after his wife from his seat at the table. "It may get the Courts off our backs. And we needed to move anyway."

"I know all that." She stacked the bowls in the sink with a sharp clatter after each one. It'd be a miracle if they all came out fine. "But exposing the kids like that?"

"Ritti is set on winning human opinion," Gabe reminded her. "Revealing your operation–"

"Yes, yes." Melissa cranked the hot water handle; steam instantly curled around her. "It'll force their hand."

"And you only need to do this if you don't hear from me or Lily by Thursday night." Gabe gave me a sad glance. "It's the only card we can play."

"Are you sure you trust Ivan?" Thomas gave me a sympathetic look. "You couldn't even tell him where you found Maria."

I swallowed the guilt and nodded. "Gabe's right, they won't risk letting humanity find out about their policy with children."

"And what if you don't save Ms. Wright? " Melissa continued to scrub, refusing to look up. "Who do we go to?"

"YouTube existed long before we knew there were vampires." Gabe snorted. "Even the FBI couldn't take down every video. Believe me, they tried."

Olive looked up with none of the uncertainty from this morning. "I'm coming."

"Olive–"

Olive glowered at me. "I owe it to them. Right?"

I hesitated. "You're still just a child."

"No!" She stood, slapping her hands against the ratty old oak table. "I'm always going to be trapped in this shape, but I stopped being a kid the minute they took me. Now I have the chance to make a difference, but you want me to wait while the sergeant's *sister* does everything!"

"Olive." Gabe's voice was cold but measured. "That's enough."

"It's alright." I kept my eyes on Olive. Her shoulders were back and her spine was straight. She'd been tortured, turned, and shaped into something else. Her body would never mature from the age of innocence, but her mind would continue to learn and grow with time. "She's right."

Everyone but Olive and the boy stared or sputtered some refusal.

"They can never be kids again." I looked back at Melissa's furiously scrubbing form. "You know this better than anyone. That's why ya stock up on puzzles and books instead of Barbie and skateboards."

Melissa stopped cleaning the dishes and turned to look at us, but she said nothing.

"And Olive has it worse than any of 'em. Unless ya count him." I gestured at the lanky boy.

"Huh?" Gabe's brows drew together as he eyed our guest. "What about him?"

The boy just sat, his long hands clasped.

"Ya said there was another child soldier." I looked away from Melissa giving the boy a once over. Aside from his raven hair and tiny ears, he reminded me a bit of Alex. His features were sharp, though far more angular than my friend, and he was so skinny he looked tall. But his eyes were like Olive's.

Solid and hollow all at the same time.

CHAPTER 28

GABE

The boy didn't respond to Lily. Instead, he looked at Olive and tilted his head. She nodded to him before he returned the nod to Lily.

"Want to tell us your name?" I looked at the boy with new interest.

Lily hadn't mentioned another soldier child, but we'd had a lot going on.

"His name is Ronald." Olive sat back down, something straining her small features.

"Can't he answer for himself?" Lily gave the boy a reassuring grin.

"No, he can't." Melissa finally turned the faucet off and came back to the table. "You may as well show 'em."

Ronald seemed to shrink, his long limbs retracting like a turtle into his shell. He looked back at Olive. She nodded again. "They'll understand."

"Understand what?" Lily leaned in with me. Ronald let out a weary sigh and opened his mouth. I thought he was about to speak, but he just sat there with his mouth open like he was waiting for the dentist's drill.

Lily gasped, her hands smacking over her lips. "Fuck!"

Melissa didn't correct her this time. I didn't get it at first. He had all his teeth. His mouth was red like mine or anyone else's.

And suddenly I saw it.

Inside the gaping cavern of this boy's mouth, there was no tongue. At the back of his throat was a flat nub, flesh connecting the stump to the bottom of his mouth. The scar tissue was a pale pink, contrasting with the deep magenta and red surrounding it.

"Dear God." I leaned back, unable to stop staring. "How?"

"He's generation one," Olive said it like it was obvious. When we continued to gawk, she shook her head. "Sorry. He was in the first group they turned. They figured removing the tongue would be handy. If one of us was caught they couldn't give anything away."

"Can't he still write things down?" The moment the question left my lips, Ronald clutched his head and started to groan. Without his tongue, the grunts were muffled and hardly coherent.

"It's okay." Olive leaned into her friend. "They're not asking you to. Don't worry."

"He does that every time we even suggest it." Thomas looked sadly at the boy. "We gave up about five years ago."

The boy shuddered a moment longer but Olive returned her attention to us. "Before they were turned, they were mesmerized. Anytime they try to write, they hear a high-pitched squeal in their heads."

"Oh, dear lord!" Melissa looked horrified. "Ronald, I'm so sorry."

"You couldn't have known." Olive's tone was becoming more clipped and formal by the minute. "That was the point, to isolate them. Make it hard to survive without the rest of their group."

"So why'd they stop?" I didn't really want to know, but I had a feeling it was important.

"Their inability to talk tended to tip off possible targets" Olive shrugged. "Also made it hard for them to relay any information."

"Can't we undo the squeal, remove it?" Surely we could do something for him.

"Vampires can't mesmerize each other." Lily shook her head. "It's irreversible now."

A thick silence filled the kitchen.

"Has anyone ever tried to teach him sign language?" I was grasping at straws and I knew it.

Same results as writing, it took Olive even longer to help calm him this time. Thomas finally got up from the table, pacing behind his wife.

I could only look at Ronald with horrified pity. He could never really reach out to someone.

Yet, he didn't look sad. He looked hopeful.

"Olive–" Lily began, "how do ya know all this?"

"The sergeant told us about the first-generation soldiers. He said they'd all been put down and we should feel so lucky we weren't them."

Apparently, they'd missed one.

"And if they could do–" I struggled for a word to encompass it all, and fell short, "that, why didn't they mesmerize ya into not runnin'?"

"Too many of the second generation died because of that command." Olive swallowed. "The Court caught a good number of them in the eighties. They didn't reveal anything, but they didn't fare well in escaping either."

"The woman hoarding children..." Lily looked at Melissa. "Is that where Ronald came from?"

The caregiver just nodded, looking suddenly ancient.

"And how did ya figure out his name?"

"I pointed to letters in the alphabet, he nodded when I hit the right one." Olive shrugged. "I didn't have much else to do last night."

"So how do they keep you from running now?" I really hated where this was leading.

"What do you mean?" Olive looked perplexed like she thought the answer was obvious.

"They eliminated isolation, they can't tell you to never run." I felt my brows trying to knit together. "What did they do to inspire you to stay put."

Olive sat tall. "They threatened to take us to the farms."

"You're shittin' me." Lily sounded sick. "We thought they were just rumors."

"They're not."

Melissa said something foul. Thomas slammed his fist into the counter.

"What's not?" I hadn't meant to raise my voice, but the tension was building like bricks on my back.

"There have been rumors for years–" Lily looked at me, "that Elias doesn't just believe in human farms but actually keeps them. Treats them worse than livestock. He uses them for food and... entertainment. "

I gagged, dry heaving as I ran to the sink. Nothing came up, but my stomach continued to convulse around bthe wave of mental images. It shouldn't have surprised me. The first time I'd ever heard of Elias, one of his flunkies was calling humanity things like cattle and calves. It made perfect sense. But the description...

Images of Tara rose to my mind. Her bruised flesh. Her cowering stance. And then, like a foul overlay in my mind, the track marks of several working girls left in a hapless heap in the corner of one crime scene early in my career.

Used like inanimate sex toys and cattle. I dry heaved again, my throat becoming sore. Never thought I'd miss the ability to vomit.

The old truck drove down the worn dirt road, several little heads poking up from the bed. Olive and Ronald stood next to us on the porch, their arms crossed.

Lily bit her cheek. "I hate kickin' them out of their own home."

"Your plan will take the heat off them while they settle elsewhere." Olive set her shoulders back.

"Yeah." Lily nodded and looked up at me. "Let's get this over with."

She pulled the burner phone from her pocket and began to dial, sticking the call on speaker as it rang. Crackling through the speaker, a dark voice with a heavy accent rose.

"Yes?"

"Hey Boss."

Ivan sucked in a surprised breath before whispering, "Kid?"

"The one and only."

The whisper changed to a harsh hiss. "Do you have any idea–"

"Cram the lecture." She looked hurt at telling her adoptive sire to be quiet, but there was no easing him into this.

"What is this about?" Ivan sounded aggravated but his tone was level otherwise.

"You're tracing the call," she snarked. "Come find out."

CHAPTER 29

LILY

Every settling thump and creak of the old house made me jump. Each time I looked up at the wall clock to see how long it had been, only another minute had passed.

Tick. Tick. Tick.

Olive and Ronald sat doing a puzzle, popping each piece into place with quick efficiency. The tiny clicks of their puzzle were in perfect rhythm with the fucking clock.

Tick. Click. Tick.

Gabe read his book, eyeing the clock far less often than I.

Tick. Click. Flip

"Gah!" I stood from the couch, tossing my hands in the air. "Can they just blow us up already?"

The group stared at me for a moment. Finally, Gabe slapped the book shut and stood.

"Come on."

"Where?" I glowered at the front door. "They'll be here any minute."

"We only called them an hour ago. They're probably preparing for a trap and assembling a team." Gabe reached into his back belt loop and ejected the clip from his gun. "In the meantime, you're getting antsy and it's going to drive us all insane."

"I'm drivin' *you* insane?" I glowered up at him.

"Besides—" he popped the clip back into the gun, "I owe you a shooting lesson."

He didn't grab my hand or pick me up. Just walked past me and headed towards the back door. I waited, hunting for fault in his logic. The two faces looking up from the coffee table made sticking around very unappealing.

"Fuck." I turned on my heel and followed him outside. It took a few seconds to catch up. "Really, ya think this is the best time?"

"We both need to blow off some steam."

At that, I stopped. "Both? You were totally calm in there."

"I just read the same two pages three times and I still can't remember a damn thing."

Before I could respond, he started walking towards the back of the house again. "Now, shooting a pistol is actually pretty hard."

His tone changed to one I hadn't heard before. Something between his official interrogation tone and Olive's clipped military manner. "In the beginning, everyone shoots like a Storm Trooper, so don't be too hard on yourself."

"What is it with you and Star Wars?"

"You're not the only one who's been to the movies." He looked along the side of the house, finally spotting his prize. "And no one in your house was getting my book references, so I found something that worked."

"Phew." I pretended to wipe my brow. "Had me worried I was dating a nerd for a minute."

"Oh yes, that would be horrible." He crouched for the discarded whiskey bottle and headed towards the fence. "Now pay attention."

I saluted him and he rolled his eyes.

"Stance is very important."

"Really, I thought ya just spread your legs–"

He scowled and I shut up.

"As I was saying–" he gave me a level look before continuing, "it's not just about spreading your legs, it's also about your knees and waist."

"Really? Never would have thought of that."

"Be quiet." His reprove was soft but firm as he set the bottle on the fence. When he came back and put the gun in my hands, I wanted to throw it across the field. "Keep it pointed down range."

I bit my sarcasm back and nodded. He crouched, repositioning my legs, turning the open space into a triangle and bending my knees slightly. I almost toppled until he bent me at the waist, leaning my torso ever so slightly forward. It felt awkward but at least it was stable. "Okay, now hold the gun in both hands."

I did and he chuckled.

"Too many movies." He reached around, his arms cradling mine. "This one is automatic, so you want your forearm in line with the gun to absorb more recoil."

He tightened his fingers over mine, forcing me to tighten my own grip on the gun and pushing my thumb away from the top of the pistol. "You want the web between your trigger finger and thumb to be as high as possible on the grip but still allow the slide to move back and forth."

He made a few other adjustments and released me, staying behind me like a faithful instructor. "Okay, shoot."

"What?"

"You've got the target ten feet in front of you. Shoot."

I shook my head, but closed an eye and squinted at the bottle. The sun reflected off it and I tried to focus the gun on the label instead of the shiny curve of the bottle. I pulled the trigger, my arms lifting as the shot echoed back to me through the field.

Wood splintered in the fence and the bottle threatened to fall, but otherwise remained intact.

"Close."

"What the fuck are ya talkin' about?" I glared over my shoulder. "I missed entirely!"

"You were in the right line, just too low." Gabe cradled me again. "You see that little green dot?"

"I know what a sight is, thank you." Did he remember I'd run a PI business before?

"Then use it. Focus on the target and keep both eyes open this time." He backed up. "Again."

I aimed again, instinct making me wink a few times before I could focus on the green dot and then on the bottle. I fired. My arms lifted. The bottle shattered.

Not because I hit it. I'd hit the fence again and the bottle had decided to imitate Humpty Dumpty.

"Fuck." Okay, I was starting to really miss my knives. Sure aiming with them was also a pain in the ass but at least they were familiar.

"Hey, I warned you." Gabe patted my shoulder and kissed my cheek. "I'll go get the bottle from the bathroom."

"I wouldn't bother." The voice was irritated and mildly entertained at the same time. "Your aim sucks, Edwards."

"No such thing as beginner's luck in shootin'." I smiled over my shoulder. "How's it going, Melody?"

The tall Asian leaned against the house, her trench coat and dreadlocks whirling lightly in the breeze. Her brief amusement vanished as she stood straight. "Drop it."

"Nope." I turned, pointing the weapon at the ground.

"Drop it, or your little darlings inside are toast." She spat. "Jesus Edwards! Is that why you ran off? To play house and become one of those freaks we chased down? I know you wanted a family but–"

"Don't bother." Ivan's distressed tone bellowed into the clearing, his heavy steps redundant in his wake. "They wouldn't have called us here unless there was a plan to keep them alive."

My adoptive sire looked tired and wounded, huge bags pooling under his eyes and onto his mismatched face. His dusky skin was darker than normal and his hair looked like it hadn't seen a good wash since the Romanovs had fallen.

My heart clenched but I tried to keep it off my face.

"Pretty much." I handed the pistol back to Gabe and walked back to the house. "Hope your men were smart enough to realize that when they found the kids."

Olive and Ronald were still doing their puzzle. Only now several soldiers were watching them. It made an odd scene, like the painting of the dogs playing poker. No one had a gun trained on their skulls and the kids looked calm, Olive giving me a simple nod of acknowledgment before returning to her task.

"Olive, Ronald, come in here please." Gabe motioned towards the old kitchen table. Ivan came up behind him and Gabe motioned to the other chairs. "You and your second can sit over there."

Ivan yanked the chair out, the wood screeching against the linoleum. "Cyrus."

The Viking spun his chair backward before sitting, jutting his chin at Olive. "Does *that* really need to be here?"

I swear I could see smoke curling from the dragon tattoo on his neck.

"Oh, shut up." I took a seat next to my ward, Ronald sitting next to her and Gabe on the other side of him. "You're just pissed you got bested by a little girl."

Cyrus glowered another moment before turning his attention to me. "What do you want?"

"Not to be cliché, but it's not what she wants." Gabe crossed his arms and sat back. "It's what you want."

"I want you in custody and *that*–" Cyrus pointed across the table.

"My name is Olive." The girl sat up straighter, placing her hands on the table and looking him in the face. "It's not hard to pronounce."

Cyrus opened his mouth to retort but Ivan slammed his big fist down. "Cyrus, enough of your pissing contest!"

The warden nodded his apology and leaned his chin on the chair back. Slowly the rest of the wardens began to crowd behind the two of them. Some I'd known and commanded and some I couldn't name if my life depended on it. Their faces were filled with a mixture of disgust, curiosity, fear, and even respect.

Eight. That couldn't be all of them.

There had to be some guards outside. Especially with Melody now missing.

Ivan eyed his lieutenant a moment longer before turning back to us. "What do you think we want?"

"We know you want to save Amber Wright and her crew." I shrugged. "Even without the moral obligations, their peril is vampire business, so vampire law prohibits leaving them to die."

"That is your fault!" Ivan's face began to glow pink under the dusky tone of his skin. "If you hadn't run—"

"You would've killed me." Olive's shoulders were quivering but her voice was strong.

Ivan, to his credit, insisted on facing his accuser. "There's more to it than–"

"Oh for Pete's sake!" I threw my hands up. "Are we really going to waste precious time debatin' this shit?"

"How long?" Cyrus again. His eyes were fixed on the table and his chin was still propped on the back of his chair. "How long have you known where to find Melissa and Thomas?"

I swallowed, trying to think of any number that wouldn't make them realize that it was the same time I'd come back with Maria. Sure, I'd sent many a tramp home and brought back my fair share of strays, but these guys weren't morons.

"It doesn't matter." Gabe rescued me. "What matters now is what they know."

That made Cyrus sit up, several of the soldiers behind him leaned in with apparent interest.

Ivan was the only one who didn't look like he might wet himself. "What do you mean?"

"We have given Melissa some very specific directions." I leaned in, giving my best shark grin. "If she doesn't hear from myself or Gabe by the end of Thursday night, she's got her own editorial to publish."

"I'm sure it'll be like every other, boring, documentary." Gabe shrugged again. "The public couldn't possibly be interested in your policies on children."

Ivan's face turned cold as stone. "This is blackmail."

"Of course it is." I let my grin expand. "How else could we expect to survive this little exchange?"

CHAPTER 30

GABE

Our headlights shone off the oncoming asphalt, illuminating barren trees and the mile markers in quick flashes. We hadn't seen another car for at least an hour and the radio had turned into some kind of noise that made static sound like Beethoven.

Less than a week ago, leaving Oregon had been daunting but necessary. As we returned, all I wanted was to turn the car around and drive straight to the East coast. But it would just be a battle for the wheel and I would be damned if I was going to let Lily drive.

"Still no GPS?" I gave her a quick glance

"Nah." Her frown deepened as she traced the lines of a map folded in her lap. "This place has been closed for so long, I don't think the all-seein' eye of Google ever bothered with it."

"I don't understand how you're so calm." Olive was staring out at the frozen night, her eyes fixed on the stars overhead.

Lily ignored the comment, pointing to an upcoming dirt road "If that's 4th Street, it's not far after that."

I nodded, my guts twisting around themselves. It wouldn't be long now.

"What if this doesn't work?" Olive leaned in the middle of the front seats. "Are you willing to let Elias have you?"

"No." I glared at Lily, not letting her answer. "This is going to work. We just keep it simple and stick to the plan."

Ronald snorted but kept playing his Gameboy. The soft light illuminated his features into a ghostly shadow.

"What he said." Olive sat back in her seat and watched the tiny screen without further comment.

"Tough crowd." Lily snorted. "Should be coming up on the right."

"I see it," I grumbled, spotting the ramshackle building ahead. Without my enhanced sight, it would have been lost against the dark slopes and night air surrounding us.

The Orange Crush Cafe might have once been prosperous, but now it sat dilapidated on the side of Highway 97, surrounded by a few more shacks. The wood roof was falling in, a large patch of shingles missing under a sign that somehow looked new but for some discoloration. Orange Crush was proudly displayed in a bold font the color of radioactive soda.

The little front porch was the only protection from the elements, covered sparsely with chipped paint the color of rotten vanilla. The other sides of the building were composed of rotting wood that appeared dark gray under the moon.

"Why here?" I pulled off the highway and killed the engine.

"Isolated and almost three hours away from Court." Lily gulped and undid her buckle. "Might as well put the four ways going."

I pushed the button, amber light blooming in and out of the night from each side of the vehicle.

In the rearview mirror, Ronald's face fell into darkness as he turned the Gameboy off. He and Olive stared ahead with an eerie calm I didn't care for.

"You two remember the plan?"

They nodded.

"You'll lure them in. We'll sneak in the back to find the reporter and her team," Olive recited. "Ivan's team will thin them out from the outside to give us a way out."

"Good, don't stray."

Ronald saluted me. Olive simply nodded.

"Kids." Lily rolled her eyes. Her hands fidgeted with the map, making it crinkle in the dark. The half of her face I could see fell in and out of shadow with the four-ways. Like she kept disappearing and reappearing before me, moment to moment.

"Come on." I dropped the keys in the cup holder and got out.

The October chill stung and a slow wind played with her hair as she caught up to my side.

"Ya didn't have to rush out."

"I didn't feel like stalling."

"Don't start." She gave me a half smile. "If this might be our last conversation, I'd like it not to be an argument."

"Keep talking like that and it will be." I gripped her elbow. "Stop."

"No." She pushed forward, making me choose between standing there or walking with her.

I walked. "It'll be okay."

Not the most original assurance. Not even the best, but I could hardly list my reasons out loud.

"Yeah, it will." She stopped. "No matter how it goes."

She kissed me. It was over too fast and I hated her, just a little, for making this the first kiss she'd initiated. All because she thought it would be the last.

A cedar shingle slid off the old roof and broke on the porch, making us both jump at the sudden crack.

"I see your taste in men hasn't improved." There he was, sitting like he was in a lawn chair instead of on a rotting roof. His scars smiled like they were waiting for a punchline.

"Oh, shut it." Lily scowled at her brother. "We're here for a hostage exchange, not for banter about my love life."

Cillian waved his hand like he was summoning a waitress. "Lift your jackets and turn."

We complied, exposing our bellies and spinning slowly.

"Why Detective…" Cillian *tsked* me several times. "Is that a pistol in your pants or are you just really excited?"

"I see vulgarity runs in the family." I kept my hands up. "What do you want me to do about it?"

"Just place it on the ground and kick it away."

It didn't slide far with the snow's traction but he seemed satisfied with the result.

"My kids will come down to check for additional weapons."

The door to the cafe squealed open with a high whine and several tiny silhouettes filed onto the porch.

"Ya wanted me, I'm here." Lily bristled like an angry cat. "Let's get to the point."

"Relax, Lí--"

"Don't call me that!"

Cillian tilted his head this way and that. "Interestin'."

"No, it's really not." Her accent was getting more pronounced as her irritation grew. "I'm just gettin' sick of the games."

"Still a sour puss." Cillian slapped his knees and stood. The moldy roof groaned beneath his weight. "Ya heard the lady."

Several children filed forth, checking our pockets, our wrists, and finally our ankles. One kid with a red mohawk yowled as he found Lily's knives.

"Come now, don't be a baby." Cillian hopped off the roof, landing in the snow with a heavy thud. "Ya were warned about those, just disarm her."

The child sucked his thumb once before starting to pull the blades free and tossing them in a messy heap. They clanged together, one at a time.

Cillian skipped, whistling a merry tune and shoving his hands deep in his pockets. He stooped at the pile of knives, picking one up and flipping it in his hand. "That nut-job in Portland mentioned these, glad she had some value in the end."

"I see your taste in employees hasn't improved." Lily's tone was deadpan as she eyed the tiny squadron, giving the kid with the mohawk a look I couldn't read.

"I don't do much hirin'. Besides–" Cillian tapped the side of his face with the tip of the blade, indicating his blinded eye, "Elias isn't a fan of being questioned."

"Speaking of your boss–" I crossed my arms, now that the search was done, "what's he want with Lily?"

"I don't remember a Q&A bein' part of the agreement." Cillian stood, still flipping the knife in his hand and turning towards me.

A shrill whistle broke the air. I couldn't help smiling.

"Sir–" One of the kids started.

"Quiet." Cillian continued to stare into the distance, his body tense. When nothing else happened he started to relax. "John, go see–"

Another whistle, this time accompanied by the tiny pops and cracks of gunfire. Several small lights flickered in and out in the distance, like a group of shutterbugs busy with some nighttime photography.

I grabbed the nearest boy and chucked him at Cillian, toppling them both. Lily bolted forward, me close on her heels as she surged towards the old rest stop.

Shots fired, closer now, several of them searing through me and setting off the tether as they rocketed through her.

CHAPTER 31

LILY

"Cease fire, you twits!" Cillian was still trying to get up from the ground when the shots stopped. "Elias wants her *alive*."

"Thank Christ for small favors," I grumbled, pushing my way into the decrepit rest stop.

The ancient floor groaned under our feet. A musty odor of rot and moss filled the space. Behind us were a bunch of kiddy soldiers with not-so-toy guns, their footfalls squishing all over the soggy porch. We didn't have long to survey the room.

"We need weapons." Gabe's eyes danced over the dark space.

"Agreed." I ran to what was left of the nearest table. Once, it had been one of those '50s-style booths. The cushions were torn, probably from a bunch of animals shredding it for nests. The tabletop was huge, but too soft and full of holes to serve even as a shield. It would only slow me down.

"Fuck." I gripped the table and tried to ignore the ache in my arms as bullets wiggled back to the surface. It was like getting shot in reverse, slowly. Gabe grunted behind me and something snapped.

The door shook from the force applied on the other end.

Our head start was over. And all we had to show for it was the putrid remains of an old table.

I yanked the tabletop up; several bugs and a giant rat ran over my feet. The door flew apart as the onset of children swarmed in. Finally, I pulled the top off leaving the supporting pole still bolted to the floor.

"Back-to-back!" Gabe backed up, a large, rotting beam in his hands. Behind him, one of the trusses was busted from the wall. "We only have to hold them off for a little bit."

I hoped the building wouldn't collapse from his weapon choice, but we didn't have time to debate it.

The kids ran in. No battle cries or anything dramatic. It was like watching a horde of well-trained zombies as they filed through the door. I threw the tabletop, knocking over a couple of them before yanking out the support pole with a loud creak. The metal was slick in my hand from years of grease and I couldn't be sure of my grip. But it would make one hell of an impact.

Another kid lunged and I swung for the fences. The boy's body crunched as he flew back into the air. A sharp pang of regret reverberated through me.

Shit, they were just kids.

The hesitation cost me. One of them bit me, running past the crowd to sink his tiny teeth deep into my arm.

"Fuck!" I flung my arm, sending the little shit into the wall opposite from his friend.

"You okay?" Gabe grunted through his own battle. Presumably, some of the beasties had come through the backdoor and were causing him the same trouble.

"Just... fuckin'... peachy," I grunted each word through a swing, my movement no longer slowed. Kids or not, they would take us down. I wouldn't kill them but I wasn't gonna lay down and die either. "You?"

The metal pole tried to slide out of my hands and my swings grew clumsy. Between Cillian's order not to shoot and our size, we were holding them at bay. But that's all we could do. This was our role.

Come on Olive. How long is this going to take?

"I think... we need to—" Gabe's words were chopped into a similar rhythm, crunches and snaps punctuating the splits, "come up... with a better... date night!"

"Yeah?" I swung down onto a kid's neck, just in time for one to clamor up my back. I yanked her off and tossed her to the floor. "How 'bout we live to discuss it."

The discarded tabletop smashed my side, as two kids used it to ram me. The back of my skull smashed into Gabe's and all I could see was blinding white for several seconds as the pain pinched every one of my internal organs.

I heard them run towards us before my vision cleared. Then I felt them kicking our legs and punching our stomachs. Gabe and I matched each other, ached for ache, groan for groan. I tried to swat them away, but there were too many and my body was still processing all the pain blinding me.

And then one of them kicked out my knee. I toppled and they piled on top of me. Elbows pelted my kidneys. Feet flew hard enough into my stomach to impact my spine.

I swung the pole, hearing the occasional grunt until I suddenly couldn't swing. The pole wouldn't move where I tried to swing it, and then it was jerked out of my hands. Something smashed into the side of my skull.

"Get off her, you little shits!" Gabe's words were muffled. He must have been under his own siege.

Someone kicked my knee again. I felt the crack, but I couldn't hear it over our cries of pain. My very insides shattered. I flailed uselessly and my hands clenched, grabbing onto whatever happened to be on the ground. One hand scraped something sharp, glass or an old nail. The other landed on something small and plastic. I didn't have time to ponder the second object as the beating continued.

Gabe grunted in the distance but it barely registered over my own agony.

"That's enough." Cillian's assured voice was emphasized by the heavy creak of his shoes dropping against the old floor.

The kids slowly stopped their assault, leaving me in a heap on the floor. I'd curled into the fetal position, with my back to the sky and spitting blood. Where the hell were they?

Ivan had to have made it through our perimeter. And Olive had to have been able to use the distraction by now.

"Good try, sister dear." Cillian walked right past me, the new-leather smell of his shoes alien with all the blood and mold in the air. "But drop the weapon, or I'll kill him."

Cillian jerked Gabe into a sitting position by his hair, one of my knives to his throat.

"Don't ya fuckin' dare!" I stood on instinct, trying to lunge for my brother. Agony bloomed in every nerve and broken bone; I crumpled.

"Then put the gun down!" Cillian slipped the tip into Gabe's skin. Gabe shook and hissed.

I looked around like an idiot. "You took Gabe's gun!"

"No, that gun!" Cillian nodded towards my hands.

I opened my arms to prove what a lunatic he was and then I saw it. The hard object I'd gripped while the kids were beating me to a pulp. It was indeed a gun. One of them must have dropped it during the fight.

And I was holding it in my clenched fist.

"Yeah..." Cillian drawled. "That gun, right there."

I smiled, though it hurt my entire face to do it. "Oh, this gun?"

"Don't even think of it, Líle." Cillian dug the blade in further, tearing a short scream from Gabe's throat and a chill from my very soul. "He'll be dead before I even start to burn."

"That's not what I had in mind." I pressed the muzzle to my own temple.

Gabe gasped something, but blood and bubbles were all I got from it.

"Let him go!" My voice shook, but there was a gun to my head after all. I laced my finger over the trigger.

Cillian stared as if he'd never seen me before and, in a sense, I guess that was true. Over a hundred years lay between us and obviously we'd both taken some interesting turns during that time.

The occasional pop of gunfire continued outside, breaking the silence in uneven staccatos.

"Now!" I pressed the gun in harder, the warm barrel singing my flesh. "Or ya can tell your boss all about how *you* lost his precious prisoner."

Cillian grinned, the gesture morphing the scars on his face. "And what makes ya think I care?"

"'Cease fire, you twits,'" I mocked. "Between you and that psycho old biddy, I can take a fuckin' hint."

He stared, weighing me in some way I found disconcerting from my lower position. He shook his head and slid the blade out from under Gabe's skin. I took a split second to take in Gabe's appearance.

His nose and cheeks were both wriggling towards their correct location. The breaks didn't make him look roguish, nor did the blood dripping from one swollen eye. Those little brats had aimed their blows almost exclusively at his head.

"Okay." I turned my attention back to Cillian but raised my voice for the others. "Where the hell is Amber Wright?"

"So you can ride into the sunset, free and clear with your boy?" Cillian twisted his lips in annoyance.

"I wasn't talkin' to you." I stood, keeping my brother in sight. "Tell me you've found 'em."

"I've got 'em," Olive's tone was still clipped as she hopped down from the rafters, Ronald landing right behind her.

Cillian sat up straighter. "Ahhh. The prodigal daughter returns."

I ignored him. "Olive, can ya get Ms. Wright and her crew out?"

"I could. Easily."

I nearly sighed in relief.

"But why would I?"

Huh? Did Olive think now was the time for a freaking ethics lesson?

Before I had time to tell her off, Olive reached behind her back, pulled out a gun, and shot my arm.

My gun fell with a thick thud.

CHAPTER 32

GABE

Lily's arm exploded and hit the floor with a solid thud. Lily didn't even scream, she just stared as the bloody stump disintegrated before looking back at Olive.

Every nerve in my body turned to ice. I think I screamed but I can't be sure. I only remember asking, "Why?"

Olive didn't answer, just kept those hazel iceberg's on Lily. "What would you like me to do, sir?"

"Keep it trained on her." Cillian stood, releasing his grip on me. "She may not value her life, but I'm sure her boy toy does."

I hit the floor with every bruised and battered part of my body, but I still didn't feel it.

This wasn't real. It couldn't be.

Cillian stood before Olive, looking down at her with a mix of emotions I couldn't name. "How'd it go?"

"Better than expected."

"I would say so." Cillian smiled down at his sister, though the expression held no joy.

"Was it all an act?" Lily croaked.

Olive tilted her head, looking like a small bird of prey. "I told you how I was trained."

We'd been fools. We seriously thought we could undo years of torture and brainwashing over a couple of days. And Olive was right. She had told us she was trained for espionage. She'd basically screamed she'd betray us any second. But we'd only heard what we wanted to hear.

"So you were just out to trap us? The whole time."

"Oh no, she was going through graduation." Cillian mussed Olive's hair. "Stumblin' upon you numbnuts was just dumb luck."

Shots still popped outside, becoming less and less frequent.

"You asked how they keep us from running away." Olive finally looked at me. "They let us."

In my battered state, it took a minute to understand. Graduation. They *let* the children go.

Just like any child who'd thought about running away, they realized how dependent they really were. They ended up cold or hungry, alienated. Even hunted. Of course, they would go back to Elias. They were lost children and he was their Pan.

The train of thought was completely derailed as the chaos outside burst inside. My vision was still blurry and vague from the beating, so I didn't understand all of the movement, only that the door and windows blew open as several new faces joined us.

And the violence started all over. The kids kicking and screaming all new targets, their faces meshing amongst the men and women gunning them down.

I crawled. I couldn't do much else. Not yet. Those kids had broken a few ribs and no matter how I moved, it was agony. But we had to get out of here.

The plan was dead. Sure the Court provided us with brute strength but Olive was supposed to be the intelligence.

Someone tripped over my body, crunching the busted ribs into my organs. God, even screaming hurt.

"Collins?" I recognized the voice in the back of my mind but the pain made it impossible to organize my thoughts. I couldn't even curl into the fetal position. That hurt too.

"Oh, you gotta be shitting me." Someone grabbed me under the arm and dragged me. I tried to pull away but all I could do was scream more. Every bump and jostle was agony.

At some point, they dropped me, swearing a bunch and pounding on something. Maybe an attacker. It didn't matter all I knew was that gravity did a great job of amplifying every burst of pain. Right as I could take in a shaky breath, they lifted me again and dragged me out into the cold night, laying me out on the snow.

They put me down swiftly and came around to look at me.

"What the fuck happened?" Cyrus was growling.

My lungs hadn't had the chance to heal. I couldn't get enough air to explain it all. I could only croak one word. "Girl."

"I fucking knew it," Cyrus spat. "Stay here."

I grabbed his sleeve, yanking him back.

"I don't have time to babysit your ass." Cyrus grabbed my hand and crushed it but not before I could wheeze out one more word.

"Lily."

Maybe it was my expression. Maybe my tone. Whatever it was, it got his attention. His face lost all expression and his eyes locked with mine.

He nodded and ran back into the building. Whatever adrenaline I'd had to keep me thinking was gone. All my bones started to slide back in place, the ribs pulling out of each organ they stabbed in slow motion. I blacked out trying to claw back into the battle, my face in the snow.

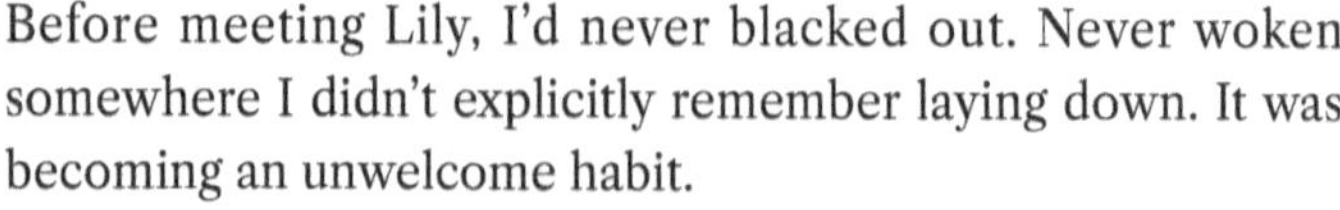

Before meeting Lily, I'd never blacked out. Never woken somewhere I didn't explicitly remember laying down. It was becoming an unwelcome habit.

Though, technically, one of those had been when I died. Maybe that didn't count, but it was still disconcerting. I guess it shouldn't have surprised me to wake up in a dungeon.

At first, I thought I was back in vampire rehab. Not sure what that says about their bedside manner. But the concrete walls and drain were all the same. Only now there was no bed and a pissed-off Viking shaking me awake.

"Get up." Cyrus nudged me again, even less gently, shoving a phone in my face. "You got a call to make."

"Where am I?"

"The dungeons, but don't worry." He pushed the phone to me again. "We have great service."

Right, the call to Melissa. We had a deal and I guess Ivan had held up his end.

I took the phone and started to dial. "How bad was it?"

Cyrus took a deep breath, thought about it, and said, "We lost seven men, but we got almost every one of those abominations before they fled."

It was the pause that made me stop dialing, my thumb over the last number.

Cyrus had taken time to consider his choice of words. Something had gone wrong. And why was he asking me to make the call?

"Where is Lily?"

He looked like he'd swallowed tar, his eyes fixing on the dingy concrete floor.

"Cyrus, where is she?"

He still didn't answer. My insides turned numb.

I held up the phone, ready to smash it on the ground. "Last chance."

Cyrus heaved a breath. "I couldn't find her."

CHAPTER 33

LILY

The rest of the team invaded and I tried to get away. But it was crowded, people tripping over each other to fight and I couldn't even crawl, my arm was still a freaking stump. I made it all of five feet when someone grabbed me by the hair and yanked me back.

"Now, now." Cillian cocked his head. "We've hardly had our family reunion."

It was all the warning I got before he slammed my head into the nearest table. My world was swallowed in a gigantic black hole.

***

The air was fragrant with smoke when I woke up. Nothing like the heavy smoke of a house fire, but the light scent you might get while camping. Something heavy and cold sat on both my wrists and ankles. Manacles from the feel of it. My arms and legs were freezing, which made little sense, considering the thick jeans and jacket I'd been wearing. Every joint ached as if I'd slept on a rock, despite the fluffy surface I found myself on. I fought the urge to open my eyes, listening for anything around me.

A slow crackle popped in the air, soft and simple. Had to be the fire. Nothing more.

When my impatience got the best of me, I popped a single eyelid open.

A giant tapestry rich in jewel tones covered the whole wall. I was on top of a thick comforter on the softest bed. Was I back at Court?

No, couldn't be. I'd be in the dungeons. Even Ivan couldn't pull rank for me this time. Could he?

I didn't recognize this room but I hadn't seen every nook and cranny of the place. Someone on our team must have found me after Cillian knocked me out. Maybe Ritti was trying to butter me up for all the juicy details. Or be certain I'd make the call. Then she'd lock me up with Gabe.

Gabe!

I sat up straight and my confusion turned to rage.

My wrist and legs were bound in thick manacles. That would have confirmed my Court theory but my clothes were gone. Instead, I was in a deep blue silk nightdress that barely grazed my thigh. They'd even taken my bra. Court had no reason to do that. None.

My own brother had fucking removed my clothes and re-dressed me!

"Can't fuckin' get it up with a conscious woman Cillian?" I shouted at the wall. "We had a fuckin' deal and my breasts weren't part of it ya sick piece of–"

"I assure you, darling, Cillian had nothing to do with your change of clothes."

I froze mid-insult. My blood slowed to sludge in my veins as I turned around. The state of my new wardrobe had distracted me from the rest of my surroundings.

The rest of the room was just as luxurious as the tapestry. Every surface was either rich wood or heavy fabric. A man sat in a thick chair, his fingers steepled in a gesture I remembered too well. He stood and sauntered towards me, making a show of a small key in his hand before shoving it into the pocket of his waistcoat.

He looked to be in his mid-forties, but that had never made him any less attractive. He was also long. Not just tall, but skinny as well. Every part of him. His angular jaw and long face were set in a small smile as he knelt on the bed, crawling towards me. I backed up, the chain of my restraints jingling as I wiggled toward the headboard frantically.

I was still asleep. Still out cold. That was the only explanation.

The man reached out, his spider-like fingers inching towards my face. I pulled away but he shushed me with a long finger to my lips. That simple touch stilled me. It couldn't be real.

My head ached as I flung my skull against the headboard, trying to merge with it. Anything to get away.

He moved his hand. I flinched until I felt his knuckles stroking my cheek in a knowing path.

"Líle," his breath caressed the old name.

I reached out a trembling hand, absorbing the familiar brown gaze. My palm cupped the line of his jaw. He was solid. He was here. He couldn't be.

"Isaac." It was barely a whisper, maybe a prayer.

"You deceptive trollop." He slapped me, my head ricocheting off the headboard. Before I could react, my sire pulled me to him. "Do you have any idea how long I've been trying to find you?"

I sputtered a response but it wasn't coherent. My brain was raging a war between mounting my defense and rejecting the reality before me.

Isaac was alive. Isaac was beating me. What fucked-up alternate reality had I fallen into?

Before I could get my tongue untangled, he kissed me.

It was possessive and rough, his teeth clashing with mine. I pushed away, my meager strength nothing. I was starving and freshly healed from a severed limb. I was weak and he used that to his advantage.

He finally backed off, laughing in a way I'd once dreamed to hear again. "Doesn't matter. You're here now."

"I... I..." I swallowed, willing my mind to release my tongue. "I thought you were dead."

"I figured as much."

"You..." I sagged, letting the weight of it all settle on me. "You changed Cillian."

"Like my upgrades?" Isaac sat back like we were gossiping girls at a slumber party.

"How the..." I shook my head and forced myself to look at him. "Why are you here?"

"Well, I came to America after that whole Famine debacle–"

"No, I mean here." I pointed at the bed for emphasis. "Right here, right now. What are ya doin' here?"

A knock came to the thick door, making me jump.

"Sir." A soldier cracked it only a little, bowing to Isaac. His tone was apologetic. "We need you outside. Do you want me to restrain the prisoner?"

"Being the boss means that I'm done when I say so." Isaac's voice was tight but controlled as he knelt in front of me. "And, unless she poses a direct threat, none of you better touch my wife again."

The soldier bowed and scurried away, nearly slamming the heavy door. Isaac stroked my cheek, a self-assured grin stretching across his features. "Does that answer your question, darling?"

CHAPTER 34

GABE

The tether yanked again, a mild ache in the black pit of numbness. Still, I clutched my chest and hissed, "God dammit."

"Again?" Melody was dropping off a new cooler of blood bags.

"Yeah."

It had just started up. Silence for hours on end, and now constant pulls. Were they torturing her for information?

Melody nodded, picking up the old cooler. "At least you know Edwards is alive."

"And in *pain*," I shot back.

"Fine, sit there in your self-pity." She turned on her heel and stomped out.

At least I was alone again. I laid back on my cot, rubbing my chest as the ache died down.

They left me alone for the most part. Maybe they figured my own thoughts were torture enough. Or maybe they thought experiencing Lily's pain saved them the effort. Every couple of days they'd drop off a new batch of blood. I was only able to tell how time passed because they turned the lights in the cell off at night. Otherwise, everything merged together.

Wake up, stare at the gray ceiling. My back would start to ache so then I'd pace. Might sit in the corner for a bit, just to examine the door, watching how they came in to drop off the blood. Then I would experience her pain. Despite growling at Melody, that was both my favorite and most hated part of every day. I waited for it. I gritted my teeth, imagining everything they might be doing to her.

Occasionally it occurred to me I wasn't the only one experiencing these daily reminders. Alex had to be losing his mind.

My door opened again. I didn't bother to look away from the ceiling. "Just once so far today."

"Long one?"

"Couple minutes."

"The kid's strong."

I finally looked over at Ivan. "You could always go rescue her."

"We don't know where she is." His whole being drooped, like the skin barely cared enough to cling to his bones.

"Like you'd go after her if you did."

"I wouldn't be able to sell Ritti on that, you're right." Ivan sat at the edge of my cot, clasping his large hands and staring down. "But Ritti would take the opportunity to take out Elias."

"Yeah right." I rolled up into a sitting position next to him. "She's probably just happy we managed to murder those kids."

Of course, I understood those kids would have killed me but I also recognized that wasn't their fault. I thought of the kids that had kicked my head in and I saw Olive, crying in the park. Maybe it was all an act, but some of it...

"Noone likes that law. Least of all the Queen." Ivan dragged a hand over his face and sighed. "You're young. I don't expect you to understand."

"I could live to be a thousand and I wouldn't understand murdering children." I stood, walking to the other end of the cell. "But seeing as I'm stuck here, try me."

Ivan looked up and I almost felt bad for him. All my misery was reflected back at me. He carried all his exhaustion in the matching baggage under his eyes. The uncertainty in that small tap of his foot. The worrying in the tear stains on his cheeks that he'd missed.

How long had he known Lily? How had they met? I'd heard Lily call him her adoptive sire but I didn't have the context.

"Death of the firstborn."

Not the answer I had expected. And, despite not moving much in the last few days, I was too tired to ask.

"That was when it started. Or so Ritti believes; it was before her time. But she's certain the plagues were one part disease and one part vampires being misinterpreted. Maybe a slave grieving her own child, turned vampire and searching for a replacement.

"I guess there were rumors in Egypt, conspiracy theories. After Ritti was changed she followed up on them. And she found them."

I swallowed, but my throat was dry. "What?"

"Starved." Ivan looked down. "You haven't seen what happens when we're deprived of food for too long. Tissue breaks down, even parts of the brain. Left long enough we can die. Before that, we become... primitive."

My other options are starvin' or terrifyin' the man. To me, that's not much of a choice.

I had wondered about it then. Here was my answer.

"Ritti found maybe thirty or forty starved children vampires in the catacombs of Egypt. No idea how they ended up down there but they couldn't rationally find their way out of the maze in that state. She tried to save them, but the brain damage was permanent."

Ivan finally looked at me.

"Even she'll admit she couldn't have found them all but she dispatched as many as she could. She's seen it happen over and over."

"No one sane ever changes a child." The words were bitter in my mouth

Ivan nodded. "And no one who does it is ever able to meet their needs."

"Fine, but why punish the *child* for that."

Ivan looked like he might puke then and there. "It deters people from doing it."

His face had turned even darker and the words felt forced.

"You hate that policy."

"Of course."

"But you enforce it!"

He was towering over me in a minute. "As I said, you're young. You haven't seen what happens when the military fails to support their leaders."

"I've lived long enough to review the history of a little place called Germa–"

The ice shot through my heart and I sank to the ground. I panted and wheezed, clutching my chest, but it didn't ebb. This wasn't the same pain as before. It held a cold edge, like a frozen blade.

"Gabe?" Ivan knelt next to me. "Gabe!"

Everything faded out of view. Even the concrete walls turn black. It was like getting frostbite deep in my soul. The tether froze over with an icy twist. Once. Twice. Three times. Each time harder and harder until...

It stopped. Leaving a cold, empty hole.

CHAPTER 35

LILY

I saac had to give up on silverware after the first night. Stabbing him with a fork hadn't done any real damage but it had made the point clear. "I told ya, I'm not eatin' this shit."

He yanked the fork out with a quick jerk and surveyed the table. He tsked me a couple of times. "I could have gotten the blood out, but I doubt we can mend the holes. Ah well, it's ruined."

He lurched from his seat, yanking my head down and slamming it into the table. I howled in pain, despite myself. I almost missed what he was saying.

"I might be rather cross with you but I'll not have you starving." He leaned in, his breath thick in my ear, his hand eased off but still held me down. "You can either develop some table manners or I can knock you out and hook up an IV."

Rock and a hard place. If I chose the IV, I'd be spared his company. And I wouldn't have to think about whoever had been tortured or killed for that meal.

I looked up at the waiter.

He stood next to his shiny cart, expressionless through the whole ordeal. Even now he looked straight ahead, as though the wall were a TV.

I took a deep breath before grinding out, "Lots of parmesan and I'd like an extra garlic stick."

Isaac put extra pressure on my neck.

I growled, "Please."

"There we go." Isaac released my neck and sat back down.

"Sir, would you like the cloth changed out?"

"No, that won't be necessary." Isaac looked at me and smiled ruefully. "It's not like either one of us is new to violence."

I stroked the back of my neck and glowered. "Maybe you've missed the memo, but that communication style is a bit outdated."

The waiter placed two large platters of ravioli with a very thin sauce down. Followed shortly by two wine glasses, filled to the brim. He started to grate the parmesan over my plate, turning the food into a winter wonderland.

"Excellent! Give Andrew my regards." Isaac sighed in pure rapture before turning back to me. "As to your comment, we both know I have never struck you before."

"You're certainly makin' up for lost time." My manacle jingled as I waved the waiter off from shredding any more cheese. It was absorbing the blood anyway. As were the two breadsticks he dipped in the *sauce*.

"You used to know your place." Isaac stabbed another shell. "You'll learn it again."

It just kept on like that. Night after night, Isaac would show up with a couple lackeys, they'd carry in a table and chairs. Then one would remain behind with a small cart, quickly trimming it with a tablecloth, candles, and fine china. Except I got plasticware.

At Court, we always recognized blood for what it was. Even Melissa only added the occasional spice.

Isaac liked to dress it up. Soups. Sauces. Marinades. Always cooked at a low enough temperature to preserve its value but made to look like the most elegant food.

Tonight was a salad with dressing. And again, I was learning next to nothing.

"So who turned Olive? You or Cillian?"

"Neither. I have people for siring. They don't go into the line of fire so the soldiers don't get distracted." Isaac dapped his mouth with the corner of his napkin. "Why do you ask?"

"Just tryin' to figure out who was monstrous enough to turn kids."

"Come now, darling, it's not all bad."

"Oh really?" I arched a brow. I wasn't sure why he tolerated the sarcasm, considering his reaction to everything else. Honestly, he seemed to find it amusing. Like tonight, when he grinned across the table and I could almost call it sweet.

The expression made my skin crawl.

"At least I don't murder them simply for existing." He pushed his plate aside and the waiter cleared it.

"They wouldn't be at risk of that if ya hadn't stolen their childhood."

"And they won't be when I'm finished. I even have homes lined up for them."

"Then why change them at all?" I scratched my arm. The sweater he gave me was itchy but at least it covered my skin. He found it funny I'd only sleep in my clothes and never that fucking slip I woke up in.

I swear he was buying the most uncomfortable materials just to convince me to try his cute little dresses. Still, he unlocked the cuffs everyday and let me have just enough time to change into something clean. I'd already spent one day pulling this place apart and searching. If he had a nanny cam, it was well hidden, so I took my chances.

Besides, he'd seen it all before. Not that knowing this was any kind of comfort.

"Can you think of a better way to expose the Court? Or make the humans hesitate." At this, Isaac's face turned grim. "No matter who I train, I will lose soldiers. This tactic has the highest chance for long-term success with the lowest casualties."

My jaw fell and I couldn't pick it up again. He really thought this was the kindest solution. No matter how hard I thought I couldn't come up with a response.

"Were you attached to her?"

I had to swallow a couple times. "Huh?"

"Olive. I could trade out your guard."

"Don't do me any favors," I grumbled, stabbing some lettuce and swirling it slowly in the dressing. It crunched in my mouth, the blood incredible on my tongue. I hated myself more with every bite.

"Now, now, darling." Isaac put down his fork, steepling his fingers and looking over his hands, patient. "Surely, by now, you understand I do want you to be happy here."

I bit back the comment that came to mind, staring at my plate. He was in a good mood tonight but antagonizing him was still a bad idea. "Why?"

"Why what?"

I simply stared forward, trying to think of how to phrase it. It was a simple enough idea but I was tired. I barely ate and hardly slept. Never knowing when I might wake up to him spooning me in an iron clutch. Waking up was the best part of my day. I could assume it was all a crazy nightmare for the first few seconds.

Then everything would settle and reality would sledge hammer its way into my mind.

Despite all the proof, even Isaac's own admission, I couldn't wrap my head around it. I couldn't even bring myself to call him Elias in my own head.

Every night he would visit and this torture would repeat. At least he didn't stay the night. I'm sure whatever room he had included a view, instead my five-star prison cell. It even included an attached bathroom, of which he continued to comment I could use to *freshen up* anytime. I washed my hair and pits in the sink but there was no way in hell I was getting naked any longer than it took to my change clothes. I was always on a razor's edge and these nightly visits were the most tiring thing I'd had to do in all my life... death... whatever.

He gazed over me for several seconds, the candlelight dancing in his eyes. "Oh, I see. You can't fathom why I'd want you to be happy."

I nodded.

He continued to look at me, calmly debating something with an expression made of marble.

"Do you remember our courtship?"

I blinked. Not what I'd expected. "Ummm, yeah. Ya spent months with my family, bringing us into your home and feeding us, before asking my father's permission."

It had been strange but sweet. Most suitors lavished attention on the girl, working to win her affection. Issac had known that flowers and jewels were useless to me then. That I'd only ever wanted my family's happiness. And he hadn't needed to bother. We didn't have a dowry of any kind and I wasn't exactly drowning in options with my promiscuous past. We would have leaped at a quarter of the price he offered.

"Have you ever questioned if it was all a ruse? If I ever just mesmerized you and everyone else to get my way."

I looked away, hating to give him this point. "Ya didn't."

"How do you know?"

"The town always remarked on our trips up to your home, even you couldn't mesmerize everyone."

He smiled indulgently. "And..."

I swallowed, the truth bitter on my tongue in this context. "Our health improved after every meal. We were one of the largest families in Castleknock, yet we were *thrivin'.*"

"So then–" he quirked a dark brow and I shuddered. I'd honestly forgotten where I got the gesture from. "why did I bother? Why do I bother now?"

I wasn't going to say it. Even in my run down state, I knew what he was getting at, but no way in hell was I going to say that.

He reached across the table, taking my fingers gently in his. I ripped it back and shoved it under the table, knocking over my glass in the process. The blood spilled out and dripped off the side.

Drip. Drip. Drip.

Neither of us spoke for a long time. The waiter maintained his silent post in the corner, waiting for orders.

"I want you with me, Líle. Surely you realize that."

"Why?" I stood unable to take it. I paced on the other side of the bed, as far as this tiny room would allow. "Why the hell do ya want me?"

"Why does anyone want anything?" Isaac smiled again, patiently. I wanted to smack him. He pulled his hand back and examined his sleeve, now covered in red, with a weary sigh. "My darling, you are *still* an absolute disaster. Two table cloths and now my best shirt."

He stood and snapped his fingers. The waiter came forth, quick and efficient, pulling the plates and cleaning the spill before loading everything back into his cart.

Isaac tugged his waist coat down, pulling out any wrinkles. "I have wanted you from the moment we met."

"But I betrayed you!" I couldn't hold it in any longer. I knew screaming, especially in front of one of his subordinates, was one of his boundaries. But dammit I couldn't take this. Night after night, having dinner with my worst demon. "And I will do it again, ya must know that! Even if I hadn't before, there is *no* way I would have gone along with this when I found out about it."

I waved wildly to gesture at his servant, the room, even the cart. Everything I could in this tiny, extravagant tomb of mine.

I waited for the slap. For him to shove me into the wall. I braced for it. Instead, he looked surprised. Those brown eyes widened and he actually looked taken aback. Every gesture of Isaac's was slow and practiced, even the violence. But at this, he jerked back like I'd hit him.

"You think I was doing this when we first married?"

"Yeah!" Of course, I'd married a fucking lunatic.

"Oh my dear." Isaac gained composure, stepping around the waiter as he finished his cleaning, and came towards me, taking a knife from the table. I flinched, I couldn't help it no matter how much I hated myself.

It was so much worse than I imagined.

He cupped my cheek in his free hand and waited until I looked at him, shaking despite myself. "All of this, I did for you."

Before I could react, he sliced my throat.

CHAPTER 36

GABE

I van's visits became less and less frequent after he confirmed Alex had felt it too. I couldn't decide if I was relieved or annoyed by the lack of company.

Mostly, I stared at the ceiling and rubbed the middle of
my chest, as though I could warm this numb ache. It hadn't
worked yesterday. Or any other time this week. But it wasn't
like I had much else to do.

That's the one thing a jail cell is good for, wallowing.

The evidence was there, chilling my core. I still couldn't *believe* it. Why would they kill her? After all the trouble fetching
her, what was the point? Had they overdone the torture? Had
she tried to escape? Maybe she'd nearly succeeded.

The scenarios played in my mind over and over.

How the hell had she survived this long just to be taken out
now? How had we found each other, across centuries, only to
have everything snuffed out before we could explore it?

Maybe it wouldn't have worked. Maybe we would have
changed the world. This was the never ending loop that
played. The *What If* reel.

What if I'd gone back in for her, myself?

The heavy click from the steel door pulled me from my
thoughts. Gray light filtered in from the hall, over my bleak

surroundings and the sounds of pain washed over me. Moans, groans, and howls of agony mixed with the sounds of chains clinking and whips snapping, the cacophony drowning my senses. The air was pungent, ash and rot mixing from years of abuse and violence.

"Collins." Melody leaned against the door frame, a stack of laundry in one arm and a plasma bag atop that. "You might want to shower."

"Why?" I didn't need to run a hand through my hair to know it was a grease trap. "It's not like I have company."

"Point of fact–" Melody came in, plopping the stack next to me on the cot, "your lawyer is here."

"I don't have a lawyer." Wasn't like I'd been permitted a phone call.

"Apparently you do, and she won't leave until she sees you."

She?

I didn't know that many vampires and none of them were lawyers.

"Look, you want to sit in a pile of self-pity, go for it." Melody shook her head. "But do you really think she deserves that?"

I sat up and ran a hand over my face. "Don't talk about her like that."

Melody leveled me with a dark, pitying look. "I doubt Elias just severed the tether. She's gone."

"I'll believe it when I see it." I rubbed over my heart again. After two rounds of loss before, you'd think denial would be an easier hurdle the third time. Nope.

"Tell you what, while you wait for a miracle, try to act like someone worthy of her time." She nudged the clothes closer. "I'll be back in ten."

I stared at the floor, waiting for the shadow of the large door to envelop me again, shielding me from the sounds and smells of the dungeon.

I debated just sitting there in my dirty clothes. I didn't know this lawyer. I didn't owe them anything.

Try to act like someone worthy of her time.

I'd already lost my dad. My mom. If Lily was gone too, then I had to stand up. They couldn't anymore.

I sifted through the pile of clothes, surprised to find I recognized them. Gray khakis and a button-up that I had bought for court days at the VPB. A tie that Michelle once said matched my eyes. I sifted through the pile some more and found the same bargain-brand shampoo and soap that I'd always stored at home, both half empty.

"Figures." Just as I started to come to terms with this new life, here were the most inconsequential parts of my old one.

I looked into the corner of the room, wondering if the cell's shower would prove just as cold as the rest of the sterile space. To my utter lack of surprise, the water froze every inch of my skin but that wicked space beneath my breastbone.

"Is this what you felt?" I placed a hand over my heart. "When Isaac died, is this all you were left with?"

She wouldn't answer but I felt better talking to her.

I forced myself through the motions, washing my skin and hair several times. There wasn't a mirror so I settled for finger-combing my hair back. It was longer than I'd liked to keep it, as was the stubble on my chin. It always would be. That had kind of annoyed me before, but now the permanent five o'clock shadow seemed appropriate to my mood.

The button-up and khakis felt tighter than before, but that was impossible. I'd worn them two days before being turned.

"Guess you got me used to jeans." I snorted sardonically and started to fix my tie. Muscle memory guided my arms as assuredly as any looking glass. I'd just finished pulling the knot in place when the heavy click of the door unlocking announced Melody's return.

She gave me a once-over and nodded. "Glad I didn't need a hose."

I sighed and set my shoulders back. "Let's just get this over with."

We walked through the corridor, the pungent odor and loud cries were as good an excuse as any for the lack of conversation. Thank God for the little things.

After several turns through the winding corridors I could never navigate on my own, the howls grew louder, as did the smell. One voice caught my attention. It was sharp and held no more or less agony than the others. I just knew it.

I stopped outside an open door, where the whipping sounds almost covered her screams. She was strapped to a cot on her stomach. Cyrus was lashing her feet with a long black cord. The short Latina shrieked and shuddered as the cord left long welts and blisters that vanished and reappeared over and over.

I couldn't stop watching. "Anna."

The moment I uttered her name, the treacherous little nurse glanced over her shoulder. She shuddered and cried but the moment her eyes found me, something flickered across them. Something I couldn't name.

"Come on." Melody nudged me, her tone calm. "Don't watch that."

Cyrus seemed to finally notice us. He dropped the makeshift whip and stepped into view, blocking me from the grisly sight.

I shook my head, but the image stayed in place. "That's barbaric."

"We are immortal, empires are not." Cyrus emphasized the *we*. "Our kind requires an extra incentive to behave."

Made me wonder why they hadn't used these tactics on me. But I didn't want to give them ideas.

Melody gave me a nudge. "Your lawyer is waiting."

I nodded and walked away with her. Cyrus waited in the doorway, only returning to his task once we'd turned a corner.

We began to ascend the stairs, the air becoming less bitter with each step. We stopped at the top and Melody laid her palm against a small screen. A green light drowned the gray surroundings in its neon glow before disappearing behind her hand.

The heavy door ahead of us clicked and concrete gave way to dark cherry wood. Rugs lined the polished floor, large sconces held the lighting, and delicate crown molding capped the extravagant nature of the room. Several people whirled about the large entryway, carrying stacks of paper, cleaning, or just walking towards their destination.

It was all too bright. I felt like a mole being dragged from its burrow.

"How long was I down there?" I'd lost count after the tether broke. It hadn't seemed relevant anymore.

"A couple weeks." Melody nudged me again and we walked on. "For what it's worth, Edwards didn't like it much either."

"Funny–" I kept my eyes on the ground, trying to avoid any more nightmares. "–she once argued for the torture of a Renfield."

"We both know she talked a lot of shit."

Melody closed the dungeon door and we pressed forward, turning sharply to walk up the large central staircase. Despite the change in temperature and scent, I'd felt more comfortable in the dungeon. Several of the people surrounding us glanced my way, scowling or making a point to turn their noses up.

"Guessing I'm not popular?" I tried to wave a few times, finally giving up at the third indigent *hmph*.

Melody glared at a few of the onlookers and they scurried back to their own business. "You're being blamed for Edwards' rebellion."

"What?"

"Don't worry, it's crock." Melody shrugged. "I didn't care for her, but I respected Edwards for standing her ground. It's why she and Alex moved out in the first place."

"And yet." I nodded to indicate a disgruntled maid before she turned away.

"You came along and Edwards broke three of our laws in a month before going rogue. It's not your fault. Wizard's first rule–"

"People are stupid," I finished the quote. "Terry Goodkind."

"Yeah." Melody gave me an appreciative glance before continuing to lead me through the decadent hallways until we stood before an ornate set of double doors, those colorful dreads swaying with her quick pace.

I gulped, vaguely remembering these halls from before. Melody's fist barreled against the door to produce a subtle knock.

"Come in." Ivan's dark accent boomed back.

Melody leaned on the door handles pushing into the stylish sitting room. Ivan stood with his back to me and his hand on the back of a chair. Over the headrest, I could barely make out the top of a woman's head, her short mass of black hair curled in a way that was reminiscent of the 1920s.

The style seemed out of place with her furnishings, all modeled for something out of a regency novel, with a long lounge sofa sitting across from a matching chair of the same deep emerald fabric. Two additional chairs had been added since my last visit.

For the first time in days, I felt hope, but I kept my eyes off the newcomers for the time being, making a point to acknowledge the greatest threat first. I walked in slowly, doing everything to keep my eyes level as I turned and bowed to the vampire queen. "Majesty."

"You are no longer one of my subjects, Mr. Collins." Her voice was a royal decree in every word, but still as inviting as candlelight to a bug.

I kept my head bowed. "That doesn't mean I don't hold you in high respect."

Silence washed over the room, all but the anxious breaths behind me. My back began to ache from the posture and my legs threatened to tighten painfully.

"Your respect is acknowledged, Mr. Collins. You may stand."

"Thank you, Majesty." My back smarted as I straightened, looking down at the vampire queen. Her clothes and makeup were as foreign and elegant as the day I'd met her, like she popped off the page from both a history textbook and a novel at the same time.

Unlike the first time we'd met, her thickly lined eyes held no humor. Something cold and calculating rolled beneath that copper gaze, measuring me as I stood before her.

I was clearly found wanting.

"I believe your friends would like a greeting." She waved her hand toward the added chairs.

"Thank you." I bobbed my head again and turned, barely having time to think before Harper barreled into me, knocking the coffee table out of place.

"Thank God, buddy." He did everything he could to crush me. It was surprisingly effective.

"Good to see you too." I patted him awkwardly, still trying to piece this together. Especially with the other addition.

"God had nothing to do with it." Michelle's sharp tone said she didn't appreciate being undervalued. That wasn't surprising but I had no idea what I would value from her at the moment. I had no idea what she was doing here. *This* was my lawyer? We hadn't ended on the best terms. I couldn't imagine what Harper had said to convince her.

"Your Majesty–" Her heels clipped violently, even over the thick rug, and her auburn curls bobbed perfectly with her stride, "we have a deal for you."

CHAPTER 37

LILY

"It'll be alright, darling." Isaac smoothed his hand over my face. "I know it hurts but it'll be over soon."

This pathetic attempt at comfort did fuck all as my body burned.

My blood had turned to molten lava, slowly devouring every inch of me. Instinct had me clutching my throat, but it was useless. My crumbling fingers only found the soft, exposed inside of my neck. I tried to scream but all that came out was a soggy croak. The fire annihilated my body one inch at a time, until my limbs couldn't support me. Isaac shouted something I couldn't hear over my own wordless garble. My blood, wet and sticky, ran over my fingers and pooled onto the floor.

I gasped, trying to edge away from the growing puddle, but my body crumbled further and I fell face first into the blood. My skin continued to turn gray and crack.

Fuck! Fuck! Fuck!

It was the only coherent word I could come up with. Every inch of me was boiling, as though a flaming snake was coiling through my body. Finally, it reached my eyes, they bubbled in my skull, searing the sockets, and the world went black.

Something cold soothed and caressed the growing flame in my body, taming it. My body ached and tingled but I didn't care, so long as it didn't burn. It started in my mouth, quenching the fire, then my throat. The soothing source spread over every inch of me far too slowly, like putting out a forest fire with a bucket. But I would take what I could get.

"Drink, darling. You're almost done."

I greedily gulped the fluid. Anything to make it stop. Someone pushed me away from the delirious drink and I ground my fangs in deeper. Fucker wasn't going to bring the pain back again. Never that. I slurped and gulped, delirious as the flames subsided.

My vision cleared and I stared down into the limp form in my arms.

"I'm sorry, darling." Isaac pulled a piece of hair from my face. "I should have done this the first night but I wanted some time with you. It was selfish of me."

I was too stunned by everything to move but that changed quickly. I shoved the body away and sprawled against the wall. Even then, I couldn't get far enough away. I could have made it to another galaxy and I still would have kept going. At least I could finally scream.

"Shhhh." Isaac gathered me to him. I pounded my fists against him, pushing and clawing like a wild animal being dragged to a cage. Nothing I screamed made any sense. Isaac took the beating, simply deflecting my blows until he could grab my chains and yank me closer, wrapping his arms around me and pulling me into his lap.

I was covered in ash and blood, all of it staining his suit as he rocked me back and forth like a child.

"I'm sorry, darling." He kissed the top of my head. "I shouldn't have waited."

All my resolve shattered and I sobbed, losing any energy to push away. He held me tighter and kept apologizing, over and over. I have no idea how long we stayed that way. Eventually nothing could stop the exhaustion.

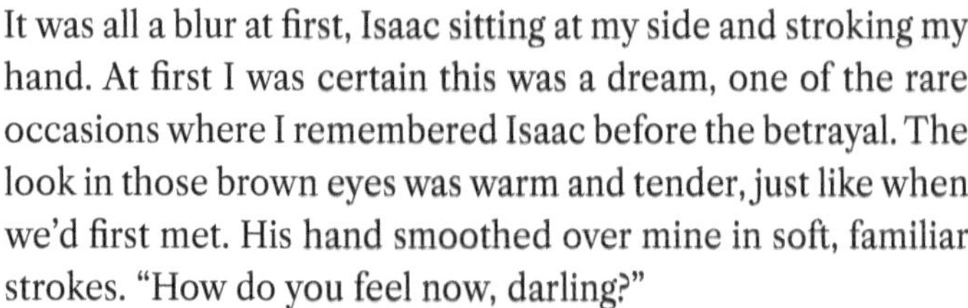

It was all a blur at first, Isaac sitting at my side and stroking my hand. At first I was certain this was a dream, one of the rare occasions where I remembered Isaac before the betrayal. The look in those brown eyes was warm and tender, just like when we'd first met. His hand smoothed over mine in soft, familiar strokes. "How do you feel now, darling?"

With those simple words, everything from the last couple days flooded my mind. I lurched away, screaming and grabbing my throat, patting it over and over. The flesh was smooth, bits of dried blood flaking away under my hands. I kept checking, waiting to find raw muscle or vocal cords.

True, when I found Isaac alive, I figured we'd actually been severed. It was either that or I had to start believing ghosts. I even understood the mechanics of severing, though I'd never seen the process in action. But I'd had no reason to think Isaac would do *that* to me.

I was still slowly crying, gasping between tears, when I asked, "Why?"

"You need to cut ties with your old life." Isaac shrugged, though it was sad and lacked his usual cavalier.

I stared at him, breathing heavily just to form the words. "Ya do realize I'm goin' to escape."

"You feel that way now." He stood, leaning in to kiss my forehead. I flinched away, getting to the other side of the bed. He sighed. "I suppose I can't blame you for being skittish."

"Skittish!?"

He nodded and straightened his ruined waistcoat. "You need time."

He offered a gentle smile as he closed the door.

I fell to pieces all over again.

I finally caved and took a shower. I couldn't stand the blood on me. I wasn't sure how much of it was mine. I leaned against the wall, still clothed, and turned the water as hot as it would go.

I immediately sank to the ceramic tile with a thud and curled in the fetal position as the steam grew thick around me. The water changed colors several times as it ran down my body, before finally turning pale pink. But it never turned cold, but I still couldn't get warm.

In my mind, I kept dropping the corpse, her head cracking against the hardwood floors and lolling toward me. Cold, lifeless eyes stared at me. Judging me within their dull gray depths.

No wonder I'd been drawn to a psychopath. I was just as much a monster as Isaac. How the fuck hadn't I seen it? In all that time, our courtship, our marriage, and turning me. Nothing had seemed out of place...

Was I just that naive?

By the time I got tired of sulking, the body wasn't in my room anymore. The rug and tapestry were both replaced. A sick part of me wondered if Isaac would bother trying to get the blood out. I started to retch uncontrollably. Drive heaves echoed back to me, my only source of company as I pictured it over and over.

I forced myself to remember her. Every detail I could. She deserved to be noticed, if only once.

She'd been young, I'd say early twenties, with a stocky frame and plush cheeks. Had her jeans been unbuttoned? They were definitely worn with a waistband that dug a visible groove into her pale flesh, bruising her with a deep-purple gouge. Her shirt had been stained several shades of red and brown, the colors bleeding into one another interchangeably on the oversized fabric.

Her hair was short, maybe shoulder length, the edges ragged and uneven with a few patches missing. It was too dirty for me to determine the color. Maybe brown or blonde.

A split of bone had poked through her skin; I must have broken her arm when I tossed her away from me. That, or they'd brought her to me injured. Maybe that's why she'd been selected, she needed to be *put down*. I shuddered at the thought and ran back to the bathroom, retching again.

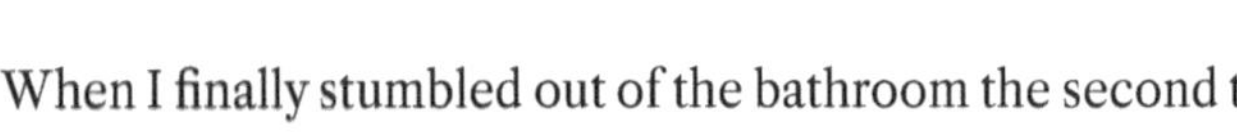

When I finally stumbled out of the bathroom the second time, Olive was sitting cross-legged on the bed, as though she'd been meditating. My clothes gave a soggy *slop* with each step.

"Get out." My demand came out in a weary tone.

"I'm to unlock your cuffs so you can change." She held up a key. "Elias didn't feel you'd want to see him right now."

I lunged for the key and she pointed a gun at my head. We sat like that, silent, for several minutes.

"Was it all a lie?"

"Not everything." Olive put the gun away and beckoned me forward.

"How do ya know I won't run for it once ya unlock these?"

"You could try." Olive shrugged as she undid the first cuff. "But there are more of us outside. Elias thought you'd handle it better if you saw a familiar face."

I snorted.

"I kind of figured that's how you'd feel." She hopped off the bed to undo my feet. "I'll be back in a bit. Do me a favor, don't hide next to the door so you can jump me."

"What *didn't* ya lie about?" I growled, more than a little annoyed she guessed my plan.

She paused, her hand on the knob, bouncing on her heels a few times.

"I really do love Cinderella." And with that, she was gone.

CHAPTER 38

GABE

I van was a volatile cocktail of anger and pain. Melody looked stony but confused.

The Queen looked... mildly amused. "You bring a *human* lawyer into my world, have her blackmail me–"

"Technically, I'm the one that blackmailed you." Harper grinned, though his eyes didn't twinkle.

"And my client did no such thing." Michelle's tone was the same indigent one she'd used to yell *objection* countless times. "We've advised you of my client's rights–"

"Yes, yes." The Queen waved an impatient hand. "And we have enough legal troubles as it is. Honestly, the more I'm around you, the more I remember why I avoid lawyers in our own legal system."

"No, you just murder innocent children," I grumbled, too tired to stop myself.

"Excuse me, Mr. Collins?"

I drew in a breath and crossed my arms at her responding glare.

"You heard me, majesty." I was exhausted and angry and just wanted to go back to wallowing. But whatever Harper and Michelle had in mind, I should see this out. "And you already made the mistake of letting Elias take control of the narrative once."

The Queen eyed me and then Michelle. To her credit, the plucky lawyer didn't cow. Then again, there weren't many people I'd have called on to walk into a nest of vampires. Michelle probably felt right at home among all the bloodsuckers.

"Fine." The Queen waved a hand to silence the stutters and protests that rose from the rest of the room. "Let them speak, I can always refuse the offer."

"As I said–" Michelle flipped open the case she was carrying, thumbing through several pages before offering one with several highlights to the Queen, "technically Gabriel Collins is still a United States Citizen."

Ritti accepted the page, skimming through something in the yellow section. "This law states that anyone who becomes a vampire automatically gives up their citizenship as they are no longer human."

Michelle pointed at something on the page. "See here, it says, 'willingly.'"

The Queen read the page again, her eyes seeming to dart over the same section over and over before she looked up. "How does this help me?"

I finally got it. "Because you can use me to set a precedent. Michelle can raise my case in court, forcing the government to address my unique situation but–"

"In doing so, she'd also be raising the first legal case for vampire rights," The Queen finished. It was the first time I'd ever seen her look stunned. "The outcome could be used as a legal argument for discrimination."

"Exactly." Michelle stood straighter, her chest puffing with pride.

I nodded, feeling a little dizzy with all this but better for getting out of bed.

The ride out was gloomy, only partly because it was well past sunset.

"We can file the paperwork tomorrow. Until then, you'll need a safe place to stay." Michelle's spunk was annoying and I glared at her from the back seat.

"I already got the okay to stay with Lily's friends. Once we get everything going... who knows what the courts will demand."

"The Court moved the whole gang." Harper gave me a pitying glance in the rearview mirror. "I think they knew Alex was helping you."

"What makes you say that?" I cocked my head curiously.

"It's..." Harper blew out an exhausted breath, "Just wait 'till you see it."

He turned down several more roads I wasn't entirely familiar with, though I knew the basic location. After the fifth turn down a street under a presidential name, I grumbled, "They moved them out to Rockwood."

"Yeah." Harper nodded. "The Court said it was all they had on short notice."

"They just didn't have proof." I looked out the window, pulling the borrowed beanie lower over my face. There wasn't any oncoming traffic but I wasn't ready to turn myself over just yet. "I've seen what they do to people when they have proof."

Something in my tone silenced the car, but it wasn't long before Michelle broke it, turning in her seat to look at me. "We'll have to meet and go over everything tomorrow."

"Sounds good." I looked into her gray eyes and realized they were scrutinizing me.

The look reminded me of a time she'd made me dinner and then spent the whole time glaring at me across the table.

I swallowed. "Thanks for getting me out of there."

"You're. Welcome." The tension eased in her eyes, but only a fraction. "Especially considering what I had to do just to get *in* there."

"She thought I was punking her about the blood." Harper laughed. "Alex had to make her do the hokey-pokey just to convince her."

Michelle grimaced and turned back around. "I can still taste it."

I shrugged. "At least it kept them out of your head."

"I don't know how you drink that stuff." She slapped her hand over her mouth. "Oh shit, that was probably insensitive or something, right?"

For the first time in days, I laughed. It wasn't gut-deep, barely a chuckle. It still felt wrong.

Michelle opened her mouth to say something but Harper placed a big hand on her shoulder and shook his head. I didn't know if he understood it all but I was grateful either way. I didn't feel like explaining.

Harper's warning kept Michelle quiet for the rest of the ride. She threatened me with an early morning meeting, then tried to smooth the offer with coffee. "Wait... can you even drink anything else? Do I need to bring a plasma bag?"

"Coffee's fine." I opened the car door. "I'll see you tomorrow."

Harper killed the engine and told Michelle he'd be right back. I didn't bother to take in much of the house, just stared at the broken sidewalk and moved one foot in front of the other. Harper met me on the cracked stoop, shoving his big hands into his pockets. "Never thought I'd see the day we'd match."

I felt my brows try to merge before I caught his meaning. It took one glance down his overstuffed suit and another up my own clothes to realize that we looked like the Blues Brothers.

"Huh," was all I could manage as I compared our shoes. His were in slightly better condition.

"Do you want me to come back after I drop Michelle off?"

"Up to you."

"Hey buddy, I don't get the whole sire thing, but I liked Lily." Harper's face fell, his laugh lines stretching with the length of his face. "She was spunky, and God knows she shoved a jalapeno up your butt."

"Yeah," I laughed, once. It still felt treacherous. "It's her smile. She has this adorable single dimple."

We sat there in silence a moment longer, Harper gawking at me. "Holy... shit."

I stopped examining our shoes.

"I knew it..." His voice was half awe and half sorrow.

I gave a pathetic snort. "You did not."

"The minute she got you on that bike–" Harper pointed at me, "I knew it."

I opened my mouth to argue, but my heart wasn't in the banter, so I just closed it.

"Sorry, buddy."

"Nope." I gave him the only smile I could. "Thanks for trying."

"I'll be back in a bit." Harper slapped my back and headed towards the car.

I watched him go, taking notice of a sharp glance in Michelle's eyes before squaring my shoulders towards the door. My knuckles barely wrapped against the hollow wood before Maria appeared in the doorway.

She was hunched and slow in a way that looked unnatural to her. Her braids were missing the beads that always clicked with her every movement. Her blouse and skirt contrasted in an ugly way.

She nodded and stepped aside. "He's in the dining room."

"Thanks." I walked past her. The familiar sectional curved awkwardly in the corner around the large entertainment center. Boxes flanked both sides, a few open but none emptied. It looked more like they'd been rummaging for a specific item.

Alex sat at a large oak table, Darren right on his elbow. He scratched the table, a tiny groove deepening under his nail.

Maria closed the front door and sat next to her fellow human, giving the chair across from Alex a meaningful look. I walked around the other end and sat.

Asking how he was doing would be stupid. His graying skin and the claw mark in the table said volumes.

"How did it happen?"

"I wasn't there. You'd have to ask Cyrus."

"I did." Alex stopped scratching and looked at me. His dark eyes were like hollow pits. "He gave me some half-assed excuse. You gonna do that?"

I shook my head. "I lost her."

Maria reached a tentative hand towards my shoulder. "Gabe..."

"Shut up," Alex growled.

"Alex..." Darren placed a hand on his partner.

"No. I want to hear this." Alex turned back to me.

I forced myself to keep looking. "I was too weak. We got separated and I couldn't find her."

He held my gaze a long time, then swallowed and looked down at his miniature path of destruction. "What are you doing here?"

"I need Lily's laptop and all her case notes."

"Court took them." Maria's face twisted. "Along with searching all our belongings for evidence. Luckily, we were prepared for that."

"They didn't get everything..." Darren blushed and pushed himself up from the table. "Give me a minute."

CHAPTER 39

LILY

My brother brought me the next change of clothes. Unlike Olive, he wouldn't leave, waiting outside the bathroom while I changed. The silence stretched, even in that short time. My curiosity finally got the better of me.

"How did he change ya?"

He let out a short, rude snort. "Not sure you want to hear that."

I opened the bathroom door, sticking my wrists out for the cuffs. "Was it my fault?"

Another snort as he latched the first cuff back on. "Always the martyr."

I grabbed Cillian's shirt collar and stared into his eyes. The milky gray one made my stomach curl. "Answer my question."

"And patient as ever." Cillian swatted my hands aside. "I'm your punishment. Is that what ya want to hear? Dad sliced his throat, almost had him too. But Elias was stronger and drank him dry."

There wasn't any passion in the description. He sounded like he was reading a history book. But everything in me turned rotten. Putrid. I'd always assumed Isaac had died that night. It had been well over a century, but to hear how our father had died. And to know the worst was only yet to come.

Cillian obviously wasn't changed that same night. Those scars took time to develop. He had suffered.

I looked at the floor. "What about you?"

"Oh no, you look at me."

I waited, hoping.

"You're going to look me in the eye if ya want to hear this."

I'd sacrificed so much and hurt so many people I cared about. I could at least get the answers I came for.

I took a breath and looked at my brother. His scars seemed to twist and twirl with every word.

"He mesmerized me. Ya didn't tell us they could do that." Cillian scoffed. He looked like he wanted to spit on me. "I stood there, stupid, and watched him kill everyone. They'd already set fire to the house, but he took his time. After his belly was full, he just–" he held up his hands and made a gesture similar to unscrewing a jar, "toyed with them."

I could only let out a wordless squeak as a reply but my brother ignored it.

"After that, we traveled. I brought him new victims, though this–" he gestured towards his wounds, "made it kind of hard to attract them. When I didn't bring him a fresh kill, he'd drain me until I was weak and send me out the next night. He got bored of that after a month; decided my face was punishment enough. That's when he changed me over."

"Why in the fuck do ya stay with him?" I clasped his hands like maybe we could pray together. Like when we were kids going through the motions at church. "Help me."

Deep in his throat, a humorless, pathetic excuse for a laugh rose.

"Yeah, just us against an army." He pointed to my broken pinkie. "That always went so well."

Okay, yes, even as kids Cillian and I had never really gotten along. I'd always kind of suspected he broke my finger on purpose. But still, he was my brother. Isaac had tortured him. Surely, he wanted better than this.

"Come on, Cillian–"

"He mesmerized me."

I choked on my sentence.

"I can't control my life, so I'll take what little fun I can." Cillian pulled his hands from mine and stormed out.

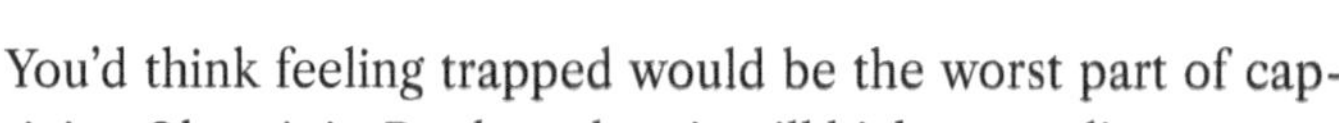

You'd think feeling trapped would be the worst part of captivity. Okay, it is. But boredom is still high on my list.

Especially now. Boredom left me time to ruminate, and none of my thoughts were pleasant.

My murder victim.

My brother's abuse.

Alex and Gabe feeling the tether break.

The fact that I'd been attracted to a monster and never realized it.

All this under some misguided thought for me, somehow. Isaac hadn't returned yet. I only saw others come in to bring me food and a change of clothes.

I could hardly touch the plates brought in, only taking a couple of fork fulls before images of my victim superimposed themselves over the plate. Even then, I was reminded that if I refused to eat, then Isaac's threat still stood.

I couldn't sleep. Before it was because I was on edge, always uncertain how I would wake up. Now I'd shut my eyes and see her again. Same short hair, same bedraggled state, same broken bone rupturing from her bruised flesh.

I've had nightmares for a while. this was nothing new, but they'd never been this violent or vivid. I guess it made a difference that I was the killer.

Occasionally I'd go back to planning my escape, but I had no idea where to start. I'd tried to watch the door for whenever it opened but that didn't tell me much. All I saw was one extra guard and a hideous Piccaso painting across the hall. Hardly enough to work with.

Plus there was the matter of my cuffs. True, I could just break my hands and pull them through. Same with my feet. But it would use a massive amount of energy to heal. And I was hardly willing to pick at my plates, eating enough to sustain such a change was out of the question.

I'd torn the room to shreds trying to find a way out. Not like I had any windows. And aside from the elaborate rug and tapestry, I had nothing to work with. Even the bathroom was useless, not even including a mirror to smash. When I dug through the bed for a spring, it turned out to be memory foam. Just when I'd shoved the dismembered foam back under the sheet, Olive came in with my next set of clothes.

We didn't talk much. She handed me my clothes and unlocked the cuffs before leaving me with an ugly purple blouse with big shoulders and a gray pencil skirt. I wouldn't have remembered anything about that outfit, including the texture, if not for a critical error on her part.

She'd left in the mini-packet with the extra button for the blouse. Attached by a nice big safety pin.

CHAPTER 40

GABE

"No." I glared across the coffee table.

"She has the same rights." Michelle flipped through her notes, not even bothering to look up. "And frankly, she's damn cute. Juries do well with cute."

"You're not using Olive," I growled with each word. I wasn't opening up about why.

"Gabriel, be realistic." She huffed and put her notes down. "Who do you think a jury is going to side with, the runaway cop or the kidnapped orphan?"

She ticked us off on her manicured fingers like she was considering items in a recipe. If steam could roll from my ears, I would have resembled a chimney stack.

"I said no." Michelle opened her mouth and I raised my voice. "That's not negotiable."

If the public learned Elias had successfully trained child soldiers, there would be panic.

Michelle pursed her lips, smudging some of her lipstick in the process. We held the staring contest for several seconds before she finally puffed out her lower lip and went back to her notes. "Fine. You've got practice speaking in front of a jury anyway."

I relaxed into the sectional, rubbing the ever-growing knot in my neck. There was a half hour of my life I'd never get back.

"I don't see why we don't just try for the Supreme Court. Legalizing vampires in Oregon alone..." I let the thought trail.

"Gay marriage." At my silence, Michelle rolled those silver eyes. "2015, Supreme Court legalized gay marriage."

I nodded. "Yeah, I remember the White House getting the rainbow wash."

"Between 2004 and 2015, thirty-six states legalized it individually." Michelle smiled, her teeth blinding in their ivory sheen. "They laid the groundwork for that case."

"Eleven years." I drew my hands through my hair.

"You're immortal, you've got time," she retorted.

I wanted to argue but I knew she was right. Harper hadn't involved Michelle because I enjoyed her company. Her cold calculation and lack of empathy grated my nerves, but the woman knew her stuff.

"Fine." I blew out a breath and stood, grabbing our now empty mugs from the table. "More?"

"Yeah." She raised her hands and held up two fingers.

"Two packets of Splenda and a dab of milk." It was my turn to roll my eyes. "You already beat that into my head, remember?"

She retracted her hand and started writing in her notebook while digging through the internet on her tablet. "Thanks."

I let the coffee brew, making extra in case Darren or Maria decided to risk going past the dragon in their living room. Alex was camped in his bedroom, trying not to tear her head off when she said something insensitive. He barely held himself together when it was just us, hard to blame him for having less control around Michelle.

The coffee started to drip and I rubbed my temples, like I could pretend that was the worst of my issues. Rolling my fingers over my temples quickly became rubbing the frigid spot over my heart.

"You need to stop that."

I looked back to the living room. This kitchen wasn't nearly as open as their previous home but you could still see the couch through the opening. Michelle's eyes were fixed on my chest.

"What?"

"Rubbing your chest." Michelle looked down to her tablet but she didn't type or scroll. "I saw the blond guy do it too. Vampire thing?"

"Kind of." Describing this would take too long.

"Well, it's distracting."

"What's that supposed to mean?" I worked very hard to keep my tone level, filling our mugs and flavoring them correctly before returning.

"Not an insult." Michelle shrugged as she took her mug. "But it looks like you're fondling your chest. So, learn to fidget somewhere else."

I drew in a long breath and forced myself to listen. If I couldn't even describe the tether to Michelle, I definitely couldn't talk about it in court. Besides, she had a point. Anything that made me less human had to go.

"Fine." I dropped my hand. "Anything else?"

She shrugged again. "I'm sure I'll come up with more later."

She didn't say it in a mean way, just matter of fact. It made it even more frustrating.

"Why not now?"

"I've got to get to the hospital if I want to see Barbara." Michelle packed every paper, book, and electronic that was sprawled across the coffee table with military efficiency. "The care center is very specific about visiting hours."

Michelle's sister, and Captain Murphy's wife, had been diagnosed with multiple sclerosis. It was his initial motivation to help the vampires.

I swallowed. "Michelle?"

"Hmmm?" She kept packing.

"How is Barbara?"

Michelle pursed her lips again, pausing in her rapid movements. "She's deteriorating fast. The precinct is looking into cutting off her Survivor Benefits."

"Jesus."

"Yeah." The single word was ice-brittle.

The silence fell between us, like an empty chasm.

She glared at me and I thought she might win this round.

"I hate you." She snatched the few remaining articles and stuffed them into her case. A few papers crumpled.

I flinched. "I'm sorry."

It was the most pathetic thing I could say. I wanted to kick myself. I'd known revealing Captain Murphy's betrayal would stick Harper in a tight spot, but having Barbara lose her Survivor Benefits...

Michelle glared up at me. "If anyone but Harper had come to me with this I would have clawed their eyes out. But we're here now, and if saving your sorry ass will save my sister, then I'll do it. I'll give you the best advice I can. I will do everything I can to get you through this."

For the first time ever, we understood each other perfectly.

We sat there, the silence swallowing us for a long moment. Finally, Michelle shrugged back into her lawyer armor.

"We still have to figure out how I'm going to present this without producing you in court."

"I don't think we should."

She looked stunned and I offered a small smile. This would go better if I didn't try to talk her into it. Especially after shooting her Olive idea down so harshly.

"Could gain public sympathy..." She looked thoughtful before nodding. "But how do we turn you in?"

The Portland Police Department loomed in the midday sun. It had only been a month, yet the black iron fences and seashell molding took on a new face for me. The Vampire Court was a lively mansion, always bustling. Meanwhile, the thick gray bricks and old-fashioned balcony turned the police department into a crypt.

Lily would have been proud of my plan, or lack thereof. The Hollywood drama probably would have produced that single dimple. After she smacked me a few times.

I nodded my thanks as someone held one of the oak doors open for me, ducking when they did a stunned double take. I had to get to the lobby before they could sound the alarm.

I rushed into the middle of the room, pushing quickly through the crowd before I pulled my hood back and put my hands up. "My name is Gabriel Collins. I am a vampire and I surrender to the VPB."

Some people stopped, stunned. Others rushed into action. Someone screamed something about a second massacre and ran for the doors, her sneakers squeaking between shrieks of terror. Several trained officers pointed guns at my head. More than a couple had once been my friends.

"Down on the ground!"

I got on my knees, threading my fingers together and cradling the back of my head in my hands.

CHAPTER 41

LILY

My excitement was short-lived. For one thing, even though this safety pin was surprisingly thick, it was still a safety pin. I would get one use out of the flimsy thing if I was very lucky. That would only handle either my ankles or wrists.

Plus, what would I do with everyone outside the room? My wit wasn't actually sharp enough to wound.

My one opportunity came just after Olive closed the door. The lock clicked. And the alarms blared.

I didn't know if it was a simple fire alarm or what, but I knew one thing. They had *never* locked my door. Too secure in their own power.

I lunged over the bed, snatching the handle and shaking it. It was rigid. If it were a standard knob, I could have just twisted the handle and snapped the whole mechanism. But this was heavy duty.

Made by vampires for vampires.

Strange though, no one had yelled at me to stop messing with the handle or quiet down. I flattened my ear against the wood and focused. I felt the subtle vibration before I heard the thunder of steps.

Something was up. Something big enough they'd had to take the guards off my door.

I looked down at the pin in my hand. I only had one chance to use this, and no clue how long this would last. If this crisis turned out to be some overcooked turkey setting off the fire alarm, I might not have time to finish.

And now I'd have to get both my cuffs and the door with this pathetic pin. Even higher chance I would weaken the metal and break it.

Unless I kept the manacles on... I might find a set of keys to unlock them once I got out.

No matter what, I needed to get out of this room.

I knelt to investigate the lock. I'd never bothered before and now I wanted to laugh. Hardcore door knob but a lock you could have found in the stone age, basic privacy but not for security. Guess Isaac had stationed me in a bedroom that simply lacked a view. No way he was this lazy with all his prisoners.

Guess I was special. My skin tried to dance off my bones at the mere thought.

I shook my head and focused back on the doorknob and examined the pin.

The sharp point would only hinder my work, sliding between tumblers like water. But I didn't exactly have any pliers to clip it. I would have to make it work. I pulled the fastener off and bent the sharp tip into an L before sliding it into the bottom of the lock. It wasn't a tension wrench but it would have to do.

I had to keep the pressure even and every time I happened to catch some change in the racket outside my door I barely caught my jump before it hit my hands.

I could feel the first tumbler give and I slapped a hand over my mouth. I almost cried out in joy but that wasn't even halfway there. Already my body was tense as I dug through the second then the third. All the while, expecting that alarm to turn back off any minute.

When the final tumbler went, a new thought struck.

This is a trap. I'm going to open this door and find Isaac, grinning like a fool.

I had to risk it. I turned the handle and peeked out. No Isaac, but a guard looking down the hall, his back to me. Just one guard. I closed the door before he noticed me and looked around.

The room was simple. I didn't even have a lamp to varnish as a weapon. Just a big ugly bed, a tapestry, and a rug.

If I couldn't get past this guard then I might as well just lock the door. The guy was huge.

I looked back at the bed, debating just falling on it. It had been too good to be true, I didn't deserve to get out. Not after everything I'd done...

You owe it to everyone you've killed. Gabe's voice echoed in my mind, a wash over my shame and self pity.

I didn't need a weapon. I just needed to make it so the guard couldn't use his. I was ripping the covers back and yanking the sheet out before the plan was fully formed. It was a bad idea. A terrible idea. But I couldn't waste this chance.

I snatched the doorknob, threw it open, and tossed the sheet over my guard's head.

"What the fuck!?" He reeled, his big shoulders smashing each side of the door frame while he floundered to get it off. I tried to slip past him, only to get a thick elbow to the gut.

I bit him. The sheet made it impossible to tell what I was biting, especially in this flurry of movement. He yanked away, taking his weight off one leg and I pushed him to the ground, crawling up to grab his head and slam it against the floor. It was hardwood, and it dented after a couple of good smacks before his body stilled.

I made quick work of his pockets. I couldn't make myself take the gun. I should, I needed it. But I just couldn't. At least he had a knife in a holster, which was handy, but no keys.

Fuck.

I looked down at each side of the hall. No nifty EXIT sign to show me the way. Fifty-fifty odds. I got up and ran as best as the shackles would let me. I ran past doors and across carpets. In the hall, the alarm was accompanied by the flashing light, strobing in and out, making everything feel all the jerkier.

Maybe that was why I tripped. Or maybe it was weakness. I hadn't had a full meal since I got here. Not unless you counted...

Either way, my toe caught the underside of some fancy rug and I crashed to the floor, smacking my head on the nearest wall. Little lights danced in my vision when I opened my eyes and I tasted blood. I must have bit something, but I didn't get time to investigate.

"What was that?"

I barely heard the cry over the still blaring alarm. I'd been lucky until now, not seeing anyone since I'd bashed my guard's brains in. I'd hoped, stupidly, this would last until I found an exit. I'm not sure what I'd expected, maybe an unlocked window I could crawl out of.

Either way, I had to get out of sight. Fast.

There were several doors in the hall but I hadn't tried any, focusing on getting as far from that room as I could. Now I crawled for the nearest one and prayed there wasn't anyone inside. I found myself facing thick double doors with ornate carvings. I reached up, putting all my weight into the lever-handle and falling into the room. Footsteps started to thunder towards me right as I shut the door, my back still against it as I listened to the steps slow and the men chatter in the hall.

"Man, you're hearing things again!"

"No, there was something."

"Yeah, sure." A rude laugh. "Come on, the boss'll kill us if he finds our post empty for no reason."

I waited several seconds and let out a slow breath to steady myself. They must have come from the opposite direction as my room. The pile of ash and clothes would have clued them in right away.

I still didn't have long. I took a second to review my surroundings.

Good news, I was alone. Bad news, there were still no windows. This room had been on the opposite side of the hall, so it wasn't about interior and exterior rooms. And this wasn't another high class prison cell either.

It was a library. A big one.

Why the fuck wouldn't Elias put windows in a room like this? Any interior designer or architect would tell you to highlight the space with as much natural light as possible. What was he hiding?

Immense bookcases lined the wall, only breaking for a large, ornate desk. Every shelf I scanned was nonfiction of some sort. Several volumes that would have had Gabe chattering on about his father, historical texts, all about various battles or civil rights movements over the millennia.

The rest were all strategy based, some older than me and some so new the covers looked like a movie poster. Sun Tzu's *The Art of War* lay on the desk with a thick notepad covered in scribbles to one side. It took me a moment to recognize the handwriting.

Element of surprise is ever important but not as important as disposable infantry. How can I accomplish this without sacrificing my men?

His proposed solutions made my stomach roll over itself. Under this question, double the size in font, he'd written *Starved,* underlining it several times.

The door clicked open behind me and my innards chilled.

Clap. Clap. Clap.

"Good show, darling."

I almost cried. Right then and there. I had to stuff my hand in my mouth to hold it in, even with my back to him.

"I didn't think you'd get this far, let alone take out poor Billy." The door clicked shut again. "Impressive."

I still shook but I was as composed as I was going to get. I walked up to him, crossing my arms. I'm sure I didn't look threatening, shaking and manacled, but I'd be damned before I'd cower before him. "What are ya playin' at?"

"No game." Isaac leaned against the door in a languid way, his eyes roaming over me. The alarms stopped. "Ah, that's better."

"Right," I snorted. "You're thrilled I made a break for it. Builds character."

"Absolutely." Isaac held up his hand. It took me a second to realize he was holding something up.

My mutilated safety pin

"Not how I thought you'd do it, but very clever." He placed the pick on a nearby end table. "You've proven yourself."

"For what?" I tried not to recoil or shiver as he neared me. "You can't possibly think I'm going to help *you*."

"Do you think there's an alternative?" He traced my jaw with his knuckles.

My skin shuddered beneath his touch and I lurched away. "I've got pride."

He chuckled, looking at the back of his hand like it held mystic properties. "But you don't have much else."

I opened my mouth to argue but he plowed right on, "First, there's that video you and the boy released. If that didn't break convention I don't know what would. Why they haven't executed him, I'll never know."

I clamped my teeth over my bottom lip. I hadn't had time to worry about Gabe. I'd assumed Ivan had kept his word. Hearing confirmation he was alive made my heart hurt and soar all at the same time.

Isaac lifted a strand of my hair, running a thumb and forefinger over the curl. "You're one of *mine*, darling."

"Am not." Childish but it was all I had as I fought for control. True, I might have to spend the rest of my life on the run like Melissa. Maybe I'd never see the others again, but anything was better than *this*.

He chuckled low, bending down to whisper in my ear. "Oh yes you are."

I backed up, trying to find some of the crazy translated somewhere on his face. "Why the hell would ya want me? Ya have to know we don't share the same values."

"I told you." He nuzzled my neck before I could pull away. "This is all for you."

I backed up to glare at him. "What the fuck are ya on about?"

"Don't you see?" He lifted his arms to encompass the extravagant room. "I never would have built this masterpiece if not for you."

"Me? What'd I ever do..." I let the words trail. Shite. The town trying to kill him, I'd caused that by disobeying Isaac in the first place. If I hadn't told my family about the change, if I hadn't tried to save them...

"You set me free." He cupped my chin, forcing me to look up with bruising force. "I was willing to play along, until you showed me everything they're capable of. We've lived like rodents, hiding and only taking what we need. What do we get for it? Pitchforks and torches."

I let out a whimper as I tried to think of an argument. Shite. I'd set the village on him. I hadn't married a big, bad monster; I'd created one. The massacres, the child soldiers, Gabe's father, Olive's kidnapping.

All of it.

I'd spent over a century assuming the worst mistake I'd ever made was getting my husband killed. Only now did I see what my thoughtless actions had cost everyone. From the raging ashes of Isaac, I'd produced Elias. My own monster.

"They outnumber us ten-to-one." I didn't know why I was bothering to argue. Maybe I just needed to talk while my mind wound itself around everything.

"There might be twenty calves in a room with one man." He grinned. "Humans are just as easy to control."

"Only if ya can get the entirety of vampire society behind you."

Hiding in the shadows was a pain in the ass, but getting the majority of Vampire Courts behind him was impossible.

"Russia and Iran are already on board." Elias stepped away, finally releasing my face but still letting his eyes roam over every inch of me. "They won't say it publicly yet, but they love my designs for the current human trafficking. Makes feeding so much simpler. China's not far behind, even offered me some of their camps. And that's just the tip of the iceberg."

He talked like a little boy opening a lemonade stand.

"So why do ya keep attacking America?"

"Because they keep sending their bloody military where it doesn't need to be." Elias shook his head. "Bunch of busy bodies."

"Poor you." I flinched at my own snark, waiting for him to smack me. When he began to laugh I dared to pop an eye open. He leaned against one of the end tables, his chuckles making his whole body shiver.

"You were always a treat when you got annoyed. Do you remember the argument over the dining room wallpaper?"

"You didn't seem that *entertained* when I woke up." I re-laxed but kept waiting for his hand to flash out.

He winced. "Yes, that was awful. But in my defense, I had just found out you were unfaithful *and* you'd just cost me several soldiers." He shrugged. "But if you join me–"

I snorted, "Ya know, I've heard this speech before, thanks."

Damn if Gabe wasn't right. There was a Star Wars reference for everything.

I shot forward, driving the heel of my hand up. The cartilage of Elias' nose crunched and cracked as I tried to shove his nose into his brain.

"I'm not joinin' your dark side, jackass."

I punched again, aiming for his chin. He caught my fist and squeezed. Pain erupted as the joints and bones splintered in his grip. I kicked and he dodged, like it was nothing.

He twisted my arm by the shattered hand, bending it at an unnatural angle. I screamed, trying to pull away. Before I could even try to twist free, he grabbed my biceps, yanking them backwards.

Both my shoulders dislocated with a shuddering pop and I screamed again as an angry pain ravaged my arms and torso.

The door crashed open and several men dashed in, looking uncertain as they stepped towards us.

Elias' breath filled my ear, his voice a low growl. "That's a shame darling."

CHAPTER 42

GABE

"Docket 3:24:cv 3:04vc000501." The clerk handed a file to the judge, her practiced monotone betrayed by several fervent glances in my direction. "City of Portland v. Collins."

My cuffs were a bit snug but at least they weren't biting. Today's officer had put them on far more gently than the day before.

"What do the People request?" Judge Andrea Taffet flipped through the folder as she spoke. I had to suppress a groan.

Taffet was brutal on the defendants. As a detective, after long hours of chasing down a perpetrator, I'd often appreciated it. Now, with the shoe on the other foot...

Karma.

"People request bail be denied, your honor." The District Attorney glared at me as he spoke. "The defendant has already fled from the law—"

"Only to turn himself in, your honor." Michelle said it like a simple afterthought.

"The matter remains." The defense lawyer snapped his collar. "Gabriel Collins was an officer of the law. He had a duty to report his *condition* to his superiors—"

"I'm a vampire," I forced a polite smile. "It's not a virus."

"Mr. Collins–" Judge Taffet glared down the gold wire of her spectacles, "please let your lawyer speak for you."

"Apologies, your honor." I nodded and clamped my jaw with purpose. Still, the defense lawyer struggled to find his verbal footing.

"Ah-hem," he coughed into his fist and looked down at the table before him. "Mr. Collins knew his status was now illegal. After all, he brought down several Renfields and vampire sympathizers while working for the VPB."

"And for all that dedicated service, my client would have been executed." Michelle stood straighter. "He turned himself over and has made no attempt to escape, despite being given no blood and his restraints being useless."

"Blood!?" The public attorney turned a few shades paler. I honestly think the idea of my food source had completely skated past his mind until this point. Maybe he thought I'd just eat the inmates.

Hell, they would have probably had me for lunch if I hadn't been in solitary this whole time. I was nobody's favorite behind bars.

"Hold your peace, Mr. Anderson." The judge raised a weathered palm and eyed my cuffs with suspicion. "Ms. King, what do you mean about the restraints?"

Michelle and I exchanged a glance before she nodded. I raised my cuffed wrists, smiling sadly.

"I hope you're watching," I mumbled under my breath as I pulled my arms apart. Several people gasped as the links flew in every direction.

The court erupted into a torrent. The defense lawyer yelled for no bail, the people watching behind me squealed in shock. The only still people were Michelle and myself.

"Order." Judge Taffet banged her gavel, ordering the bailiffs to show the hysterical people out of the courtroom before glaring back down to us. "Mr. Collins, was that really necessary?"

"Sorry, your honor." I kept my hands up, high where everyone could see them. "We didn't see another way to get my point across. And that's not my only ability."

"Oh?" The judge squinted at me. Something in her gaze made me think of an archaeologist uncovering a lost tomb. "Do you have another *demonstration* planned?"

"I believe it would be best if I gained the court's permission, as this would require a volunteer." I swallowed.

"Volunteer?" The judge looked curious and annoyed.

"Yes, your honor." Michelle nodded. "We promise no harm will come to this individual."

"Fine." The judge sat back, clasping her thin hands, like she was waiting for a play. "Do you need me to come down there?"

I'd expected that response, but I didn't like it. "No, your honor."

I concentrated my gaze on the judge, trying to let the power pulse into my eyes. "Your honor, please pick up your gavel."

She gave me an annoyed look. "What for?"

I swallowed a lump of sandpaper in my throat, trying to remember the feeling of controlling the pimp. I'd *wanted* him to stand still and stop abusing Tara. Now, I *needed* the court to let me out on bail. I *needed* to be free to investigate.

"Pick it up."

She looked affronted now. "First, tell me why."

People chuckled behind me and she reached for the gavel to silence them, stopping short and eyeing me heavily.

"Why, Mr. Collins?"

I *needed* to be free to feed. It had already been a week since my last meal. I might be ravenous, if Maria hadn't forced me to take fresh blood right before I'd gone in. If I didn't get out soon, I might starve and I wasn't sure what that entailed or how to warn anyone.

I wasn't even sure the solitary cell, or the heavy metal door would hold me. Who I might hurt...

My eyes pulsed, like a slow thunder building below the frail surface. "Pick it up, please."

The judge became rigid. Her whole body shook as she reached for the wooden mallet. It quivered on the podium in her still shaking hands, tapping out an irregular rhythm that slowly replaced the giggles behind me.

The defense lawyer started to shout something about my eyes, Michelle retorted. People kept making indiscriminate sounds of fear behind me. I couldn't take my eyes off the judge. There was too much at risk.

"Wave it like you're conducting an orchestra."

The judge did so, the large sleeves of her gown flapping as she waved her arms clumsily. Several more gasps omitted from the crowd, and maybe even a small scream.

Michelle placed her hand on my shoulder. "That's enough."

I let out a breath as the power depleted from my gaze. "Thank you, your honor."

The judge stopped with her hands still raised, staring at the gavel. Her lip quivered, like words couldn't form.

"As you can see–" Michelle raised her voice to be heard over the commotion behind us, "my client could have escaped custody in a number of ways."

The judge looked down at me. Her lip continued to shake. Her eyes were big as serving trays.

Shit, I'd gone too far. She wasn't going to give me bail. I'd have to mesmerize the guards to feed. The very idea had my stomach coiling like I'd drank spoiled milk with chunks of old meat.

The noise of the courtroom continued to swallow all thought, Michelle and Anderson bickering violently over the ethics and logistics. Anderson said that they simply had to keep me in solitary confinement and my world shattered.

Would I have to run for it? I could get out of here. I was certain. No one knew to aim for my head. They'd aim for my body. And the ammunition wouldn't be silver.

But then this case would end. I would leave this world even worse than I found it.

I gave the judge my best pleading look as I shouted over the crowd. "If I didn't want to be here, I wouldn't."

The judge looked at her still-raised gavel then back to me. Her lips tightened as she smashed it into the wooden sound block below.

"Order!" She belted the command several more times, her eyes continuously fixed on me as she did so. "Court is set for December the 10th, bail is set at $350,000."

CHAPTER 43

LILY

Elias forced me forward, barking orders at his men and pinning my arms behind my back. I couldn't hear him over my own cries as he twisted my arms. I kept waiting for him to rip them from their sockets; that would have been preferable.

"You won't suffer long, darling." His voice was stern.

We walked along the hallways; the people we passed didn't even bother to look interested as he propelled me forward, directing me with my twisted arms. I shuddered and cried in pain. Drool slathered my chin and I couldn't stop screaming.

We rushed down stairs and I was vaguely aware of them turning to concrete, hard and cold against my bare feet. Elias grunted and one of the men walked around us. I was slumped forward, supported by his fingers digging hard into my flesh. Something metal squealed. Elias barked an order and heavy footsteps retreated; the thumps mixed with my wordless sobs.

He guided me inside, before lowering me to the ground. "There you go."

Pop. Pop.

I cried out as one of my arms found its socket, then again with the other. I curled into a ball on the cold floor.

"Get up." Elias' voice stiffened me.

I hadn't realized he was still there. I slowly got to my hands, taking in my surroundings. No bed or books. Just gray concrete and a thick metal loop in the middle of the floor with a thick chain attached. Decaying blood stained the concrete in various shades of red and brown.

"No." I glared up at him.

"Fine." Elias strode forward, grabbing the huge cuff from the floor and linking it around my ankle. Pain sliced into me and I screamed again.

I stared in horror as my ankle bled freely; unlike the manacles Elias was removing, this set had silver barbs. I was already half starved. I wouldn't last two days. I wouldn't have the strength to get out.

"I'm sorry." Elias gripped my face, forcing me to look at him. "I can't sacrifice everything for one woman. Not even you."

I yanked my chin away but even that hurt now. "I'm not tellin' ya a goddamn thing!"

"I don't need to torture you. And I don't want to." He shook his head, smoothing a lock of hair from my face. "But I can't let you leave, not now. So, you're going to be one of my infantry."

"Fuck you." Raving fucking lunatic. I just wanted him to leave me alone.

"You saw my notes." He waved his hands like he was conducting a symphony. And finally I noticed the cries of pain, coming up like some horrible crescendo. "Why do you think we kept focusing on Oregon?"

"I don't fucking know!" I was starting to shake uncontrollably. Not all of it was pain or hunger.

"Yes you do." Elias ran his fingers over my cheek.

I swallowed and tried to think. Everything hurt. I was already exhausted, all the adrenaline pouring out of my body with the blood.

"Think, darling. You're going to die for this. I think you deserve to know."

"The Court?" It was all I could come up with.

"Almost. I mean weakening those morons is certainly an advantage."

I layed down on the ground, even sitting up took too much energy. "Just get to the point."

"Of course, you're tired." Elias stood and dusted his waist coat. "I'll leave you with this. How did the humans feel about the vampires after The Massacres?"

He walked out and reached up, grabbing a metal door. It rattled down and I was left in the dark with my thoughts and a pathetic sliver of light at the bottom of the door.

CHAPTER 44

"I still can't believe you put your parents' house up for bail." Michelle dug through her brief case before handing me a laptop.

She'd been pretty good to me, bringing a burner phone and going back to Alex for all of Lily's files. I only interacted with two people recently, and I doubted the guy who dropped off my blood bags was about to do me any favors.

"Thanks." I started clicking through the files without looking up.

Worrying about the house wasn't going to solve anything. If the case went well, I would get it back at the end. If not, I wouldn't care.

Thank God I'd lost my apartment upon the landlord learning about my new status, the single room would have driven me insane by now. Not that being confined to a single level home was any vacation. If I won, I might finally sell it.

The ankle monitor itched but I tried to ignore it.

I don't know how neither of us saw this coming. Maybe I was just assuming they'd keep me locked up; I hadn't even considered what release would look like. But house arrest and the ankle monitor hadn't calmed the public. They were still outraged.

I didn't have cable in my parents' old house, but Michelle constantly complained about our news coverage. Even without her, there was always a small protest on the sidewalk outside my home. They started stationing marked cars outside. The court said it was to keep the protesters in check. I kind of doubted that was their priority.

Even without them I wasn't interested in going outside. I needed something to do while we waited. I sat at the kitchen table with the laptop while Michelle kept talking about Channel Five's coverage. We had a system, I could solve puzzles and she could think out loud and construct counter measures. I only had to say *uh huh* once in a while.

Kind of like dating again but without the pressure of romance.

No matter how I examined the maps and patterns, Lily's files weren't making sense. "I don't get it."

"What's not to get?" Michelle pulled a glass from the cupboard and started to fill it from the sink. "We need interviews to counter balance all the media."

That caught my attention.

"Wait, what?"

She held up a finger as she drank from the glass, letting out a deep sigh. "Your first one is scheduled for next Monday."

I groaned, cursing myself for not listening.

"Even if I wanted to, you know I can't." I indicated the itchy contraption above my shoe.

"Good thing you already agreed to do it by Zoom."

"When?"

"The third 'uh-huh.'" She rinsed the glass, even though it had only held water, and placed it in the sink. "What's so mesmerizing in those files, anyway."

I debated arguing the interview but it wasn't like I was low on free time. The files were another matter. I slid the computer closer to me on the table.

"Seriously?" She leaned on the counter and crossed her arms. "You trust me to defend your life in court, but not to look over some files."

She wasn't trying to save me. Not really. But that was all the more reason to trust her. Besides, all my issues aside, I knew she was a good lawyer. That included attorney client privilege. It hadn't come up often with her representing the state, but there had been occasions where she came out for a date and could only tell me it had been a rough day.

We still weren't right for each other, but I was starting to realize she wasn't as shallow as I'd thought. She'd just had to compartmentalize the most compassionate aspects.

I slid the computer back across the table, waving her on. She sat. "What am I looking at?"

"The ramblings of a crazy girl." Her look clearly said glibness wasn't appreciated. "You remember that girl I lost right before I went missing?"

She nodded. "Kimberly Ash-something."

"Yeah, well Lily and I found these files with her. It's some kind of map showing missing kids across the United States." I bit my tongue, debating how much to tell her. Trust still took time. "Olive is on there."

Michelle grimaced at the map. "All these kids were changed?"

"Yeah, that's my guess."

She scanned the map. "And they're *all* over the states?"

I pointed to Oregon. "Yeah, but there's no other concentration like ours."

She covered her lips, still scanning the page. "Why?"

"All I can think is they're weakening the Court."

Michelle stopped scanning to look at me. "Wait, they *know* where the Court is located?"

"You know where the White House is, right?" I shrugged. "Court is the vampire capital."

She scowled. "And they didn't move, even after the massacres?"

"I doubt it's easy to get an estate like that." I shrugged, though her guess was as good as mine. "Who knows what kind of paperwork and tracks they have to cover to make everything work."

"True, and I guess we didn't move the White House after Nine-Eleven. Would have made us look weak."

I nodded. It was a good point.

"Yeah, so this Elias knows where the vampire capital is, because that's common knowledge. He focuses his own resources here trying to deplete theirs." She looked down at the maps, her lips twisting. "That doesn't make sense."

"What do you mean?"

"I mean if he's trying to deplete vampire resources, why did he have the massacre in the first place?"

Shit. I hadn't thought of that. "Because it made it harder for the Court to stay in the dark and put a strain on them?"

"Yeah, but it's not like he's strutting down the block while you're hiding." Michelle sat back, pulling up something on her phone before turning the screen to me. It was the crime stats for Portland. "See, vampire crimes are growing but not at a rate that says Elias isn't worried about getting caught."

"That's only the ones humans know about." I almost smacked myself as I said it. Michelle was glowering. I swallowed. We'd come this far. "Lily once told me, those stats are usually kind of off. You should check missing persons cases to see how that's going."

"What?" She looked at the city's pie-chart in disbelief.

"Yeah, missing person cases are a big indicator for extra vamp activity." I shrugged. "At least that's what she always said."

She stared at the screen, open mouthed. "Of course."

That had been my reaction when Lily had explained it. Missing people could easily be vampire victims. If a vampire did a good job of cleaning up after themselves, law enforcement would have no reason to tag it as known vampire activity. Lord knew we'd tried and failed...

Suddenly, my brain felt like it was on the edge of a cliff, about to fall over.

I yanked the laptop back and started typing furiously, looking for the city website and its crime stats.

"Shit."

"What?"

The missing persons rate had been slowly inclining since the end of September, when the Cheri Coke had spread. Around the beginning of October, when we'd slowed the business down, the missing persons cases were still on the rise.

"It's gone up by four percent, and has kept rising." It didn't sound like a lot, but when you considered that there were over four-million people in Oregon, especially with the Doll Maker nonsense...

"What's at four percent?"

"How the hell did the news miss this?" I started to scan the stats more thoroughly.

"Hello..." Michelle waived her hand over the screen. "Would you tell me what you're talking about?"

"Oh shit," I said again, ignoring her glare. I ran into the living room and grabbed the burner phone. "Shit!"

I punched in the only Court number they'd given me. It went to voicemail. I hung up and dialed again. "Come on, come on."

Every ring was louder and longer, even though that was impossible

Michelle had stopped asking anything, just followed me, open mouthed, and watched.

Finally it clicked. Ivan growled, "What?!"

"Let me talk to Cyrus or Melody."

"You're not a member of this—"

"I think I know what Anna's been up to!"

The line went silent for a long moment. "You had better prove your worth, especially after that stunt."

The other end of the line clicked and clacked, as though Ivan were on the move. He barked some orders and something squealed. Maybe the metal door.

The sounds of pain were amplified. Listening so closely for the next voice on the phone wasn't helping. Based on Michelle's occasional flinch, it wasn't just me.

Ivan bellowed on the other end of the line. "Cyrus!"

The snaps of chains stopped just before a new, confused tone came on the line. "Collins?"

"Where's Anna?"

"Why?"

"I have a hunch."

He waited a moment, the phone dead silent. Must have muted his side to talk to Ivan. "Explain."

That would take too long. And Michelle didn't need to know the worst of these details.

"Just ask her how many *soldiers* are hiding out in the city?"

He knew what I meant but he was still confused. "What are you talk–"

"Just. Ask. Her." My tone turned arctic.

Even Michelle stepped back.

He waited a moment, then answered. "I'll put you on speaker."

He went in and Michelle came closer, tentatively. "Gabe?"

I let out a breath and covered the speaker on my phone. "The recent hike in missing persons, it lines up perfectly with the first Doll Maker death."

"Yeah, so?" She shook her head, confused "There was a killer in the–"

"No, don't you see?" I went back to the laptop and pointed at the screen. No point telling her who the Doll Maker was, especially not now. "It shouldn't have. The Doll Maker was feeding on the families. Unless..."

Michelle looked like she'd swallowed a bug. Cyrus was on the line but far away. "You've been keeping secrets, Anna."

"Don't be boring, Cy." She spat in the background. "It doesn't suit you."

A sharp snap and an awful cry shattered the stillness on the line. Michelle turned green.

"You're gonna tell me how many brats Elias has in the city, or I'm going to whip those raw and have you standing on them until they heal." Chains rattled again. "That interesting enough for you?"

Michelle glared at the phone. "Is this normal?"

I couldn't just nod or shrug. I turned away.

"I know there are more of those little monsters here. You thought we wouldn't notice because of the Doll Maker sensationalism."

Anna laughed. "There's nothing you can do about it now."

"Do about what?" Another whip. Another shriek. "It all makes sense now. You wanted Lily to find you. That's why you used the cards."

Shit, I hadn't thought of that but he was right. Anna wasn't one of the ancient biddies who didn't age with technology. She worked with humans everyday as a nurse. She'd had to keep up. Anyone who watched TV knew a credit card could be traced.

"Took you long enough." Anna's chuckle was dark.

Cyrus growled, "You wanted out."

"I wanted front row seats." Anna grinned. "You or Elias, either way I wasn't going to last long. Not after my fuck up. I didn't want to die without seeing the look on your faces."

"What are you talking about?"

"Failing to recognize Lily's name earlier."

"Huh?" It was both me and Cyrus that time. That made no sense. They'd been friends, what the hell was Anna talking about?

"Elias, he's been looking for a Líle Edwards for *decades*. Didn't think his wife would be that Irish brat."

I almost cursed. "His *what?*"

Cyrus must not have responded on his side because Anna responded to me.

"Oh, you didn't know about that." Anna's voice filled with a note of glee. "I figured you coming back without her meant she'd finally reunited with her husband."

I didn't get it. It was a lie but what was the point?

Maybe the two were having nice chats and reconciling in Heaven, but her past had nothing to do with the here and now.

"That's okay, you won't have to live with that for very long."

"What do you mean?" I growled. Something thumped outside, making Michelle jump a mile in the air with a shriek. She looked at the front of my house several times, before casting me a furtive glance and going to check on the noise.

Someone shouted Cyrus' name in the corridor. He ignored it, "What are you talking about?"

"Come on, Cy, you know why vampire and zombie lore line up so well." Laughter broke all of Anna's words. "Hey Detective, what happens when you starve a vampire?"

My other options are starving or terrifying the man. To me, that's not much of a choice.

Before I had time to consider what Anna was insinuating, another sound came from outside, this one closer. Like something had been thrown at the front of the house. Maybe a protester had tossed garbage against the front window. Wouldn't be the first time.

Then Michelle screamed.

CHAPTER 45

LILY

My nails shredded across the concrete as I clawed at the little shaft of light. My yowls blended with those of the Starved around me. I strained, trying to pull my ankle through the loop of the cuff.

The barbs scraped against my tibia, the grinding noise swallowed by the metal clank as I shuddered from the silver poison. Even when I broke my foot, I couldn't get the damn thing off. The barbs were too long. Too deep in my flesh.

Hours passed.

A thick foam pooled in my throat, becoming a heavy lump that swallowed my cries. I forgot where I was. I couldn't understand why everything was so loud. I just knew that everything hurt, radiating from my leg into my belly, and then through my head.

Everything but my brain. There was no brain.

Agony continued to wrack me and I shook on the floor, out of control and starving. Suddenly, the shallow beam became a large beacon, only to be blocked by a hulking shadow.

Life.

I smelled life. It was faint and just out of reach. I lunged, the chain snapping me back and tearing into my ankle. I didn't care, the pain didn't compare to the growing beast in my belly.

I growled. Snarled.

Something smacked my face and something cold clasped my neck. I clawed at it, growling and hissing. The source of life neared and I reached for it like a desperate babe reaching for their mother. The source stopped, stooping before me. I could smell the life, lingering and dying in the cells before me.

Let me feed. I need to feed.

I snapped as the source's hand drew closer, my fangs burying deep in my lower lip. But no blood greeted me. My own body was sandpaper. I yanked my mouth open, dislodging the fangs for another try. The source chuckled and shouted to something behind it.

It left, I clawed and spat, the heavy clamp around my throat wouldn't release me. Then glory as three sources replaced the lost one. They released my ankle from the cuff and the lower pain stopped. The roaring beast of my belly kept calling, beckoning for the life just ahead of me. But none of them got near enough. They moved me through the clamp, keeping me just out of arm's reach, chasing them at a staggering pace.

Still I tried. I followed, barely registering the other hulking shapes that followed next to me. We hobbled up the stairs, tripping and scrounging. Light stung my eyes and the air froze my skin.

The flesh of my hands was broken and torn; crawling was excruciating. I didn't care. If I could only feed, it would be better. I didn't know how, but it would. We were herded in a large box that echoed and rumbled. Still, we weren't released

The ache burned in me, unsatisfied and teased by the nearness of life.

Let me feed. I need to feed.

The thought came out as another agonized growl, mixing with those of the hulking gray forms alongside me as the container rumbled under us.

The box finally stopped rattling. Light blazed and heat seared my skin, but amidst it all, there it was. Life. A fountain of it, never ending.

Someone screamed as we all surged forwards.

The cries of pain grew with the sounds of satiation. Flecks of blood flicked my skin and I lapped at the tiny drops. I was so thirsty...

CHAPTER 46

GABE

"**C**ollins, what's going on over there?"

I didn't answer Cyrus; I was too busy rushing to the front of the house. Just in time to see it slam against the window again with a soggy thud. Michelle was sprawled on the floor, crawling backwards and unable to take her eyes off it. I stood there, phone in hand, just trying to comprehend.

What happens when you starve a vampire?

This thing couldn't be that. I had no other explanation but this couldn't have once resembled a human. It was withered and dry, the gray skin hanging from the bones like a loose sack.

The worst was the face, gaunt and bony with shreds of flesh clinging to hollow cheeks. It all made the fangs look even larger, elongated and yellow against that ashen skin as it hissed and spat before making another rush at the window.

The glass fractured and my instincts woke up. I grabbed Michelle's arm and pulled her to her feet. She still screamed as I shook her shoulders.

"Do you remember my birthday?"

"What?"

"My birthday." I shook her again. "Say it."

She rattled it off, confused, side eyeing the monster and shivering.

"That's the code to the gun chest in my parents' night stand." I shoved her down the hall. "Grab it and lock yourself in the bathroom."

The master bath didn't have any windows. I had no idea where this thing came from but I knew I had to be stronger for Michelle. She faulted, looking back at me and tripping in her heels.

"GO!"

That got her. She ran, leaving one shoe behind. The door to my parents' room slammed shut just as the glass broke and the thing scrambled over the carpet, shards splintering from its face and hands. Brown blood covered everything it touched.

It ran without hesitation. Not even the most basic animal instinct to survey the scene. I wish it had been slow like a zombie, but this thing didn't lumber. Even as the elbows bent at unstable angles, it crawled rapidly, like a rodent.

I ran into the kitchen. It had to chase me. I was closer. I could get to the knives, it wouldn't be easy but it was the best I had.

I grabbed the biggest knife from the block, berating myself for never sharpening them as I turned back. And found an empty room.

Boom.

Michelle screamed as a heavy thud slammed again down the hall. Fuck.

I ran out to find it clawing and banging against the door, trails of dark blood oozing with every slap. It had ran right past me, focused on Michelle. Even now, with me running at it screaming, brandishing a chef's knife, it still clawed at the door, hissing and spitting between each of Michelle's screams.

"Hey!" I slashed its arms.

It screeched, a crazy sound, too dry to come out of any living thing. But then again, it wasn't alive.

The wretch kept banging at the door, dogged in its focus. Michelle's screams grew as the door shuddered. Despite its decaying bones for arms, the thing was making progress. This door wasn't meant for fortification; the hollow wood was starting to splinter and reveal a hole.

Think of us like zombies in a video game. Aim for anythin' but the brain, we keep comin'.

I grabbed the thing's head and smashed it into the wall. It snarled and spat, rotted blood oozed through my fingers and I threw its head into the wall again. And again. And again.

Until the whole head fell apart in my hands and it finally stopped moving.

I sagged against the wall, steadying my nerves as it dissolved into a pile of ash I'd have to clean later. Michelle was still screaming. I'd have to go in and calm her before checking the front.

"Very efficient."

All the heat left my body and I snatched the speaker up by her collar, holding her a few feet off the floor. "Give me one good reason."

Olive's hazel eyes were steady even as her feet dangled and her shirt stretched. "You should kill me right here."

I glared, unsure what to do. It wasn't worth the breath to ask what she was doing here. She would just lie again. She was nothing more than a well orchestrated trap.

"I can take you to Lily."

I laughed so hard I almost shook her. "That's really the best you have?"

"It's why I'm here."

"Don't lie!" I shook her once, her little legs swaying.

"Gabe..." Michelle had finally stopped screaming. Must have heard me shout. "Who are you talking to?"

"Get in the bathroom," I gritted through my teeth. "I'll come back for you."

I heard a second door click as I kept my eyes locked on the girl in my grasp. "You should have come up with a better trap."

I wasn't sure where I could hide her or how I would get her to the Court. The images of what Cyrus would do... Even after everything... But where else could I send her?

"I tried to help her escape but she was too slow."

I pulled Olive closer to my face, hissing, "Lily is dead. I *feel* it."

I hated myself for saying it. Guess I'd finally hit the stage of acceptance.

"Elias wanted you to. But there's still time."

I doubt Elias just severed the tether.

I hadn't questioned what Melody meant by that. I hadn't cared at the time. But now the words came to life. In an instant I took their meaning even if I didn't know how such a thing was possible.

My glare darkened. "Why would I trust you?"

"You shouldn't. Elias sent me to take care of you while the first wave takes the city."

A new scream tore the air. I could only spare a furtive glance at the front of the house as more rose from outside. Along with gunfire. Shattered glass. The quick footsteps of people running for their lives.

"She's out there."

I gave Olive a dark look.

"She needs you."

I didn't understand her play. Was she just here to lure me into whatever chaos was erupting outside? But better to keep her in my sight, no matter what this was.

I dropped Olive and she landed on her feet. "Lead the way."

She only nodded and headed to the front of the house. I didn't have time to look out the window before she flung the door open.

The first massacres had happened at night. This was broad daylight. Somehow that made it even worse. Such gore didn't belong in sunshine.

People were running, all in one direction. They tripped and scrambled over each other, some stepping right on the fallen. I recognized a few faces on the ground, battered and bruised. They'd been my neighbors. A couple of them had held Pickett signs while marching outside my house.

"This way." Olive yanked my sleeve, pulling in the opposite direction of the crowd.

We ran past the police car, but it was empty, a small ding chiming over and over that the doors were ajar.

The officers were out, trying to help everyone they could, too busy to close the damn door. And here I was, more than likely following Olive into a trap and running past people in need. The same people I'd also vowed to serve and protect.

I yanked my sleeve out and ran to the scream of a woman, high and frantic, but muffled. I found her hiding under a truck, clutching her child to her chest. The kid was sobbing and the woman's screams grew every time something bumped the car.

She was stuck in her panic. I layed on my belly and reached under the truck, nudging her shoulder. "Ma'am."

She jolted, smacking her head on the bottom of the truck with a metal thud, and screamed, "Get away!"

"It's not safe here." I held out my hand. "Let me help you."

She shook her head violently. "You're one of them."

She'd seen the news. Of course she'd seen it. Dammit.

"We don't have time for this."

I peered out from under the truck and scowled at Olive. "I'm not leaving them."

"We can't save everyone." She knelt by me. "And if we try, then we might lose Lily."

I let out a breath and glared at her. "I'm not leaving them."

Olive seemed stunned by this. Bobbing up and down on her feet. "You're willing to sacrifice her for a stranger?"

I didn't have time to keep debating with her.

"If I know I can save the stranger, yes." I turned back to the woman and reached again. "I only want to help you."

She started to swat my hand away and screamed until Olive spoke. "Stop screaming and get out from under the truck."

The woman looked petrified as she scooted away from us, pushing herself into the light of day.

"Olive!"

"Your way was taking too long." Olive looked back to the woman and pointed in the direction of the crowd's stampede. "Take your child and run to the end of the street, until you find the fire trucks."

The woman scampered away, almost tripping twice, sobbing in relief as she clutched her child to her chest.

"Fire trucks?" It was all I could get out.

"They started to drive in but all the people clogging the road made them park. Same with the police. It's made a thick barrier at the end of the road."

I nodded. We stared at one another. The chaos kept growing around us.

"We can't save everyone."

"I won't *pass* everyone."

The sounds of shattering glass and screams replaced every argument we might make.

Olive turned sharply. She lunged on the next party needing help, yanking one of the creatures off an old lady and smashing its head into the ground. "We have to move fast."

The thing writhed and spat, even after I stomped on its head. It took several times before flesh and decaying blood squished under my shoe.

And so it went, wading through the mass of rot and violence. Most of them crawled more than walked, their backs arched towards the sky. The skin ranged from gray to black, peeling in purple or brown strips. They didn't speak, but they made plenty of noise. Their battle cry was a unified mess of wordless groans and mummified hisses.

They covered the block, hunting alone and fighting each other for every scrap of human meat. In the road, two of them were pulling at a screaming man like starving dogs at a steak. His screams only grew as Olive and I tore each of them away, their nails gouging deep grooves in his skin. It took forever to get them off. He left a trail of blood when he ran away

I turned and sped to catch up to Olive. She was so easy to lose in the chaos, being so short. We turned a corner and the violence grew exponentially.

Bodies littered the road, ash circulating with every breeze. A desperate car alarm blared over the faint echoes of screams. Houses were torn, bricks and glass covering the littered street in layers of debris. The creatures crunched over the broken garbage, the feet and hands bleeding as they crawled and lunged.

Swarms, all pounding against structures while the few remaining residents cried in terror. Some had broken windows or doors,the creatures flooding into the bungalows like a stream flowing backwards into the home.

"Where the hell did he get all of them?"

"He made them." Olive swallowed. "He would have made Lily too, but I managed to sneak her out. I think we can reverse it."

Before I had a chance to consider her words, Olive shot down the road. One of the creatures smacked against a window with fervor, Olive pulled a gun from her pocket and aimed, calmly. The head exploded and the window shattered.

"Why don't they come after us?"

"They need life. Our blood doesn't have enough."

Meaning the police and firemen were only adding fuel to this fire.

The air stank of ash, bile, and urine. The scent grew stronger as the piles of bodies and trash continued to grow and the sounds of panic quieted.

Some of the dead looked like raisins, puncture marks littered their bodies like freckles. Others had been torn apart or skipped entirely, possibly missed in the initial chaos as these things had been let loose.

Olive slowed. "One more block."

That block had enough carnage for a warzone.

Three dark-blue semi-trucks were parked, the way to them paved with a heavy pile up of cars. A car alarm blared under the rubble. Clearly, the semis had blocked many people from their exit. Arms, legs, and partially chewed up bodies hung from open car windows, all limp and dripping blood on the asphalt. A few of the car windows were broken inward, red smeared on the shards.

I had to force myself not to look inside the cars we passed. There was no one to save here.

Instead I focused on the semis. Two were open, empty caverns that echoed the faint sounds of chaos.

"She's in there." Olive lifted her chin and my guts turned chilly.

The third shook, quivering with excitement.

I think we can reverse it.

"No..." I backed away, one step.

Olive grabbed my sleeve. "I can't get her out on my own. The guards will overpower me."

"I knew this was a trap!" I yanked my arm free and glared. I should have never come. There was no way. No way she was one of... them.

"I could have shot you before you noticed me." Olive looked at me in earnest.

"But *why* should I believe you?" I pointed at the truck in the distance. "Give me one reason to get close to that thing, one reason to believe your lying mouth!"

Olive stared for several moments before looking down at her feet. She muttered something.

"What?!"

"The nightmares got worse!" Olive looked up, red tears rimming her eyes. "I thought they'd go away once I was back but they got worse!"

I gaped. It was so simple. And something told me it was true. I nodded. "How many guards?"

"Only two. The Court is in the opposite direction, so after each release, the two in charge ran off for fun."

I suppressed the urge to shake her. Her calm tone and the description infuriated me. "Give me the gun."

She flinched back.

"You have a lot more reason to trust me, than I you." I held out my palm. "Go lure them out."

She waited a moment before handing me the gun and marching away. It probably only took a minute. God knows what she said. I wasn't thinking. I was too busy trying to answer an impossible question.

What if?

What if she was in there? What if this was a trap? What if I couldn't save her?

The sound of running feet brought me to this moment.

Olive screamed, "You have to help! He's got my gun!"

Fucking traitor! Then I saw her running out of the trailer and to the side, two men chasing her towards a house. Clever.

The men followed her without question as I took aim. It's always harder hitting a running target. I didn't need to do it often in the real world. It would be easier to let them keep chasing Olive. But she'd sacrificed herself. Despite my arguing and accusing. And when they found out she'd lied...

I aimed, tracking as best I could. I wouldn't have long to adjust after the first shot. The back runner's head exploded.

"What the fuck?!" The front runner screeched to a halt at the crack of the gunshot, turning just in time to see the result.

He figured out where I was too fast, ducking down as he shot towards me and that's when Olive lunged on his back. He wiggled and raged trying to pull her off as he called her every name in the book.

"Shoot!" Olive screeched as he hauled her over his head and flung her to the ground.

I didn't have enough time to aim. I got extremely lucky. His head blew apart and ashes covered Olive instantly.

I ran up to her, hauling her off the ground by an arm. "You alright?"

She nodded and ran for the truck. "We have to let the whole truck out. I anchored her to the back."

"What!?" I halted.

"It was the only way I could get her out!" Olive shouted.

So if I let her out, I'd be releasing more of those monsters. How many more would die so I could save her?

If she was even alive.

CHAPTER 47

LILY

The light stung my eyes. We'd been in the rumbling dark for so long.

All the others surged forward, but I couldn't. I tried and tried but hard as I pulled I couldn't follow the others.

Why?

They ran, but all I could do was hiss and spit, pinned to the back and unable to go anywhere. After the container emptied, two more entered. Not like the others, but not sources. They didn't matter. I continued to claw and fight for freedom. For food.

The two stood in front of me, muttering something between them. The taller one knelt before me. Something about it was familiar, but it wasn't food.

"Jesus..." It backed away as the little one stepped forward and yelled at it. It nodded and walked behind me and suddenly I could move. Only a little. It was like pulling the world behind me but I didn't care.

I could hunt, I could find food. Pain prickled my stomach, urging on my need.

The two continued talking behind me, once in while I was pulled away from the path I chose.

CHAPTER 48

GABE

I winced, pulling the chain like the leash of a wild dog. She clawed at the ground, crazed and pulling, singular in thought. I hadn't been certain it was her. Even when I knelt before her and looked in her eyes. The blue was almost swallowed entirely with red and black.

But then I saw that crooked pinkie. And I knew.

I stumbled along as Olive surveyed the cars before looking up and shouting, "This one is fresh."

I swallowed bile and disgust.

I'd failed. I'd fucking failed. I could hear the screams rising in the distance. How many of those were my fault. I'd let those things out. I'd killed as many as I could but there were so many, and they moved so fast.

I shouldn't have agreed to this. But seeing her, even in this decrepit lurching form, I couldn't think of anything else I could do.

"Come on." I pulled the chain, watching her limp after me as the link on her foot pulled. We staggered along.

"You know—" I said to Lily, "I kind of imagined a nicer place for our first dinner date."

She didn't respond, just kept hissing and spitting. I almost lost it, just pulling her to the car.

God, please let this work. I need this to work.

I couldn't have sacrificed those people for nothing.

Olive's plan made sense. I'd drank from blood bags, so obviously blood didn't lose life the minute it left the body. Therefore, a fresh enough corpse would also have something left to offer.

The idea of feeding her some poor sap probably should have tied my stomach in knots, but I was just too damn tired and overwhelmed by what I'd already done.

Finally I made it to the car. Olive had chosen a plump man, half-hanging out of his window. At a glance, I couldn't tell exactly how he'd died. Maybe a broken neck, judging by the way his head hung, but his body obviously had some blood left.

"Alright." I grabbed Lily and pulled her close. She resisted, clawing the air mindlessly as I finally got my arms around her waist and shoved her towards the dead man.

Lily sprang, falling on the remains. I didn't look, just stood there listening to the heavy gulps and slurps.

I leaned against the car, watching her intently and checking the gun. Three rounds. Hopefully nothing else attacked us. Not to mention if she didn't come to...

"How long?"

"Shouldn't take more than a couple minutes." Olive shrugged, surveying our surroundings. "Elias only started the process a couple days ago."

A couple days? So what had broken the tether? What had she endured that whole time?

As I popped the clip back in, Lily's languid gulps began to slow. Then they halted. And she screamed.

"Oh fuck!" She bolted backwards from the corpse, slamming into the asphalt screaming something over and over. It took me several repetitions to catch what she was saying.

"Not again! Not again!" She shrank into a ball, rocking her body back and forth and chanting. For a moment, I could only watch in shock. Lily's hair was still filthy, but it started to lighten in hue beneath the grime. Her skin began to stitch back together, the soft cream color slowly returning.

"Not again." She stared at the corpse in the car as she continued to rock. "Not again."

"Lily!" I ran forth, falling to the ground and grabbing her by the shoulders. She was so cold in my hands. She finally halted her maniacal rocking, but kept chanting. I moved, blocking her view of the corpse. "You didn't kill him! You wouldn't kill someone. You never could."

She lifted her head, slowly meeting my gaze. She didn't seem to register me for several minutes, just looked right through me. Her bottom lip shook and she bit into it hard enough to draw blood.

I kept telling her she didn't kill him, that he'd already been dead, unsure if the words were reaching her. Right as I considered shaking her, she lunged forward, cradling into my arms. Sobs wracked her body, shaking her so hard I could barely hold on.

But I could never let her go again.

I brushed my hands over her shivering body. Between her sobs and the continuous sounds of death and massacre, I could only distinguish a few words.

"I already have."

CHAPTER 49

LILY

Portland crumbled under the falling snow. I stared out the window of my room, watching it fall onto the broken landscape, building in glittering waves, the light powder too heavy for the ruined buildings.

The TV played in the corner of my room, but I hardly listened as I watched the glistening sheet build, curled under a thick quilt and nestled into the chair. On the end table beside me was a full mug of blood, cold and untouched. And my phone, though I'd been warned it would be monitored.

Like there was anyone I wanted to talk to.

Out of my peripheral, Queen Ritti filled the screen, her posture straight and regal. Her eyes were puffy red orbs as she spoke, *"Hello, My name is Queen Ritti of the American Vampire Court. Many of you were to be introduced to me through an interview video with Ms. Amber Wright. Let me assure you that video will still be released. However, given the events of yesterday, I feel a conversation is necessary."*

A knock sounded at the door. I nestled further into the quilt, trying to block it out. Maria had tried last time, it was Darren's turn. He hated confrontation, I only needed to wait him out.

I couldn't take anymore of their concern.

He knocked once more, quieter, muttering my name. Finally he gave up and left.

I let out a breath and gathered myself. Ritti continued her speech, *"The tragic deaths of last night can never be justified. No, my Court did not unleash that hoard. This was done by the man you now know as Elias. He believes humanity is nothing more than cattle. That your lives are disposable."* At this, Ritti paused. *"My kind have lived among yours since the Garden. Our laws were built with the intent to protect humanity and vampires alike."*

The phone buzzed on the end table. I flinched at the unexpected motion before reaching over. I was going to press *ignore*, until I saw the caller ID.

Gabe didn't wait for me to answer, taking silence as his queue. "Hey."

I should have let it go to voicemail.

A single tear rolled down my cheek and I managed to choke out, "Hi."

Silence filled the chasm between us, thicker than anything we could say.

"Lily..." He drew my name out. "You need to rebuild your strength. You're still not fixed up."

Of course they'd called him.

"Fixed up," I snorted.

I thought I was broken before. Now...

"We do not all share Elias' twisted faith." Ritti's voice rose from the television with authority. *"Most of us believe our races to be equals. Two sides of one coin."*

"Lily." His voice was soothing, like a caress.

His soft tone broke me, and I fell apart. Would I ever stop crying? I'd never been one of those weepy girls. But now, I could fill Niagara falls. The stupid tears overflowed through my hands, staining my clothes and the blanket.

He was quiet for a long moment. "It's okay, I get it."

"No!" Anger filled the single word. I hated myself with everything I said, but I was powerless to stop. "Ya don't 'get it.'"

Something about his bloody sympathy, his *compassion*, it just made me feel that much smaller. I didn't want it, and I certainly didn't need it.

Ritti sighed heavily in her TV speech, *"We have gotten so used to being in the dark. I see now that is more than just impossible. We can never go back to the shadows and must learn to live in peace."*

"I didn't mean–"

I didn't let him finish, "It doesn't bloody well matter what ya meant! Ya don't get it!"

And how could he? How could I ever expect that of him? Still, that he would even suggest he could...

"I'm seriously fucked up right now, but at least I wouldn't compare my shit to somebody else's."

Gabe took in a breath, like he was trying to figure out what to say.

I wanted to go to him. I wanted to shout.

I hung up on him and threw the phone across the room.

Yes, we had both lost so much, and given even more. But there was a core difference. All of this, the war, Olive being turned, the ruined city outside, the death of Gabe's fucking father, it was all my fault. If I hadn't lied to Isaac, if I hadn't sicked the damn village on him, then none of it would have happened.

So no, Gabe couldn't possibly understand. And I never wanted him to.

Ritti's voice boomed from the TV, startling me with new viement and volume, *"Let our races fight together. Fight for what is right. Fight for freedom. Let us fight for love and kindness. Let us fight for a new world, one that is decent and built on the backs of hard labor and the courage to go forward in the face of the unknown. Elias offers his men such a world but it is a lie. Let us show him what that promise would look like fulfilled. Let us fight for a world free of his intolerance, instead filled with reason. People, in the name of all that is good, let our two kinds unite."*

"Oh, fuck off." I switched the TV off and buried my face in my hands.

I should call him back and apologize. Maybe we weren't together... or were we? This was all so fucked up. But I didn't want to lose him in my life. I didn't have much good left.

The phone buzzed from the other end of the room. My heart soared. I sprawled out of the chair and crawled to the phone, hitting the *answer* icon without bothering to read the screen. "I didn't mean it. I'm so sorry!"

He'd called back, he had to understand.

My veins froze as a dark chuckled filled the speaker. "Not yet, you're not, darling."

About the E.H. Drake

Visit our publishing website at www.ehdrake.com to learn about E.H. Drake's next fantastic book or join our Discord. You can also follow the **E.H. Drake** Podcast of Spotify or YouTube for free audiobook samples, videos essays, and more.

If you love the cover, please check out our artist's website https://nicoleyork.com, check out her amazing photography and art work. Thank you again!

ACKNOWLEDGEMENTS

I owe a serious thanks to so many people (again.)

Firstly, to my new business partner, The Editor, who prefers their privacy. You know who you are but I doubt you realize how *amazing* you are. It is a rarity in this world to offer criticism with such a heavy dose of kindness.

To Dallin & Kennedy Bradford, the voices of Lily & Gabe in our audiobooks. Listening to your interpretations of my work has been a Masterclass in writing all on its own.

And finally, to my friends, beta readers, and critique partners who kept reading my story long before editing. Over and over. You all make me a better person, let alone a better writer.

Thank you.